SOMETHING HIDEOUS WAS WAITING, JUST OUT OF SIGHT ...

One of the men let out a strangled scream as he jerked his sword from its scabbard. All at once, these *things* were coming out from behind the bushes. A dirty yellow haze covered the true hideousness of their forms.

The fighter ahead of me stood where he was, rooted to the spot, so frozen with terror that he couldn't even move to arm himself. Someone else broke and ran, screaming, and he was the first of us to be cut down. His screams broke off quickly and suddenly, *chopped* off.

Then the creatures rushed us. There were so many of them we didn't stand a chance. The fighter next to me and the one frozen in place went down almost together. That left only four of us to face the horror alone.

They were going to kill us all, and there was nothing we could do to stop it.

WIND WHISPERS, SHADOW SHOUTS

SHARON GREEN

AVON BOOKS • NEW YORK

WIND WHISPERS, SHADOW SHOUTS is an original publication of Avon Books. This work has never before appeared in book form. This work is a novel. Any similarity to actual persons or events is purely coincidental.

AVON BOOKS
A division of
The Hearst Corporation
1350 Avenue of the Americas
New York, New York 10019

Copyright © 1995 by Sharon Green
Cover art by Donato
Published by arrangement with the author
Library of Congress Catalog Card Number: 94-96775
ISBN: 0-380-77724-X

First AvoNova Printing: July 1995

AVONOVA TRADEMARK REG. U.S. PAT. OFF. AND IN OTHER COUNTRIES, MARCA REGISTRADA, HECHO EN U.S.A.

Printed in the U.S.A.

RA 10 9 8 7 6 5 4 3 2 1

This one is for my daughters, the former Valerie Engel and the former Maria Pisani. I love you, guys.

WIND WHISPERS,
SHADOW SHOUTS

CHAPTER ONE

It was much too quiet. The sky was filled with sullen, threatening clouds, there wasn't the slightest breeze to relieve the heavy, mid-summer heat, and the silence was all wrong. The woods around us should have been filled with *some* kind of noise, even if it were just birds warning each other about the coming rain.

"They're waitin' for us," Cadry observed in a murmur from my left, obviously feeling the same thing. "They know we're after 'em, and they stopped to set up an ambush."

"Too bad it won't help them," I answered in the same murmur, keeping my eyes on the woods around us. "But they'd better not have hurt those girls, or they *will* live to regret it."

Cadry grunted her agreement, and then we joined the general silence while we waited for half of her group to make their way around to the other side of the fugitives we were after. Just how many of them there were wasn't certain, but the three squads of Cadry's group, about thirty fighters, were good enough to handle twice or more their own number.

How good they were had been proven more than once during the last three weeks. That was how long Tiran and I had been king and queen of that realm, and all of Tiran's fighters had proven themselves. We'd had some losses, of course, all good men and women, but considering the fact that we'd been fighting our predecessors' army of

1

guardsmen, we'd been incredibly lucky to have so few casualties.

And now we were chasing individual bands who had turned outlaw rather than surrender, bands of men who thought there was no reason for them to stop their depredations just because there was a new king and queen. They'd been allowed to do whatever they pleased to the people of the realm, but we meant to break them of the habit no matter what it took to do it.

"That's it, Alex," Cadry said when we heard the sound of a scolding bird in the distance. "My men are in position, so it's time to move."

"Cautiously," I qualified, having no desire to lose any more fighters. "They've got *something* set up and waiting for us, so let's find out what it is in some way other than walking right smack into it."

"You're the boss," Cadry said with a grin, the sort of mocking grin she'd been giving me lately. Just as if I were getting too careful in my old age, but she was determined to humor me. Cadry was the biggest woman I'd ever seen, even a little bigger than *me,* and we were both glad we were friends rather than enemies. But there was no confusion over which of us was the better fighter, and I happen to like the idea of being a live better fighter.

"Damn straight I'm the boss," I said, giving her grin no more than a glance. "And that slime grabbed two village girls to entertain them, little girls who won't have a chance without our help. Do you really want to go whooping and hollering into that camp, giving the slime a chance to get *us* before we can get *them?*"

"No, can't say I do," Cadry admitted, the grin turning to a sigh. "Had more fun three days ago, when the band was alone. Weren't as many as we thought there'd be, but we still had fun. Guess it's time for work instead."

And with that she turned to the fighters around us, giving them their orders in a brisk, professional way. All the fighters in Tiran's company were professionals, but they also had a small but definite core of juvenile wildness. It was probably what let me get along with them so well.

Within another minute we were ready to move, so we spread out through the woods and advanced cautiously.

We'd left our horses a short distance behind us, along with the boy who had come to tell us that his sister and another girl had been taken from their village. No one else in the village had made any effort to ask for our help, even though they knew we'd be in the neighborhood today. That was because they didn't trust Tiran and me yet, something else we were trying to change.

Even with moving slowly and carefully, it wasn't long before we reached the clearing the outlaw band had stopped in. The rest of our fighters came up on them from the other side at about the same time, and we all paused to look over the "trap." It didn't seem possible that that was all there was to it, but one of the eight men in the clearing spoke up before any of us could begin to ask questions.

"That's right, these girls are dead if you do the wrong thing," he said, grinning at Cadry and me. He stood with an arm around the neck of one of the girls, the knife in his other hand right at the girl's throat. A second man stood next to the first with the other girl held and threatened in the same way, with three more men in front of them, and three behind. If we attacked, even with bows, the two men in the middle would certainly have enough time to kill the girls before we were able to kill *them.*

"What do you consider us doing the *right* thing?" I asked the man, at the same time studying him and the other seven. Most of them still wore pieces of their old uniforms, but the spokesman wore it all. His collar markings said he'd been an officer, but all eight of them looked like the shabby sneak-thieves they were.

"The right thing is being smart and doing what we say," the man responded, still enjoying himself enough to show that grin. "We don't really want these pretty little girls, so we'll trade them—for a pretty, *big* girl. Our new queen ought to be worth a good bit in ransom, and *that's* what we want. If we don't get it, you can explain to their families why their daughters had to die just to save the king some gold."

"Don't do it, Alex," Cadry said at once while the fighters around us stirred in silent outrage. "They heard we were comin' so they set this up, but you can't trust 'em even as far as you could throw a horse. Gold ain't all they want, and I'll bet on it.''

I didn't say it out loud, but I would have bet the same. That set-up was not only lame, it was all wrong for what the band of men said they wanted. They could have demanded ransom directly from the villagers, forcing them to appeal to Tiran and me. Instead they'd put themselves at risk to demand a trade, which meant they did have more in mind than gold.

"You seem to be assuming I *care* what the villagers think," I drawled to the man, folding my arms as I stared directly at him. "And even beyond that, how would they know what happened here? If we tell them you killed the girls before we were able to catch up with you, how would they know any different?''

"They already know different because one of my men is right now telling them all about it," the leader answered, his good humor completely undisturbed. "And if you *didn't* care what the villagers think, you wouldn't be wasting your time and effort visiting them personally. If these little girls die they'll blame *you,* but even more I think *you'll* blame you. I don't really understand stupidity like that, but I don't have to understand it to take advantage of it. You've got two minutes to make up your mind, and after that I get to make it up for you.''

"You tryin' to get us to believe you're that hot to die?'' Cadry demanded of him, annoyance clear in her voice. "The only thing keepin' you alive right now is those two girls. You kill 'em, and we do the same for you. You *got* to know that, so why waste our time with empty threats?''

"There's nothing empty *about* the threat," the man countered with a laugh. "We're as good as dead anyway with the way you've been hunting us, so what have we got to lose? Either this works or it doesn't, and if it doesn't we'll take these girls with us—and die knowing we did you damage with the villagers. That's worth a good bit to us all by itself, so you do whatever you think you have to. We'll be happy whichever way it goes.''

He really sounded as if he meant what he said, and most of the others looked just as ready to die as he did. I didn't believe it for a minute, not with men who'd spent their time plundering the lives and possessions of others, but I needed to know what they were really up to. Not to mention the fact that I couldn't let them hurt those children. If they wanted me, they would get me.

"All right, we'll do it your way," I said, putting a hand up to silence Cadry's immediate protest. "But there's something you'd better understand, and more than that, believe: if *anything* happens to those children, even by accident, you'll die so slowly and horribly that even executioners won't have stomachs strong enough to watch. That's a solemn promise from me to you, and if you look around you'll see that no one who knows me doubts my word on it."

Some of them did look around, but if it was something encouraging they looked for, they didn't find it. Their leader had finally lost his grin, but an ugly kind of satisfaction now showed in his eyes.

"Don't worry, nothing will happen to these two as long as you don't try any fast ones," he said, working to sound casual but actually showing intense excitement. "Now here's how we'll do it: you'll—"

"No," I interrupted before he could start handing out orders. "*Here's* how we'll do it. I'll move to a point halfway between you and my people, and that's when you'll let the girls go. Once they're safely out of your reach, I'll come the rest of the way. You have my word that I won't try to escape, and that my people won't try to interfere with my reaching you."

He thought for a moment, all but biting his lip, and then he snarled, "All right, I *will* take your word for it. But first you'll get rid of that blade. I've heard about how well you can use it, and I'd hate to tempt you into trying to show off. We want you alive, not stupidly dead. And let's get started *now*."

I shrugged as if none of the details concerned me now that I'd gotten what I'd wanted, and then I took off my swordbelt. Going up against eight armed men without a weapon wasn't something I enjoyed the idea of, but *no-body* is so good that they can face odds like that and win even *with* a weapon. If I survived it would be because

I was able to surprise them, something I fully intended to do.

Cadry took my swordbelt when I handed it to her, her expression telling the world how frustrated and shackled she felt. Only the glance she sent me said differently, showing instead that she understood what I'd given my word about. I'd promised not to run, and I'd promised that my fighters would not try to keep me from reaching those eight men. After that all bets were off, and Cadry was more than ready to back whatever I did.

Which still didn't make for that pleasant a situation. I used the back of my hand to wipe at the sweat on my forehead as I began to walk forward, hoping the eight thought the sweat was from fear rather than the heat. Some men believe a frightened woman is the perfect victim, and you don't get ready to defend yourself from a victim. I'd need every edge I could get once I was in amongst them, and if they wanted to think of me as helpless, who was I to argue?

When I reached the halfway point between my fighters and them, I came to a stop and said, "Okay, now's the time. Let the girls go."

Those two poor children were terrified, and had been the entire time we'd all stood there. When they were finally released one began to run, but the other just stood there as if she were still being held. It took a shove from the second man to get her moving, and then she ran as if she never intended to stop. I waited until two of Cadry's fighters snagged her and pulled her toward the first girl and out of harm's way, and then I looked at the leader of the eight and began to walk toward him again.

I kept my face expressionless, but only because I'd nearly grinned and called out, "Ready or not, here I come!" I hadn't really expected to get the girls back without a lot more trouble, and now that they were safe I felt positively lighthearted. Tiran would have jumped on my head for dismissing what *I* was about to walk into, but I wasn't really dismissing it. I just felt that I was a lot better at handling a situation like that than two little girls, and I was also ready to prove it.

"That's it, come right over here to me," the leader of

the group urged as I moved past the endmost man in front, his grin almost back. "I knew I could count on you keeping your word, your sort always does. And you're even better to look at up close than you are from a distance."

The last of his words was more like a spoken thought, a personal observation filled with all sorts of anticipation. If I'd needed anything to make me suspicious that would have done it, but since I'd started out suspicious I paused near the second man who'd held a girl captive.

"How much ransom do you intend to demand?" I asked, just to be saying something while I took a better look around. The man was calling me to him rather than coming over to me, and that didn't make sense. The sooner he had me as a shield the safer he would be, but he just stood there waiting. Something was wrong, even though I couldn't imagine what it might be.

"Our ransom demands won't be too high for the king to pay," he assured me quickly, now trying to project friendliness and calm reason. "And you have *my* word that you'll be perfectly safe the entire time you're with us. Now come right straight over here."

Well, that clinched it. I couldn't have been more than five or six feet away from the man, but he still wanted *me* over where he was rather than coming himself to where *I* stood. He was a fairly big man with light brown hair, gray eyes, and a handsome face, and very clearly did not need to make gestures just to prove who was in charge. He had another reason for wanting me over there, which meant I had every reason to stay right where I was.

"But what do you mean by not too high?" I persisted, not moving an inch. "Right now I'm not sure *what* Tiran would pay to get me back, considering the last argument we had. He's so stuffy and conservative now that he's become a king, and sometimes he bores me silly. Why, just the other day . . ."

I'd been babbling along and playing the empty-headed female, an act certain men seem to expect from a woman no matter what else they know about her. I could see the spokesman of the group struggling to hold his temper, but the man closest to me on my right didn't bother trying.

"Stop talking and start moving again, woman," he or-

dered with strong annoyance, reaching to my right arm
with his left hand. He obviously intended to hurry me on
my way, but that wasn't the way *I* wanted it. I pulled free
of his grip and side-kicked him in the crotch, then took
his right arm and shoulder-tossed him at the spokesman.
I fully expected the two to collide and go down in a pile,
but I didn't stop and wait to see it. As soon as I tossed
the man, I dived for the ground myself.

Which was, of course, what our archers were waiting
for. The multiple *fssst-thunk!* of arrows reaching their
mark came almost immediately, and the six men who had
been playing outer defensive wall went down and stayed
like that. The only ones left were the two in the center,
and I wanted *them* for questioning before they got what
was coming to them. I got to my feet fast, expecting a
fight before they were taken—and then just stood there
for a minute in shock.

"Where in hell did they go?" I demanded once I'd
pulled my jaw up off the ground, turning to look in every
direction possible. "And how could they have disappeared
so fast? And last but certainly not least, how could the
bunch of you have let them get past you?"

"They *didn't* get past us," Cadry said as she and most
of the others walked up, every one of them looking very
bothered. "You were too busy gettin' out of the line of
fire to see it happen, but *I* saw it clear. When that second
one hit the first they didn't go down, they just—disappeared! There was a little bit of smoke, but not so much
that I couldn't see through it. One minute they were here,
and the next they were gone."

"So that's why he wanted me to come to him," I said
after taking a deep breath and letting it out slowly. "Whatever made him disappear involved the place he was standing, and also obviously involved magic. It looks like there
was more of a trap than we were expecting."

"And somebody is out to get *you,*" Cadry added very
flatly, giving me an odd kind of stare. "When the boss
hears about this, you won't be goin' out visitin' any more.
And he *will* hear about it, so I'd advise not sayin' what I
think you were about to."

Swallowing the words was hard, but Cadry was right to

ask me not to put her in an untenable position. I *had* been about to say that Tiran didn't need to know how close they'd come to getting me, but Cadry's first loyalty was to the company and Tiran. If he eventually found out about the incident, which he probably would, and learned that Cadry hadn't told him about it . . .

"Okay, all right, I won't ask," I grumbled. "I know you have to tell him, so I'll save my arguments about whether or not I go out again to use on *him*. Right now we'd better get those girls home again—and see if we can't get our hands on that man who was supposed to be telling the villagers about what was happening here. Not that I expect him to know anything even if there really is such a person. That would be too much to hope for."

Cadry grumbled her agreement, and then we got ready to leave the clearing. The six outlaws were dead, of course, a tribute to the ability of the group's archers, so we had no prisoners to worry about. We found the two girls over by the horses, both of them holding tight to the teenage boy who had brought us to their rescue. The boy himself looked absolutely delighted, and his arm around each of the girls was protective and filled with pride.

"I knowed you could do it, ma'am," he said as soon as he saw me. "C'n we take 'em home now? Our momma an' Addie's is gonna be mighty worried."

"You bet we can take them home now," I said, returning his smile. "But don't give me all the credit for the rescue. These fighters did their share, just the way they'll be doing from now on. We'll be forming and training a *real* guard, men and women who will protect you rather than take advantage, so tell everyone in your village. If they ever need help again, they now know who to call on."

The boy nodded happily, but before he could say anything else one of the girls whispered something to him. It was a fairly long something, so we almost had everyone mounted before she finished. By then the boy looked— bothered, impressed, I couldn't quite tell what, but he stayed silent even when one of the fighters pulled him up to ride double.

It wasn't far to the village, and although there were

people working in the fields and among the houses, it wasn't hard to see that most of them worked with the spirit drained out of them. Those among the houses looked up as we approached, their expressions frightened and wary, but then they saw who we had with us. Word began to spread with shouts and with children sent running to spread it, and by the time we reached the center of the village there was quite a crowd.

"M'baby, m'baby!" one woman screamed as she pushed her way through, and the second girl slid off the horse she'd been on and ran to her. They were laughing and crying at the same time, and then a woman appeared who must have been the boy Callor's mother. His sister slid to the ground and ran to her while Callor followed more slowly with a big grin, watching while the two hugged and kissed and cried. I wouldn't have minded watching all that for a while longer, but a small deputation of men stepped forward.

"Looks like we owe ya our thanks," their spokesman said, apparently trying to ignore the happy carrying-on. "Ya done us a good turn by bringin' them girls home."

"Don't kill yourself showing all that gratitude," I couldn't help saying, the words coming out very dry. "And you don't owe us anything. Those girls needed help, and we were able to give it so we did. Since you didn't *ask* for our help, you're not bound by having gotten it."

"I didn't mean we ain't grateful," the man protested, apparently having enough decency to feel embarrassed. "We just ain't had much luck with sayin' thanks. Tried t'do it with guardsmen a couple years ago, an' got robbed a everythin' worth havin'. The favor they done us waren't no such thing, 'cause the kids they found was took, not lost by accident. Tell th' queen we ain't bad folk here, we just learned better'n t' trust real easy."

"You and everybody else in this kingdom," I answered with a sigh. "We're finding it the same everywhere we go, and it certainly isn't *your* fault. We know we'll have to earn your trust and that it will take time, but right now we want you to know we intend to try. And that we'll be there to call on if you ever need our help. The people in this kingdom have had enough of the bad. Now it's time for some good.''

The man still looked faintly skeptical, an expected reaction for someone in his position, but at least he looked ready to wait and see. He also looked ready to say something else, but before he could one of the men with him touched his arm. The boy Callor had hurried over to speak to the second man while I spoke to the one who was probably village headman, and now the second man passed something along to the headman. I didn't know what it could be, but it didn't take long before I found out.

"Is that right?'' the headman asked me with a disturbed frown. "Did they take them girls 'cause they knowed you'd go after 'em, an' it was you they wanted? You traded yoreself for them two little girls, an' yore th' *queen?*''

"It's not as big a deal as you're making it sound,'' I said, suddenly feeling uncomfortable with all those stares on me. "Yes, I traded myself for the girls, but what else could I do? They were in trouble because that slime wanted *me,* so how could I *not* get them out of it? Besides, they may have traded for me, but they didn't get to hold onto me for very long.''

I tried a grin then, hoping to lighten all those very intense stares, but it didn't work. Everybody looked even more upset, including the headman.

"Never heard nothin' like it,'' he declared, staring as if he were trying to memorize me. "Two village girls ain't worth a *queen,* never was an' never will be. They was crazy t'think you'd do it, but you did do it. Looks like they know you better'n us, but not anymore. Could be they done us a bigger favor 'n you done, Yore Majesty.''

And with that he went to his knees, quickly followed by everyone else in sight. I'd been raised as a princess and was now a queen, but I've never liked the idea of extreme subservience.

"I'm sorry, friends, but you're doing it wrong,'' I said, raising my voice a little in order to be heard by as many of them as possible. "Tiran and I believe that no man or woman should have to go to their knees for *anyone,* so from now on a simple bow or curtsey will do as a sign of respect. The choice of which you'll do is yours, of course, but I've got to warn you men that you'll probably look kind of funny if you curtsey . . ."

I let my voice trail off, wondering if they'd loosen up enough to laugh at a bad joke, and they actually did. The men chuckled and the women giggled as they all got to their feet, and then the headman gave me a very deliberate bow.

"Gotta say it looks like we're gonna like havin' a new king 'n queen," he told me with a grin. "You find you need somethin', you 'r the king, you let *us* know. If we c'n do it, it's yourn."

"I really appreciate your saying that," I told him as warmly as possible, and then I asked about that other outlaw who was supposed to have visited the village. No one had seen anyone like that, but the villagers seemed even more impressed that I'd told them the whole story. By the time we left, children were standing in groups waving goodbye, and their parents were full of smiles.

"Did a real good job there," Cadry observed as we took the road in the direction back to the city. "Too bad it won't be smart for you to keep on doin' it with other villages."

"How about giving me a break?" I said sourly with a glance for her very neutral expression. "You know Tiran is busy learning how to be a king—and cleaning up the city—so visiting the villages is *my* job. I just wish I knew why that lowlife wanted me so badly. It was probably as a lever against Tiran, but what do they want to force him to do? Not just pay them, I'm sure it isn't that."

"And there's magic involved," she reminded me, wisely dropping the subject of whether I'd go on to other villages. "You oughta talk to your sorcerer friends about that, and maybe get *their* help."

"Chalaine and Bariden have enough to do with straightening out their own kingdom," I answered with a headshake. "They left us that very powerful truth spell so we'd know who could and couldn't be trusted, and in all fairness we can't ask any more of them. I think Tiran and I need our own magic users, like the ones my father has at *his* court."

''Worth lookin' into,'' Cadry agreed, and then we each retreated into our own thoughts. The air was heavy with heat and even heavier with humidity, and it was really surprising that the sky hadn't already opened up. We still had a couple of hours' ride before we got back to the city, so it was bound to happen before we did get back. We'd walk into the palace looking like a troop of drowned cats . . .

Which would not make the argument I was bound to have with Tiran any easier. He hadn't been all that happy about my riding around the countryside without him to begin with, and now something like that kidnapping attempt had to happen. On top of that, I'd already visited all the villages within a day's ride of the city, starting with the farthest out and working my way back. For the next ones I'd have to stay at an inn or camp out, and Tiran would just love *that*.

So I spent my time marshalling every argument I could think of, storing them in categories according to whatever objections *he* would make. Most of the ride went by without my noticing, but I did notice when the rain started. We were already in the city by then and almost to the palace, so it wasn't *too* bad. We got wet, of course, but we managed to get under cover before the skies really opened up.

''Today's your lucky day, looks like,'' Cadry commented as we dismounted under the overhang next to one of the palace entrances. ''You want me to come with you to talk to the boss?''

''No, Mommy, I can talk to him all by myself,'' I said as I handed my reins to a groom. ''But do feel free to talk to him yourself later, just to make sure I didn't forget to mention everything.''

''I'll do that,'' she agreed calmly, a look of amusement in her eyes. ''If *you* don't have the sense to look after yourself, somebody's gotta do it.''

''I swear, you sound more like Tiran every day,'' I grumbled, finding it impossible to blame her for caring about me. ''I think I'll take one of the other groups the next time I go out.''

She didn't say anything to that, but her expression suggested that Hellfire would turn to icicles before that happened. But it wasn't something to argue about on the spot—even if I decided I might be smart to do exactly what I'd only been joking about—so we separated. She and her group would see to their horses before going back to their quarters, but I had nothing to do except tell my husband that someone had tried to kidnap me.

CHAPTER TWO

I sighed as I entered the palace, acknowledging the bows and curtsies I got with automatic nods. Tiran had spent a week riding out after guardsmen-turned-outlaw with some of the company, and then he'd been faced with the fact that *someone* had to stay home and run the kingdom. He'd tried to foist the job off onto me, but I'd flatly refused. *He* was the one who'd wanted to be king, and it was time he started to do the job.

I used the nearest stairway up to the second floor, remembering how he'd tried to resist sitting on the throne he'd risked his life for. Tiran was a born leader and did really well with his company and even an army, but being a king is another matter entirely. The protocol is daunting, the deference discomfiting, and how good you are has nothing to do with your position. Even if you turn into a drooling idiot, as long as you still have your fighting force you'll still have your throne.

So Tiran began his reign cautiously, trying to do everything right and cause the least amount of upheaval. He knew as much about running a kingdom as the next man— which is to say he had no idea at all about what it took— and hadn't had the benefit of watching a good ruler—like my father—to see how *he* did it. So far I hadn't made any attempt to interfere, and hoped to be able to keep to that indefinitely. I *did* know what it took to run a kingdom, and had long since decided I had no interest at all in doing it.

At that time of the afternoon Tiran was usually in his

conference room, speaking to one or more of the multitude who always want to see a ruler and who have enough standing for a private appointment. The fact that two uniformed guardsmen—new recruits rather than members of the company—stood outside the double doors told me he *was* in there, but when I tried to pass them one of them put a hand up.

"Excuse me, Your Majesty," the man said respectfully but firmly. "Our orders are to keep this meeting private unless there's an emergency. Is there an emergency?"

"Not really," I allowed, suddenly curious. "Who's in there, that they need so much privacy?"

"The nobles of the realm, Your Majesty," the guardsman answered. "They've come to consult with King Tiran on a number of very important matters, they said. And we've been instructed to tell you that their ladies await *you* in the conference chamber across the hall."

He nodded in the proper direction, and I couldn't help raising my brows. Tiran and I had received a couple of the nobles not long after we'd taken over, a small delegation sent to see if there really had been a change for the better. We'd reassured them and they'd left to pass on the happy news, and now they were back in full force and apparently accompanied by their wives—who wanted to see *me*.

I blew out a short breath as I looked at the room where they were waiting, trying to decide whether or not to join them immediately. I'd been looking forward to soaking in a bath for a while before getting into clean clothes, but there was no telling how long those women had already been waiting. Making them wait even longer would have been inconsiderate, and chances were they just wanted to introduce themselves to the new queen.

So I shrugged and headed for one of the doors, waving back the second guardsman who was about to run ahead and open the door for me and probably even announce me. I've never gotten along well with most protocol, but in my father's kingdom making a fuss accomplished nothing. But this kingdom was supposed to be half mine, which meant I was free to do anything I pleased.

Inside the room were eight women, some of whom

looked at me as I entered and closed the door behind myself. They sat in chairs in a loose semicircle, only partially filling the fairly large room. A nearby table held four trays for them, two with snacks and the others with coffee and chai pitchers as well as cups and sugar and cream. The women were all dressed in expensive and beautifully made gowns, but they seemed to have been listening to the one woman on her feet. That one finished whatever she'd been saying, then turned her attention to me.

"Well?" she demanded. "Is there any word on how much longer the queen will be? We happen to know she *is* in the palace, so you people needn't try telling us again that she isn't. Hasn't she any idea how insulting this is, making us wait like a crowd of commoners? That, I think, is the first thing we'll need to discuss."

"So you know the queen is in the palace?" I said, trying not to feel completely put off by the woman's attitude. "It so happens she *has* gotten back, but how did you find out?"

"How dare you question me?" the woman returned coldly, her light eyes flashing indignation. She was a tall, really beautiful blond with what looked like a good figure, and she drew herself up trying to match *my* height. She didn't make it, of course, and that annoyed her even more.

"How dare you question me?" she demanded again, tossing her head in a way that most men claimed to find incredibly attractive. "I am the Duchess Ravina. Tell me this moment when the queen will be with us, and then report to whomever your superior is and tell him you're to be punished. Appearing before ladies clad in such disgraceful clothing will not be tolerated."

"I hadn't realized that you—ladies—were so delicate that less-than-elegant clothing would harm you," I commented as I headed for the tray with drinks, suddenly feeling a great need for some coffee. "And I hate to tell you this, but I don't *have* a superior. I'll grant you that makes for something of a problem, but there's nothing I can do to change it."

"Don't you dare use that cup!" Duchess Ravina snapped, even more outraged now that she saw what I was about. "And if you think lying will save you, you're very much mistaken. All of you disgusting little tramps in the king's special guard have superiors, undoubtedly the same men whose beds you warm. If I have to ask someone else who that is it will just go harder for you, so you'd better give me his name at once."

"Oh, you want the name of the man who shares my bed," I said as if I'd been hit with revelation, then took a slow sip of coffee. "You confused me by asking for my superior, but I understand now. But why would you want the name of the man I sleep with? Wouldn't it be easier to ask mine?"

"*Your* name?" the woman repeated with a laugh of ridicule. "I don't care *what* your name is. Haven't you the wit to understand that I mean to report you? Now tell me the man's name!"

A couple of the other women had been trying to interrupt the magnificent duchess, but she made an imperious gesture meant to silence them, then ignored them completely. It was fairly obvious those others had realized who I was and were trying to tell the dumb blond to close her mouth, but the woman clearly took her hair color very seriously. She'd decided to report me so I'd be punished for insolence, and wasn't interested in hearing anything else.

"All right, I *will* tell you," I agreed pleasantly. "The name of the man I sleep with is Tiran."

"Oh, don't be ridiculous!" Ravina snapped, even more annoyed. "Why would the king sleep with *you*, when everyone knows that the queen is a beauty? And not particularly understanding, is my guess, as queens seldom are. And don't try to tell me there's another man named Tiran, because I happen to know there isn't."

"Oh, really, Ravina, you're being quite impossible," another, older woman said as she rose to her feet. "At first it was amusing to wait for you to see the truth, but now it's become quite embarrassing. Hasn't it come to you yet that this is Queen Alexia?"

The blond Ravina started to protest with a ridiculing laugh, but then she noticed that none of the others was laughing—including me. That made her indignant again, and she tossed her head a second time.

"That was awful of you," she said to me with heavy accusation, the pink in her cheeks more from anger than embarrassment. "You could have *said* you were the queen, and how was *I* supposed to know when you didn't? You certainly don't *look* like a queen."

"I look like the queen of *this* realm," I pointed out after taking another sip of coffee. "And you *could* have known who I was if you hadn't been so busy trying to throw your weight around. As it is, you're lucky I'm *not* a servant or a member of the special guard. If any of my people had been punished on *your* sayso, whatever happened to them would also have happened to you. In this palace you don't *have* any weight to throw around, and you'd better remember it."

The stupid woman looked affronted and deeply insulted rather than at all sorry, and began to say, "You're insane if you think my husband would allow that," but wasn't given the chance to put her foot in it any deeper. The older woman stepped forward smoothly and got between us, and then performed a curtsey.

"Your Majesty, I'm Duchess Tiraya," she said in a sweet, kindly way. "We've asked to meet with you for a reason, and arguing certainly isn't it. With your permission, I'll introduce the rest of the ladies."

I nodded to tell her to go ahead, and had the rest of the group pointed out. Countess Fandra was an older woman, as were Baroness Tovail and Viscountess Bonnea. Countess Leestin, Baroness Iltaina, and Viscountess Kindoran were all younger, and that was the only distinction I could make in that crowd. Four were older like the Duchess Tiraya, and four were younger like the blond Ravina, but I did notice that they weren't sitting according to age groups. Either they were all solidly together so they'd taken seats anywhere, or there were factions in their small, exclusive group.

"One of our reasons for coming here was to meet you, of course," Tiraya said after the last of the others finished her curtsey, all of them now on their feet. "Our main reason, however, was to offer our help. Our husbands tell us that the king is the first of his line to establish a dynasty. Is that true?"

The way she put the question made me smile, but only because I admire superior diplomacy. What she'd really asked was whether or not Tiran was a commoner, a much cruder question that could easily cause insult. I freshened the coffee in my cup, idly wondering what they'd been talking about that had caused them to send away whoever had brought the refreshments rather than let them stay to serve—and listen—and then walked to a chair and sat.

"Yes, your husbands are right," I said with a neutral smile while they all reclaimed their own seats. "Tiran's expertise was in great demand in any number of worlds, but this is the world—and the realm—where he belongs. Why do you ask?"

"Only because, as I said, we want to help," Tiraya answered with her own warm smile. She was still a handsome woman with dark brown hair and eyes, and the manner of a wise, benevolent matriarch. "And you, Your Majesty. May I ask what your own antecedents are?"

"You could say one of my major involvements was with horses," I told her, pretending I didn't see Ravina's quickly swallowed flash of vindictive satisfaction. "And I repeat: why are you asking?"

"For the simple reason that we're now your loyal subjects," Tiraya answered soothingly. "As such we're here to help you and His Majesty to a complete understanding of the requirements of your new positions. Your—predecessors—were never offered this assistance, since we knew at once that they would be unable to appreciate it or learn from it. You, however, are so far superior to them that we hesitated not at all in coming to you."

Her smile was echoed on a number of the faces of the other women, making them seem like one big group of happy helpers. I happened to know that none of them had come anywhere near our—predecessors—because they'd known it would be worth their lives to leave the protection of their various residences, but I'd gotten curious about where this offer was going.

"So, with all that in mind, we'll begin your lessons at once," Tiraya went on in that same light, happy tone. "First is the matter of your equals, meaning we of the nobility. We are your only friends in this kingdom, and we have nothing but your best interests in mind. That's the reason you must never ignore what we say, or keep us waiting when we come here to the palace. *We* know it isn't being done on purpose to insult us, but our husbands are as touchy and militant as all men. It would be best, we think, if you shared *that* truth first with His Majesty."

"How odd," I couldn't help commenting, needing to do something definite to clear the air of all those sweet, helpful smiles. "If you know being kept waiting isn't a deliberate attempt to insult you, why was Ravina so furious? She said she *knew* I was in the palace when it so happens I've only just gotten back. When someone *knows* something like that, they *have* to feel that they're being taken advantage of."

"No, no, not at all," Tiraya denied pleasantly while a couple of the others sent dagger glances toward Ravina. "The duchess is rather young, you must remember, and the very young are forever impatient. The rest of us knew Ravina was mistaken, but that does bring us to another point. The people of this kingdom expect their queen to be here, in the palace, fulfilling her obligations to the realm in the proper way. If they learned you were out riding around, doing who knows what, it would do terrible harm to both your reputation and the king's. Since we certainly don't want *that,* from now on you must remain here, where you belong."

"Doing who knows what?" I echoed, looking around at them again. "I can't help noticing that your second point is even stranger than your first. Are you telling me you don't *know* what I've been doing these last couple of weeks?"

The woman's sparkling smile faltered, but only for a moment. She had control of herself again so fast that senior diplomats would have been green with envy, especially over how quickly she'd decided on how to proceed.

"Well, yes, we *have* heard a rumor or two," she allowed in a kindly, sympathetic way. "I see no reason to repeat those rumors and cause you embarrassment, not when they'll die out rather quickly once everyone sees that you've changed your ways. Which I'm sure you will, and immediately. It would distress us all if it reached the point where the *king* was *also* embarrassed.''

''I have a feeling I know exactly what you're likely to be distressed over,'' I commented, then gestured away her attempt to interrupt. ''No, we'll go into *that* in a few minutes. First I want to know about these rumors you claim to have heard. Since I've spent my time hunting down renegade guardsmen and talking to villagers, we can assume no one is accusing me of throwing too many parties. What I want to hear is what I *am* being accused of.''

This time Tiraya paused a good deal longer, obviously thinking hard, and when she finally looked at me again her smile had turned faintly sleek and self-satisfied.

''I'm afraid, my dear, that you're being accused of the worst a woman *can* be accused of,'' she said, her sympathy now a shade too thick to be sincere. ''Enough of us have heard the same thing that there can't be any possible doubt, and if the need arises to speak to the king about those rumors we'll have no choice but to tell all we know. It would be a shame if it came to that, considering that it covers a subject which would cause you a great deal of trouble with the king.''

''So that's the way it's supposed to go,'' I said, showing a bit of my own satisfaction. ''Either I take your orders and stay put from now on, or you swear to Tiran that you've heard I've been sleeping around. One way or another you intend to keep me here in the palace.''

''Now, now, my dear, you mustn't make it sound as if we're plotting against you,'' Tiraya scolded happily and gently. ''We're doing this for your own good, after all, to preserve your reputation with the people as well as with the king. We—''

''Oh, spare me,'' I interrupted, putting my cup aside before standing. ''You're doing this because I'm scheduled to begin visiting villages on *your* estates. Until now I've only gone to the ones nearest the city, which owe fealty directly to the crown. The next ones are supposed to be under the protection of you people, and I can't wait to find out what I'm not supposed to see. It must be positively stomach-turning, if you've gone to these lengths to keep me away from it.''

"You seem to forget that you won't be seeing anything, or the king will have to be told about those rumors," Tiraya said, now fighting to keep her tone even. All signs of amusement and sweetness were gone, and she looked up at me as though *she* were the queen. "Once he hears what we have to say, he'll either sequester you here in the palace himself, or he'll put your marriage aside and choose a new queen. Either way—"

"Either way you're dreaming," I interrupted again, this time with disgust. "Go ahead and tell Tiran anything you please, but I strongly suggest you arm yourself first. He has this silly idea that I need to be protected ... and there's one other thing: *Get to your feet!*"

I barked those last words in my best drill-sergeant-to-new-recruits imitation, and it worked like a charm. Every one of them jumped to her feet, most of them paling as they did, their gazes going to the way my left hand rested on my sword hilt.

"Since you're all so interested in lessons, I've decided to try *my* hand at teaching a few," I said, looking at each of them in turn. "To begin with, you people are *not* my equals. Your husbands owe their titles and lands to my husband and me, which makes them our vassals. You girls are just along for the ride, and the next time *any* of you dares to sit in my presence without my permission, you'll learn that the hard way. The same goes for the use of names like 'my dear,' and for rising out of a curtsey before being told you can. I am the *queen* here, and you'll by damn show the respect due me, or I'll do what my great-great grandfather did when he took the throne in my home kingdom."

"Your great-great grandfather?" Tiraya blurted, now looking appalled. "But you said ... you're just a commoner!"

"What I said about horses was a private joke," I informed her coldly. "If you'd asked about the dynasties in *my* family, I would have told you that my father was the fourth to rule under his name, but not just from our branch of the family. My great-great grandfather was a younger brother who fought for the throne and won it, defeating his nephews who'd had their own father killed. That branch was ruined by inbreeding, something *you* people ought to keep in mind. I'm ready to leave now.''

They took the extremely unsubtle hint and immediately curtsied just the way they were supposed to, staying down and keeping their heads bent in the proper way. I stood there for a moment before turning to leave, for the first time in my life getting a hint about why some of the protocol was there in a royal court. If you keep the barracudas bent near the floor, it's harder for them to go for your throat . . .

The guards on the door across the way looked up when I came out, but I didn't give them a chance to say anything. Marching across took me directly to the door *they* guarded, and my expression must have convinced them of the wisdom in keeping quiet. I opened the door just as quietly, stepped inside, then shut it behind me. Eight men were in the room with Tiran, and one of them, of middle years, was speaking.

''. . . and so there's no other choice, Your Majesty,'' he said with the same sort of smooth mildness Tiraya had used. ''We *must* remain insular and independent, else the rulers of our neighboring realms will consider you weak.''

''And you surely know what *that* would mean,'' another man, about the same age but a lot harder, added. ''We would be plunged into war even before we recovered from the depredations of your predecessors, which would certainly mean the end of all of us. And that's another reason why we each mean to raise an armed force comparable to your guard. If—no, *when*—one of our neighbors decides to attack, we'll be more than ready for them.''

Tiran sat listening expressionlessly, but I knew him well enough to tell that he didn't quite know what to say. I knew he was anxious to have a good relationship with his nobles, but I'd specifically refrained from giving him advice so that he'd be free to find his own way to do it. Now I could see I'd left him vulnerable to ''help'' instead, so it was time to do an about-face.

''And how do you intend to pay your own private armed guard?'' I asked as I came forward from the door. ''Out of your own pockets? You all must be rather well off to attempt such an undertaking.''

The man who had been speaking turned quickly to look at me, and if the expression on his face meant anything he was about to demand that I be thrown out as the low-class interloper I so obviously was. He was luckier than the women, though, in that two of the men with him had already met me. When those two jumped to their feet and bowed, the others had no choice but to do the same.

"Alex, I'm glad you're back," Tiran said with a smile too full of relief for my liking, also standing to put his arms out toward me. "These gentlemen have a lot of plans for the kingdom, and I'd like you to listen to them with me."

"My pleasure," I murmured as I reached him, leaning up to exchange a kiss. "Or at least it *will* be my pleasure." Then I turned back to the man who was still scowling and said, "I repeat. How do you intend to pay for your private guard?"

"That, young woman, is a matter to be discussed among men," he came back in a growl, as crusty as the first man had been smooth. "Now that you've greeted us, your proper place is across the hall, with the other ladies."

"I've already *been* across the hall," I growled back, looking him straight in the eye over the table between us. "My proper place is for *me* to decide, not you, and the next time you address me as 'young woman,' you will heartily regret it. Have I made myself clear?"

He stood there all but choking on fury, and there certainly would have been trouble if the first man hadn't hurried forward to put a hand on his brother noble's arm.

"Your Majesty, please forgive my friend, Duke Pavar," he said in that smooth, professional way. "The upheaval in the kingdom has brought us all a great deal of pain and anguish, and Pavar has suffered greatly. I am Duke Selwin, and completely at your service."

His bow was lavish and courtly and meant to disarm, but I wasn't in the mood to be disarmed. Beside me, Tiran was using a cold stare on Duke Pavar, who was too busy still glaring at me to notice. I looked around and saw that the only drinkables available were alcoholic, so I went to the bell cord and yanked on it three times, then walked back to Tiran. He'd pulled a chair over for me next to his so I took it, and once he was also seated the rest reclaimed their own chairs.

"All right, Duke Selwin," Tiran said once everyone was settled. "Since you've volunteered, I'm taking you up on it. *You* answer my wife's question."

"Your Majesty, the answer is in one of the first requests we put to you," Selwin replied with an easy smile. "After the devastation caused by your predecessors, we are forced to pray relief from the crown. A short while of the suspension of taxes we asked for, and everything will be put right again."

"In other words, you expect *us* to finance your raising private armies," I said, being as blunt as possible. "Do we look that stupid to you, Duke Selwin, or were you just hoping?"

"Your Majesty, you wound me!" Selwin protested, looking hurt rather than insulted. "We are all of us loyal to the crown. Any armies we raised would be for the benefit of the kingdom and your royal selves."

"*You* may be loyal, Duke Selwin, but we haven't the same guarantee about your successor or those of the others," Tiran picked up, finally letting what he'd learned during all those campaigns he'd fought guide him. "Private armies aren't a good idea, so we'll move on to other things."

"Like the fact that you can now use your gold to pay those taxes instead of army salaries," I put in with a smile for the suddenly expressionless Selwin. "If you could have afforded one, you can certainly afford the other. And what was that nonsense I heard as I came in, that other kingdoms will consider us weak if we aren't insular and completely independent? Kingdoms that don't engage in commerce are at the mercy of local suppliers in everything they need, and the suppliers grow rich while everyone else grows poor. How can men like you not know that?"

All eight of them shifted in their chairs, but even the glowering Duke Pavar wasn't stupid enough to try to argue. They'd been hoping to sell an inexperienced ruler a bill of goods, and pressing the point would just show how flatly they'd been caught at it.

"And now would be a good time to discuss some things

we *will* help you finance,'' Tiran said into the general silence, then was interrupted by a knock at the door. The knock was followed by the door being opened by two servants, who brought the same kind of chai and coffee service that the ladies across the hall had. The palace servants had quickly learned that three rings meant either Tiran or I—or both of us—wanted coffee, but the full service and quick delivery meant someone was paying attention to where we were and anticipating possible needs. I made a mental note to find out who that someone was, and reward their intelligence and efforts.

Our guests refused the coffee and chai, but Tiran put his glass aside to join me. The servants brought our cups—and little sandwich snacks for me, which I discovered were exactly what I wanted—and then retired to the side of the room. Duke Pavar looked at the servants and cleared his throat loudly, but Tiran chose to ignore the demand that the servants be sent away. Duke Selwin waited a moment to be sure of that, and then moved smoothly into the breech again.

''You were saying, Your Majesty, about something the Crown *will* help to finance,'' he prompted before Pavar could start another argument. ''Can you be referring to the aid we requested for repairing the destruction done to many of our summer homes?''

''I think it's much more important to repair the destruction done to the kingdom,'' Tiran answered smoothly. ''And to repair inexcusable oversights. We've discovered that the only real schools in the realm are here in the city and in some of the larger towns, and only your children and those of the wealthier merchants get to attend them. That has to change as quickly as possible, so we're drawing up districts that will contain three or more villages. A school will be built in each of those districts, and the village children will attend it. That's what we mean to help finance, something to benefit the people.''

''You'll throw the gold away on *them?*'' Pavar demanded with an incredulous snort before Selwin could put forward his own objections. ''Those commoners don't want schools, and won't send their brats even if they have 'em. They need their brats to work the fields, and that has to come before anything else.''

"What a shock that you think so," I couldn't help saying, drawing the man's spiteful glare again, which bothered me not at all. Pavar would never be loyal to anyone but himself, and pretending otherwise wasn't something I cared to do. "I wonder what you would say if we required *your* brats to work in the fields as long as the village children were made to. But that won't happen, any of it, because my husband's plans provide a solution. The schools will be built *and* attended.''

"And what solution do you have, Your Majesty?" Selwin asked Tiran before Pavar could come back to me. "I'm sure we'd all be interested in hearing about it.''

"We'll go into the details of the plans once we're closer to putting them into effect," Tiran said, having gotten my signal not to tell them now. "Was there anything else you gentlemen wanted to discuss at this time?''

The so-far silent noblemen exchanged a lot of glances while Pavar and Selwin had a low-voiced but animated discussion. Pavar seemed to want something that Selwin refused to consider, which earned Selwin the kind of murderous glare I'd been getting. Then Selwin said something that ended the argument on *his* terms, and a moment later he smiled at Tiran.

"Thank you, Your Majesty, but we feel we've burdened you enough with our problems for one day," he said as he began to gather himself. "With your permission—''

"Just a moment, Duke Selwin," I said, interrupting before he got to his feet. "If you have nothing else to discuss, then I do.''

"Why, certainly, Your Majesty," Selwin said at once, switching his smile to me. "How may we assist you?''

"You can start by telling me what you and these others have done in the villages under your protection," I said, looking around at the other men as well. "It's already been established that you're desperate to keep me away from them, and I want to know why.''

"What can you possibly be referring to?" Selwin asked with very obvious bewilderment that meant nothing. The way two of the others paled and Pavar reddened said a lot more, but not in the sort of detail I needed. "Your Majesty, I assure you we have no idea what you mean, and what's more—"

"Save it," I advised shortly, sticking with the bluntness. "I mentioned when I came in that I'd already been across the hall, and I wasn't joking. Your women tried to run the same scam on me that you tried with Tiran, but when *their* plan failed they shifted to blackmail. If I don't stay out of the villages, they'll be forced to tell Tiran they've heard rumors about my sleeping around with members of the company. *That* says you're desperate, so stop playing games and tell me why."

By then my words were being drowned out by every man in the room but the servants, and that included Tiran. The man I'd married was on his feet and roaring, which eventually caused our "guests" to stop their yammering. Pavar was furious again—big surprise—but now Selwin was shaken out of his cool self-possession, especially when Tiran leaned his fists on the table and glared at the much smaller man.

"Now *I* have something to ask about," Tiran growled, causing every one of them but Pavar to flinch. "I want to know which one of you was stupid enough to say something like that about the woman I love. Speak up! Whose idea was it?"

None of them said a word, but they worked so hard at *not* looking toward Pavar that they might as well have held up signs. Tiran saw that as quickly as I did and moved his stare, but the man was too stupid to be frightened.

"If she runs around acting like a slut, you can't blame people for calling her one," he announced in that brash, brainless way that he had. "A decent woman stays home where she belongs, seeing to her husband's comfort and needs, not gallivanting around pretending to be a man. And not sticking her nose where it doesn't belong. You can't sit that throne without *our* backing, you fool, and if these others don't have the spine to say it, I do. You'll both stay off our lands and out of our villages, or you'll be tossed back into the gutter where you came from and belong!"

He was on his feet by then, trying to match Tiran glare for glare, but Tiran had stopped glaring. Somehow he'd changed from being an angry captain of mercenaries to an angry—and self-assured—monarch.

"Guards!" he bellowed, and when the two men in the hall rushed in, he pointed to Pavar. "*That* man is under arrest for treason against the throne, and I want him thrown into the deepest dungeon this pile of stone has. And make sure you pass the word: if he happens to escape, the man or men responsible for letting him go will get to take his place on the execution block. Now get him out of here."

The other noblemen were also on their feet, but shock kept them wordless as the guardsmen advanced. Pavar, still a fool through and through, snorted and began, "Who do you think you're impressing with orders like that? You can't have me arrested, not when I'm— What are you idiots doing? Take your hands off me! Don't you realize who I am? Let go of me, let go of me at once!"

At that point one of the servants closed the doors on his ranting, since the guardsmen had already dragged him out into the hall. The servant didn't say a word, of course, but if there wasn't a gleam of satisfaction in the man's eyes, I've never seen the emotion.

"I think—that might have been the best thing you could have done," Selwin said then, his voice as unsteady as his hands. "Pavar was inexcusably rude, Your Majesty, and we'll be the first to admit it. When you release him in a few hours, or even in the morning, he'll certainly have learned his lesson. One just does *not* speak so to one's sovereign. He'll . . ."

Selwin let the words trail off when he saw Tiran's slow headshake, and that made the man sweat even more.

"Save your breath, Duke Selwin," Tiran said, and his own voice was rock steady and very cold. "Only a fool leaves an obvious enemy to run around loose and make trouble, and I can't afford the luxury of being a fool. And since the subject has come up, we'd better get a few things spelled out clearly between us."

Tiran sat back down in his chair, but deliberately withheld permission for the other men to do the same.

"It's time to choose sides," he said, now looking at everyone *but* Selwin. "The two dukes in your midst had some sort of grand plan to control or take over my throne, but it isn't going to happen. Pavar isn't sane, and I mean to put him down the way you would a rabid animal, but that won't teach Selwin anything. In a day or two, once he gets over his shock, he'll be back to plotting and planning."

The six men he spoke to glanced at Selwin in a way that confirmed what Tiran had said. They all knew Selwin well enough to know Tiran had spoken the truth, but they were also very impressed. They had no idea *how* Tiran knew, and he didn't tell them the worlds were filled with Selwin's kind.

"So that means the rest of you have to choose sides," Tiran continued, reaching to his coffee cup. "Unless and until Duke Selwin actively does something against us, I won't have him arrested or even punished. That isn't the kind of kingdom I want to rule, but this attitude of mine makes it much more likely that he and I will meet on the battlefield. By then it will be too late for anyone who hasn't cast his lot with me, and after the fight there won't be any pardons. Those of you who decide to join me are invited to stay for the feast tonight, and the rest of you are excused."

They stood there for a moment looking very sober, and then they realized they'd been dismissed. They began to bow their way out of the room, a very pale Selwin being the last to start, and the two servants saw to the doors for them. Once the nobles were gone Tiran gestured the servants out as well, and when we were finally alone he leaned back with a sigh and rubbed his eyes.

"So how was *your* day, Alex?" he said, sounding horribly weary. "I can't wait to tell you about mine."

"Tiran, you have to look at the bright side of this," I said as I reached over to take his hand. "If we actually manage to survive and keep our thrones, we'll have started a brand-new kind of government: telling it like it is instead of prettying it up and dancing around the awkward spots. We could end up famous in every civilized world in the universe."

"Did you say famous or infamous?" he asked, but at least he was grinning as he tightened his fingers around mine. "And doing it like that did have an immediate benefit: they were so shocked at what I'd said and done, they left without making any more trouble. Do you think I *should* turn Pavar loose? You know, to show royal mercy?"

"That would be showing royal stupidity," I said with a snort. "The man said in so many words that *he* means to run this kingdom, which probably means him and Selwin as long as Selwin can keep him calmed down. Turning him loose would tell the others that you're weak and uncertain, that any threats you make can be ignored because you'll end up backing down. But the final decision is yours, so you do what *you* think is right."

"Damn it, Alex, you're not being fair!" he complained, looking at me with annoyance. "All the books say I'm supposed to be fighting *you* as well as them, because you don't see why I should do all the ruling. Instead you're making no effort to take over, and you're letting *me* make all the decisions! What kind of a wife and queen do you call *that?*"

"The intelligent kind," I answered with a grin for the way he was actually half serious. "If this whole thing falls apart, I can honestly say, 'Hey, it was all *his* doing. I just sat back and watched.' Do you want to tell me what's really bothering you?"

"You're getting to know me too well," he grumbled, paying a lot of attention to my hand as he traced the bones with one finger. "What's bothering me is this business of having someone arrested and executed. I can't help feeling it's the coward's way of doing it, but you're right about it not being possible for me to change my mind. If I let Pavar go I might as well hand over the crown at the same time, and I'm not prepared to do that. So what *can* I do?"

"You might take advantage of the fact that he's a duke and grant him the privilege of facing you in personal combat," I suggested slowly. "You'd have to point out that you're doing it only because of his former status, and don't plan to make a habit of doing your executioner's job. If he accepts, that will make *you* feel better, but your putting him down personally will also remind the others of who they're messing with. It could save you some trouble, especially since he's probably thick-headed enough to jump at the offer.''

"And if he doesn't, the others will still be impressed because they'll believe he's afraid to face me,'' Tiran said with brows raised, definitely looking happier. "But I'll bet he does agree, because he's used to having a sword to lean his hand on. It annoyed him every time he found the weapon gone, which should mean he tends to rely on it. Alex, you're wonderful.''

"It's about time you noticed,'' I told him comfortably, liking the way he now held my hand with both of his. "And don't worry about who does and doesn't show up for your feast tonight. If all of them decide to leave instead, I'm hungry enough to take up the slack. But I still wish I'd gotten an answer to my question about what they're doing in their villages.''

"If we don't get the answer tonight, we'll have to make checking personally a priority,'' he said, the grin gone again as he leaned back. "Even if I didn't trust your instincts, the way that group behaved says they're hiding something important. So how *was* your day? Aside from sleeping with every man in Cadry's group, that is.''

There was amusement in his beautiful green eyes when he said that, and I couldn't help laughing a little.

"I'll bet they still have no idea how stupid an accusation that was,'' I said with a headshake. "Half of Cadry's male fighters are afraid of me, and the other half are afraid of *you*. And on top of that, I happen to be in love with the man I'm married to. That kind of limits my options, but so far I haven't been *too* disappointed. I guess I'll keep you for a while.''

"You'd better make that a *long* while,'' he ordered, pretending to growl, but the look in his eyes was pure delight. "Especially since a miracle happened today, and I actually heard you refer to me as your husband. I hadn't expected to live long enough for that, and right now I'm still in shock. I expect to come out of it soon, though, and when I do we'll take a royal break. But right now I'm still waiting to hear how your day went.''

"Not badly at all," I said, silently cursing the fact that he seemed to have some kind of instinct where me running into trouble was concerned. It would have been nice being able to put off telling the story for a while longer . . . "We visited those last few villages, and there was a problem only with the very last. They'd had two young girls kidnapped by renegades, so we went after them and got the girls back."

"Unharmed," he said with satisfaction even as he frowned. "If you'd gotten there too late, you'd never be telling it so calmly. But I have the feeling something else happened. What was it?"

"Damn, Tiran, how do you do that?" I demanded, more annoyed than I'd expected to be. "I make a simple statement, but instead of just accepting it and moving on, *you* immediately want to know what else happened. How did you know that that isn't all there was to it?"

"I know because kings know everything and I'm a king," he said, but there was no real joke involved and he certainly wasn't laughing. "Tell me what happened, Alex."

"They kidnapped the girls only because they knew I'd be there with the group," I grudged. "When we caught up to them they offered to trade the girls for *me,* so naturally I accepted the offer. Once the girls were in the clear we took them, killing all but two of the eight. Those two got away, and they used magic to do it. They said they wanted to hold me for ransom, but I still don't believe it. They had something else in mind, but I don't know what."

"You say that so calmly and dismissively," Tiran commented, but the look in his eyes had changed considerably. " 'They tried to kidnap me, Tiran, but they missed so why worry about it? You know nothing can hurt me, Tiran, so let's talk about something important.' Damn it, Alex, are you sure they didn't hurt you?"

"Do I *look* as if I were hurt?" I countered, still trying to minimize the whole thing. "And I never said *nothing* can hurt me, it just takes a lot more than *they* had. I'm perfectly all right, Ti, but I don't like the idea that they used magic. I've been thinking that we need magic users of our own."

"I've been thinking the same thing, and now I'm convinced of it," he said, one hand to my face as he continued to look me over. "But that's for when we can find somebody suitable. Right now I'm giving you notice that we'll be swapping jobs until I find out what that kidnapping attempt means. You'll take care of things here in the palace, and *I'll* take a couple of squads and go check out those villages."

"But you can't do that," I immediately protested. "We agreed that this would be a kingdom, not a queendom, so you have to be *here*. Besides, the kidnapping attempt was probably nothing but those nobles trying to keep me out of their villages. Once I've gone into a few, there won't be a reason for them to try it again."

"Nice try yourself, Alex, but it won't work," Tiran said after taking a final swallow of coffee and getting to his feet. "This *is* a kingdom, and since I'm the king I get to do things *my* way. You'll stay here and look after the city projects I've started, and I'll see about those villages. I can use the break from routine, and you can stand handling some of it. Now let's go find you that bath you probably want."

I let him drag me out of the chair and along with him, but not because the argument was over. I did want that bath, but taking over his city projects wasn't my idea of something to do. We hadn't finished talking about that, not by a long shot.

CHAPTER THREE

Tiran escorted Alex into the main dining hall, pretending not to notice how empty the giant room looked with just six guests waiting. The servants easily outnumbered them, and they seemed very aware of it.

"I'm shocked there are actually that many," Alex murmured from his left, breathtaking in a golden gown covered with blue-green lace. "They look as if they expect to be attacked at any minute, but I suppose that's only natural. I wonder which of them are Selwin's spies."

Tiran smiled faintly without answering, since he'd been wondering the same thing. Duke Selwin was far from stupid, so it wasn't likely he'd let the chance go by to slip a listener into his camp. But depending on who'd been chosen, Tiran might find it possible to turn the pretend supporters into real ones. If he decided the man was worth turning . . .

Their six guests were busy bowing and curtseying after the announcement of "King Tiran and Queen Alexia," an announcement Tiran still wasn't used to hearing. He kept getting the urge to look around for the king with his name, and still felt the mild thrill of shock when he realized it was him. But the thrill disappeared fast when the work started to pile up, a dirty trick if ever there was one. It should be possible to be a king *without* the work, and still have things run smoothly. Yeah, right. That'll be the day . . .

"Welcome to the Palace of Promise, my lords and ladies," Tiran said formally, allowing them all to straighten.

"We hope you've found your accommodations to your liking."

"They came as a pleasant surprise, Your Majesty," Baron Sandor, the oldest man among them, answered. "We'd heard that your predecessors had stripped the parts of the palace they didn't use themselves, and I for one hadn't expected you to have gotten around to restoring the guest quarters yet. I have to say I'm grateful you have."

The man grinned a friendly grin, showing a fairly strong personality now that Pavar and Selwin weren't here. He wore the same sort of finery Tiran did, only in brocade and silk rather than leather and silk, exactly the same, except for color, as the other two men. Sandor's dark hair had quite a lot of gray in it, and he and the others looked like the nobles they were. Tiran had chosen to play the role of warrior-king, and none of them seemed to have missed the point.

"Actually, the guest apartments didn't need much in the way of restoring," Tiran told him with something of a smile. "Our predecessors ignored anything that wasn't made of gold or silver, or didn't have precious jewels all over it. The few items they'd taken out of the other apartments were easily replaced, and that left only the sheets to change before your arrival."

"Now that's amusing," Sandor said with a wider grin as the other two men smiled dutifully. "Not many kings ever find the need to discuss dirty linen. Your Majesty, I would like to present my wife, Tovail, whom you haven't met as yet."

"Baroness Tovail," Tiran said with a nod while the woman curtsied. "We bid you welcome to Our court, and hope you and the baron will return many times."

"Thank you, Your Majesty," the woman said, glancing at Alex uncomfortably. "I'm afraid all of us have gotten off on the wrong foot because of the overambition of some, and we appreciate this opportunity to begin again. And may I say I wish Ravina was here? Seeing the way the queen looks in that gown would have absolutely killed her."

They all laughed out loud at that one, especially Alex. The Baroness Tovail was a still-handsome woman, less

gray showing in her light brown hair, but there was still
some. Her gown was a bright violet trimmed here and
there with white, and it seemed to suit her personality.

"At first I was surprised that Ravina is Duke Pavar's
wife," Alex said after the laughter died down. "Then it
came to me how well they suited each other, the dirty old
man and the supreme spoiled brat. Tiran thinks *I'm* bad,
but that's only because he hasn't met *her*."

"From what I hear I don't *want* to meet her," Tiran
put in, doing his part to put that meal on a friendly, relaxed
basis. "If she's worse than my wife, I feel intimidated
already."

That produced more laughter, especially from the men.
Only Baron Sandor was slightly larger than Alex, which
meant Tiran towered over everyone in the room. Intimidat-
ing him was something only Pavar had been foolish
enough to try.

"Baron Obrif, Count Nomilt, I'd like to meet *your* ladies as well," Tiran said after the laughter. "Once introductions are over, we can sit down to the meal."

"Then, by all means, let's get the introductions done,"
Count Nomilt said before either of the other two men were
able to comment. "Your Majesty, allow me to present my
lady, Leestin."

Nomilt had red hair almost as bright as Alex's, and
Tiran noticed a faint nervousness behind his attempted
friendliness. His wife Leestin was a saucy-looking brunette
with a good figure, but all she did was curtsey. The smile
on her pretty face was friendly without the nervousness,
and Tiran was willing to bet they'd hear from her later.

"And last but certainly not least is *my* lady," Baron
Obrif said, leading his wife forward. "Your Majesties, my
lady Iltaina."

The other two men stirred while Iltaina curtsied, and
Tiran didn't have to wonder why. Baron Obrif had included Alex in the introduction, which the others hadn't.
It might be true that Alex had already met the women,
but Obrif had definitely gotten one up on his friends by
"forgetting" that fact.

And looking at the man, Tiran wasn't surprised he'd
managed it. Obrif was a handsome, self-possessed man,

taller than his age peer Nomilt and showing more confidence. He and his wife Iltaina had the same shade of light blond hair, making them both look almost like porcelain dolls. Iltaina's smile was more neutral than the others', but also seemed faintly triumphant. She'd enjoyed her husband's ploy—or had she instigated it?

"And now we can eat," Alex said firmly, taking his arm again. "I'm feeling positively hollow, so maybe it's a lucky thing the others didn't stay. Any more introductions and I'd start to go transparent."

"Which would be a terrible loss, Your Majesty," Obrif said with a courtly bow. "Beauty such as yours should be preserved at all cost. The former queen, before your immediate predecessors, was an older lady, I'm told, and quite plain."

"Weren't you at court then yourself, Baron Obrif?" Tiran asked, mostly to keep Alex from needing to respond to the man's compliment. Alex didn't like flattery, and wasn't above letting people know it. Tiran also kept them walking, to make sure Alex didn't lose patience and leave them all behind to go to the table alone. He should have ordered her something to eat before the bath, the bath she'd fallen asleep in . . .

"No, Your Majesty, I *wasn't* at court with the old king and queen, and neither was Nomilt," Obrif answered. "Our fathers had the titles then, but have since passed away. Viscount Coptil is in the same position, or would be if he were here."

"Coptil finds it impossible to take a step without Duke Selwin's approval," Count Nomilt commented, almost in passing. "Coptil's father was a martinet much like Duke Pavar, and never allowed Coptil a mind of his own. Now his lands might as well be in Duke Selwin's name; his son certainly doesn't have the final say over them."

No one spoke up in the absent Coptil's defense, so the ladies were seated in relative silence. Tiran had decided to make the meal almost informal—at least in the seating arrangements—so he and Alex took one side of the long table, and their guests were given the other. Alex sat to his right, of course, and directly across from them were Baron Sandor and Baroness Tovail. To Sandor's right was

Countess Leestin, her husband Count Nomilt to her own right. To the left of Baroness Tovail was Baron Obrif, and his wife Baroness Iltaina to *his* left.

"Your Majesty, there's something we agreed earlier to discuss with you," Baron Sandor said as the servants began to bring the food. "If you prefer to have serious conversation put off until after the meal, I'll say no more at the moment."

"If the topic is of that much concern, there's no sense in waiting," Tiran said, certain he knew what was coming. "Please go ahead, and if I find the subject a problem, I'll be sure to let you know."

"Thank you," Sandor said, then took a deep breath before plunging in. "It's about Pavar, of course. We'd like to know if you meant what you said to Selwin, or were just trying to frighten him. Is Pavar really to be executed, or eventually released?"

They all seemed to be holding their breath while they waited for his answer, and again Tiran wasn't surprised. He'd known the subject would come up at *some* time, and there was no sense in putting off answering.

"I won't be releasing Duke Pavar," Tiran said calmly but firmly, looking around at all of them. "He declared himself an enemy to me and mine, and if I freed him I'd deserve whatever trouble came because of it. But I also won't simply have him executed. As a noble of this kingdom, he deserves the right to personal, individual combat. If he agrees to face me, we'll fight to the death. If he refuses, *then* I'll have no choice but to have him executed."

"But what if he bests you?" Nomilt blurted, clearly upset. "Duke Pavar is the best and strongest swordsman to come along in this kingdom in ages. Why do you think we all put up with his autocratic ways without a word of protest? *No* one has ever faced him with swords and lived, not even younger—and larger—men."

"Age and size—and gender—have only a very little to do with ability," Alex said with serene confidence, pausing in her eating long enough to do it. "A man who's a fool talking will be a fool fighting, through overconfidence if nothing else. I'd say Tiran could handle a dozen like him, but that wouldn't be true. He couldn't handle more than five or six.''

Tiran chuckled as Alex reached over to pat his hand in qualified approval and support. The joke was a private one between them, but the confidence in him was completely real and equally as obvious.

''My queen is somewhat biased, but that's only to be expected,'' he told their guests, who were in the process of exchanging unreadable glances. ''But the fact remains that I'm *allowing* him to face me, and I don't expect—or intend—to lose. It will be done within the week, and it will be done in public.''

There was another stir over *that*, and then the blond Obrif leaned forward.

''And once you've bested him, Your Majesty, what do you mean to do with his holdings?'' he asked. ''Pavar had three sons by his first wife, but not even his heir was willing to stay with him. That's one of the reasons he tossed his first lady aside and married Ravina. He intended to hold on more tightly to his next heir, but so far she's given him only girls.''

''Actually, what happens to his holdings—and those of the others who currently oppose me—concerns all of *you*,'' Tiran commented, privately amused at how quickly *that* got their attention. ''As I said this afternoon, I don't expect Duke Selwin to be able to refrain from trying to take over. That means his holdings and those of his supporters will be thrown into the pot before this is all over, and I don't expect to take *any* of it for the crown. The nobility will be expanded, and those who remain loyal will be at the top of it.''

''And you really ought to understand that neither Selwin nor Pavar have any sort of claim on the throne at all,'' Alex put in while their guests silently considered what they'd just been told. ''They may be the highest nobility here and may even be related by blood to the last legitimate rulers, but those rulers were kicked off their throne by interlopers, and no one in this kingdom was able to unseat them. Tiran and I unseated them, which makes *our* claim to the throne the most legitimate one around. Do you understand the point?''

The three men nodded thoughtfully. They might not like the idea, but Tiran knew they understood it completely. When it comes to a throne, if you can't keep it or take it back from thieves, you lose all rights and claims on it.

"And now I wonder if one of you gentlemen can tell me what Pavar and the others are hiding in their villages," Alex went on. "It must really be something if they've gone to such lengths to protect their secret."

"To be frank, we don't know for certain," Sandor answered after glancing at the others, now looking uncomfortable. "Selwin hinted once that there was something he and Pavar had started in order to help advance their cause while at the same time make up for the crops and income we lost to the interloper's guardsmen. A good portion of what our villagers produced was confiscated and sold cheaply, the proceeds going only to the Crown. I let him know I had no interest in anything he and Pavar thought was a good idea, and he never mentioned the matter again."

"Going along with Duke Selwin's ideas usually ended with you being beholden to him in some way," Baron Obrif added after Nomilt nodded to show he'd done the same. "The man would come by with a 'friendly' suggestion, and before you knew it you were in some sort of debt to him. and if you tried to deny the debt, Pavar came visiting to explain how ignoble a course like that would be. My father fell to their tricks, and they've been trying to get me to acknowledge his indebtedness ever since I came into the title."

"It sounds to me as if they planned to make a try for the throne themselves before our predecessors beat them to it," Tiran commented with interest. "Put all the rest of the nobility under your control, and then make your move. Would they have succeeded?"

"Probably," Sandor agreed wryly, the other two men also listening with interest. "King Dobros inherited the throne from his father, who lived to be a fairly old man. That means Dobros was getting on in years himself when he took the throne, but he was also ... odd. Nothing extreme enough for people to point to and talk about, just a number of small strangenesses. Like the fact that even

the heirs of his nobility were unwelcome at court. He
hated to have young people anywhere around him, and
some said it was because his own youth had been thrown
away waiting for his father to die.''

"My father belonged to the group that thought it was
because he had no children," Nomilt contributed. "Baron
Obrif mentioned earlier that the queen was plain, but according to my father's description of her, Obrif was being
kind. Queen Gronna was considered out and out ugly, and
the king reportedly never showed any feelings for her at
all. Considering the fact that she had never given him even
a daughter, let alone an heir, everyone wondered why he
never put the marriage aside and remarried."

"There was a rumor he meant to do exactly that,"
Sandor put in slowly and thoughtfully. "Pavar visited me
and mentioned it, saying something about it being surprising only in how long Dobros had waited. The marriage
had been arranged by his father, of course, and refusing
would have meant being disinherited. Now that Dobros
was king in his own right he could do as he pleased, but
Pavar and Selwin weren't precisely happy for him. I had
the impression they meant to make their move before
Dobros managed to produce an heir."

"Assuming their childlessness was the queen's fault,
that would be understandable," Tiran said with a nod.
"It's possible the fault was the king's, though, and that
would have made things easier for them. But they couldn't
afford to wait and see, not when they aren't young men
themselves. They wanted the throne personally, not just to
pass on to their children. Which one was supposed to
actually have the crown?"

"That's a point no one ever mentioned," Sandor replied
with a snort. "And I, for one, would hate to have to guess.
I can't imagine either of those two stepping aside for the
other, but it's possible Selwin proposed that Pavar be in
charge of the army they would have to build up. Dobros
had nothing more than a palace guard consisting mainly
of middle-aged men—another of those little quirks of his.
He saw no reason to spend any gold on 'useless decora-
tion,' his definition of an army in a kingdom uninterested
in conquest."

"My father told me Dobros refused to consider the possibility of anyone trying to dethrone him," red-haired Nomilt put in with a frown. "He was the lawful monarch, and it was inconceivable that anyone would try to change that. My father thought the attitude was a result of how long Dobros had had to wait for the throne."

"Understandable, but not at all a sane attitude," Tiran said with a headshake. "If the interlopers hadn't come along, someone else probably would have. I'm sure you know that my people have been recruiting for weeks, and we've got the beginnings of a very respectable force. Most of them are completely untrained, but we've already begun to take care of that. And you don't have to worry about when we begin to recruit in *your* villages. We're not so much *taking* men and boys as trading for them."

"I don't understand," Obrif said, apparently speaking for the other two men as well. "What do you trade for them *with?*"

"Since she's been in charge of the project, I'll let my queen explain," Tiran said, looking over at Alex. "That is, if she's had enough to eat to hold her for a short while. She's been eating more trail rations than regular meals, so she needs a chance to catch up—and rest up. I won't have her falling over from exhaustion."

"I don't have the *time* to fall over from exhaustion, not when there's still so much to do," Alex commented with a glance for him, knowing exactly what he was saying. Tiran had taken the opportunity to show that he was *not* going to change his mind about having her stay in the palace and city for a while, but her glance had told him she hadn't said her last word on the subject.

"Tiran should have said the project is a joint one that both of us are working on," Alex continued to their guests. "He's been taking care of the city, and I'm working with the villages. The biggest problem has been getting the villagers to go along with it, but being able to use a truth they can see for themselves has helped enormously. The truth I'm talking about is, not everyone is cut out for village or farm life. Can any of you argue the point?"

Faint smiles showed as their guests shook their heads, the point being *too* basic to argue. There have been dreamers and fighters born into villages ever since there have *been* villages, and either they ran away young to challenge the outer world, or they stayed and made life unpleasant for themselves and everyone else.

"Well, none of the villagers could argue it either," Alex said after taking a sip of wine. "They certainly didn't like it and most couldn't understand it, but it's a fact of life they'd learned to accept. What I did then was point out how much better off they'd be *without* those who didn't want to be there, especially if they got people who did want to be there in their place. Just think, people who were villagers at heart but who had been born into a town or city, knowing village life was forever beyond them because they were outsiders and would never be accepted in a village. Or those who had left their own village, mistakenly thinking they would prefer city life, forever deprived of returning and admitting their mistake."

"Those are rather moving pictures of desolation and pathos," Countess Leestin, Nomilt's wife, commented with a smile. "I should think many villagers would respond to them without hesitation."

"They aren't stupid or easily manipulated," Alex answered, keeping the words mild to also keep them from being a rebuke. "Most of the villagers *did* respond positively, but only because I asked them to imagine *themselves* in such a position. For the most part they're warm, caring people, and they were disturbed at the thought of people needing to live in lifelong exile because of a mistake in birthplace or a mistake in judgment. But they're not fools, and it took the guarantee to make them go along with the plan."

"And what guarantee was that?" Baroness Iltaina, Obrif's wife, asked with a faint, cool smile. Apparently everyone thought it was more proper for the women to respond to Alex—or they were trying to make sure that their husbands didn't respond in any *wrong* way.

"We guaranteed that those were the only two kinds of people we would send to their villages," Alex replied with her own faint smile. "No thieves looking for easy pickings, no slackers looking for a place to relax and put their feet up, no dissidents looking to make trouble. Just people who *wanted* to be in a village, and people who belonged there. Those in the first group might not all work out, not when there's a big difference between *wanting* to be in a village and really understanding how much work is involved. If any of them don't fit in, the villagers will tell us and we'll swap them for someone else.''

"You still haven't said where you're getting the people to trade to them," Sandor pointed out, using his wife's turn but too involved in frowning to realize it. "Obviously they're coming from this city and the larger towns, but how are you choosing them?"

"We're finding more than choosing," Alex said, then she laughed at the expression of confusion on Sandor's face. "I know the distinction doesn't explain anything, but we'll have to start with some basics of city life. To begin with, there are an awful lot of poor and unemployed people around, even more than there would be normally because of the efforts of the interlopers.''

"We've all noticed that," Nomilt agreed dryly. "But you also have to remember that old saying that tells us the poor will always be with us.''

"That old saying is garbage," Alex came back with a snort of ridicule. "Whoever said it was really saying he'd make no effort to change the situation, not when it let him feel oh-so-superior and also gave him a good excuse not to part with any significant amounts of gold. What he and too many other people don't understand is that you don't give money to the poor, you give them help enough to let them earn their own money. Then they aren't poor any longer.''

"An interesting philosophy," Sandor said as neutrally as it was possible to be. "I can't say I've never heard it before, but I *have* never heard of it working.''

"That's because those who tried it were idealists, and you'll never find an idealist who's in touch with the real world," Alex came back, unbothered by his silent but obvious scepticism. "Tiran and his people have been sifting through the city's population, interviewing not only the poor and unemployed, but also those who are unhappy doing what they're currently doing.

"This man works as a clerk in a butcher shop, but in

his heart he's always wanted to learn to use weapons and wear a uniform. That man is in a uniform, but his creative sense of style and color has always made him want to design women's gowns. That man was apprenticed to his uncle in the uncle's dress shop, but he cooks in his spare time and would make a superb chef. That man is a chef, but his real talent lies in being able to cut meat just right and know when it's prime. I'm simplifying, of course, but that's approximately what we're doing: giving people the chance to do what they've always wanted to.''

"You still haven't said how this is being accomplished, Your Majesty," Obrif put in, in a friendlier way than his wife. "And what will happen when the guarantee you gave the villagers fails?"

"Why should it fail?" Alex asked, now showing amusement. "Tiran and his people are interviewing prospective villagers and new government employees with a truth spell. The deliberately shiftless are given the choice of finding a job within the week, or leaving the kingdom. The seriously incompetent are either being retrained, or placed as servants in situations where they're under constant supervision. Those who want to do nothing but steal or take advantage of others are being escorted out of the kingdom. Everyone else is being put to work."

"A truth spell," Baron Sandor said, no longer looking skeptical. "So no one can lie their way into something they have no true interest in, and that's how you were able to make that guarantee to the villagers. But what will happen once all this rearranging is done? Perhaps I'm mistaken, but I have the feeling there may well be a shortage of workers."

"You're very perceptive, Baron Sandor," Tiran said, taking over again so that Alex would be free to give her attention back to the new food being brought. "It so happens a shortage was projected when we first began this project, so we've taken steps to avoid the problem. Women are being recruited as well as men, not only for city jobs, but also for our new army."

"You're joking," Baron Obrif said with a small laugh, obviously expecting Tiran to agree and laugh with him.

"Women in important jobs and in the army? What fool thought *that* would work?"

"This fool," Tiran answered, following Alex's example and keeping the words mild as he leaned back. "As the captain of a very successful mercenary company, I can tell you just how good female fighters are. Of course, if you don't believe me you can challenge any one of them, but I strongly suggest the use of practice weapons if you do. My male fighters respect them, and there's rarely any trouble. And if they're that good at fighting, how hard will the competent ones find doing work in a shop or office?"

"But that's ridiculous," Count Nomilt protested, unthinkingly taking Obrif off the hook. "If women go traipsing off to jobs, what will happen to men's homes? Who will be left to clean them and cook the meals and—and—all the rest? And what about the children? Who will have and look after the children?"

"Have you any idea how foolish you sound, Nomilt?" Baroness Tovail, Sandor's wife, said with a laugh. "You and Obrif together. If men find it impossible to look after themselves because they're helpless, they'll just have to *pay* someone to look after them. And women will still *have* the children, but someone can be hired to look after *them* as well. Queen Alexia: is there anything *I* can do to help you and the king execute your plans?"

"Tovail!" Sandor exclaimed in shock and horror, which made Alex pat her mouth with her napkin to keep from laughing out loud. All the rest of them were making similar sounds of indignation and disbelief, which meant Tiran had to use his own napkin for the same reason.

"I appreciate the offer, Baroness Tovail, and I also accept it," Alex said as soon as she had control of herself again. "There really is a lot left to be done, and finding people to help enthusiastically as well as capably is now our biggest problem. If the people running these projects don't believe in them, neither will anyone else."

Tovail was delighted with her acceptance, but her husband and fellow nobles clearly felt less than pleased. Tiran took that as the strongest possible indication that all serious discussion should be put aside for a while, and happily began to apply himself to his food. Casual talk at a meal is fine, but the intense sort that keeps you away from eating should be made illegal.

The rest of the meal went pleasantly enough—at least for Tiran—and it really was a fairly respectable feast. There was certainly enough food for everyone, and every dish was more than just good. The six guests slowly relaxed as they ate, and by the end of the meal they were chatting a little again. The conversation was the least bit stiff, but at least it had started again.

After dinner they had brandies by the fire in the nearby informal reception room, and Tiran's three male guests seemed upset when their wives were not only not sent elsewhere, but were offered the same.

"I see you mean to depart from tradition in any number of ways," red-haired Nomilt commented to Tiran, clearly fighting to keep a frown off his face. "I should think that someone in your position, new to the throne and the crown, would prefer to reassure people by adhering to it."

"Tradition doesn't spring out of nothing," Tiran answered mildly, looking down at the much smaller man. "At some point in time *it* was the new way of doing things, and then people continued with it because others convinced them it was the 'right' way. But times have changed, and any tradition that isn't flexible enough to change with them doesn't deserve to be followed. In this instance, you happen to have a very capable—and very independent—queen. Would *you* like to tell her she isn't good enough to join the men after dinner and drink with them?"

"But she *refused* the brandy," Nomilt complained, turning a bit to look at Alexia. "She's drinking coffee, and she's talking to Baroness Tovail with the other ladies near them. If she's going *that* far, she ought to go the rest of the way and be in another room."

"For what purpose?" Tiran tried again, also trying not to lose his patience. "If you need to be given a separate room before you can feel important, the sad truth is you're *not* important. What you *do* makes you important; what room and company you have drinks in and with doesn't. Can't you see that?"

Nomilt shook his head very slightly, not in answer to

Tiran's question but to show that he was struggling with a new, outrageous idea. Tiran understood and didn't try to press the point, but someone else felt it necessary to take up the gauntlet of argument.

"But those who are important are *entitled* to certain privileges," Baron Obrif, standing beside Baron Sandor, put in. "When one is born to the nobility, that birth endows the person with certain rights that are his automatically. Any attempt to deny those rights can also be considered an attack against his status, an attack meant to make him less than he is. Do you believe in ignoring attacks against you, Your Majesty?"

"That depends on whether or not the attack is real," Tiran returned, now looking at his new adversary. "To begin with, what family you're born into isn't nearly as important as what ability you're born with and how well you put it to use. My own family wasn't considered noble, but before I came here I'd amassed a personal fortune larger than those of the nobles clamoring to hire my services. And they were the ones who needed *my* help, not the other way around."

Obrif glanced at Sandor, obviously hoping the older man could counter what Tiran had said, but Sandor was too busy frowning in thought.

"The second point is, of course, what nobles are *supposed* to be," Tiran continued. "They began as the warriors of a kingdom, and their job was to protect the ordinary people in return for being supported by them. Then the first generation of noble children grew up, and somehow they'd gotten the idea that what they were given was *due* them. By and large that attitude caused a lot of them to find out they were wrong the hard way, and then new people joined the ranks of the nobility. No kingdom interested in thriving needs a drain on its productivity that gives nothing beneficial in return."

By now Nomilt had joined the others, and all three of them stared at him soberly. Tiran knew he was reaching them, but whether it was for good or ill he couldn't yet tell.

"And the final point is this matter of status," Tiran said, glancing at each of them. "No one will ever question the status of my nobles, because everyone will know who they are and what they've done to make this kingdom a better place to live in. That means I expect anyone who supports me to *work*, not just stand there and demand things because they happened to be born into a particular family. I'm being completely frank and open with you gentlemen, so that later no one can say he didn't know what would be expected of him. Whether or not you support me is up to you as individuals, but how you support me is entirely up to me."

"Well, I think I see at least one benefit in your new policies, Your Majesty," Sandor said ruefully after a moment of utter silence. "We don't have to guess about what you're after and what you expect of us, we now know. I hope you'll forgive me if I say I'll need some thinking time. This won't be an easy decision for any of us."

"Certainly, Baron Sandor," Tiran agreed affably after sipping at his brandy. "You have to choose between Duke Selwin, who will almost certainly adhere to tradition in everything, and me, who will establish new traditions whenever the old don't suit me. Everyone wants to be on the winning side of a fight, but the trick is to figure out which that will be before it happens. Afterward will be much too late."

Peculiar expressions fleeted across the faces of the three men, certainly because of what Tiran had said for the second time: if they chose to support Selwin and Tiran defeated the duke, they would *not* be allowed to swear allegiance to the crown in the time-honored tradition of forgiving one's nobly born enemies. If Selwin went down they would go with him, and it was unnecessary to add that no one would be allowed to remain neutral. Sides had to be taken, and once taken there was no turning back.

Even casual conversation flagged after that, at least among the men. Alex kept it going with Baroness Tovail and then with Countess Leestin joining in, but after a few minutes it became clear that Baroness Iltaina had also joined in and had managed to say the wrong thing. Alex kept her voice down, but it wasn't hard to tell that she was wading into Iltaina with the other women silently cheering her on. Tiran let it go on for only a couple of minutes, and then he walked over to the small, quiet battle.

"Excuse me," he said when he reached them, interrupting whatever Alex had been saying. "I know it's rude to intrude on a serious conversation, but it's been rather a long day for me. Alex, would you really mind if we called it a night?"

"I suppose not," she grumbled, her glance at Iltaina saying she would have preferred to go back to her argument. "I've also had a long day, and the more tired I am, the touchier I get. Have you men made any bottom-line decisions yet, or is it still up in the air?"

"Up in the air," Tiran admitted readily enough, and then he looked more closely at Alex. "Don't tell me you women have outdone us?"

"Some of we women have outdone you," Alex answered with another glance for a tight-lipped Iltaina. "Tovail and Leestin have both decided they want to be put to work, but Iltaina has been raised to believe that breaking a fingernail could well become fatal. We were discussing the merits and drawbacks in letting yourself be pampered to death when you came over, but I suppose we can pick up where we left off at another time."

"I appreciate that, and I think our other guests will too," Tiran said, sending his own glance to the men. They stood in a cluster and spoke in very low voices, which made it impossible to tell which of them was for or against anything at all. "At least they'll appreciate it when they find out about it. Ladies, I hope to see you all again very soon."

The women all curtsied as Tiran gave Alex his arm, and a moment later the men came out of their cluster to bow. The actions of the six were all very proper, but once he and Alex were out in the hall, Tiran murmured, "I wonder how many of them actually mean it. They *all* think they're better than I am, but that doesn't mean they might not decide to support me anyway."

"It would be nice to have their support, but we don't really need it," Alex commented, holding to his arm now with both hands. "None of them has an armed force worth mentioning, but they might have enough gold among them to hire a mercenary company or two. Do you think your reputation is enough to keep them from getting the best?''

"My reputation along with all the recruiting and training we've done," Tiran said with a short laugh. "I know the captains of just about every first-rate company out there, and a good number of the second-rate captains along with them. I can't picture any of them coming against an army of mine, not when I'd have a personal stake in the fight. Selwin and his allies might find some ragtag outfits willing to take the chance for a fortune in gold, and I almost hope they do. Once I mop up their forces, they'll be out of mercenaries *and* money."

"Somehow I don't think it will be that easy," Alex said, sounding faintly disturbed. "I listened to everything everyone had to say about Selwin, and I got the impression he isn't the sort to do the obvious. If he does move against us, it will be in a way we aren't expecting."

"What do you mean, *'if'?*" Tiran asked, feeling his sudden frown. "You said you heard what they told me about Selwin, and you were there this afternoon after I had Pavar arrested. You don't seriously think he'll give up his ambitions to pledge loyalty to *me?* If he ever tried *that,* I'd probably find it impossible not to laugh in his face."

"And I'm finding it impossible not to *yawn* in *everyone's* face," Alex said after trying unsuccessfully to swallow the yawn. "The only thing keeping me awake at the end there was Iltaina's infuriating attitudes. I don't think there's a man alive who can match a real, true, male chauvinist *sow.*"

"Oh, yes, your discussion on pampering," Tiran said with a grin for the phrase she'd used. "But there's a question I have to ask about that, one that's very relevant. I gather you were arguing against letting yourself be pampered, but how do you know how terrible it is? When were you ever pampered?"

"What do you think being raised as a princess is like?" she came back with a sound of ridicule. "Years of hard labor? You *do* remember my father's palace, the one I grew up in?"

"Yes, I remember your father's palace," Tiran agreed,

nodding to the guards who stood their post outside the royal apartment. Two of the six men immediately opened the doors for them, then closed them again once he and Alex were inside. Their arrival brought servants out of the woodwork to help them undress, so Tiran abandoned the conversation until it was done. Once they each came out of their dressing rooms in nightwear and the servants were gone, though, Tiran plunked Alex into the middle of their giant bed and stretched out next to her to pick it up again.

"You can't use being raised as a princess as evidence that you know what pampering is like," Tiran said, using one finger to trace the features on Alex's beautiful face. "A pampered princess isn't started on weapons skills at the age of four, and given over to a Master Combat Instructor for training lessons at the age of ten. I know people who will swear that even the prisoners on roadgangs have it easier than you did."

"But prisoners on roadgangs don't have a choice about what's done to them, and I did," Alex pointed out, one of her hands reaching to the bottom of his very proper nightshirt. "Now that the servants are gone, why don't you get rid of this? And I want to talk to you about tomorrow. There are reasons why I should be the one to visit the villages, and it won't take me long to list them."

"Alex, we *are* talking about tomorrow," Tiran told her gently, ignoring—or mostly ignoring—the way her fingers tickled at his thigh. "The point I was trying to make is that it's time you did get to be pampered, at least a little. The start of it will be you staying here in the city while I go out to the villages, and when I get back there will be more. As your husband I have the *right* to pamper you a little, and you can't refuse until you see what it's like."

"But, Ti, I don't *want* to be pampered," she protested, starting to show impatience. "I don't have to be run through with a sword to know I won't like *that,* so—"

"Now that's not fair and you know it," Tiran interrupted at once. "You can't really know you won't like pampering until you try it, and there's another, even better, reason you can't refuse."

"Oh? What?" she asked, trying to be annoyed but finding it impossible now that he had begun some touching of his own. Her skin was smooth and soft and warm and alive under his hand, and her body was heating up just as fast as it usually did.

"The reason is that, at *your* insistence, I'm the king and the final word around here," Tiran murmured, leaning down to start kissing her neck and throat. "What I say has to go, and I say you *don't* go. And that you agree to spend some time being pampered. After you try it for a while, we can discuss the matter again."

"But . . . you haven't even . . . listened to my list," she tried to protest, but her hands were already moving over his body in the same way his were over hers. "Tiran . . . stop . . . this isn't right . . ."

"Of course it is," he murmured as he began to slide her out of her nightgown. "We're married and everything. It couldn't be more right."

And then he used a kiss to cut off the rest of her arguments. He was absolutely crazy about her, and knew without doubt that she was just as crazy about him. Their lovemaking was always marvelous and that time was no exception, but afterward Tiran held a deeply sleeping Alex in his arms and looked down at her face.

"You haven't spoken about leaving for good in weeks," he whispered, stroking her hair gently. "I don't know if that's because there's still so much to do or because you've changed your mind about going, and I'm afraid to ask. But that doesn't mean I won't *do* everything in my power to keep you here forever. I would *not* be better off without you, not in any way at all, and I've got to make you understand that."

Even in the middle of a probable war to keep the throne, he added silently to himself. And with people who seem to be interested in kidnapping you. The thought of someone doing that sends me closer to mindless rage than I've ever been, but I've got to stay in control if I intend to find out who it is. And I *will* find out . . . and then kill him with my bare hands . . .

Tiran had to spend some time calming down after that, but it was necessary so he did it. He had to be up early tomorrow and it would be an even longer day than usual, so he needed to get some sleep. And there were special orders to be left, a number of special orders . . .

CHAPTER FOUR

When I woke up the next morning, I discovered that I'd slept later than usual. That was Tiran's doing, of course, cancelling the orders I'd left to be awakened early. I'd known I'd probably want another chance to argue him out of going to the villages in my place, but it probably wouldn't have done any good anyway. Not with some unknown out to kidnap me, so that was another one I owed them even beyond the try itself.

I stretched lazily in the big, empty bed, watching as the servants who had appeared as soon as I woke up opened the drapes on the terrace doors to show a dismal, rainy day. And then more servants came with the breakfast-in-bed Tiran had also ordered for me. I remembered then about the pampering, and couldn't help sighing. You'd think if a man went so far as to marry you, he'd have *some* idea about what you were basically like . . .

But men are strange creatures even at their best, and I had enough strangeness to occupy my thinking time. I had the breakfast tray moved to a table while I took a quick bath and got dressed, and then I sat down to eat. The first thing I'd have to find out would be what Tiran had scheduled for today, and how much of it should be postponed. Things that were a matter of policy were *his* to decide, and I had no interest in interfering.

And as I ate my eggs, I wondered what I would do with Baroness Tovail and Countess Leestin if their husbands hadn't managed to talk them into taking back their requests for jobs. I'd almost fallen over when Tovail had volunteered out of the blue and I hadn't had the heart to turn her down, but I seriously didn't know what she could help *with*. Or Leestin, for that matter. The younger woman had seemed just as eager as the older, but I couldn't decide about her motives. Had she volunteered as a ploy to make sure nothing happened with any of the other noble families that she and her husband didn't know about, or was she seriously jumping at the chance to get out of the rut? It made a difference, and not knowing bothered me.

"How can you mutter to yourself while you're eatin'?" a too-pleasant voice asked from behind me. "Chewin' problems along with your food does nothin' but give you a bellyache."

"It's more like a headache, and not all problems are small enough to be chewed," I told Cadry as she pulled a chair over to the table and sat in it. "What are you doing here so early? You know I can't stand morning-people cheerfulness before my eyes are even open."

"It ain't early and I was told to be here," she answered comfortably, reaching for a piece of toast to chew on while a servant brought her a cup for the coffee she'd probably want. "The boss left word for me to show up fast and stay until you threw me out, so I don't have to ask if you told him about yesterday. And I'm not your only visitor. There's two ladies out there in the anteroom waitin' for you to be officially up, and I never seen such—*determined*—expressions on their sort in my life."

"Shit," I muttered as I slumped back in my chair and reached for the coffee. "Tovail and Leestin. And I wish you'd make up your mind about whether you're going to be folksy or grammatical. Your switching back and forth is starting to drive me crazy."

"I *used* to shift back and forth dependin' on who I was talkin' to, but not payin' attention and just mixin' it up is easier," she commented, then looked at me curiously. "You sound like you know who the ladies are, so what do they want?"

"Jobs," I answered shortly, deciding I hadn't really lost my appetite and would finish breakfast after all. "I was in the middle of telling them last night about what Tiran and I were trying to do, and I guess I did too good a job of it. The older woman, Tovail, volunteered to help, and later on in the evening the other one decided to do the same. I couldn't very well refuse, but now I don't know what to do with them.''

"They don't look stupid, so if they really mean it you ought to be able to use 'em *somewhere*," Cadry said, but the doubt in her voice was an exact match to what *I* felt. "What do they teach women in their place in life?"

"You don't want to know," I said with a grimace for the memories, then shook my head. "Actually, its only a little different from what most women are taught, only with less physical labor. What we really need is a retraining program for the hopelessly domestic, but right now we can't afford to start one. I think I'll have them walk around with me while I'm catching up on how far Tiran has gotten in the main projects. Maybe *they'll* see something they can do."

"Or maybe I will," Cadry said very blandly. "Don't forget I'll be comin' along, me and one of my squads. Parts of this palace have too many strangers wanderin' around, and I'd rather not have to stand in front of you all by myself."

"Stand *where?*" I asked, looking over at her with no amusement whatsoever. "Do you have any idea what would happen to you if I ever found you standing in front of me during a fight? Let me give you a hint: your greatest danger would *not* be in what was coming at you from in front."

"And let me give you a hint right back," she countered, her tone easy but very, very serious. "It looks like you missed it, but you're the *queen* of this place. Not a damned good fighter who also happens to be married to the captain of my company, but the queen to his king. That means you do get to have people standin' in front of you if there's trouble, and you got nothin' to say about it. Everybody's got their job in this life, and that's part of yours."

"Not even close," I said, finishing my coffee before wiping my mouth. "Since Tiran and I are making all those changes, that might as well be one of them. You're welcome to fight *beside* me and always will be, but don't let me catch you trying to handle it all by yourself. If you do and you survive, you'll wish you hadn't."

I gave her a look that was supposed to say I wasn't joking and then stood up, but I had to ignore her own look back that said she didn't care. She would do things *her* way, and to hell with what I wanted. I hadn't expected to have trouble from Cadry, and it made me want to sigh. Or plan to commit regicide when Tiran got back. If he hadn't insisted that I stay in the city, the only thing I'd be worrying about now would be how to stay dry in the rain.

Leestin and Tovail got to their feet with big smiles when I appeared, the two of them only glancing nervously at the sword I wore before forcing themselves to ignore it. They glanced at Cadry in the same way, and then their attention was all mine.

"Good morning, Your Majesty," Tovail said while they both curtsied. "We're here and ready to begin, just as we promised."

"So I see," I agreed, gesturing for them to rise. "There was no trouble with your husbands, then? They smiled and nodded when you said you were off to find jobs?"

"Not quite," Tovail answered dryly while Leestin made a face that was half way between amusement and exasperation. "Sandor was completely impossible, and Leestin tells me Nomilt was the same."

"He actually ordered me to stay in the apartment," Leestin added, and there was no doubt about the annoyance she felt. "My birth and upbringing were every bit as noble as his own, and he had no right to treat me as if I were a slave. I told him that just before I walked out."

"There's a definite benefit in dealing with a man who's used to the idea of women not being helpless," I said with a smile. "But even men should be capable of learning, so let's look around for what you can do to show them there's a new part of you for them to learn about."

They agreed enthusiastically, so after exchanging a glance with Cadry I led the way out of the anteroom. The men of her squad were waiting outside in the hall, so we turned into a fairly large procession. I toyed with the idea of turning into something myself, like a cat or a dog or a mouse, and taking off on my own, but the idea wasn't practical just at that moment. Later, though . . .

I headed us downstairs and toward the part of the palace that had been given over to new governmental concerns, and after a few minutes of walking we reached it. But before that we also reached the end of a very long line, and the people standing on it looked as if they'd been in the same place for hours. Even as we approached, one man spat something under his breath and walked off, abandoning his place and intentions at the same time.

"What *is* this?" Cadry asked as we began to see just how long that line stretched. "Don't remember anybody sayin' they wanted a whole bunch of people with roots."

"They do look like they've been standing there long enough to grow roots," I agreed. "Let's see what's happening to cause that."

The line apparently originated inside a large conference room that had been supplied with a long table and chairs behind, but at the moment only one man sat in one of those chairs with a second man standing behind him. It turned out that the second man was actually looking over the seated man's shoulder, and when we got close enough we heard what he was saying.

". . . must be legible," he seemed to be lecturing in a slow, dry voice. "I *have* told you that over and over, but you insist on writing much too quickly. These people will wait because they must, and if I need to reprimand you again I may well send you away with the others and replace you myself."

The seated man looked furious and frustrated, but he also looked helpless. The man standing at the head of the line looked the same, but all *I* must have looked was confused.

"What's going on here?" I asked, addressing the man who was standing. "Who are you, and why is everything going so slowly?"

"One *must* proceed slowly if one is to perform without error," the man answered pedantically—and *slowly*. "It's quite fortunate I was placed in charge, else—"

"You, sir," I said to the seated man, finding it impossible to listen to the other one. "Can *you* tell me what's happening in less than an hour?"

"It's the new man in charge," the seated one said, his frustration pouring out along with the words. "We'd been doing fine for days, and then yesterday afternoon the new man showed up. He didn't say anything, only looked around, then he came back this morning. That was when he told us he was in charge, sent the other clerks home, and set Ardry here over me. Filling out these forms should take only a few minutes, but Ardry makes a career out of every one."

"And rightly so," the round, slow-speaking Ardry said with a frown. "And who, may I ask, might *you* be to—"

"This man who said he's in charge," I interrupted again to ask the seated clerk. "Where can I find him right now?"

"He's in the room he took for an office," the clerk responded, turning to point to a closed door in the wall behind him. "After I sign people up, they have to go in and talk to *him*."

"Do they," I murmured, looking at the door, then I turned to Cadry. "Send for more of your men while I take care of the 'man in charge.' And get that fool Ardry out of the way."

She nodded and began to give orders, but I didn't stay to listen. I was already on the way to the "office" that had been established, and when I reached the door I opened it slowly, quietly, and just a crack.

". . . so there's really no use in complaining to me or anyone," an amused voice was in the midst of saying. "The king wants all these changes made, but you can't expect *him* to pay for them. I can accept those measly ten coppers *now*, but once you're working and earning regular pay you'll have to do much better. We'll expect half of everything you earn for the first year, a third the second year, and a quarter the third. After that it will only be ten percent, which you must admit is modest enough for anyone."

"Modest!" another voice said, this one sounding rougher. "Highway robbery's whut it is! Whut if I won't do 'er?"

"Then you can stay unemployed," the first voice answered, even more amused. "It's *your* family that will starve, not mine or the king's. Make up your mind right now and give me an answer."

"Suppose *I* give you an answer," I said, pushing the door open and walking in. The roughly dressed man standing in front of the small table turned, but the sleek one sitting down behind it shot to his feet.

"How dare you barge in here?" he demanded, justified outrage in every line of his body. "I've been appointed to this post by the king himself, and now I'll be taking down your name. He's certain to have something rather sharp to say to you for interfering where you don't belong. Now tell me your name!"

"You do that very well," I observed mildly, feeling as if I'd gone through that scene once before. "If I didn't know better, I might actually believe you do belong here. And to answer your question, my name is Alexia."

He opened his mouth again as if to snap something, but then he paled and swallowed the words. It had obviously just come through to him who he was threatening to report to the king, and he didn't hesitate. He took off for the door I wasn't quite blocking, his short, compact body really moving, and when two of Cadry's fighters caught him as he ran through, he screamed and struggled.

"Have him locked up somewhere," I called to the men, then walked the rest of the way to the small table. A neat stack of completed forms stood on one side, and a large leather pouch filled with coins stood on the other. The form on top of the stack had the name Lornd on it, with a note of "ten coppers" in the margin.

"Mr. Lornd, it looks like ten coppers of this money is yours," I said, now giving my attention to the tall, strongly built man who stood there frowning at me. "Whoever that man is, the king did *not* appoint him to rob people blind. There are no charges of any sort for signing up for work, and any taxes you pay won't be in the amounts he mentioned."

"Thought there wus sumthin' funny goin' on," the man said with a satisfied nod, but held a hand up when I reached toward the money pouch. "Cain't take thet 'cause ain't none uv it mine. Ten copper's whut he said I *hadda* give 'em, not whut I did."

"Well, it's nice to meet an honest man as well as a smart one," I said with a smile I really meant. "Some people would hand over their heads if someone who seemed to be in charge told them to. Please let all your friends and neighbors know about what happened here, and that we'll be returning the money in this pouch according to the names on these forms. And if you see or hear about anything like this happening again, please do me the favor of coming to tell me about it. If I'm not available, ask for Cadry or Damis or Hadar. One of them will be sure to make the time to listen."

"Ah'll shore do thet, girl," the man agreed affably before starting to leave, then he turned back to me again. "If'n *Ah* ever git t'talk t'th' king, Ah'm gonna tell 'im yore all right."

"I appreciate that, Mr. Lornd, I really appreciate it," I said with a grin, then watched him leave. It had been obvious the man didn't know who I was, and there was no need to make him uncomfortable by telling him. Once he was gone, I went out to take care of the rest of the problem.

"Cadry, when your other men get here, have two of them get the forms and money from the table in that room," I said. "Names and addresses are on each of the forms, and the people get back the amount written in the margin near the names. And make sure everyone knows it was a thief taking advantage, *not* the new king's money-grubbing policy."

"Don't believe that twerp had the nerve to set up right here under everybody's nose," Cadry said with a nod for the orders I'd given. "How'd he get away with it even this long?"

"He got away with it because nobody was watching," I answered sourly, having already asked myself the same thing. "We don't have enough people to actually do what needs doing, let alone have a bunch of them stand around watching everybody else work. It was this one's bad luck that we spotted him so quickly, but next time the luck could be on the other side—if it hasn't happened already.

Something has to be done, and I think I'm getting an idea about what that should be.''

It was the sight of my two lady companions that began to give me the idea, but there were other things that had to be done first. There were twenty or so people from the line actually in the room, so I asked if any of them were able to read and write well. Only one tentative hand went up, so I sent one of Cadry's people to repeat the request down the length of the rest of the line, then took my two lady nobles aside.

"I need you ladies to do me a very big favor," I said to them in low tones. "As soon as I find out who the rest of the clerks are I'll send some people to bring them back, but until they get here I'll need as many literate assistants as I can get. I'd like you two to play clerk for a while, but as soon as the real clerks get here I need you for something much more important."

"Such as?" Tovail asked, indecision on her face along with skepticism. "I know we said we would help, but *this* . . .''

"*This* is just a small part of the overall plan, but if *it* doesn't work, the rest might not either," I explained, also speaking to Leestin, who seemed to be thinking about being outraged. Then I lowered my voice even more. "What I'll really need you for is a special guard service I'll want you to put together and run. Do you think you'll be able to do that?"

"A *guard* service?" Tovail echoed, and now her eyes were as round as Leestin's. "You want *us* to find men to do something like that?"

"Yes, but not with men," I answered, glancing around to make sure no one was close enough to overhear the conversation. "There aren't *many* women in that line, but there are enough to get you started—especially if you use the ones you recruit to bring in friends who can also do the job. And the job won't be easy. What you'll be doing is arranging to keep a regular eye on everything going on in this part of the palace. But I don't want anyone to *know* that's what you're doing."

"You want us to build a *spy* force," Leestin whispered,

delight now filling her shining eyes. "Oh, I *knew* I was
right to volunteer, I just knew it!"

"And what we'll be looking out for is things like this,"
Tovail said with a general wave of her hand, just as delighted. "Oh, Your Majesty, I don't know how to thank
you. Sandor said I'd end up as nothing but a glorified
servant, running to fetch you things whenever you decide
you needed them. Wait until he hears about *this*."

"Actually, I think Baron Sandor and Count Nomilt
should hear that you *have* been given unimportant, meaningless little tasks to do," I suggested slowly, watching
their expressions. "I think we all know how men gossip,
even if they swear they don't, and they're also prone to
boasting. If word gets around about what you're doing,
you might as well forget about doing it."

"You're absolutely right," Leestin said with a frown
as Tovail's brows went up. "But if we pretend to be bored
and unhappy, won't they insist that we stop doing whatever we're doing? And when we refuse, won't they become suspicious?"

"Not if you point out that what you're actually doing
is getting into the good graces of the queen," I said with
a grin. "The silly woman is running around handing out
useless orders that most people just ignore, but *she* thinks
she's really important. Having two members of the nobility
around to give dull little jobs to has made her feel even
better, and if you sound resentful but resigned when you
say that, your husbands might even *insist* that you stick
with it."

"No matter *how* boring and awful the time is," Tovail
said with a laugh, then she sobered a little. "But now it's
time to get started, and I have a request. If we're going
to be making sure everything is going right, we'll need
someone to tell us how they *should* be going."

"Excellent point," I told her, happily impressed. "I'll
have Cadry assign you two of her more discreet fighters,
and you can send one of them to find out. But once you
get started, don't limit yourselves by thinking that the only
way someone can take advantage is by using the way used
here. Investigate everything that looks even a little odd,
and don't worry about wasting time or effort. If even one

little oddity turns into something important, all the effort will be worth it.''

"I suggest that those two fighters be male," Leestin said, her tone and expression thoughtful. "We're bound to run into situations where a woman's 'silly little request' will be ignored, and we won't want to make a fuss. Having someone male—and armed—to make the request *for* us will eliminate the problem before it happens.''

"You know, I'm beginning to think the EverNameless made you two volunteer," I said, not joking in the least. "I want you to know how grateful—and relieved—I am that you're here to help me out. We'll get together later so you can tell me how far you've gotten.''

They showed flattered smiles as they curtsied, but even as I walked away they already had their heads together, suggesting things to each other. If that went as well as it promised to . . .

"You're lookin' a lot happier now," Cadry observed as I walked up to her. "Considerin' that we only found two men on the line who are up to playin' clerk, I wonder why that is.''

"It's because the ladies have also agreed to play clerk until we can get the missing men back here," I told her. "They'll also be doing something else for me, so I want you to assign two of your more closed-mouth men to them for detached duty. And until the full crew of clerks does get here, use those two men to hurry the process here by keeping the single line and sending people one at a time to the first available temporary clerk. Except for the women. The women on line are to be directed only to one of the ladies.''

Cadry raised her brows at me, but when my only answer was a mild and friendly smile, she gave up asking and went to arrange things. I *wanted* Cadry to know what was happening, but telling her would have to wait until later, when no one else was around. Once she finished giving the necessary orders—including making sure our temporary clerks were paid and our one overworked real clerk got a bonus—we left the room.

It took a while to check out the other things being done in that wing, like the registering of *all* children for school, and interviewing people to teach them, but there didn't seem to be any more *obvious* trouble. On a hunch I looked in on the paymaster Tiran had set up in an office, and discovered that someone unknown but "with authority" had ordered that the people working for us were to be given pieces of paper called "credit notes" instead of silver or copper. The credit notes would be redeemed once a month rather than daily, and anyone who didn't care to wait could find a job somewhere else.

The paymaster, a gruff older man who had once served in someone's army and had lost a leg doing it, hadn't liked that order but also hadn't seen any way around it. I showed him the way by tearing up the order, then told him not to change his procedures for *anyone*. If someone came in to say something different, he was to smile pleasantly and agree with whatever they said, then doublecheck the order with Tiran or me. I left behind a much happier man, but when I left his office I took his former unhappiness along as my own.

"That's twice," I said to Cadry once we were out in the hall. "If people thought we'd be paying once a month rather than every day, we'd be lucky if as many as five people showed up tomorrow to do their jobs. Someone is trying really hard to wreck things for us, but I didn't recognize the description of whoever came by here. Did you?"

"Not even a little," Cadry agreed as she looked around. "Had a word with the two guards in there, though, and if the cheeky son tries comin' by a second time they'll grab him. Ain't it funny that all this's happenin' right after the boss leaves?"

"I think it's safe to say you and I don't find the same things funny," I told her sourly. "And in fact I'm starting to get mad. They're all but saying Tiran would have caught them immediately, but since I'm here instead they can do as they please."

"Maybe they just didn't expect you to check so soon," Cadry suggested, clearly considering the idea seriously. "The boss made a habit of lookin' in on things every day, they tell me, but you've been out huntin' renegades and talkin' to villagers. First day back you oughta be restin'

up, so the fox figures he's got a clear road into the hen-
house. Even if you got around to it tomorrow, most of the
chickens would be down his throat by then.''

"You know, I'll bet you've just seen more than I did,"
I said slowly, thinking the idea through. "This was a set-
up, and they *did* expect me to take some time off before
getting down to it. The most interesting part, though, is
how they knew I'd be here at all. Those two scams weren't
spur-of-the-moment, especially not the first one. That lone
clerk said the man we arrested came by yesterday afternoon, to take a look around.''

"That's right, he did," Cadry said with a frown that
changed quickly to surprise. "But that would mean—that
kidnappin' attempt wasn't for real!''

"Exactly," I agreed, but actually felt like cursing.
"They knew I'd never be taken so easily, and really didn't
expect me to be. What they wanted was to give Tiran a
good reason for insisting that *I* stay in the palace while
he goes out in my place. And like a damned fool, he fell
for it. I *told* him they were after something more, but he
went ahead and did it his way anyway.''

"But the plan still didn't work," Cadry pointed out.
"You *didn't* sit around with your feet up, or even ignore
things because you were pissed. So what do we do now?''

"Now we go to have a talk with that man we arrested,"
I said, suddenly not quite as unhappy as I had been. "It's
too bad I didn't realize sooner that he isn't your ordinary,
everyday con man, but we do have him. And take my
word for it: he *will* talk to me about who's doing this.''

Cadry made a sound of amusement, knowing I meant
exactly what I'd said. When someone declares himself
your enemy, you no longer owe him anything including
consideration. I found out that the man had been taken to
the highest dungeon area that was now being used as a
lockup, and also got directions for finding it. We went
down one level, and torchlight showed us three of the
company's fighters playing jailer. They knew the man I
wanted, and one of them led me to his cell.

"You can see through the bars that it ain't too bright
in there," the guard said, gesturing to a dark, narrow space

enclosed by a rusted iron grating with fairly wide gaps. "You want I should go in and haul 'im out for you?"

When I nodded he matched the nod, then unlocked the cell and stepped inside. It was gloomy in there even with the grating out of the way, and when the guard hesitated, Cadry stepped over to the entry area and came back with a torch. Once it was brought into the cell, though, it showed us more—or less—than we'd expected to see.

"Damn!" the guard growled, looking around everywhere including up at the bare stone ceiling. "He can't be gone, but he is! How in hell could he have got out?"

I thought I knew the answer to that one, but unfortunately it made more problems rather than fewer.

CHAPTER FIVE

Tiran peered through the grayish mist and rain, wondering if his imagination had taken to playing tricks on him. After a full day of riding through the steady downpour he was more than ready to find an inn for the night, but the flash of light he'd seen—or thought he'd seen—a moment ago seemed to have disappeared.

"Ha! I *wasn't* imagining it," Rhodris said abruptly from Tiran's left, his voice filled with triumph. "There *is* a light ahead, and it looks like a torch. If there's any justice in this world, the thing will be attached to an inn."

"I hope it's an inn even without the justice," Tiran commented, amused by Rhodris's manner. The man was relatively young, but he'd still earned the position of group leader in the company and was popular with the fighters. Black-haired and brown-eyed and almost as large as Tiran, he'd proven to be a good choice for riding through the rain with.

"You're right, Captain," he said with a laugh. "I'm willing to take it without the justice, too. And, if necessary, share a room with half our men. As long as it's dry."

Tiran nodded to show he agreed completely, even with the part about sharing quarters. They only had twenty men with them, but depending on how many rooms the inn had and how many previous guests, they might *have* to share. It was a good thing he'd decided that morning to travel as a captain of mercenaries rather than as the king. Captains were free to share quarters as necessity required; kings usually weren't. You'd think that the higher a position you had the more freedom you'd get with it, but that wasn't proving to be so.

In another few minutes it became clear why the torch both he and Rhodris had spotted had kept disappearing: there was a grove around the inn, and the wind had moved branches and leaves from the trees to occasionally block sight of the torch. Or torches, as it turned out. The inn was large and sported three, but the rain had managed to put out one of them.

The adjoining stables were just as large, but the two boys who appeared were far from adequate for handling twenty-two mounts. Tiran and Rhodris handed over their reins along with a few coppers, but the rest of the men stayed to see to their own mounts. The boys looked relieved, but also a bit nervous. They obviously weren't used to having this kind of company in the stables, even for a little while.

"I don't like the way those boys reacted," Rhodris said low as they walked toward the front door of the inn. "They should have looked awed and impressed as well as nervous, but all they were was wary. That could mean they've had less than pleasant experiences with men of our sort."

"This inn could well be the closest one to Duke Pavar's estates," Tiran told him, pausing at the door to glance at his current second. "Since we still don't know what's going on there—or who the duke has working for him—let's make sure we watch our backs."

Rhodris nodded and opened the door, then stepped aside to let Tiran enter first. Tiran did, but he strutted in like the captain of a fighting company rather than strolling in like a noble. He also made sure to look around as he went, pulling off the hood of his raingear to make it easier.

The door had opened into one large room, with a polished bar along the wall straight ahead. There were small tables scattered across most of the floor, with benches arranged around the fireplace to the left, and half a dozen men had taken their drinks to those benches. Two more stood at the bar and three shared one of the tables, but none of them did more than glance up at the newcomers, if that. Tiran knew of only one thing that made men act like that, which meant they could well see action even before they reached any of the villages.

"Welcome to my house, gentlemen," a surprisingly educated voice said. "Do step up to the bar and have your first drink on me."

Tiran couldn't see the source of the voice until the man stepped away from the two standing at the bar. He was behind the bar and was a good deal smaller than average, but the way he held himself said that that could matter only to other people, not to him. His smile was friendly and his manner open, which made him the only man in the room who wasn't trying hard to be invisible.

"We appreciate the offer," Tiran said, walking closer to the bar. "We'll also need food and rooms for the night, the best you have."

"My best rooms are kept under a standing reservation, but the rest are available," the man said, anger ghosting briefly through the expression in his eyes before a smile banished it. "I'm Gandro, your host, and the meals will make up for the lesser accommodations. Are there just the two of you?"

"The rest of my men are out seeing to our horses in your stables," Tiran answered, accepting the mug of brew that had been set in front of him. "They should be in in just a few minutes, and they number—"

The sound of the front door slamming open interrupted Tiran, but he and Rhodris were the only ones who whirled around. The other patrons of the inn did no more than twitch before drawing even more deeply into themselves, and Tiran could see why. The five men coming in acted as if they owned the place, and possibly the rest of the kingdom as well. Arrogant was too mild a word for their behavior, and even as Tiran straightened in reaction, he glimpsed Rhodris doing the same beside him.

"Get your peasant brats out there to see to our horses," the leader of the five ordered flatly, obviously speaking to Gandro. "And this had better be the first and last time they don't run out as soon as we ride up. If it isn't, we'll make sure it's the last time they do anything else in this life."

"The boys are busy seeing to *our* horses," Tiran said,

immediately drawing the newcomer's attention. "If you don't like that, don't talk to *them* about it, talk to us."

The leader of the five was tall and husky, larger than his men and more hard-faced. He also had that almost-fey look in his eyes that said he killed without hesitation or regret, a look that most people trembled back from. He turned the look on Tiran, obviously expecting him to do the same, but it wasn't about to happen. Tiran had learned many years earlier that a man who killed without hesitation usually died just as quickly and easily as his victims.

"You don't belong around here," the man said flatly and emotionlessly when his stare had been ignored for a moment or two. "Take your horses and move on, or this will be where you're buried."

"It looks like you get a lot of mileage out of threats," Tiran remarked calmly, then deliberately grinned nastily. "I wonder how long it's been since you had to back up those threats—assuming you ever did."

The man stiffened at the insult while the men behind him stirred, all of them well aware of the fact that Tiran was deliberately starting a fight. The other four men looked uneasy, which probably meant it had been a *very* long time since their authority had been challenged.

The leader of the five wordlessly pulled off his rain-cloak, so Tiran quickly did the same. The other patrons of the inn hurriedly retreated as far from the coming fight as they could go, and Tiran knew they were reacting to the husky man's silence just the way he wanted them to. It was a trick meant to terrorize, as if staying silent made the man better with a weapon than someone who spoke. Tiran had never yet seen a fighter who gained skill simply by keeping quiet, but nonfighters had trouble understanding that.

But Tiran had been a fighter for many years, so there was only caution and the usual eagerness in him when he stepped out to face the husky man. His sword hilt felt good in his fist after so many weeks of playing administrator, and his mind rode the usual high that came when he stepped between ordinary people and those who enjoyed pushing them around. Bullies usually aren't fighters; a fighter proves nothing by picking on people without skill, so why would he bother? It was most often twisted non-fighters who made all the trouble, them and the crippled who were born without emotions.

And that could be what this *one is,* Tiran thought as the husky man stood with weapon ready. *One of the soulless ones who don't care* who *they face.* That sort made life hard for normal fighters, since the fear people felt for the twisted ones carried over to include all fighters. The only way to solve the problem was to eliminate the cause of it, which Tiran was more than ready to do.

And this particular cause didn't keep him waiting long. The husky man paused only briefly, probably to see if Tiran would be foolish enough to jump in recklessly. When Tiran didn't oblige him he immediately began his own attack, one designed to startle an inexperienced fighter and drive him into retreat. Tiran parried the flurry of vicious slashes and chops and then replied with attacks of his own, all the while holding his ground. The husky man *was* good with his weapon, but not so good that Tiran had to let himself be pushed around.

The husky man wasn't pleased to have his attacks turned aside before they could accomplish what he wanted them to. The fey look in his eyes grew fractionally more intense as he increased his efforts, now obviously determined to kill Tiran as quickly as possible rather than make him an example by toying with him. Tiran could almost see the man's cold thoughts, still more than arrogant and completely unafraid. He'd made up his mind to kill, and nothing would keep him from doing it.

He is *insane,* Tiran thought as he automatically adjusted his fighting style to his opponent's latest efforts. *He'd slaughter anyone in his way just to get what he wanted, and never think twice about it. Or he would if he lived.*

And with that realization Tiran was completely on the offensive, using every bit of skill he had. The husky man was able to defend himself only for a moment, and then Tiran's steel thrust through his chest and out his back. The husky man faltered, trying to stay on his feet and continue fighting, but blind arrogance means nothing to death. It claimed the man completely between one breath and the next, and Tiran was able to withdraw his blade and watch the body fall.

And that seemed to be the signal for the other four men to draw *their* weapons. Their expressions said they knew they'd never survive a loss of standing, which gave Tiran some idea about the sort of thing they'd been doing. If you need to keep people terrified to keep *yourself* from being hanged or worse, you've been doing more than simple bullying.

It didn't take long for the new attackers to reach Tiran, but by then Rhodris stood beside him with a weapon in his own fist. The four seemed fairly confident that their numbers would overcome any disparity in skill, but the two who engaged Tiran weren't particularly impressive. He cut them down one after the other, and when he stepped back from the second he found that Rhodris had had just as little trouble. There were now five bodies on the floor, and once Tiran cleaned his blade on the tunic of one of them, he turned to Gandro.

"Who *were* these fools?" he asked, making sure he showed only mild annoyance. "And how long have you had to put up with their nonsense?"

"Too long," Gandro muttered, looking only faintly shaken. The rest of what filled him seemed to be satisfaction, along with a touch of regret. "I can't say I'm sorry to see them lying there, but now *you* gentlemen will have to move on. When the others hear about what you've done, they won't hesitate to come after you."

"Others," Tiran echoed, exchanging a glance with Rhodris while the locals in the common room muttered softly among themselves. "Somehow it doesn't surprise me that these aren't the only pieces of trash in the neighborhood. But now that you have a new king, why do you people put up with it? Why don't you ask the king for help?"

"Really, friend, you're most naive for someone who looks to be a worldly man," Gandro replied with a snort. "These five—and the rest—are in Duke Pavar's employ, and when have you ever heard of a king supporting ordinary people against a duke? It doesn't even matter that none of us owes fealty to the duke; his people still do as they please, with none to say they can't.''

"I'd say these five have been given a rather forceful no," Rhodris commented with a faint smile. "Who you work for doesn't really matter in the end, not unless that someone can keep you alive even with three feet of steel through your guts. Besides, everyone in the capital is talking about how Duke Pavar's been arrested for treason. The king had him thrown into a cell, and he'll be as dead as these five within the week."

That started all the locals talking at once, and this time out loud rather than in a mutter. Tiran gave Rhodris a small nod of approval for timing the announcement so well, and then he looked back at Gandro.

"And since you're probably wondering, I have it on very good authority that your king won't be changing his mind about that at the last minute," Tiran said. "Pavar shouldn't be a problem for anyone ever again, but the same doesn't yet go for the rest of his hirelings. What does he have them doing?"

"Something in the villages," Gandro supplied after a brief hesitation, still looking shocked and half disbelieving. "We don't know precisely what, since those who tried to find out never came back to tell us what they saw. And occasionally even people who weren't trying to pry have disappeared . . . Look, who *are* you men, and what do you expect the two of you to be able to accomplish? You—"

Gandro's words broke off at the appearance of more men at the still-open front door, but Tiran's hand relaxed away from his hilt at the first clear sight of them. They were the rest of his own men, who came in to stare down at the bodies with expressions of mild curiosity.

"Part of the answer you want is that there aren't just two of us," Tiran said, turning back to Gandro. "As I tried to tell you earlier, we number twenty-two in all. We need beds and food, and we'll pay in gold for what we get. And I'm sorry to have to say it, but you'll be having more guests than just us tonight."

Tiran glanced at the locals in the common room, and Gandro seemed to understand immediately. When you deal with those who are terrorized, it's impossible to know which of a group of innocent bystanders might run to tell of whatever they happen to know. The locals should have found out *something* of what was happening on Pavar's lands, and if they hadn't it could be because someone was keeping very close tabs on their doings. And that someone had to be one of them, otherwise secrets would never have been spoken aloud.

Tiran had some of his men take the bodies outside and then see to the horses the five would never need again, and even before that the locals had gone back to muttering among themselves. It was also necessary to post a watch outside, but that watching could be done from the shelter of the stables. There was a door at the back of the house that led directly into the stables, and the outside men were warned to keep an eye on that as well.

And then he and the rest of his men could relax and have a drink and a hot meal, pretending they were off-duty and completely unconcerned. In the middle of the meal three of the locals tried to leave together, and were upset when two of Tiran's fighters immediately stood themselves between the three and the door. Tiran had been expecting that, though, and he left his table to stand beside his men and smile at the locals.

"I'm sorry, friends, but you won't be going home tonight," he told them gently. "In the morning my men and I intend to visit the former Duke Pavar's villages, and we'd dislike finding the men in them ready and expecting us. Once we leave, you'll be free to do the same."

"You sayin' we talk outta turn?" one of the three demanded with nervous belligerence. A second of the trio simply looked nervous, but the third had gone almost white. "We live in these parts, man, an' we don't say nothin' t' nobody. All we want's t'be left in peace."

"Peace isn't bought by ignoring what's going on around you," Tiran countered in an even voice. "The only thing you buy that way is a worsening of whatever trouble it is you're trying to ignore. And if no one in these parts talks out of turn, why is it that *no* one has managed to find out what's happening in the duke's villages? At least one of the men who tried should have made it back after getting an eyeful—unless the men in the villages were warned to expect them. You don't see it that way?"

The spokesman of the group looked as if he wanted to argue, but was being kept silent by having thought the same thing himself. And from the furtive glances cast by most of the others, he wasn't alone. Most of them had apparently worried and wondered over the same point, but hadn't been able to accuse a lifelong neighbor without proof.

"So you all might as well make yourselves comfortable," Tiran said, raising his voice slightly to include every local in the room. "You'll be my guests here tonight, and tomorrow you'll be free to leave. But those of you who are completely innocent had better keep one thing firmly in mind: if any of your number tries to talk you into leaving together tonight, his reason isn't innocent no matter how good it sounds. If you decide to ignore what I've said and believe him anyway, whatever happens is on your own heads."

That started the muttering again, but as Tiran went back to his table he decided it sounded more disturbed than angry. The locals weren't fools, and more than one of them was looking at the third man of the three who had tried to leave. He was the one who had gone really pale at being stopped, but he didn't seem to notice the glances. He was deeply into his own thoughts even as he rejoined the rest with his two companions, just as though he searched for a way around the warning Tiran had given.

"Let's keep a really good eye on that tall, thin one," Tiran murmured to Rhodris, nodding at the man he meant. "I'll bet gold he talked those other two into trying to leave with him, and now he looks like he's fishing for a way to get all of them to back his next play. If there's any trouble, it will come from him or any confederates he might have among the others."

"The way they're all looking at him, I'd guess he's on his own tonight," Rhodris murmured back, watching the group out of half-closed eyes. "I noticed him doing some talking earlier, so no bet on his being more than a simple dupe. If he was being *forced* to report on the doings of his neighbors, he would be more terrified and less calculating.''

Tiran nodded his agreement, then went back to his meal. There would probably be trouble during the night, but hopefully not from the entire group. And he'd decided to get a really early start the next morning, one that would put them in the first village shortly before dawn. Then they'd be right on the spot when things began to happen, but that meant their suspect local couldn't be released with the others. They'd have to find a way to leave him locked up, but without one of Tiran's men as guard. He couldn't spare any of his men ... well, he'd solve the problem in the morning.

After arranging rooms and assigning guard watches, Tiran went to bed. The room was clean and comfortable and the bed felt great, but it took a couple of minutes for Tiran to fall asleep. He'd already gotten used to having Alex beside him at night, and he almost wished she were there. But that was almost, which turned into not-at-all when he thought about the fighting they'd almost certainly do tomorrow. Better that Alex stay in the city, where the danger was minimal.

Tiran was awakened from a dream about Alex that had made him grin even in his sleep. It was one of his duty fighters doing the awakening, and the man had news.

"That local we were told to keep a eye on,'' the man said as Tiran stretched and rubbed sleep from his eyes. "He don't need watchin' no more. Durin' the night, somebody done for 'im.''

"He's dead?'' Tiran said with a frown, glancing at the fighter while he climbed into his clothes. "Which one of ours did it, and *why?*''

"Waren't none a us done it,'' the fighter answered with a headshake. "Ibris found 'im in the blankets they was give, eyes wide open an' starin'. Somebody put a blade in 'im, an' it took 'im a while t'go. But we din't hear or see nothin', so we don't know who done it.''

Tiran looked directly at the man again, the way he'd spoken his piece bringing thoughts of suspicion. That complete and very neutral disavowal of any knowledge of the murder was probably meant to tell him his men did know who had done it, but had chosen not to say so. He thought about that while he finished dressing, and by the time he stood to buckle on his swordbelt he knew why that course had been chosen.

"So the fool tried something to get the others stirred up, and that answered the question they'd all had," Tiran said, pretending to speak only to himself. "They knew for certain that he'd been betraying them to their enemies, so they made his death a community project. And we'd do best not to notice, since their effort probably saved most of *our* lives as well. All right, that's the way we'll handle it."

Tiran's fighter kept silent, but the look in his eyes showed the man was properly impressed. The captain had figured out what was going on in no time, and what's more he'd decided to back his fighters. Those two qualities, intelligence and loyalty, were important to men who risked their lives at the order of their leader, and Tiran made a policy of encouraging them as often as possible.

He led the way downstairs, and half the common room was dimly lit near tables laden with a good breakfast. Gandro calmly presided over the meal, but none of his unofficial guests, silent and unmoving in their blankets, was in the least disturbed by the activity.

"Good morning, Captain, even though it isn't quite morning yet," Gandro greeted him softly with a smile and a gesture. "Please seat yourself there, and I'll go and prepare you a special breakfast."

"What you have here will do nicely, Gandro," Tiran told him with an answering smile, taking the indicated chair. "As soon as all of my men have eaten, we'll be on our way. After that your other guests can leave whenever they wish, but I'm hoping they'll stay until after sunrise and pause to eat the breakfast I'll be paying for."

"I'm sure they will, Captain," Gandro said with a slightly wider smile, still making no effort to look toward the "sleeping" forms. "But you needn't worry about paying for their meal. It will be theirs with the compliments of the house."

"Let's share the cost," Tiran said, and Gandro accepted the compromise with a bow, then began to pass platters of food to Tiran. The breakfast was just as good as dinner had been the night before, even though the food was just warm rather than hot. The last group of Tiran's fighters joined him, and the five of them left nothing on the table but dirty dishes.

"It's time to leave, but you just may see us again," Tiran said as he got to his feet. "Your hospitality has been excellent, Gandro, and I'll be certain to tell everyone I know about your wonderful cooking."

"All referrals are greatly appreciated, Captain," Gandro answered with a soft laugh as he took the pouch of gold Tiran handed to him. "And if one particular friend of yours should happen to stop by, I'll be certain to treat him like a—king."

Tiran grinned at that before turning away, finding the comment even funnier than Gandro knew. The man had been hinting that he'd realized who was behind Tiran's "visit," but apparently his guesswork hadn't gone quite far enough. Which wasn't terribly surprising. Having a king send a group of fighters to help out the people of his realm wasn't hard to imagine; having that king *lead* the fighters was another matter entirely.

But that depends on the king, Tiran thought as he and his men went out into the predawn darkness to their waiting horses. *And on the king's queen. If I hadn't grabbed the privilege, it would be Alex out here right now rather than me. And I'd still be ears deep in administrative problems. Obviously it's a damned good thing I do have the queen I do.*

Tiran almost felt like whistling as he mounted, and that despite the trouble that lay ahead. The rain of the previous day had stopped, a man who routinely betrayed his neighbors was no longer a problem, Alex was safe in the city, and *he* was about to do what he did best. And for people who were now his. Did life get any better than that?

The good mood lasted until Tiran and his men reached the first of the villages on the former Duke Pavar's estates, where they dismounted and made their way in closer on foot. Rhodris had gotten excellent directions from Gandro, and once they were in close enough it became clear why no one from the area knew what was going on in the village.

"Armed sentries around a village?" Rhodris whispered in confusion. "What are they afraid might be stolen?"

"I think it's more complex than that," Tiran answered in a return whisper. "What I'm wondering now is whether to replace those sentries with our own men, or— Everybody down!"

Tiran's whispered command was obeyed immediately by everyone including himself, which meant they weren't seen by the yawning, stretching replacement guards coming from the village. He and his fighters had gotten into position just in time, and now the question was answered. As soon as the guards who had been relieved were no longer in a position to notice, the replacements would be replaced.

By the time the last potential witness stepped into a house, Tiran had one of his men positioned in the tall grass near each of the four sentries. When the farthest away whistled to say he was ready, all four moved at the same time. The faint morning light showed no more than two brief scuffles, and ten minutes later there were four new sentries. The men guarding the village had worn rust leather and swords and had carried bows, and now did again.

"I'll bet they thought they would never be in rust-colored leather again," Rhodris murmured with a chuckle and a nod toward their men. "Now that we're the king's special guard rather than mercenaries, rust leather is no longer appropriate."

"But a distinctive uniform would be," Tiran said, frowning at the thought. It was something his fighters had earned and deserved, but the idea hadn't occurred to him before. "That's one of the first things I'll have to see to— once all the trouble is over and a distinctive uniform won't make our people targets. If I forget about it, make sure you remind me."

Rhodris nodded dutifully, but Tiran could see the amusement in the man's eyes. He obviously considered the point minor, but Tiran couldn't do the same. If something was important to even a small number of his people, a king had to at least be aware of it.

With the sentries taken care of, Tiran and his fighters

were able to move up really close to the village without being seen. They'd realized almost immediately that the sentries hadn't been around the entire village, only one relatively small part of it, so that told them where they wanted to be. They settled into position behind a wagon which seemed to have been abandoned months earlier, and simply waited.

It took only until dawn had clearly arrived, and then the village began to stir. But not in the normal way, with kids shouting and playing, women at their hearths cooking, and men getting ready to start the workday. It began with two armed men coming out of the house the former sentries had gone into, and stopping by a gong which hung just outside. One of the men struck the gong a single time, and immediately women and children hurried out of the houses nearest to him.

But not just women and larger children. Old people and small children came out just a little more slowly, and when the houses seemed to have emptied, the gong ringer strode through the gathered people and headed for the fields that began on the far side of the village. The people shrank out of his way and then followed as quickly as possible, which for some was no more than a shuffle. The second armed man waited until the entire group had begun to move, and then he followed to kick and shove anyone who wasn't walking fast enough to suit him.

Tiran exchanged a glance with Rhodris, but his second seemed just as confused as Tiran felt. Why would women and children and old people be forced out into the fields? What had happened to the younger men of the village? All of the men sent to the fields had been white-haired and unsteady on their feet, and there hadn't been a boy older than ten or eleven.

Tiran could see that the question bothered his fighters as well, but it took another few minutes before they got an answer. Ten more armed men appeared from a different house, but they waited until the women and children were far out into the fields before heading for the guarded houses.

And those houses had to be unlocked. They were also shuttered, Tiran noticed, and when men and boys began to file out of them the reason was only partially explained. What made village men so dangerous that they had to be kept under lock and key? The question twisted at Tiran—until he saw two of the guardsmen carrying wooden practice weapons out of one of the houses.

"Son of Chaos!" Tiran swore softly, now knowing what Pavar was doing in his villages. "Hiring an entire army was probably too expensive for him, so he volunteered the men in his villages and forced them to cooperate by holding their families hostage. Those two guards out in the fields have bows, and anyone trying to run for it would never outrun an arrow. Assuming any of them would desert the rest of their family, which I seriously doubt."

"So how do we break them loose?" Rhodris whispered back, now looking furious. "Pavar isn't just using them to make sure the crops aren't lost, so those two out in the fields are watching double closely. How do we get around *that?*"

"By doing something they aren't expecting," Tiran answered, gesturing over two of his men. He didn't have many Shapeshifters like himself in the company, but he'd brought along two of them on a hunch. "The first step is to take out those field guards," Tiran explained to the group of three. "You two will have to Shift to get close enough to them, but I want them down at the same time. Once they are, it becomes my turn, and I'll take out the two with bows watching the men. Then you bring in the rest of the men, Rhodris, just in case those villagers don't grab the opportunity to use the weapons they'll be holding."

"And wooden weapons *are* real weapons, if you know what you're doing," Rhodris agreed with a grin. "They seem to be calling the roll right now, but after that they'll be handing out the practice stuff. I suggest we hold off until they have."

"Hold off, yes, but we can use the time to get into position," Tiran said with a nod. "You two get started now, but don't let those guards see you no matter how small you have to go. They're probably bored enough to let fly at just about anything, just for the sport. Wait for the whistle, and then go.''

The two men nodded with grins, and then they Shifted to fox form and sped away through the grass. The two were friends, Tiran knew, and obviously thought quite a lot alike. Not to mention the fact that they were good fighters who could be counted on.

"They'll get it done right," Rhodris said, echoing Tiran's thoughts. "What I'm wondering is how *you* intend to handle it, Captain. Those two archers in the village are on opposite sides of the group."

"I *have* to make it work, so I will," Tiran responded, having already considered the question himself. "Wait until whatever number of villagers are going to be armed *are* armed, and then whistle the signal to start."

Rhodris nodded, knowing the whistle signals of the company as well as Tiran did, so Tiran was free to take up his own position. He Shifted to house cat form to do it, knowing a dog might be shafted if seen, but not a cat. There were always cats around a village, and people ignored them as a matter of course.

But he still took advantage of what cover there was, running across open stretches to pause behind something like an empty, broken box before running to the next shelter. A normal village would never be that cluttered, but apparently the men who had taken it over didn't believe in picking up after themselves.

Tiran made it to his first objective, the back of the nearest house that had an archer in front of it, and that was where he ran into trouble—from an unexpected source. A big tan tomcat appeared from around the far side of the house, saw him, and immediately began his howling challenge. Strange black toms weren't welcome in his territory, and he announced that clearly.

Tiran felt his back rising in automatic answer to the challenge, something he didn't need or want. In that form he'd be howling himself in a minute, but he hadn't come here to fight a *cat*. A quick glance around showed no one in sight, so he hurriedly Shifted into his fighting form— of a *giant* black cat that couldn't be called *anyone's* house pet. The big tan tom suddenly became a small tan tom, and one who abruptly stopped howling, hissed as if to say, "*That* was a dirty trick," and then disappeared back in the direction from which he'd come.

And that let Tiran Shift back down to smaller form. He'd been showing his fangs in a grin before Shifting, and it would have felt good to stay in fighting form. Fangs and claws were what he wanted to use on the invaders, but a man's form was more versatile and that's what he would need. Along with a lot of luck. Tiran crept around the side of the house, heading for the front of it and his first target, hoping hard for the luck.

By the time he was around the front and only a few feet from his target, most of the villagers already had wooden swords in their fists. They spread out in double rows along that part of the main village street, more than fifty men in each row. The first of the training would be general exercises and moves, then, he told himself, taking up a position directly behind the archer. The trainees would do those exercises together, and then would come individual work. That arrangement ought to be very much to his benefit . . . *ought* to be. It all depended on how far the training had gone.

It wasn't long before all of the villagers held wooden swords, and Tiran spent the waiting time stretched out long and relaxed in plain sight. As expected, no one paid the least attention to him, not even the man he lay behind. The villagers had been lined up in an exercise formation, and Tiran understood why most of them looked more than ordinarily unhappy. The formation was on the tight side for men not fully trained, their closeness to one another guaranteeing that anyone who moved improperly during the drills would be hit with a neighbor's weapon. It was an effective way to teach a large group quickly, but wasn't likely to be popular with the trainees.

The guardsman at the front of the group shouted, and the villagers all raised their wooden weapons to the ready. That, of course, was when Rhodris whistled, and Tiran was completely ready. He flowed to his feet even as he began to Shift, and by the time he was back in natural form he was also only a step behind his target. His left arm went around the man's neck, his right hand to his head, and one sharp snap eliminated the first opponent completely.

But that was only one. Tiran had the man's bow even before the body fell, and he quickly added a shaft to its string. The other archer was on the far side of the group of villagers, so now was the time to try the luck he'd been hoping for.

"Everybody down!" Tiran ordered in a shout, and the harsh training the guardsmen had subjected their victims to suddenly worked against them. Every villager hit the dirt without hesitation, leaving Tiran a clear view of his second target. He already had the nock drawn back to his ear, and only had to loose. The second archer went down with an arrow in his chest even as he reached for a shaft of his own, and that just left the training guardsmen.

And the village men were quick to understand that. A good number of them jumped back to their feet and headed for the nearest intruder, wooden swords raised again at the ready. Only now they were ready for more than practice, even though the intruders had drawn their own weapons. They were prepared to go up against steel with nothing but wood—or would have if not for the help that was already racing toward them.

Tiran only glanced at his running fighters, then ran himself toward the group of villagers that was farthest away from incoming help. Five men—two of them still boys—fought with one of the intruders, trying to get past his steel and reach him with a hard blow from their wooden weapons. The intruder, furious over the attempt, worked to knock the practice weapons aside and reach the villagers, who had almost all they could do to keep it from happening.

"All right, men, good work," Tiran called hurriedly as he reached the melee. "You've done your part, and now you can leave him to me."

The purpose of that announcement had been to draw the intruder's attention and give the villagers a chance to withdraw without getting hurt. When it worked Tiran grinned, enjoying the flash of frustration the intruder showed. The villagers had been able to scramble clear, and now the man armed with steel had more than a wooden weapon to face.

"Put up your sword and buy a few more days of life, or throw it all away by choosing to fight," Tiran said flatly to the man. "Those are the only two choices you have, so make your decision fast."

The intruder made a brief suggestion and attacked viciously, but he'd spent too much time among untrained men. His attack was sloppy and overconfident, and two breaths later he was dead and falling. Tiran withdrew his sword fast and looked around for the next intruder, but his fighters had beaten him to it. The last intruder—as well as the four previous perimeter guards, who had come rushing out of the house they'd been in—fell to Rhodris's and other men's blades even as Tiran watched, and it was all over.

Or at least the fighting was over. The two Shapeshifters Tiran had sent to see to the field guardsmen had done their jobs with the expected efficiency, and now were helping the women and children and old people back to their homes. The men dropped their wooden weapons to run out and meet them, and the laughter and happy-crying and shouts of relief would have made even twice the effort more than worthwhile.

"I'd say this was worth getting up early for," Rhodris commented with a grin as he joined Tiran, also watching the glad reunions. "It's too bad we couldn't keep one of those overseers alive for questioning, but I can't honestly say I'm sorry that they're dead."

"I'm not either, since questioning them wouldn't have gotten us much," Tiran told him with a glance. "We couldn't have relied on anything they said about the other villages, and we would have been left with the problem of having to guard them. I would have enjoyed seeing them tried and convicted of enslaving these people and then hanged, but this way I *know* they won't escape to do the same to other innocents at another time."

Rhodris nodded emphatically, but that was all the time they had for private conversation. A heavyset man in his middle years who had found and embraced a woman and three children—as well as two of the boys who had been training with him—now left them to approach Tiran and Rhodris wearily.

"Don't know who you men be, but just words cain't say our thanks," he told them with deep sincerity. "We had no way t'fight 'em, not with 'em holdin' our famlies. I'm Korat, headman a this village, an' anythin' we got is yourn fer th' askin'."

"Don't worry about it," Tiran reassured him with a smile. "We didn't do this expecting to be paid. And you shouldn't have to worry about others coming to take the place of *this* trash. Duke Pavar has been arrested for treason against the crown, so he won't be back to bother you people again. Let's check around to make sure everyone is all right, and then my men and I need to get on to the next village."

Korat nodded and walked with Tiran, taking the opportunity to also mention everything he knew about the next closest village. Tiran filed the information away in his head, then mentioned the new policy regarding trading people with the cities and towns. Most of the folk in the village would want to resume their normal lives, but if any of them didn't there was now a way to work things out.

They had to wait while everyone thanked them, but after that they were able to leave. Tiran made plans with Rhodris while they rode, so a few hours later, when they reached the second village, they were ready to act.

The same method of handling the people was being used in this second village, leading Tiran to suspect that Duke Pavar had developed the idea and then had ordered all his men to use it. The major problem facing Tiran was the four perimeter guards, each of whom was in sight of two others. With only three men in the group able to Shift, that left one guard unattended to and therefore able to give the alarm.

So they had to supply that fourth man with something to occupy his attention. One of the fighters in the group looked rather young and harmless, so he was the one who wandered curiously across the open field to approach one of the guards. He was unarmed and carrying a hastily prepared blanket-roll, but the guard he ambled toward still stayed completely alert.

Which did nothing to help the man. Tiran and the other Shapeshifters had already put themselves close to the remaining three guards; once the young-looking fighter had reached the fourth man and began to ask silly questions, they each Shifted back to natural and moved. The three guards went down almost as one, the fourth followed as soon as the young fighter saw the others taken care of, and no one in the village noticed a thing.

Tiran and the other Shapeshifters played perimeter guard until three different fighters relieved them, and then they repeated their performance at the first village. Everything went exactly the way it was supposed to, and once the villagers were freed and reunited with their families, the group moved on toward the third village. They stopped at a roadhouse for a late but well-earned lunch, and reached the third village just at dusk.

"At least this is the last one," Rhodris said with a sigh as they tied their horses in a stand of young trees. "I never realized how tiring it is to ride around saving people all day."

"Obviously we're not cut out to be epic heroes," Tiran said with a nod of agreement. "I feel like something trampled by a herd of wild horses, and the rest of the men look like they feel the same. The trouble is we don't usually have to fight and travel, fight and travel, over and over again. But since this *is* the last one, at least on Pavar's estates, let's get it done and behind us."

"What about Selwin's villages?" Rhodris asked, his expression saying he both did and didn't want to face a second day like today. "If they're having the same thing done to them—which they probably are—we can't just walk away and let it continue."

"I agree, but we aren't just talking about Selwin's villages," Tiran pointed out as he rubbed at the back of his neck. "Every noble who threw in his lot with Pavar and Selwin has probably done the same, which means about twelve villages and at least a thousand forced recruits. We can't be everywhere at once, but I've been thinking about it and maybe there's a way we *can* be everywhere at once. Since Pavar went to all this trouble to train his villagers in how to fight, wouldn't it be a shame if they never got to practice their new skills?''

"You expect to use the villagers we freed to break the others free?" Rhodris asked with brows raised. "But they're completely green, not to mention probably unwilling. Most nonfighters are smart enough to recognize their limitations and stay *out* of fights."

"But they're not insensitive," Tiran countered. "They know the horror *they* went through, so they don't have to be convinced that the job needs doing. And they're certainly not above being angry enough to want to get even for what was done to them. Besides, we need them mostly for window dressing. Our men will do the bulk of the real fighting, and only the archers among them will need to actively help."

"And afterward they can *claim* to have done it alone," Rhodris suggested, brightening with the idea. "That should increase their future safety, since Selwin and the rest will think twice before trying the same again."

"Now *that's* good thinking," Tiran approved, clapping him on the shoulder. "Until we get things settled with the nobility, the villagers will *have* to take care of themselves. So let's go and get ourselves another group of fearsome warriors."

Rhodris chuckled and gestured to the men, and they all left the stand of trees to move closer to the village. It was just about full dark, but the women and children and old folk were only now being brought in from the fields. The men and boys were already locked up, of course, and the ones who had been training them were helping to get the field workers separated to the various houses. Torchlight showed the activity clearly, so Tiran and his men simply waited.

Once the field workers were settled in for the night, most of the intruders headed for the houses *they* were using. One of them, probably their leader, came out to check on the four sentries at their posts before following the others into the house. Tiran thought about bringing the sentries together by Shifting to look like the man and then ordering the four in, but quickly decided against it. He was too tired to play involved games when there was really no need for them.

Tiran left four of his men to use the darkness to get as close to the sentries as possible, then led the others around to approach the houses the intruders were in from the far side. Once the houses were surrounded he whistled the attack command, then did his part by breaking into the house the leader of the men had entered.

Tiran and his men numbered just about the same as the intruders, but it still didn't turn out to be an even fight. Most of the intruders were relaxed after a hard day of pushing around helpless people, and their leader was to the side of the front room of the house. A blanket had been strung up to provide privacy, and the man was behind it nuzzling a naked young woman who wasn't being allowed to struggle. Another woman, dressed but still looking terrified, was near the hearth getting ready to serve whatever had been cooked.

Tiran noticed all that in an instant, and even as Rhodris jumped toward the woman at the hearth to stand in front of her, *he* was on his way toward the man behind the blanket. The sudden attack had caused most of the intruders to freeze momentarily in shock, but not the man behind the blanket. Instead of freezing he grabbed for the sword he'd tossed aside, right after throwing an arm around the neck of the woman he'd been getting ready to enjoy.

"What a surprise," Tiran drawled to the man insultingly as he came to a stop, ignoring the sound of fighting in the rest of the house. "You're the one I'd decided was in charge of this scum, so what else would you do but hide behind a woman? If you were anything like a real man, you wouldn't be here in the first place."

"What I'm not is a fool," the man rasped, looking as if he held himself tightly in check. "You can't reach me without going through *this* slut. Toss that sword away and then call off the rest of your pack, or the first blood on my steel will be hers."

"Whatever you've been drinking, it was the wrong choice," Tiran countered with a snort, fighting to make himself sound and look uncaring. "I'm not dropping my weapon or calling off my fighters, so if you mean to kill the woman, do it fast. Then there won't be any petty distractions to get in the way.''

The intruder frowned with frustration, undoubtedly noticing that Tiran kept his gaze on *him* and hadn't even glanced at his shield. That should help to make him believe that Tiran didn't care whether the woman lived or died, the only thing that might save her life. And then the man growled wordlessly and shoved the woman at Tiran, following immediately behind her with his sword up and ready. He meant to attack from behind his living shield, and if the shield died in the process that was just too bad.

But Tiran was ready for just that move, and so, apparently, was the woman. As Tiran jumped to his right the woman threw herself down and to Tiran's left, giving the intruder an easy choice. If he turned to finish her off he would present an undefended back to his enemy, which meant he snarled with fury but still had to face Tiran squarely. Which was exactly what Tiran wanted. He grinned as he closed with the intruder, and although the man was no novice with a sword, the fight was over in a very short while.

''I don't know who you are, but I'm glad you're that good,'' a woman's voice came as Tiran cleaned his sword on his late opponent's shirt. ''I'll have to remember to thank you formally as soon as I stop shaking.''

Since the fighting was over in the rest of the house as well, Tiran was able to finally study the woman. She'd pulled down the blanket to wrap herself in, and now stood huddled into it while she studied *him*. She did look shaken over how close she'd come to death, but it didn't seem to be anything she couldn't handle.

''Informal thanks do a good enough job,'' Tiran commented, noticing how well dark hair and eyes suited the woman. And from what he'd seen earlier, her figure matched the rest. ''You live in this village?''

He'd been trying to keep the question neutral, but the woman must have heard his skepticism, which made her laugh.

''No, you're right, I *don't* live in this village,'' she said with a smile. ''My horse's shoe came loose a couple of miles away from here, and although I hammered it back into place with a rock, I still wanted a blacksmith to look at it. Like a fool I rode right in, and didn't even get a chance to draw steel when I finally woke up to what was going on. With two archers aiming straight for me, I was taken like a toddler by its mother. The only good luck I had was that it was late enough in the afternoon for that moron to decide to wait until dark before he had his fun. And my name is Caldai Moyan.''

"I'm Tiran d'Iste," Tiran supplied, then nodded toward the area which had been behind the blanket Caldai now had wrapped around herself. "If those are your clothes scattered over the floor near the cot, why don't you rehang that blanket and get back into them. I'll make sure no one interrupts before you're through."

"Thanks, I appreciate that," she said with relief and another smile, then immediately went to follow the suggestion. Without "accidentally" lowering the blanket, or asking him if he'd like to help, or doing any of another dozen or more things he would have found awkward and unwelcome. The idea of a woman traveling alone had made Tiran suspicious on general principles, but it was possible he was wrong. The other two villages hadn't had any female intruders, so maybe her story would turn out to be true.

In a short while Rhodris came over, looking as exhausted as Tiran felt but also as satisfied.

"We got them all, and now the men are in the process of letting everyone know they're free again," he told Tiran. "And it was a good thing I got in front of that woman at the hearth. That filth would have cut her down just to make sure she didn't interfere on our side. Is the other woman also all right?"

"Thanks to you people, the other woman is fine," Caldai answered before Tiran could, then she stepped out from behind the blanket. "I'll need another tunic from my saddlebags, but aside from that there's not a problem in the world."

Her smile moved back and forth between Tiran and Rhodris, a neutral smile to match the simple ripped sleeve of her tunic, along with breeches that were no more than rumpled. Again Tiran felt relieved, especially when she looked toward the hearth and brightened.

"Hey, that's my sword," she said, pointing before heading toward a scabbarded weapon lying abandoned to one side. It was plain and workmanlike and well-kept, and when Caldai picked it up and unsheathed it to look it over, it was obvious she was no stranger to the weapon.

"If I'm not mistaken, we aren't far from Gandro's inn," Tiran said to Rhodris. "We rode pretty much in a circle today, so let's ride a little farther and close the circle right. We all need a good meal and a good night's sleep, and that's the best place I can think of to get it."

"You're going to an inn?" Caldai said as she rejoined them, buckling on her swordbelt. "Do you mind if I go with you? If the morons didn't go through my saddlebags, and I don't think they did, my money ought to be right where I left it."

"If it isn't, you'll have to do me the honor of being *my* guest," Rhodris told her with a smile and a courtly bow. "It's the least we can do for you after the terrible experience you had."

"You people really *are* nice," Caldai said with an answering smile that was all Rhodris's. "Something tells me this 'terrible experience' is one of the best things to ever happen to me. I'm Caldai Moyan."

"And I'm Rhodris Khay," Tiran's second answered with a grin, then offered his arm. "May I escort you outside?"

"You certainly may," Caldai responded with her own grin, taking the offered arm. "And you can tell me all about yourself—after I tell you all about *me*."

They laughed together as they left the house, neither one of them paying the least attention to Tiran, who found the relief of that exquisite. The woman hadn't tried to gain *his* interest, and hadn't even really come on to Rhodris. They were playing the after-battle game of delight in being alive that most fighters played, which might or might not turn into something serious. Usually it didn't, but they certainly both knew that. Caldai was obviously a fighter, and that's why she'd felt safe traveling alone.

Tiran stretched gently in an effort to ease the soreness

in his back and shoulder muscles. It had been much too long since the last time he'd had this much exercise in one day, and now he paid for not having kept in shape. Outside he could hear the noise of laughing and crying people who were in the midst of reuniting their families. It was a good sound that banished some of Tiran's weariness, but he couldn't quite fool himself into believing all the trouble was behind them.

"If we don't move first, Selwin and the others will use their own villagers in the way these people were supposed to have been used, as expendable bodies meant to fill the ranks of an army," he muttered as he walked to the door to watch the happy celebrating. Rhodris would have to point that out to them tomorrow, and to the other villagers as well. Selwin and his allies had to be neutralized, otherwise every one of these people could find themselves back in the slavery they'd just been freed from. They'd be able to take one day's rest, but the day after they'd have to move.

And tomorrow *he* had to head back to the city. They'd been busily training an army for the last few weeks, and it was time for the trainees to get some practical experience. He'd have help on its way to Rhodris an hour after he got back, and depending on how Alex was doing, he might even be able to come back with it. That thought brightened him quite a lot, so he headed outside to get his fighters free of the grateful villagers and on their way to a hot meal and beds.

CHAPTER SIX

I arranged for lunch to be served to my noble-lady assistants in the room where they were playing clerk. Then I decided that everyone involved, including the people standing in line, deserved some sustenance in return for their efforts and patience, and arranged for food to be brought to them as well. I took my own meal with Cadry and her people in a small but comfortable meeting room not far from the governmental area, and Cadry was no more pleased than I was.

"I know those men standin' guard in the dungeon," she muttered for the third time after finishing only half the food on her plate. "They ain't the sort to take silver or gold to let a prisoner go free, but there ain't no other way that lowlife coulda gotten loose. Looks like Damis is gonna have to replace 'em and bring charges, but—"

"No," I interrupted, drawing her immediate attention. "Don't replace the guards and don't charge them. If you know them to be honest men and loyal supporters, we'd only be harming ourselves by accusing them—which is probably what that lowlife wants us to do."

"But how can we let somethin' like that slide?" Cadry demanded, now outraged. "Our people are good, Alex, but they're still just people. If they see those three gettin' away with takin' a bribe, sure as Hellfire some of 'em'll start doin' the same."

"Then you'll have to make sure everyone hears the truth about what happened," I told her after taking a swallow of coffee. "That prisoner didn't bribe his way free any more than Tiran or I would have had to. He just Shifted down to something small, and scurried out when the guards weren't looking.''

"But—Shifted?'' she echoed, now looking confused as well as bothered. "But if he was a Shapeshifter, why didn't you tell us?''

"Because I didn't know,'' I grumbled, feeling extremely stupid. "Magic users can tell each other at a glance, but if a Shapeshifter doesn't have the typical silver, gold, red, or yellow eye color, there's no way to tell until you actually see them Shift. Or find a situation that suggests they Shifted, like not recognizing the description of the man who tried to make the paymaster hand out promises instead of money. I shouldn't have assumed there were two men running around trying to sabotage us when one Shapeshifter could have accomplished the same thing.''

"And now he's free and can be lookin' like anybody or any thing,'' Cadry summed up, no happier now that she knew our people were innocent of taking bribes. "I'd better spread the word, just to make sure nobody gets jumped just from not knowin'.''

"While you're at it, see if someone can fix up a cell that will hold the slime if we catch him again,'' I said, stopping her on her way over to the table holding her fighters. "I'm going to spend a couple of hours this afternoon looking around the palace in my own way, and if I trip over him I want someplace to put him.''

"I'll pass on the word about the cell, but we'll hafta talk about those plans of yours,'' she said, giving me that certain look before continuing on to her fighters. Her look had said that I wasn't going anywhere without her and the rest of my bodyguard, which helped me to make up my mind. Running out on friends and supporters wasn't very nice, but I'd had enough of being smothered. A couple of hours of being alone would do wonders for me, and then I'd be able to come back to the smothering.

Finishing the last of my coffee and then getting up and heading for the bathroom adjoining the conference room earned me no more than a glance from my babysitters. They knew where I was going—they thought—and it wasn't a place they would be welcome to go with me. I went in and closed the door behind me, used the facilities, then began to examine the baseboards around the room. The only door out of it led back into the room where Cadry waited, but sometimes rooms come equipped with unofficial exits.

It took a couple of minutes, but I finally spotted the mousehole I'd been looking for. It wasn't very big so I had to Shift way down, but at least the floor was solid enough to hold my compressed mass without cracking or buckling. I scampered through the hole before Cadry came in to see what was taking so long, then Shifted back up to house cat size. That let me thread my way through the between-walls passage without worrying about rats, and also spread my mass out a little. The floor still seemed solid enough to hold me, but there was no sense in taking chances.

I followed the narrow passageway for quite a distance, then Shifted down again briefly to use another mousehole. This one led into what looked like a pantry, with people hurrying in and out in a very businesslike way. I Shifted back immediately to a house cat to keep from getting bashed, since mice are never welcome visitors in pantries. But I also made myself long-haired, regal and gray, which would hopefully keep me from getting chased. Everyone knows long-haired cats own whatever world they happen to be standing in, so trying to chase them away is a waste of time.

And everyone *did* seem to know that. I strolled out of the pantry into what had to be the palace kitchens, and the hurrying servants stepped around me rather than making me get out of *their* way. I waved my fluffy tail in satisfaction as I looked around, trying to remember why I'd been thinking about visiting the kitchens, and then it came back. That very efficient servant who didn't need instructions to do things right; I wanted to know who he or she was.

And I also wanted to make sure that escaped Shapeshifter hadn't decided to stop in here for lunch before going back to whatever other sabotage plans he had. It would be difficult to check that out as a cat—or, considering the size of the kitchens, as anything smaller than an elephant—but I still meant to try. We needed to know *why* someone was working against us as badly as we needed to know who, and that escaped prisoner was someone who could answer both questions. It was highly unlikely that Selwin and Pavar were responsible, not with the amount of subtlety involved. Selwin certainly must have considered himself subtle, but these sabotage attempts were on another level entirely.

I wandered through a jungle of preparation tables surrounded by hearths and ovens and more pantries, but the only other cat I saw was dining on a mouse. For an instant I worried that the mouse might be my escaped prisoner, but a moment's thought banished the possibility. Shapeshifters turn back into their natural forms when they die, and the mouse was only two-thirds of a mouse. I also looked more closely at the cat, but just got hissed at for my trouble. The gray, black, and white tabby was female, and the protective paw on what was left of the mouse was no put-on. Actually the mouse looked rather tasty, but I'd already eaten lunch.

So I continued my wandering, and eventually reached an area where people were giving out orders rather than carrying them out. There was a large arrangement of bells just behind them with neat tags under each bell, and even as as I watched, one of the bells rang twice.

"That's the baron, and he's ringing from his apartment upstairs," a harried man with short brown hair fretted at once. "Brandis, how have you been handling all this while I was ill?"

"A call through the speaking tube to the servants' quarters in that wing gets a servant there without delay, sir," a nondescript young man answered promptly, politely— and slowly. "That's the reason speaking tubes were installed in this palace, but I don't believe you've ever used them."

"Of course I've never used them!" the harried man snapped, his pale face reddening. "If you start being too efficient, *they* start wondering what you're up to. Well, they won't be wondering that about *me*. Send someone up from the servants' quarters down the hall."

That order was given to one of the serving girls standing around, and she bobbed a quick curtsey and then hurried toward the door. The man Brandis opened his mouth as if to say something, realized the harried man was now whining at someone else, and gave it up with a headshake. Which, considering what the harried man was like, was very wise of him.

"And someone get that hairy *creature* out of here," I heard, then looked up to discover that *I'd* taken the harried man's attention. "Those animals are disgusting, and I won't have one of them near me. Shoo, you horrible creature, scat!"

He was actually trying to chase me by waving his hands in the air from six or eight feet away, but that wasn't the surprising part. What really took my attention was the fact that the man Brandis was now also looking at me—but not the way you'd look at a cat. Somehow the man knew I wasn't what I seemed, and the next thing he did apparently proved it.

"I'll take care of the cat, sir," he hastily assured the harried man, cutting off two of the girls who had started forward flapping their aprons. "Cats like that are very intelligent, so I know I'll have no trouble getting her to follow me. Come on, pretty puss, follow Brandis over this way, that's a good girl, right this way."

He'd begun to lead the way to the right, toward what looked like a storage area for pots and dishes, so I decided to take his suggestion and follow like a "good cat." He kept calling me that as he coaxed me after him, and I couldn't help grinning. The man was both covering for me and protecting me, and if he wasn't the one I'd been looking for, I'd Shift into termite form and eat the nearest wooden table.

He edged into the storage area first, walking backwards and holding his hand out to me, and I ambled along after him. Unlike the pantries, this area seemed deserted, which means that once we were both inside he dropped his arm and gave me a stern look.

"I don't know who you are, but that wasn't very smart," he lectured with slight annoyance. "Figler has been known to throw knives at cats, so the people here try to keep all cats out of his sight. Most of the workers don't know he just got back, or they would have simply tossed you out. You should have chosen a different form to go sightseeing in."

A glance around showed me no one was watching or listening, so I Shifted back to natural and gave him my own stare.

"If anyone had tried to pick me up and toss me out, they would have hurt themselves rather badly," I pointed out mildly. "And anyone without the sense to know the value of cats in kitchens this size doesn't even belong in charge of a pig sty. Who hired that fool?"

"Whoever did the hiring for the old king and queen," Brandis answered automatically, looking me over with raised brows. "And I can see you're right about what would have happened to anyone trying to pick you up in cat form. But you look familiar somehow, although I'm certain we've never met. Who are you?"

"My name is Alex," I answered, briefly wondering how many times I'd have to say that while I was in the city. "But let's get back to that fool Figler. Does he make a habit of coming to work halfway through the day? And where has he been for the last couple or three weeks?"

"He tends to stay home 'sick' a lot," Brandis replied with a disgusted shake of his head. "Not that any of us here really mind, since the workload doubles whenever he shows up. He has his own way of doing things and his own ridiculous reasons for doing them, and doesn't care how much unnecessary effort he causes. He must have been related to whoever did the hiring for the old regime, otherwise he never would have gotten the job. And I suppose he came back this afternoon because one of his cronies told him how smoothly everything has been going."

"So he came back to cause chaos, and afterward will pretend he fixed the chaos after someone else caused it," I said with a nod. "That means he'll need someone to blame and fire, which probably means you. What will you do once he fires you? Go back to being a magic user?"

"What are you talking about?" he asked quickly. "I'm a kitchen worker, not a magic user. You don't—"

"Please," I said, holding up one hand to stem the flow of protest. "I can't imagine what you're doing working in this place, but there's only one way you could have known I wasn't a real cat. And come to that, you probably have to be fairly powerful to have noticed. Care to tell me what's going on?"

He hesitated visibly, as though trying to decide whether or not to come clean, then made up his mind.

"You probably won't understand or believe me," he said with a sigh, slumping back against some heavy wooden shelves. "I'd taken a break from my studies to go traveling among the worlds, just bumming around and seeing whatever there was to see. I got to this place just before those interlopers took over, met a girl, and decided to stay for a while.

"The girl is Sighted, but with the study of magic being discouraged in this whole area, she's completely untrained. There was instant attraction between us, but as far as I'm concerned, for someone Sighted to remain untrained is like stopping up your ears because everyone around you is deaf. I wanted to take her back with me to be trained, but she kept hesitating."

"Are you saying she's Sighted but her family isn't?" I asked, remembering Chalaine's situation. "I'd think that would make her eager to go rather than reluctant."

"That's what *I* expected, until I met her family," he agreed with a nod. "Rather than giving her a hard time because she's different, they all supported and protected her. She does want to learn how to use her ability, but leaving her family to do it is another matter. I'd just about decided to start her training myself, right here, when this kingdom and the one next door were taken over. And to make matters worse, the new king and queen in the neighboring realm were Sighted who began to track down and destroy every trained Sighted in both kingdoms."

"I hadn't realized they'd done that, but I suppose it makes sense," I said with a frown. "They wanted to train their helpers in their own methods, which I'm told were inferior to standard methods, so they'd *have* to get rid of any potential troublemakers. So why didn't you take the girl and leave *then*?"

"Because she refused to desert her family," he answered with another sigh. "Trouble started as soon as those four took over, with so-called guardsmen stealing and raping and killing as they pleased. I offered to take her family as well, but they had friends and other family spread out all over the kingdom. Since I couldn't take everyone, none of them would go, and if they were staying, so was she. She said the Sighteds in the next realm wanted only men or really aggressive women as recruits to be trained, and since she wasn't aggressive she would be safe from them. But I wouldn't be, so she insisted that I leave alone."

"But you obviously didn't agree," I commented. "So how did you end up *here?*"

"It was the safest place I could think of," he responded with a shrug. "I spoke a spell of familiarity, which made everyone here believe they'd known me for years, and then I settled down to work. But I kept a close watch on Ariella and her family, and was able to help out once or twice to keep them safe. While I cursed the fact that I hadn't gone on with my studies. If I could have reached wizard level before any of this started ..."

"You probably would have ended up destroyed, like the one wizard who did go up against those two twisted losers," I finished. "But they've been defeated and things are starting to change back to some kind of normality, so why are you still here? Grown overly attached to the job, have you?"

"You're getting kind of pushy for someone talking to a man she knows is a sorcerer," he said, his skin darkening slightly with annoyance. "How would you like to be turned into something a lot less attractive than a cat?"

"I have an edge you don't know about yet," I said with a brief grin. "But you haven't answered my question. Since the crisis is over, why are you still here?"

"Because the crisis *isn't* over," he came back, frowning. "If you know so much, you ought to know that as well. Things are far from peaceful and settled in *this* kingdom, but there's even more going on next door. I can feel the magic being used even from here, and there's nothing casual or everyday about it. I considered offering to help the new king and queen, but just standing on the riverbank and looking over into *their* city tells me I'd be way out of my league. My staying here is all but useless, but I can't just walk away and leave Ariella without *any* protection.''

His expression of frustrated helplessness was too familiar, but what he'd said had given me something else to worry about.

''You're telling me they're really up against it over there,'' I said, sorting quickly through options and possibilities. ''Do you think ordinary fighters would be of any help to them? Sometimes magic does best with nonmagical help.''

''I don't know,'' he admitted, now staring at me closely. ''Depending on the situation, fighters might be totally useless. So that's who you are. I got a glimpse of your predecessor once, but not down here in the kitchens—where I also never expected to see *you*. Are you waiting for me to bow before you order me out?''

''Actually, I'm waiting for you to say you can get a message sphere through all that magic you mentioned,'' I said, finally deciding on a plan of action. ''If you can, we'll let Bariden and Chalaine tell me if they need those fighters. Do you think you can get through?''

''I don't know,'' he repeated, but now his frown was thoughtful rather than disturbed. ''It all depends on how well they're doing over there. If they're surrounded by enemy magic I won't be able to reach them, but if they're not surrounded . . . What do you want me to say?''

''Say . . . 'Is it time for another walk through the fog?' '' I finally decided after thinking about it for almost a minute. ''They'll understand what I mean and answer properly, but their enemies won't be able to. Assuming their enemies can intercept a message sphere. I don't know if they can or not.''

''We'll have to hope they can't,'' he said, leaning off the shelves and straightening. ''If they can, your friends are probably beyond anyone's help. Okay, you'll have to think about them now, as clearly as possible.''

I obliged by picturing Chalaine and Bariden, two people I'd gotten to know rather well and whom I both liked and respected. And worried about, no matter how silly that sounds. Two powerful magic users didn't need *me* to worry about them, but still . . .

"Okay, it's on the way," Brandis said after muttering something I didn't understand. "Now all we can do is wait to see if it's answered."

"How long will it take?" I asked, wishing there was a cup of coffee handier than somewhere out in the kitchens. "Are they likely to answer right away, or—"

"So *this* is why you aren't out there making your usual mess of things!" a triumphant but still whiny voice interrupted to announce, and we turned to see Figler in the doorway. "Sneaking around meeting a *woman* when you ought to be doing the work you're paid for. Or should I say, the work you *used to be* paid for. If I needed additional grounds for your dismissal—which I don't!—this would more than suffice, so get your things and get out. You don't work here any longer."

"Told you so," I said to a furious Brandis, then looked at Figler and smiled sweetly. "This fool doesn't want anyone around who might become a potential replacement for him, which has to mean anyone with more ability than a dead goat. Is there anyone left around here besides you who could take over for him right now, or has he gotten rid of *everyone* who's competent?"

"Look here, just who do you think you are, girl?" Figler sputtered indignantly, but Brandis decided it was his turn to interrupt.

"As a matter of fact, he's overlooked the one who's better than everyone, including me," Brandis told me with a grin, now enjoying himself quite a lot. "She's the one who trained me, and she knows more about the kitchens and how to run things smoothly than anyone else here. Her name is Ollela, and that's her standing behind Figler."

The woman Brandis gestured to was in her early thirties and mouse-like, meaning she blended into wherever she stood and did nothing to bring attention to herself. Now she looked startled and confused, but her reaction was nothing compared to Figler's.

"Ollela?" he echoed with a snort that somehow still came out like whining. "A woman? Better than *me?* You're not only a lout, Brandis, you're also stupid. No one in their right mind would give a responsible job to a woman, and especially not on *your* sayso. Now take your trollop and get out of here, or I'll summon guardsmen to throw you out."

"Guardsmen sounds like a good idea to me," I said brightly before Brandis could get in his say, then looked beyond Figler to the growing audience we were attracting. "Would one of you be so kind as to call a couple of the guardsmen out there in the halls? Tell them there's someone here who needs to be thrown out into the street."

"And also tell them to hurry, because I'm being threatened," Figler added quickly, then turned back to me with a smirk. "When they get here I'll tell them you threatened to draw that sword you probably don't even know how to use, and every man and woman here will back me up. That means they'll certainly arrest you, so take my advice and leave this instant. Trying to make a fuss and telling lies about me won't get either of you anywhere; no one is *ever* believed over me, and it's been tried more than once."

"That I *do* believe, but I'll still take my chances," I told the vindictive satisfaction in his dull brown eyes. "But while we're waiting for the guardsmen, don't you want to ask me what my name is? Or even the name of the man I sleep with? If you don't, I'll be very disappointed."

Figler glared at me, naturally missing the very private joke, but he also didn't ask anything. I *was* disappointed, but only until Brandis touched my arm.

"I've just gotten an answer to the question you sent," he murmured, keeping the exchange private. "The return message is, 'It's the farm and town all over again. Try to keep in touch in case that changes.' I take it you know what they mean?"

"Yes, and it makes me feel a whole lot better," I murmured back. "But it also means you have a new job, if you'll take it. It should be easier than working in the kitchens, but no less interesting. Think about it and let me know."

He nodded expressionlessly, agreeing to nothing but the thinking part, and I had a moment to do my own thinking. I'd asked Bariden and Chalaine if we needed to team up the way we had in the fog on our way to this world. They'd answered that they *were* having trouble, but it was a setup the way it had been in the places we'd "created" in the fog. It wasn't terribly odd that they were having trouble, but why did they consider it a setup? Was it a matter of being set up the way Tiran and I were having done to us, or—

"Oh, thank the EverNameless you guardsmen have come!" I heard, and looked up to see Figler talking to someone I couldn't yet see. But the man's voice had changed slightly, so that now he sounded more pathetically helpless than petulant and whiny.

"I asked them politely to leave, but they flatly refuse," he went on, actually wringing his hands. "I was forced to dismiss the man for incompetence—and for having a liaison while he was supposed to be at work—and now the woman has threatened me. I feel very much the coward having to ask for your help, but . . ."

"That's what we're here for, pal, so don't let it bother you," another, deeper voice said when Figler's trailed off in misery. "Just step out of the way, and we'll take care of it."

Figler turned to shoo everyone in our audience out of the way, but not before I caught the gleam of vindictive satisfaction in his eyes. Once again someone with strength and authority had believed him, and now he just had to stand back and wait in order to get his own way. Or so he thought. I happened to recognize the voice of the guardsman who had spoken, just as I thought I probably would.

The two guardsmen, a hard look on their faces, stepped forward to fill the doorway. One of them was a new recruit, but the other was Dentro, a fighter from the company. Dentro and I had sparred with practice swords once—for about a minute and a half—and when he saw me he grinned, then immediately looked confused.

"What's going on?" he asked, turning his head toward Figler as well. "I can see this is a joke, but I don't get it."

"My dear sir, this is no joke!" Figler protested, still sounding innocent and helpless. "When I dismissed the man he began to make all sorts of wild and terrible accusations, and his trollop supported him. Then she began to threaten me with that weapon she wears, and I became terribly frightened. I dislike asking this, but if they won't leave quietly I must insist that they be locked up.''

"And now for *my* side of the story," I said neutrally as I leaned off the shelf I'd been resting an arm on. "I came to the kitchens to find out who was doing such a good job running them, and got here just in time to discover that the one who *should* have been running them had also heard about how well things were going. For that reason he came back from being 'ill,' immediately began to screw things up, then used the opportunity to fire the man who was such a threat to his position. Three guesses who the screw-up is."

"That's a lie, and I simply won't stand for it," Figler said at once, injured dignity covering smouldering anger. "I told you there were wild accusations being made, sir, and now you've heard them with your own ears. If you doubt my word, you may ask any of these good people standing about. They'll tell you I'm speaking the truth."

He turned then to look at the kitchen workers in our audience, obviously expecting them to back him up. Some looked doubtful, others angry, and a few secretly amused, but none of them spoke up to support his story. Figler frowned, not understanding, but I suddenly did.

"How about that," I remarked, smiling at the workers. "I guess they've all heard about the new employment program, and how good workers will be in high demand. That means they don't have to lie for you any longer, Figler, not when they don't want to. See what you miss when you spend your time at home rather than at work? But that's not all you've missed, so now you get to spend *all* your time at home—but without pay. You have ten minutes to put your things together and get out."

"Don't be absurd," Figler snapped, shifting his glare from the workers to me. "Only the man who hired me can fire me, and you, trollop, are not him. And despite the rest of this nonsense, I can assure you that that man will *not* fire me. Guardsmen, get these two people out of here, and then you can come back for the rest of this dross. I want them all out of here right now, and as long as I remain in charge here you must obey my wishes whether you care to or not.''

Figler was back to being whiny and triumphant, and the new guardsman looked seriously bothered. Dentro, however, simply shook his head and grinned.

"But you're not in charge here, not anymore," he told the smaller man who immediately began to frown in outrage. "The 'trollop' fired you, and as far as I'm concerned, what she says goes. But at that, you're lucky the captain didn't hear you call her that. If he had, he wouldn't have just thrown you out. And since you only have nine minutes left, you'd better get a move on with collecting your possessions.''

"This is absolute insanity!" Figler whined in disbelief. "How dare you take a trollop's word over mine? I insist that you call the third seneschal, who happens to be the man who hired me. *He'll* set you straight in a hurry!''

"Wake up, fool," Dentro growled, making Figler jump. "Anyone else would have figured it out by now. That's the queen you keep calling names, and if you do it again I'll put your lights out myself. Now, get your stuff and get out of here.''

Figler was open-mouthed with shock, but everyone else in our audience cheered. Some of them had known who I was, of course, and they'd been waiting eagerly to see Figler get what he deserved.

"And don't waste your time running to the third seneschal," I advised as Dentro locked a heavy fist into the top of Figler's tunic, getting ready to haul him out of there. "He was fired over a week ago, for refusing to be questioned under a truth spell. Now I'm beginning to understand why he refused. I'll have to look around to see what other incompetents he put into positions of authority.''

Figler was babbling as Dentro pulled him away, the new guardsman trailing after them with a grin. Some of our audience had started to curtsey or bow to me, so I waved a hand and shook my head.

"Since I'm here unofficially, you can all save the bows and curtsies," I told them. "I apologize for taking so long in getting around to Figler, but things are kind of busy these days. And if any of you know about others like him, write down their name and position and we'll check it out. People can't do their best work if they're saddled with idiots who live to make their lives miserable."

Everyone cheered again, but I wasn't through.

"The new head of these kitchens is Ollela, the woman standing right over there," I said once the noise died down, pointing to the mousey woman. "I know you'll all give her as much help and support as she needs, and she in turn will try to make your lives easier."

"But what about Brandis?" Ollela protested, looking seriously bothered. "He's been doing the job for Figler, Your Majesty, so he should be given the first chance to take the man's place."

"Brandis has been offered a different job," I reassured her, noticing how everyone now looked at her with respect. "I admire you for speaking up in favor of fairness, Ollela, but in this case it wasn't necessary. If you want it, the job is yours."

She had to look at Brandis first, who smiled and nodded his own reassurance, but that's all it took. Once she was sure no one was being done out of things, she lost the mousey look and grinned and nodded eagerly. There was cheering for the third time, and then everyone followed their new boss away.

"I'd better remember to tell the paymaster about this," I muttered, then turned to inspect Brandis myself. "So? Have you made any decisions of your own yet? I'm not trying to rush you or anything, but if you take the job we'll have to get you settled into a nice big apartment. That means the housekeeping staff will have to be notified, and the guard, and then we'll have to—"

"Okay, okay, I get the point," he interrupted with a laugh. "I'm holding up everyone in sight. But first tell me what you'd expect from me if I did take the job."

"Why don't we discuss that over cups of coffee while we're sitting in comfortable chairs?" I suggested, glancing around at the storeroom. "What do you say?"

"I suppose I might as well," he agreed with a sigh after only a brief hesitation. "It won't commit me to anything, and I'll admit I'm curious about what you have in mind. Did you want to go somewhere, or would you prefer that *I* provide the amenities?''

''You're not on the payroll yet, so let's go somewhere and both be served,'' I said, beginning to lead the way out of the storeroom. ''If memory serves, there's a meeting room only a short distance away. We can go there and ring for what we want.''

''I know the room you mean, so let's save some time,'' he countered, suddenly moving ahead of me. ''I'll speak to Ollela, and the refreshments will be there almost as soon as we are. Would you like anything besides the coffee?''

When I shook my head he nodded, then trotted off to find Ollela. By the time I reached one of the doors out of the place he had rejoined me, and we walked together to the meeting room. When we went in Brandis snapped his fingers to light the lamps, showing the room to be small with only a few chairs around a central table and with an unlit hearth to the back, but it was perfect for comfortable, private discussions. The coffee—and a selection of small sandwiches and cakes—*was* there right behind us, so Brandis and I were able to settle into chairs with cups in no time at all.

''You want to know what your duties would be if you became the Crown's Chief Sorcerer,'' I began, then noticed his startlement. ''What's wrong? Are you surprised at the title? Actually it would be a lie, because you'd be the Crown's *only* sorcerer. Do lies like that bother you?''

''Not really,'' he said with a headshake and a faint smile. ''I had just begun to picture these hordes of Sighted, and couldn't figure out where they'd come from. Please go on.''

''Well, without the hordes, the entire burden would be on you,'' I continued after sipping at my coffee. ''You'd have to try to keep Tiran and me out of any traps, you'd have to be on the lookout for saboteurs, and you'd have to lend a hand in any of the dozens of situations where the help of a strong magic user is vital. Aside from that, your time would be your own.''

''Well *that's* a relief,'' he said, amusement dancing in his dark eyes. ''For a minute I thought you'd be expecting me to work all the time. But what about helping against your enemies? Wouldn't you want me involved with *that?*"

"Only if they use magic first," I said, looking directly at him. "That's something you do have to understand if you take the job, Brandis. Some of our enemies are very nasty people who deserve whatever is done to them, but the whatever does *not* include something they would be totally helpless against. We have to win this fairly, otherwise Tiran and I will spend the rest of our lives fighting off takeover attempts from people who *know* we can't win without special help."

"I suspect that's only part of your reason, but I'm still relieved to hear it," he said with a warm, honest smile. "If you'd wanted me to do all your fighting for you, I'd already be out that door. But I'd still like to know what makes you think you can trust me. In case you don't know it, I don't *have* to refuse to be questioned under that truth spell you mentioned. I'm strong enough to ignore any truth spell not set by a wizard."

"I thought you might be, and I'm glad you confirmed my guess," I said with a nod. "I was told that someone with enough strength might even be able to manipulate the spell, so take that as reason number one for my trusting you. You could have kept quiet and simply used the spell to put yourself beyond suspicion."

"But my admission, noble as it was, came only a minute ago," he pointed out dryly. "You offered me this job while we were still in the kitchens. How do you know I wasn't planted there by your enemies, just biding my time until I found the opportunity to do you and the king serious damage?"

"Well, if that happens to be the case, just tell me and I'll put you back where I found you," I responded just as dryly. "While you were working in the kitchens everything ran smoothly, and if that's your idea of doing us harm we could do with a little more harm. But on top of that, if you are a plant I don't want you even if you've decided to change sides. I'm afraid I can't see working with a really stupid magic user."

"Stupid?" he echoed with a frown. "Why would you say something like that?"

"Because you're the one who told me what you were, by recognizing me in cat form and getting me safely out of Figler's way," I reminded him. "If you're a plant but still did that, you're too dumb to come in out of the rain. But just for form's sake, I'll ask the question: *are* you a plant?"

"Am I working for your enemies?" he repeated, back to being amused. "I can give you my word that I'm not, and also that I do usually come in when it starts to rain. I'd forgotten about the way we met, which makes me feel foolish. Now it seems to be time for *me* to give an answer, so here it is: I'll be glad to work for you and the king as long as I can. If something comes up that makes it necessary for me to leave, I'll have to reserve the right to go."

"That sounds fair enough," I allowed, watching him reach for one of the sandwiches. "Welcome to the team. Do I tell the paymaster to add your name to the list, or what? I've never hired a magic user before."

"No, all you do is provide me with comfortable surroundings," he answered with a grin. "And make sure I don't have to protect myself from mobs of magic-hating lynchers. I could do my own protecting in that kind of situation, but it makes for even harder feelings when a Sighted acts against the unSighted. I don't expect many mobs around *here*, but it's best to be prepared."

"I didn't realize people still did that sort of thing," I told him wryly. "But this kingdom hasn't had much experience with magic, so I guess we *should* be prepared. I'll have the word spread among the guard and the army, but if a problem comes up you'd better find some of our company fighters to stand behind. They, at least, are used to the idea of magic and magic users."

"I'll do that," he agreed around the last mouthful of sandwich. "So what's my first assignment?"

"I'd suggest you start thinking in terms of batches," I answered with my own amusement. "Your first *batch* will include keeping in regular touch with Bariden and Chalaine, keeping alert for the use of magic in *this* kingdom, looking around for a Shapeshifting saboteur who recently escaped from the cell we had him in, and thinking up a way to keep Tiran and me in touch even when one of us is out of the city. In your spare time you might want to think about training some of our Sighted citizens to help you, and then you might actually *have* some spare time.''

"I'm sorry I asked," he muttered ruefully, then grinned to show he was just kidding. "Actually it will feel good to be using my talent again, but first I'm going to finish these sandwiches. I have the feeling I'll need all the strength I can muster.''

"I have the feeling you're right," I agreed, then sat back to give him the chance to finish eating. As soon as he was through I'd have to hunt up Cadry and the others, who were probably turning the palace upside down looking for me. And this first day was barely more than half over . . .

I finished the coffee in my cup, then leaned forward to refill it. I knew that what I was doing was necessary and I wasn't *really* bored, but I also expected that soon I would be. Bored and restless and ready to see what lay beyond the next mountain or gate, just the way I'd felt for the last few years.

But this kingdom was what Tiran wanted, and the thought of leaving him behind was enough to give me nightmares. I couldn't bear the thought of losing him . . . not after what had happened with the intruders . . . so what in hell would I do when those wanderlust feelings *did* start?

I didn't know, and luckily didn't have to think about it yet. Plenty of time to worry once I did have to think about it . . . and hope one of the EverNameless came by with an answer . . .

CHAPTER SEVEN

It turned out that Cadry wasn't turning the palace upside down after all. She and her fighters were just stalking around, giving a bad case of nerves to anyone who saw them, looking for me and their other escaped prisoner both at the same time. When she saw me coming she just stopped and waited, fists on hips and expression grim, making me glad we both knew who the better fighter was. My father had once looked at me like that, and I'd lost no time disappearing fast and staying lost for a while.

"Hope you got that out of your system now," she growled as soon as I reached her, sparing no more than a glance for Brandis. "If it happens again I get to put it in my report, which the boss means to read as soon as he gets back. Am I comin' through to you?"

"As loud and clear as a threat to my life," I answered dryly. "But don't worry about it, Cadry. We'll both do whatever we have to, and if Tiran disagrees with that it's for me to worry about. Right now I'd like you to meet Brandis, our newest associate. He'll be watching out for any magical trickery, and also giving us a hand in whatever other way he can. Brandis, this is Cadry, formerly a group chief in Tiran's company and now my official babysitter."

"Which is exactly what you need," Cadry said after nodding to Brandis, no happier now than she had been. Strange the way her grammar got better the angrier she got . . . "Even a baby would know better'n to walk away from her guard when there's troublemakers around . . .

Well, no sense beatin' a dead horse. You see any sign of that Shifter?''

"No, which doesn't mean he isn't still around," I said, annoyed all over again. "Brandis, do you think you can locate the man we're looking for? We need him to supply some answers to this large block of questions we have.''

"Frankly, I can't think of a spell that would help you,'' he answered, now frowning in thought. "With all the people coming and going these days, even setting up an exclusion field could be tricky. Someone who wishes that all rulers would just dry up and blow away could try to come in, for instance; a person like that might have no intentions of causing harm personally, but their general attitude could very well make a protective exclusion field keep them out. Is that something you'd want to have happen?''

"And turn them personally and solidly against us?'' I countered with a snort. "Thanks anyway, but we have enough enemies without producing a batch by accident. But think about the problem, and let me know if you come up with any ideas.''

He nodded to show that he would, and then it was back to touring the palace, checking on things and keeping an eye open for our escaped prisoner. As though we'd recognize him if he took the face of someone he knew and we didn't ... or the form of an animal ... or even of a blank wall. It was supposed to be possible for us to do that kind of Shifting, but I'd never tried it myself ...

The rest of the day wore on slowly, but finally it got to be dinnertime. I'd already had Brandis shown to his own apartment, so only Cadry and her people were still with me—until Tovail and Leestin showed up. They were tired but very pleased with their progress, which reminded me I hadn't told Cadry what they were up to. I took care of that chore and listened to what the ladies had to report, discussed possible next moves with them, then reminded them about the act they had to put on for their husbands. Happily that turned out as an encouragement for them to leave, and I was finally able to collapse on a couch in the reception room.

"Got to admit I'm surprised," Cadry said when she came back from seeing the ladies out. "Not only have they got fifteen women recruited already, those fifteen are also assigned and now they're waitin' for the others they expect to get tomorrow. Maybe we oughta put them in charge of recruitin' for the guard.''

"Don't kid yourself," I said with as much of a grin as I could manage, not moving from the couch. "Before they're finished, they'll be completely in charge of palace security. And I like their idea of trying to get some of the city's working girls into their group. Once they do, they'll have every secret in the city worth having inside of a month. Damn. I'm too tired to get up and ring for dinner, and I don't understand why. I didn't *do* anything today."

"All that walkin' instead of ridin' has *me* flattened, so why should you be different?" Cadry asked, going over to yank on the bellpull before lowering herself into a chair. "It ain't what you do that gets you, but what you don't do, and what we don't do is enough walkin'. Startin' tomorrow we oughta change that."

"Starting tomorrow we're back to riding," I said, closing my eyes only because it was easier than keeping them open. "Tiran was scheduled to ride around all over the city, making sure there aren't too many problems that aren't being taken care of, so we get to do it for him. But we won't leave until our ladies' auxiliary is here and in place, and that reminds me. There should be three shifts of ladies, and I forgot to tell that to Tovail and Leestin."

"Tell 'em tomorrow," Cadry said, then levered herself out of the chair when the servant knocked and entered. We ordered dinner for ourselves and the rest of Cadry's fighters, didn't quite have the chance to fall asleep before it came, then forced ourselves to eat. After the meal Cadry and her people searched the entire apartment—that escaped Shifter was still on the loose—and one of them even brought in a cat. To keep the man from coming into the apartment as a mouse, I was told, and I was much too tired to keep myself from laughing hysterically.

"Go on and laugh," Cadry told me as she herded her fighters out while I rolled around holding my sides. "If that cat catches him, then it'll be *my* turn to laugh."

She slammed the bedchamber door behind her, obviously insulted, but that was only because she couldn't see things from *my* perspective. I hadn't stayed in mouse form any longer than it took me to go through the mouseholes, and our fugitive couldn't be expected to either. I mean, if you have attack in mind, the only one you would stay in mouse form for is an elephant.

That thought set me off again, making my new feline companion look at me as if I were crazy. And then I took another look at the cat, and laughed even harder. They'd brought in a tom, for Pete's sake, when everyone knows the best hunters are female. Toms usually consider them-selves too good to hunt, and this one proved the point by jumping up onto my bed, finding a spot right smack in the middle, and settling down to sleep.

But that didn't bother me at all, since I had no intention of sleeping in the bed myself. With Tiran gone the over-sized thing had very little appeal anyway, and I had no interest in lying awake all night, imagining that escaped prisoner sneaking up on me. I turned out most of the lamps and gathered some extra blankets, arranged most of them under the quilts to make it look as if I were in bed, then took the last blanket and threw it casually over a chair on the other side of the large room.

"So it looks like it was tossed here in passing," I mur-mured as I stepped back to inspect my work. It did look completely normal, and even more it hid the wide seat of the chair. Then I got out of my clothes, tossing *them* over the back of the chair, and lastly positioned my sword lean-ing against the front of it.

"And now for me," I said, sliding carefully into the chair to keep from knocking down the sword. Tiran had told me how he'd once Shifted down to a much smaller version of himself in order to sleep comfortably on a short and narrow lounge chair, and that had given me the idea. I Shifted myself small enough to fit under that blanket, and the chair seat was very comfortable—despite the rather deep impression I made in it. After that it must have taken me a good minute or less to fall asleep.

I slept deeply all night, and woke up early to match the early hour I'd gone to sleep. That let me take a leisurely bath before dressing, and by then my breakfast had been delivered. I shared the meal with my cat friend, who was mostly white with patches of gray stripes, and who hadn't stirred from the bed all night. Mouse didn't seem to be to his taste, but bacon and eggs definitely were. Cadry came in just as we were finishing up, and she frowned at me and the cat both.

"Somebody said you're not supposed to feed 'em," she observed after shaking her head to the offer of coffee. "That makes 'em even more eager to go after the mice."

"This guy is too important to chase mice," I said while I stroked the tom, then let him alone when he began to wash. "If you don't believe *me,* ask *him.*"

"Yeah, I guess I can see it," she conceded with a shake of her head. "He's too big to chase *anything* that can run, so tonight we'll look for a skinnier one."

"We'll talk about it, but not right now," I said after finishing the last of my coffee. "We've got a lot to do today, so let's get to it."

She nodded as I stood, and we both went out to pick up the rest of the fighters in my escort. First stop was downstairs in the administrative wing, and to my honestly great surprise, Tovail and Leestin were already on the job.

"We decided we *had* to be here early," Tovail told me while Leestin spoke quietly to a woman in the line that had already formed. "These people get here early, and we didn't want to miss anyone who might be really good. We've told everyone that we're in charge of putting together a really superior force of chambermaids trained especially to deal with the nobly born. Strange how no one doubts that."

"How did your husbands react last night?" I asked as softly as she'd spoken, also matching her wry smile. "Do they still want you two to stop the nonsense and come home?"

"Oddly enough, they've both now changed their minds," Tovail replied, her smile now too innocent. "Leestin said Nomilt told her that stroking the queen's vanity was absolute genius, and now that she's in such an enviable position it's her duty to stay there. Sandor said almost the same thing, just in different words. How did you learn to understand men so well?"

"That was an understanding of politics, not men," I

told her with amusement. "I grew up watching my father's nobles jockeying for position in his court. He kept them from playing at it too hard, but they still played the game. Your ladies will need to be especially alert today, since I'll be out of the palace most of the day. Tell them there's a Shapeshifter at work against us, and he could show up as anything from a man to a woman to a child or even as an animal. If any of them sees anything in the least suspicious—including someone they happen to know who doesn't look quite right—they're to send one of your fighters for Damis. Cadry here has already spoken to him, so he'll know what's happening."

She nodded with a calculating look, curtsied in a distracted way, then headed for Leestin. Cadry waited until she was out of hearing range, then touched my arm.

"If that Shifter tries anythin' with *her* around, he'll be back in a cell before he can blink," Cadry murmured. "Glad it's not me she's after."

"She's finally being allowed to use her intelligence and ability," I answered the same way. "Sometimes being born to money and position is almost as bad as being born to poverty. Let's take a quick look around and then get going."

She nodded and gestured her fighters after us, but everything seemed to be going smoothly and the way it was supposed to. That meant we were free to leave, and in fact our mounts were waiting for us outside—along with an even larger number of the fighters from Cadry's group.

"Ridin' around the city ain't like walkin' around the palace," Cadry said when I stopped short. "Won't hurt havin' 'em, and they'll be right there if we happen to need 'em."

"And anybody with a problem can just fight his or her way through them to talk to me," I said sourly with a nod. "I'm supposed to be doing this to let people know Tiran and I intend to be available to *all* the people, Cadry. How available will I look surrounded by a million fighters?"

"Ain't even a hundred of 'em, and there's a difference between bein' available and bein' an easy target," she returned calmly. "The boss would've had the same size

escort, but he would've had the good sense not to argue.
You comin' or not?''

Since I had no choice about going I went to my horse,
but not with very good grace. I couldn't shake the belief
that Tiran would *not* have had that large an escort, but
had made sure I did. Pampering and protecting, he would
have called it, but to me it was coddling and smothering.
He and I would have to have a long talk as soon as he
got back.

But at least it was a nice day. I climbed into the saddle
smelling that early-morning freshness that hadn't yet disappeared, thanks to the presence of grass in front of the
palace. Once we reached the city streets that would
change, but at least I was able to enjoy it until we rode
through one of the gates. Then I paid attention to the city
itself, letting all other considerations go.

The area around the palace was fairly affluent, with only
a few people out and about. That changed slowly as we
changed neighborhoods, and by the time we reached the
fringes of the main marketplace we were kneedeep in people. Our parade attracted quite a lot of attention, and there
were even a few tentative cheers. Most were warily unsure
about why we were there, and I couldn't blame them for
being cautious. Their last rulers had taken great pleasure
in hurting them, and for all they knew Tiran and I were
no different.

So I picked a spot with an abandoned booth, climbed
onto the top of it straight from my saddle, and began to
make a speech. I told my quickly growing audience that
things had now changed, so Tiran and I wanted to know
it if anyone was still being taken advantage of the way
they'd been under our predecessors. If they were we'd
take care of it, starting right now.

That brought a lot more cheering and, after something of
a hesitation, a few people coming forward. My bodyguards
brought them to me one at a time after I'd jumped off the
booth counter, and three of the people simply wanted to
tell me how glad they were that Tiran and I were making
things better. I thanked them warmly and accepted their
bows and curtsies, and then the last two were brought
forward.

"We thought on this hard, Yer Majesty, me an' th' old woman," the man said, sounding as if every word was being dragged out. He had a battered old hat that he kept turning around and around in his hands, and the woman's fingers kept bunching up the material of her skirt. Neither one of them looked directly at me, or even seemed to want to.

"What he means is, we're tired a gettin' robbed an' bein' pushed around," the woman said when the man's words didn't continue. "We wus thinkin' on comin' to th' palace t'tell somebody, but now yer here an' askin'. Where we live—there's them as takes frum alla us, them as usta be guardsmen. Said they'd kill us if'n we told, but . . .''

They still hadn't looked up and there was something odd about their accents, but none of that was important. What mattered was that we seemed to have flushed out more of that human garbage who had had so much fun destroying people's lives.

"Tell me where the men are, and we'll be glad to get rid of them for you," I said, keeping my tone gentle so as not to frighten the two. "Where do you live, and how many former guardsmen are hiding out in the area?"

"I seen five," the man grudged, still turning his hat. "They took over this house with a alley an' small back garden, two streets over frum ourn. Whole neighborhood knows where they're at, but nobody dares t'say nothin'."

Then he gave us directions to an area that lay a short distance beyond the far side of the market. I thanked the people and gave them each a silver piece, and then we all remounted and headed for the next street up that paralleled the market street.

"With only five of 'em, we'll take 'em easy," Cadry said as we rode, her expression of anticipation matching what *I* felt. "Glad those two had the guts to speak up."

"You and me both," I answered, "but we'll have to surround the area before we go in. Cities have a lot more boltholes than the woods, and we don't want to lose any of the trash."

Cadry nodded absently, and when we got close to the street where that house was supposed to be she sent some of her fighters around the long way. The rest of us dismounted and continued on on foot, and by the time we got there the house *was* surrounded, and the one immediately next door as well. All those extra fighters were coming in handy, but I'm not partial to crowds. That made me take myself around to the alley, to join the smaller number of fighters there. If any of our quarry tried to bolt the house, there would be less competition in reaching them.

I heard a few whistled notes, and then sounds of breaking in came from both the front and back of the house. No one came to the window on the alley that we stood near or over the wall from the enclosed garden despite shouts and scuffling noises from inside, and then—

And then I heard a really odd whistling from behind me. I turned to see an opening in the building on that side that seemed to lead to some sort of courtyard, and the whistle had come from there. I also caught a flash of dirty yellow, the same shade as the uniforms worn by our predecessors' guardsmen. There were half a dozen fighters in the alley with me and a couple of them cursed with pleasure, obviously having seen what I had. Some of our quarry had escaped the net, but they wouldn't stay free for long.

One of the male fighters pushed his way ahead of me as I started forward, and it was annoying but I didn't argue. The opening we moved through wasn't very wide and had a strange smell to it, but we were beyond it in a minute and into the courtyard, where we were able to move forward fast and spread out. Waist high bushes surrounded a number of lovely flowerbeds in the corners of the yard, and stone benches stood near the beds, looking as if they were inviting use.

"They could be hiding behind any of those bushes," the male fighter who had pushed in front of me said softly, his eyes moving over the entire area. "I don't think you ought to be in here, Your Majesty, at least not without the rest of the escort."

"You sound like Cadry," I grumbled back, but something in that peaceful, lovely courtyard-garden was beginning to give me the chills. The benches and bushes had begun to shift and blur a little in my vision, as if they'd suddenly decided to sneak around behind us. And that thought frightened me, the idea of having them *behind* me where they could do just about anything. *All* of it felt as if something hideous was waiting just out of sight, waiting to flow out and do something unspeakable . . .

"I don't think any of us oughta be in here," another fighter said, wiping his mouth with the back of his left hand while his head jerked from one side of the courtyard to the other. "It's gonna get us, I know it is, an' we won't have a chance."

"But we came so far in!" a third man, bigger than the others, whispered in a terrified voice. "We'll never make it out again, I know we won't!"

Most of the others moaned their desperate agreement, and it was all I could do not to join in. It had gotten so *cold* in that place, and I knew the cold meant that something terrible was about to happen. The others were absolutely right, and we'd been fools to go in there in the first place. *IT* had us now, and we'd never live to get out again.

And then one of the men let out a strangled scream as he jerked his sword from its scabbard. Others echoed him as I fumbled at my own sword, so terrified that I was close to wetting myself. These THINGS were coming out from behind the bushes, coming at *us*, and the twisted weapons they held were meant to destroy us. They were all over dirty yellow, the THINGS, mostly haze that covered the true hideousness of their forms.

Someone was whimpering as the THINGS got closer and closer, but it wasn't the fighter who had pushed in ahead of me. He just stood where he was, rooted to the spot, so frozen with terror that he couldn't even move to arm himself. Someone else broke and ran screaming, and he was the first of us to be cut down. The way his screams broke off quickly and suddenly, *chopped* off . . . ! I wanted to be violently sick, and didn't know what was keeping it from happening.

And then I was screaming along with everyone else as the THINGS rushed us. There were so many of them we didn't stand a chance, and the fighter next to me understood that and didn't even try to defend himself with the sword he held. He and the fighter frozen in place went down almost together, and that left only four of us to face the horror alone.

My hands were trembling so hard that I almost dropped my sword, and my breath came out in gasps to match the hammering of my heart. When the first THINGS slashed at me I nearly missed getting my sword up in time, and that added to the terror. They were going to kill us all, and there was nothing we could do to stop it.

The other three fighters with me really tried, but one by one they all went down. There were so *many* of the THINGS that I couldn't understand why I wasn't dead yet, but that time wasn't far off. Something inside made me defend myself frantically, but there were so *many* . . . ! I screamed as two weapons reached me, cutting my flesh open and freeing my blood. The pain was worse than anything I could have imagined, and it made me want to cower in a corner . . . It hurt, it *hurt* . . . !

But that something refused to let me stop fighting, to stop trying to defend myself. Another sword edge reached me and at the same time I heard the wind, whispering in many voices and ordering me to stop trying to resist. *Give up and find peace and safety,* the wind whisper urged, *you know you can't win.* I did know that and I did want to stop, but I just couldn't. I wasn't strong enough to override the something that kept me going, the something that drove me on despite all the sword points and edges that now reached me.

And then, suddenly, even more madness erupted. Fighters appeared around me as if by magic, and the THINGS weren't able to reach me any more. I'd stood against them so long that it had felt like forever, and pain burned and beat at me even harder than it had. I was so dizzy and weak . . . couldn't stand any longer . . . had to fall down and let everything go black . . .

It was very quiet, so quiet that I just had to open my eyes. When I did I discovered I was in my own bedchamber, lying in bed. I could feel something like the echo of pain, far away and very faint, but still there somewhere. The linen around me was fresh and the quilt comfortable, but somehow a distant chill managed to touch me with the very tips of its fingers.

A sudden movement came on my right, making me want to cringe away, but then I recognized Cadry and the magic user Brandis, quickly coming up to the bed.

"Alex, how're you feelin'?" Cadry asked, sounding really worried. "We've been waitin' for you to wake up . . . Are you okay?"

"What happened?" I asked in the loudest whisper I could after swallowing from a dry mouth. "Why am I *here*?"

"We brought you here once we pulled you outta that trap," Cadry answered while Brandis raised a hand and murmured something. "We were set up, Alex, and I still don't understand how. That house we broke into belongs to a small-time merchant, and there was no sign of any ex-guardsmen. I was busy apologizin' to the man and his family, when we heard screams comin' from outside. That's the first I realized you weren't with me . . . Damn, Alex, don't you know how close you came? You and that misbegotten *need* to take off alone . . . !''

"Calm down, Group Chief," Brandis advised her gently when her ragged voice broke off. "There's more going on here than we've been able to figure out, and I don't like what I'm Seeing when I look at her. Your Majesty, how do you feel? I healed your wounds, but something still seems to be wrong. Can you tell me what it is?"

"I don't know what you mean," I answered Brandis, pulling the quilt up to my chin as memories began to return about what had happened. "Cadry . . . are they really all dead, the six who were with me? There were so many of them, the THINGS . . . they hurt me . . ."

"Alex, there were only the five ex-guardsmen we were told about," Cadry said slowly, now looking really worried. "They were all around you when we got there, and my fighters were dead without even one of *them* bein' touched. You were hurt bad but still defendin' yourself well enough that they couldn't get all the way through your guard . . . Can you tell me why none of you was able to take even one of 'em, not even you? What happened?"

"It—was a nightmare," I got out, closing my fists tight

on the quilt to keep them from trembling. "All we could see was these—THINGS, and we knew they were going to kill us. There were so many of them and we were all so *afraid*—"

I'd started breathing so fast that I couldn't go on, and I felt nausea begin to rise in me again. This time I knew I'd never be able to stop it, but Brandis quickly raised his hand and said something. Peace and safety began to wash over me, along with sleepiness, but I was still able to see Brandis turn to Cadry.

"I knew something was done to her, I knew it!" he all but growled, the savagery in his eyes making Cadry look even more worried. "This isn't the woman I met yesterday, the one who talked me into working for her. Something was done and I'll find out what, *damned* if I don't!"

Cadry looked as if she wanted to believe him, but I would have gotten out of there if I could have. Brandis hadn't been that savage yesterday, and I felt disturbed even through whatever he'd done. He frightened me and I tried to get up, tried to ask what was happening, but I was just too tired. My eyes began to blink and then a blink turned into sleep . . .

CHAPTER EIGHT

"**W**ell, we made it," Tiran said to Caldai Moyan when they topped the last rise before the city. "My home and your . . . what?"

"Temporary stopover, I guess," she answered with a shrug and a smile, only glancing at him. "I'm not ready for a home yet, but I don't mind visiting other people's. And I'm glad I had your company for the ride today. When you travel alone the temptation's there to start talking to yourself, and once you do that your friends stop inviting you over for dinner."

"And strangers do even worse than that," Tiran said with a laugh. "I've enjoyed your company too, and not just because I still want my friends to invite me to dinner. It was nice to have everything said even before we started the trip."

"Everything like the fact that you're happily married and I'm delighted that you are?" she said, now turning her head to look at him. "I've learned to recognize men who are capable of committing themselves to a woman, and I usually avoid them like death. For me, a committment right now would *be* like death, only not as kind. I need to find what I'm searching for first, right after I find out exactly what that is. Am I making any sense to you?"

"More than I care to think about," Tiran replied, all amusement gone behind a sigh. "My wife felt the same way, but I still managed to talk her into marrying me. If she ever decides she made a mistake, I don't know what I'll do."

"You'll do what's right and best for both of you," Caldai said firmly, giving him a look to match. "And most women are *not* cut out for my kind of life, even if some are silly enough to think they should be. If you want me to, I'll have a talk with your wife and explain that in a way she can't just brush aside."

"Where mistakes are concerned, *that* would be one of the biggest," Tiran said, suddenly trying very hard not to laugh. "You don't know my wife, and believe me when I say you don't want to try telling her something she might not want to hear. People have been known to get hurt doing that."

"She's a fighter, then," Caldai said with a wry smile, shifting in her saddle. "Somehow I hadn't expected that, and now I understand why you're worried. But you'll see, everything will work out right. Where in the city do you live?"

"Ah, pretty much right smack in the middle," Tiran hedged with a partial smile of his own. "And there's lots of room for guests, so spend some time now deciding whether or not you'd like to stay with us. I can even provide hire if you happen to need the silver."

"Because you're the captain of a mercenary company," she said with a nod, now looking at him soberly. "It wasn't hard to pick *that* up, but I got something else as well. You and your people are a special guard for the new king and queen, doing the jobs they won't trust to anyone else. Is that what you're offering me a chance to join?"

"In a manner of speaking," Tiran allowed, choosing his words carefully. "You can't be part of the special guard you mentioned because you weren't with us from the beginning, but trained fighters are given preferential hire and as much responsibility as he or she can handle. After things settle down there will be promotions *into* that special core group, as present members of it are shifted elsewhere. If what you're looking for happens to be a place to exercise your ability without interference from *too* many fools, this is it."

"I'll have to think about it, but you could be right,"

she said, glancing away before looking at him again with a smile. "I'll accept your offer of hire while I'm looking around, and let you know my final decision as soon as I make it."

"Fair enough," Tiran agreed, then let his horse pick up its pace. It knew they were close to home, and it wanted its comfortable stall and a binful of oats. It was close enough to sunset that Tiran wanted the human equivalent of the same, not to mention seeing Alex again. The three days they'd been apart felt like a year or more, and he couldn't wait until his arms were around her. There were things that had to be taken care of first, but as soon as they were done . . .

Tiran led Caldai to a side entrance to the palace grounds, one that took them straight to the wing housing Company HQ. Damis, Tiran's former lieutenant, was in overall charge, while Gann, one of Tiran's former sublieutenants, saw to the training and disposition of their fighting force. Eventually Gann would be in charge of the army all by himself, while Damis and Hadar, Tiran's other sublieutenant, would be awarded places among the nobility. It was what each of them had chosen for himself, and they'd more than earned it already.

"Captain," Gann said when Tiran entered his office after knocking. "How did it go?"

"Successfully, but not far enough," Tiran answered, gesturing Caldai in with him. "We cleared Pavar's villages, but the men will need help with Selwin's and any others of the nobility who have done the same. Send Rhodris as large a force as you can spare, in groups small enough to make good time. And this is Caldai Moyan, a fighter who will join us at least for a time. I'd like you to get her settled in, but first you need to know what we found."

Tiran helped himself to a cup of coffee while he filled Gann in, and then he completed the introductions between Caldai and her new boss. With all that done he was finally free to leave, to find his version of the stall and oats his horse had gotten almost as soon as he'd dismounted. He'd thought about telling Caldai that he wasn't simply a captain of mercenaries, but as much as he'd enjoyed her company he still wasn't completely certain about her. If it turned out eventually that she worked for his enemies, he'd be able to deal with her more easily once he saw Alex and got some rest.

Walking through the corridors of the palace took more time than he liked, but it also wasn't something he could do anything about. At least the crowds were gone for the day, leaving before sundown the way they usually did. He passed occasional servants who bowed to him and various guards who came to attention, but finally, *finally,* he reached his apartments, where there seemed to be a heavier guard than he'd asked for. He frowned as he walked through the doors two of them opened for him, but didn't question them as he'd originally intended. Cadry was in the reception room talking to a man he didn't know, and she should have the answers ordinary fighters wouldn't.

"Cadry, what's going on?" he asked at once as he strode toward her. "Why are there so many fighters stationed out there, and where's Alex?"

"Boss, am I glad to see you back," she said as she stood, but relieved would have been a more accurate word to describe her. "Alex is okay, but this time we came real close. They tried for her again with a really nasty trap, and it almost worked."

"Where is she?" Tiran repeated, and the unknown man who had also stood flinched just a little.

"In the bedchamber, sleepin'," Cadry answered as quickly as possible, clearly recognizing Tiran's rage. "Once you see her, we'll tell you what happened."

He nodded curtly and headed at once toward the bedchamber, fighting silently but wildly to control what stormed inside him. This was the second time those bastards had tried to hurt his beloved, and when he caught up to them he would kill them with as much pain as it was possible to give. He didn't even know who they were, but he would find out. And when he did . . . !

Tiran opened only one of the bedchamber doors, and that as silently as possible. Inside the room were half a dozen of his female fighters, who were already beginning to clear steel even before seeing him. Once they realized who he was they went back to simply standing guard, but not one of them looked in the least relaxed. Their being there disturbed Tiran more than it reassured him, especially when his searching gaze finally found Alex.

She lay asleep in their very large bed, just as she'd been when he'd left three days earlier. But three days ago she'd been sprawled under the covers, spread out comfortably and enjoying being asleep. Now . . . now she lay all drawn in, one fist closed tight on the top of the quilt, a small frown marring the smoothness of her beautiful face. And somehow she seemed to be *working* at sleeping rather than enjoying it, braced rather than relaxed.

Tiran paused where he stood, wanting to go over and take her in his arms, but he couldn't help noticing the dark smudges under her eyes. She needed the sleep she was currently getting, and waking her would be criminal. Besides, he still hadn't heard the details of what had happened. If there was any justice in the worlds, the story would lead him to the people responsible for trying to harm his Alex.

He went back out as quietly as he'd entered, and saw that Cadry and the stranger were still on their feet. But more to the point there was also a pot of coffee, and Cadry had already poured him a cup.

"Thanks," he said to her, taking the cup before going to a chair and sitting wearily. "Now tell me what happened."

"It was yesterday," Cadry began, sinking back down onto the couch she'd been on, the stranger doing the same after a brief hesitation. "We started ridin' around the city the way the schedule called for, and at the first stop these two people came over to tell us about ex-guardsmen holed up in their neighborhood. We had a strong escort so we went right over there, only it was a trap. The five we were huntin' weren't in the house we broke into, but in the courtyard of the house next door. They lured Alex and six fighters in after 'em, and by the time the rest of us got there only Alex was still standin', with the five tryin' hard to change that."

"Five of *them* took six of ours *and* almost took Alex?" Tiran echoed in disbelief. "Cadry, if that's some kind of joke, I'm missing the punchline. It couldn't possibly have happened like that."

"There's one point you haven't been told about yet," the stranger put in, leaning forward with his hands locked between his knees. "There was a walkway Alex and the others had to go through to reach the courtyard, and I'm sure that's where the heart of the trap lay. Alex remembers noticing a funny smell when she walked through, which means a scattered powder or a mist. That has to be what did it to them."

"What did what?" Tiran asked, suddenly lost. "And who are you? I don't remember ever seeing you before."

"Boss, this is Brandis, a magic user Alex found," Cadry said, looking briefly annoyed with herself. "Should've introduced him sooner, but with everythin' goin' on . . . He saved Alex's life by healin' her, then kept diggin' till he found the rest of the problem."

"Your Majesty," the man named Brandis said, standing up to bow. "I'm a sorcerer, and two days ago I agreed to help the queen and yourself. What happened here can only be considered my fault, since I should have been watching over Alex. Instead I was in the midst of checking through this palace, trying to locate an escaped prisoner. If one of the fighters hadn't ridden ahead to alert me, my healing might have reached her too late to do any good . . ."

His words trailed off as he sank down onto the couch again, obviously fighting against useless self-recrimination—and losing. The man clearly blamed himself for the incident, but Tiran had a sudden question.

"I don't understand how you could have healed Alex," he said, drawing more of the man's attention. "She's been warded against the use of magic, and as far as I know that warding hasn't been cancelled. Are you that strong a sorcerer that you were able to *break* through?"

"Of course not," the man answered quickly, and then he showed a faint smile. "I keep forgetting how little most of the unSighted know about magic. It's true that warding will stop all magic from an equal or lesser source than the caster of the warding, but that doesn't apply to healing magic. Warding won't stop it because its purpose is to help rather than harm."

"I see," Tiran said, although that wasn't quite true. He'd never heard that about healing, but there were a lot of things he didn't know about magic. "Let's get back to that powder or mist. What did it do to Alex and the others?"

"It made them terrified," Brandis answered, slumping back on the couch. "It also apparently distorted their perceptions to the point that they didn't even know who was attacking them. They saw horrible monsters of some kind, and were so afraid that they weren't even able to defend themselves. But we did get one lucky break."

"He means that one of the fighters pushed his way in ahead of Alex, and went through the walkway first," Cadry explained. "She told us about that, and also that when the attack came the fighter was so terrified he couldn't move at all. Just stood there whimperin' while he was cut down, which is what we figure was supposed to happen to Alex. They expected *her* to be the first one through the walkway, so they set it up that first one through got the heaviest dose. And whatever that stuff was, it hung on even after the healin'."

"Which was my second clue that something besides wounds was wrong," Brandis said with a frown of memory, taking up the narrative again. "The first clue was the length of time it took Alex to come around after I healed her. She should have been awake in a matter of minutes, and instead it took hours. When she did wake up she was disoriented and obviously frightened, but talking about what had happened brought her close to panic. I put her to sleep again, and went looking for what I'd missed the first time."

"And you found it," Tiran said, both hands tightening around the cup he held. "I mean, she *is* all right now? You got rid of whatever was affecting her, and she's fine?"

"It took most of the day today, but she should be," Brandis confirmed, bringing Tiran staggering relief. "Whatever they used spread all through her, but it should be gone now. The process was exhausting for her but she withstood it, and afterward she told us what happened. She'd be out here with us now if I hadn't put her to sleep again."

"That sounds like my Alex," Tiran said with a smile, then remembered the coffee he held. He took a long swallow, but in a moment the smile was gone and he turned again to Cadry. "But if she's all right, why are there fighters stationed in our bedchamber? And female fighters at that?"

"Brandis made sure she wouldn't wake up till the mornin'," Cadry answered, her face expressionless. "That means she can't see to takin' care of herself, and just because she's in her own bed, that don't mean she's safe. And as far as the rest of it goes ... I got a lot of respect for my male fighters, Boss, but there are times and situations when men'll hesitate before killin', especially decent men, which most of ours are. Those girls were told to kill *anythin'* that don't belong in there, and you can bet they'll do just that."

Tiran nodded, understanding the point and appreciating it. A female protecting her young is the most dangerous animal in the forest, and most human women had the same potential for deadliness. Too many of them were raised in such a way that the potential was never realized, but that didn't apply to trained fighters. As long as those six women lived, Alex would sleep soundly and safely.

"Let's go back to something Brandis mentioned," Tiran said to Cadry after leaning forward to refill his coffee cup. "There was something about an escaped prisoner ... Is that why you have so many guards posted? And I hope we're not talking about Duke Pavar."

"No, the duke's still where they put him," Cadry said with a headshake while refilling her own coffee cup. "The one missin' is somebody Alex caught tryin' to mess up your new system. We didn't know he was a Shapeshifter, so he got put in an ordinary cell in lockup. When we went to question him he was gone, and Alex decided Shiftin' was the only way he could've gotten out."

Cadry then went on to tell Tiran about the scams Alex had uncovered, and their theories about that original kidnapping attempt being staged just so Alex would be left in the palace instead of Tiran. It had looked like a fairly safe bet—until the second attempt nearly worked.

"So now I don't know *what* to think," Cadry grumbled, clearly more than just physically tired. "They *were* ready for you to be gone and for her to be too pissed to bother lookin' around, but that setup in the courtyard wasn't just a grabbed opportunity. It came at our first stop, not the last, so it had to be already arranged when those two phonies came to talk to us. And those five *were* wearin' raggedy, dirty-yellow uniforms. I would've been happier keepin' at least one of 'em alive, but they wouldn't surrender. Killin' 'em was the only way to get 'em to stop tryin' to reach Alex.''

"Which also doesn't make sense," Tiran said, absently shaking his head. "If they really were ex-guardsmen, they should have scattered as soon as you and the others got there. Where they would have gotten that powder or mist is another story, but they shouldn't have stayed to fight. It almost sounds like they were under a compulsion, which means they didn't have to be ex-guardsmen."

"Or maybe they were, and were just so filled with hate it was *like* a compulsion," Cadry suggested, looking disturbed. "They had a good thing goin' before you and Alex got here, and now they're a scattered pack of hunted animals. That would make for the crazy kind of hate, like decidin' to get one of you or die tryin'.''

"Whatever it is, so far they've been way ahead of us," Tiran said, temporarily pushing the question aside. "We've got to sit down and do some thinking and planning, not just react to whatever *they* do. And tomorrow I'll take a close look at the new programs. Chances are good that they grabbed the opportunity to mess things up again."

"This time they only got to try," Cadry said, and there was finally a trace of satisfaction in her voice. "Alex set up a spy network, and it almost got us that Shapeshifter back."

And then she told Tiran about what Baroness Tovail and Countess Leestin had been put in charge of. Tiran remembered that the two women had volunteered, but hearing about what they'd accomplished almost made him blink.

"So they've got a capable, eager group," Cadry summed up, "and one that started meshin' right away. The ladies had their recruits separate into partnered groups. Each group was assigned to a different part of the palace,

and once in it they broke up into pairs. The more innocent—or dumber-lookin'—one of the pair stumbled around
pretendin' to be lost, while her partner kept an eye on her.
If the first one spotted somethin' she signalled her partner,
who then went runnin' for help while she stayed and kept
an eye on whatever she'd spotted.''

"That sounds like it should have worked well," Tiran
said, trying to get the surprise out of his tone. "I guess
I'm as bad as everyone else, expecting high-born ladies
and ordinary women to be helpless. So how did they almost catch our fugitive?"

"He turned up where they were signin' kids up for
school and interviewin' teachers," Cadry answered. "First
thing he did was try to tell people there would be a fee
for sendin' kids to school. The woman there had already
sent her partner for help, so she piped up that she *knew*
there were no fees because her sister had already enrolled
fifteen or sixteen kids. Then she started talkin' about her
made-up sister and all those kids, and wouldn't let the
Shifter get a word in edgewise. After a couple of minutes
he got disgusted and walked away.''

"I wish I could have seen that," Tiran said with a grin
that Brandis shared. "If there's anything a man can't stand
against, it's a talkative woman going on about her family.
I suppose the fighters showed up right after he left."

"Not right then, no," Cadry denied, just as amused as
her male listeners. "Once he disappeared the woman went
and headed off her partner and my fighters, tryin' to keep
the Shifter from findin' out what was goin' on. But the
fighters stayed close and the woman swapped places with
her partner, to keep the Shifter from recognizin' her.''

"Smart," Tiran commented, more impressed by the
minute. "I used to wonder if *all* women are born with a
talent for strategy and tactics, and now I'm beginning to
believe they are.''

"Well, those two did well enough," Cadry said, clearly
and definitely refusing to comment on what Tiran had said.
"The second one spotted the Shifter in the room where
they were interviewin' teachers, and she signalled fast before goin' in after him. He was tryin' to tell everybody
that there would be a real hard test for all the applicants—

unless they paid a fee to get themselves exempted. So the woman went over and started askin' him what would be on the test.''

"I'm beginning to feel sorry for that man," Tiran said with an even wider grin while Brandis chuckled. "How long did she have to keep it up?"

"Long enough that he looked like he wanted to scream, she told us," Cadry answered with her own grin. "Seems like she *could* be a teacher, so she acted like she *wanted* to take the test. When he couldn't stand it anymore he headed for the way out, but my fighters were already on the way in. He took one look at them and headed for an open window, then dived through. By the time they got to the window, he'd Shifted and was gone."

"And trying to keep him gone was what *I* was in the middle of," Brandis contributed with a sigh. "This happened the day before yesterday, while Alex and the others were out, and as soon as I was told the man was around again I formulated a find spell. There couldn't be many men running from pursuit and hiding to keep from being discovered, so I was able to use those generalities for the search. When it turned up nothing, I decided he'd left the palace. Or had changed his looks, and had good enough control of himself not to be worried any longer. I had just begun to think about what else I could use for a different search, when word reached me about what had happened."

"I think those women deserve some recognition and reward," Tiran said after nodding to what Brandis had told him. "Tomorrow, Cadry, tell the Countess and Baroness that I've declared a bonus for all of them, but twice the bonus for the two who came so close to catching that fugitive. And when this is all over and they're no longer a secret weapon, we'll have a reception with all of them as guests of honor. Do you think they'll like that?"

"They'd probably like the promise of permanent jobs even more," Cadry suggested as she watched him. "Don't mean to be makin' decisions for you, Captain, but—"

"Hey, you're right," Tiran interrupted, delighted with the idea. "And see if you can find someone to remind me every couple of hours that women have the same needs as men. If they'd been a group of male agents, I would have thought of that jobs thing myself. You can add that they'll have jobs with us as long as they want or need them.''

"Then that about covers it," Cadry said, rising to her feet. "Now that you're back, I'm goin' to my quarters and droppin' into bed. You want me to take some men off that guard detail at the door?"

"Take half of them, and put them in a room where they can watch the ones at the door," Tiran decided after a moment's thought. "And tell their reliefs to watch themselves, since right after changeover is the best time to attack. And make sure they all know about that powder-mist thing. It won't matter how many fighters we have available, if none of them are able to fight."

Cadry nodded and headed for the door, but Brandis stayed where he was on the couch they'd shared. Tiran had the feeling the magic user had more to say, and once they were alone he discovered he was right.

"Your Majesty, I don't quite know how to say this," Brandis began, obviously groping for words. "I'm not used to being in the middle of things like this, where people are attacked and their good work is sabotaged for nothing more than individual gain. I've traveled fairly widely so I never considered myself a sheltered scholar, but I'm coming to believe that that's exactly what I am."

"If you're trying to tell me you've decided to leave, I can't really blame you," Tiran said with a sigh as he got up to ring for a servant. "I *am* used to situations like this, but there's something about this one that seems to be waiting to turn around and bite me in half. I'm grateful for the help you did give, and if there's anything I can do for you—"

"No, no, Your Majesty, you misunderstand me," Brandis said with an odd expression, one hand held up toward Tiran. "I was trying to apologize for doing so little to help, and meant to add that I intend to do better in the future. But you were ready to let me go if I felt I had to leave, and with thanks rather than accusations of desertion. There aren't many men in your position who would do that, and you have my word that I won't forget it. And there's something else I think you should know."

"Go on," Tiran urged, seeing the man's very obvious hesitation. "And I'm about to order dinner. Would you like to join me, or have something else brought if you've already eaten?"

"Thank you but I *have* already eaten," Brandis said, then laughed just a little. "What I mean is I ate a late lunch, and I'm not yet ready for dinner. I won't stay once your meal is brought, but please see to the ordering of it before we continue."

Tiran was about to say the servant hadn't arrived yet, but a knock at the door kept him from making a liar of himself. One of the guards opened the door to let the servant in, and the man took Tiran's order quickly and efficiently and left again. Once he was gone, Tiran turned back to Brandis.

"I see more has improved around here than just the security," he commented. "Now what do you have to tell me?"

"Something that probably won't help you, but I still feel I ought to mention it," Brandis answered, his expression now disturbed. "Something feels ... *wrong* around here, I suppose is the only way I can put it. In most places the balance of the universe isn't noticed because it's there and in its proper place, but here ... I had the feeling that that's what you meant when you said something is waiting to bite you in half."

"That the universe is out of balance, yes," Tiran said, finding the definition very accurate. "But Alex and I were told that we're supposed to be here, so what could be out of balance in the situation? Our enemies? What they're trying to do? But that doesn't make any sense. I've seen people try takeovers before, and it was nothing like this. So if we're in the right and our enemies wrong, why is the universe so far out of balance?"

"Maybe it has something to do with the times," Brandis said with a shrug that suggested it was too far beyond him. "Whatever, I'm here to do the magic, not the thinking. Would you like to know why service has improved in the palace, especially kitchen service?"

Tiran nodded, so the man told him how and where Alex had found him. It was an amusing story, and lasted until

Tiran's food was brought. Brandis waited until the servant's back was turned, then spoke some nearly silent words and gestured at the food. Whatever he saw seemed to please him, as he stood and bowed to Tiran.

"I think it's safe to leave you to your meal, Your Majesty," Brandis said with a wink. "As I mentioned earlier, I've never done this before, but making sure your meals are nothing but nourishing must certainly be part of my normal duties. Rest assured that I intend to keep a watchful eye out, for both you *and* Queen Alexia."

Tiran thanked him and watched him leave, then sat down to the meal served by the man who had brought it. He would have been happier to have Alex there to share it with him, but she needed the sleep she was getting. Tomorrow she would be there to join him for meals, but that was all she'd be joining him in. She'd certainly argue and complain about staying in bed, but she'd had a really rough time of it, and it was all his fault. He should have sent Rhodris out alone to check on those villages, but the idea of getting out from under the workload for a while had been so damned tempting . . .

The food was delicious, but Tiran ate it only because it was necessary. Guilt tried to fill him more than anything he put down his throat, but it was forced to make room for the raging fury he'd only been able to push aside for a while, not dismiss completely. Fighting angry meant fighting stupid, but that was something his mind knew. His gut wanted the deep satisfaction of catching whoever had almost killed his Alex, and tearing them apart with his bare hands.

Or with claws and teeth, if they were able to form fight. Tiran finally gave up on the meal and dismissed the servant, then took his silent rage to the bathing room and a bath. He was bone tired and needed to sleep, but his mind refused to quiet down. It kept demanding to know who was at the bottom of their major troubles, and what Brandis had meant about the strangeness having to do with the times. It was such an odd, meaningless comment that it had stuck in his mind.

Having piped-in hot water was a luxury Tiran had gotten used to in Alex's father's palace, but not one he had stopped being grateful for. He filled the giant tub full and then lowered himself into the hot water, hoping it would do the job of making him relax. Alex didn't need someone tossing and turning all night in the bed next to her, and he was *not* going to sleep elsewhere. If anyone was stupid enough to try for her again, he would be right there to stop it.

Along with his female fighters. He'd thought about dismissing them once he was ready to get into bed, then dismissed the idea instead. When he did fall asleep he would sleep deeply, and it would be stupid to gamble Alex's life on whether or not he could wake up fast enough. No, the fighter guard would stay, and he just regretted he didn't have enough female fighters to make it an around-the-clock assignment.

And he'd have to remember to tell Gann not to include Caldai in the assignment, not until they knew more about her. Coincidence bothered him, and she'd turned up just a little too conveniently. It was too bad it would be days before he'd be able to find out how things were going for Rhodris and the others with the villages, but maybe Brandis would be able to help with a little long-distance viewing ... What did they call that? ... Scrying ... ?

Tiran snapped awake before he slid under water, realizing that the hot bath had done its job. Now he just had to wash and dry off, and then he could get into bed. But tomorrow ... yes, tomorrow he'd think about everything ...

CHAPTER NINE

I woke up expecting to feel pain, and in a strange way I did. It was the echo of pain remembered, a whisper of wind blowing through the leaves of memory. Ordinary, incidental hurt doesn't stay with you long, but the spectacular kind tends to hang on for longer than it should. And also tends to walk your dreams, which mine certainly had. I now remembered everything that had happened to me, and felt as if I'd relived it over and over again during the night.

Which meant I really needed a bath. I'd noticed that my female fighter guard was still in the room despite the fact that I'd told Cadry I didn't want them, but when I shifted around before sitting up I made a different discovery. Tiran was in bed with me, but all the way over on the far side. He must have gotten back after Brandis put me to sleep, and hadn't wanted to disturb me.

My first urge was to wake him up so I could hold him, but then I saw how deeply asleep he was. He must have gotten back either really late or really tired or both, and it would be cruel to wake him early. Besides, I really needed that bath.

Bathing and dressing didn't take long, but the silence encouraged my mind to go back to the fight again, reliving it for the thousandth time. The worst part about it was the way I'd just stood there, scared out of my mind, watching those fighters die. I'd done nothing to try to save them, but when it came to my own life I'd somehow managed to do what was necessary. *They'd* died only because they'd come along to protect *me,* as though one life could be so much more important than six ...

"Alex, are you all right?" I heard, and looked up to see a rumpled Tiran there in the bathing room with me. "You were just standing there and staring into space ... what's wrong?"

"Nothing's wrong now," I said with a smile and hurried into his waiting arms. "I'm so glad that you're back and unhurt. You don't mean to go right out again, I hope?"

"No, I'm back for good," he answered, and I could hear his frown even though I couldn't see it. "I wanted to wrap you in my arms like this last night, but they said you needed your sleep. Are you sure you're all right?"

"I'm a hell of a lot better than those six fighters who went into the courtyard with me," I said, suddenly feeling the urge to move back out of his arms. "You have to promise me something, Ti, and this is one point I won't accept any argument on. I don't ever want guards around me again under any circumstances, and especially not Cadry. That could have been *her* lying dead with the others, and the next time it probably will be—unless *you* reassign her. She won't take that kind of an order from me, so you have to do it."

"You expect me to be more concerned about Cadry than I am about you?" he demanded angrily. "I'm sorry as hell that six good men had to die because someone wanted to get at *you,* but Alex, that's what they were there for! I'd see every man and woman in my company go down rather than see you harmed, every man and woman in this entire kingdom! Don't you understand what I'm saying? I love you!"

"And I love you, but that has nothing to do with it," I told him bleakly, feeling that ghostly ache of banished wounds again. "We're just two people, Ti, of no more value than any other people unless you count being better at killing as being more valuable. It's pushing it to ask other people to stand *with* us in a fight, but to have them stand in front of us? When we're better than they could ever hope to be? I shouldn't have let it happen before, and you can be damned well sure it won't happen again."

I walked past him back out into the bedchamber, and that group of female fighters was actually still there. I tried not to snarl as I ordered them out, but they disappeared so fast I couldn't have done a very good job of smoothing my tone. When the door closed behind the last of them I began to pace, trying to figure out what to do next. Part of me wanted to spend time breaking things, but one part also wanted to crawl under the bedcovers and pull them up over my head.

I paced back and forth for what felt like a very long time, but that was only because the ambush had come back to me again. Everyone alive knows what it's like to be frightened, even though different people fear different things. I'd once scared the hell out of my combat instructor, Gromal Sihr, a man I would have sworn couldn't even spell the word fear. I'd been a teenager at the time, and I'd substituted practice swords for the real ones my sparring partner and I were supposed to be using.

When Gromal saw me being run through with what he thought was a real weapon, he went so white it was a miracle he didn't pass out or have a heart attack. He actually staggered trying to rush over to me, and that was the end of my thinking the joke was funny. I immediately stopped pretending that I was dying and apologized quietly and sincerely, and he just stared at me for a minute before turning and walking away. For days after that I expected him to suddenly blow up and hand me my head, but he never did. In all the years that had passed, I'd never been able to figure out why.

But now I thought I knew. I ran a hand through hair that hadn't had enough brushing lately, finally understanding what it meant to be touched by a horrible fear you had no control over. To just stand there, helpless, while someone you cared about—and who counted on you—was struck down. Those fighters *had* been there to protect me, but they'd also been counting on me to put up a better fight than any of them possibly could. And I'd been too afraid to move . . .

"Damn it, Alex, you're doing it again!" Tiran said, and I looked up quickly to see that he was all bathed and dressed. "You're just standing there and staring into space, and there's no telling how long you've been doing it! I'm getting Brandis back here, and don't even think about not cooperating with him."

"There's nothing wrong with me that Brandis can fix," I said, turning to follow Tiran with my gaze as he strode across the room. "I told you what was bothering me, but you refuse to understand how I feel. But one thing you'd *better* understand is that this isn't something I'll let go. I'm not going to be changing my mind, so you'd better get used to the idea of changing yours."

"Discussing important things on an empty stomach is always a bad idea," he returned, pausing at the door to turn back and look at me. "We'll have a decent breakfast, and then we'll talk about it again."

And with that he went out to the reception room, as though the promise to "talk" about the problem meant something. What he'd really said was that he'd explain why things were going to stay just as they were, but he was mistaken. This time he was very much mistaken.

I followed him out into the reception room, but he'd gone to the door to speak to the guards there. I waited the short while it took him to give whatever orders he meant to, and when he came back to where I stood he'd apparently changed subjects.

"You know, I've been doing some thinking, and I think we should move upstairs to the real royal apartments," he said, glancing at me as he took a chair. "We weren't ready to occupy that much space when we first got here, but now I think we've earned the right to spread out a little. After breakfast we'll go up and take a look."

"I've already looked, and I'm not interested," I told him flatly, staring down at him where he sat. "Now that that's settled, let's get back to our original discussion. There are guards in the anteroom outside that door, and I want to see them sent on their way. The order will sound better coming from you, but if I have to I'll do it myself."

"Alex, we haven't even had our coffee yet," he pointed out, obviously trying to stay calm and reasonable. "I gave orders to have that brought first without waiting for the food, so why don't you sit down until it gets here? I'd suggest we sit down together, but I don't think you're in the mood for necking."

"That's very observant of you," I commented as I folded my arms where I was. "Now let's see if you can answer my question: do you get rid of them, or do I?"

"Alex, I've already told them not to take orders from you about leaving," he said with a sigh, standing up to come toward me. "You're being completely unreasonable about this, but I *am* willing to discuss it. If you can give me good enough reasons I'll rescind the order—but not until we've gotten some food in us. *No* one can be reasonable until they've had their first cup of coffee."

I'd taken one step back from his advance, but he didn't come all the way over to me. He stopped a couple of paces short, so I didn't move any more either. But I also didn't get to answer him, because a knock came at the door, announcing the arrival of Brandis and a servant with the coffee.

"Ah, wonderful timing," Tiran declared, going to meet both the magic user and the servant. "Put the coffee down on that table, please, and then you can go. Brandis, there should be a cup on that tray for you as well."

"I appreciate that, Your Majesty," Brandis said with a bow that didn't quite hide his frown of confusion. "It's still too early to do without coffee, and pouring it takes less effort than producing it with magic."

By then the servant was heading for the door, and once he was gone Tiran dropped the hail-fellow-well-met routine.

"Brandis, I'm afraid you're going to have to have another look at Alex," he said, his hands and eyes busy with pouring three cups of coffee. "She's decided she won't have any more guards around her, and twice this morning I've found her standing and staring off into space without any idea that I was there. I'm afraid that isn't what can be considered normal behavior for her."

"Now that's what I call clear thinking," I said as Brandis shifted his frown to me. "After everything that's happened, *he* expects things to be what he considers normal. It's too bad you have to be jarred out of your dream world into the real one, Ti, but like it or not, that's life."

"Insisting on being completely unguarded is your idea of dealing with the real world?" Tiran countered with a snort while handing Brandis his coffee. "Have you forgotten that there are people somewhere nearby who aren't very fond of you? What do you expect to do if they suddenly show up with a dozen or so of their friends for company?"

"What I *won't* do is stand around watching another bunch of innocent people die for me," I answered clearly and slowly, determined to make him believe I meant what I said. "If you're waiting for me to change my mind about that and be reasonable, you have a long wait ahead of you."

"You see?" Tiran said to Brandis after putting down a filled cup on the side of the table closest to me. "She doesn't see anything wrong with what she's saying, which has to mean there's still something wrong with *her*. Isn't there something you can do?"

"I can take another, closer look," Brandis answered in a troubled voice, then turned his head toward me. "Would you mind if I did that, Your Majesty?"

"I don't care one way or the other," I said as I reached for the cup Tiran had filled for me, wrapping both hands around it. It wasn't at all cold in that room, but for some reason I still felt chilly.

Brandis came over and muttered at me in that strange language magic users use, but whatever his spell was about it didn't affect me directly. He just stared for a couple of minutes while I sipped coffee, and then he turned back to Tiran.

"I can't See any outside influence affecting her in any way," he reported, still sounding and looking disturbed. "I wish I had a better answer for you, but it must be the incident itself that's affecting her. It's not an easy thing to be wounded that extensively and deliberately."

"Deliberately," Tiran echoed after a moment, studying Brandis thoughtfully. "That's a strange word to use, and I wonder why you did. Aren't all wounds from a fight deliberately given?"

"You're right," Brandis granted him with brows raised. "It *is* a strange choice of words, so let me think about it for a minute. *Something* made me use them, and I'd also like to know why."

His voice trailed off as his thoughts turned inward, but I didn't much care whether or not he found anything. I had my own things to think about, like what I would do if Tiran refused to see reason. *My* version of reason, the only version I'd be able to live with. My options were clear but not terribly easy to accept, but I was almost there when Brandis came out of it.

"I think I understand now," he said to Tiran, then turned his head toward me where I sat in a chair a short distance away from them. "What I have to say won't be pleasant for you to hear, Your Majesty. If you'd rather retire to the other room until I'm through . . ."

"If you say anything I can't handle, I'll think about leaving then," I told him when his voice trailed off. "It so happens I understand a couple of things more clearly myself, and I mean to discuss them as soon as you're through."

"Very well," he agreed with a sigh, then turned his attention back to Tiran. "Apparently I noticed something when I healed the queen's wounds, but didn't realize consciously that I'd noticed it. She was cut and bleeding all over, sliced up the way a single fighter against five blades could be expected to be, but . . . the pattern of wounds and their severity leads me to believe her attackers were *trying* to wound rather than kill."

"I don't understand," Tiran said while I fought to push away the memory of sharp edges cutting into me. The pain had been so incredibly intense, the fear twisting my insides into knots, and the cold . . . that terrible, awful cold along my nerve endings . . .

"I don't understand what you find so unusual," Tiran said to Brandis while I clutched my coffee cup and struggled not to shudder. "When fighters have to face someone really superior in a serious way, one of the safest things they can do is go for the wounding rather than for the kill. Even the best fighter can be taken eventually if he's lost enough blood to enough minor wounds."

"I'm sure you're right, but that's not what I mean," Brandis said, faint frustration in his tone. "You're forgetting the same thing I did—that the queen was under the influence of something that let six seasoned fighters be taken without more than a token struggle. That she was able to fight at all is incredible enough, but I can't believe she was able to use anything like her usual skill. She shouldn't have survived and wouldn't have—if they'd really meant to kill her.''

"But why would they arrange something so elaborate and spend the lives of five of their people if they didn't mean to kill her?" Tiran asked in bewilderment. "If they'd murdered her I would have been devastated, which is exactly what most people want their enemies to be. There's even a good chance that I would have taken my company and left."

"But there's an equally good chance that you would have decided not to rest until you found the ones responsible and took *their* lives," Brandis pointed out. "No one in his right mind would want to make an implacable enemy of someone like you, Your Majesty, not if they had any choice. I'd say it's fairly clear that their plans run in another direction."

"But *what* direction?" Tiran said, taking over Brandis's earlier frustration. "If they'd used the opportunity to kidnap her instead, I definitely would have agreed to leave in order to get her back safe. Why didn't they do something like that?"

Brandis shook his head and gestured, showing he didn't have a clue. I suddenly had more than a clue, but I couldn't see where knowing it would do any good.

"Wait a minute," Tiran said, straightening in the chair where he now sat. "That's what the rest of this is all about. There's no sense in taking out one of a pair when you can get to them both by *not* taking one out. That's so obvious I should have seen it right away."

"Would you mind translating that?" Brandis asked, his expression confused. "It sounded like ordinary language, but it didn't make any sense."

"He means they let me live because they expected me to mess *him* up in some way," I supplied before Tiran got the proper words in the proper order. "He thinks that that's what our argument is about, something *they* caused me to feel which was guaranteed to make trouble between us. That could actually be what they had in mind—except that they're *not* responsible for what I feel in any way but indirectly. And with that being the case, nothing has changed.''

"How can you say nothing has changed?" Tiran demanded, now looking outraged. "If you feel a particular way and that way hurts us and helps them, it *has* to be their fault whether you think it is or not. Are you going to do exactly what they want you to, Alex? Are you going to help them win against us?''

"If our winning depends on me letting myself be guarded, then we might as well give up now,'' I said to his intensity, choosing my words carefully. "I just can't do it, Ti, because if the same thing happened again it would kill me too, even if no one so much as raised a weapon to me. I can offer to leave, right now and alone, but I can't offer to change my mind.''

"There's got to be a different way out of this,'' he answered, immediately shaking his head against my proposal. Most of me was disappointed to see that, but one small part trembled in relief ... "We can't just sit back and let them have everything their way. Damn it, who *are* they? This isn't Selwin and his friends, not unless I've read them completely wrong. You said it has something to do with the times, Brandis, and although that makes no sense it somehow *feels* right. But *what* does it have to do with the times, and why are they playing such a roundabout game?''

Brandis shook his head and gestured again, the expression in his dark eyes faintly haunted. I knew how he felt, but in my case there was nothing faint about the sensation. Even thinking was hard, as though my mind sat encased behind layers of ghosts. It wasn't a pleasant sensation and the silence of the others didn't help, but then a distraction came. Servants had arrived with our breakfast, and set about putting it on the table.

I moved to the table with Tiran and let myself be served, but I had nothing in the way of an appetite. Brandis had muttered and gestured while the food was being put out, probably checking for poison or something, but the condition of the food wasn't what bothered me. My problems went a lot deeper than that, and after only a few minutes of pretending to eat I couldn't stand it any longer.

"I've just discovered that I'm more interested in going back to bed than I am in food," I told Tiran as I stood. "I won't be sleeping, only resting, so . . . I'll see you later."

I think he nodded as I turned away from the table, but nothing but silence followed me into the bedchamber. Tiran had probably expected me to stay with him, but he'd be walking around checking on things and the thought of that was more than I could stand. All those people, some of whom might even decide to attack . . .

I hurried to the bed and got into it, then pulled the covers up high with trembling hands. The fact that I hadn't even taken my boots off meant nothing, not when I needed the safety of the darkness so badly. I'd meant it when I said I couldn't let myself be guarded again, and that was what was turning me sick with terror. I couldn't let anyone else die for me, but I was also terrified of being alone. Because I knew, deep down where the central *me* lived, that I couldn't fight again.

Chills rolled through me, so strongly that I shivered violently and felt sick to my stomach. I'd spent most of my life learning to fight and had been hurt any number of times in the process, but nothing had even come close to what I'd experienced during that ambush. The whispered agony had touched my mind as well as my body, burning itself into my memory so deeply that I knew I'd never be able to face the same again. I was worse than dead, a handicap to Tiran that he didn't yet know he had.

But I'd have to tell him; somehow I'd have to find the words to get it said. Our enemies' plan had worked better than they'd probably dreamed was possible, and there was nothing left for me. Except to hide shivering under the covers, wishing I *was* dead . . .

CHAPTER TEN

Tiran watched Alex hurry out of the room, wishing he knew whether to be glad or sorry that she'd decided to go back to bed. No matter what Brandis said there *was* something wrong with her, but maybe a lot of rest and love would make it right again.

"I've never felt so helpless in my entire life," Brandis said tightly after the bedchamber door closed behind Alex. "There aren't any spells or poisons working on her, but that isn't the same woman who found me in the kitchens. It's as if everything inside her has been removed, so she has to work really hard to keep the rest of herself from collapsing inward."

"Don't you have *any* idea what could have done that to her?" Tiran asked, trying not to sound accusing. "It couldn't have been that ambush alone, or even something connected with it. Alex is too good and experienced a fighter."

"It has to be something well beyond my ability to See, and something other than magic," Brandis fretted, obviously too absorbed with the problem to notice anything like accusation. "You don't have to be able to unravel a spell to know it's there, and I'm ready to swear there's nothing like that affecting her. I'll have to spend some time thinking about this. If you need me, Your Majesty, just send someone to my apartment."

"While you're thinking, there's something I'd like you to do," Tiran said as Brandis got to his feet and bowed. "Some of my people are currently engaged in working with villagers a good day's ride from here, and I'd like you to keep an eye on their progress. I've already sent more men to give them a hand, but if they run into anything unexpected I'd like to know about it before the situation gets beyond their control.''

"Of course, Your Majesty,'' Brandis agreed with another bow. "Just give me their current location as closely as possible, along with descriptions of one or two specific individuals, and I should have no trouble keeping tabs on them.''

Tiran described Rhodris and where he and the others ought to be, and then Brandis left. Tiran looked down at what food was left on his plate, thought about finishing it, then realized he couldn't. Alex had barely touched her breakfast, and her lack of appetite seemed to have spread to him. He refilled his coffee cup instead, then carried it to a chair where he could be comfortable while he thought.

He'd only just gotten started when there was a knock on the door, and one of the guards opened it to admit Cadry and Damis.

"Glad to see you back, Tiran,'' Damis said with a grin as he came forward, a cylinder of rolled parchment in his hand, and then the grin disappeared. "What I'm not so glad about is the news I have. If Gann hadn't told me last night that you were back, I would have had to send someone after you.''

"That means something major has happened,'' Tiran remarked, waving the two of them to chairs of their own. "Since this day can't get much worse, you might as well tell me what it is.''

"Yesterday afternoon a communication was delivered from that Duke Selwin and the bunch who have sided with him,'' Damis said, waving the parchment and folding his big body into the chair without paying any attention to the process. Damis was nearly Tiran's size but with blond hair and blue eyes, and the two of them had worked together for years.

"*I* know,'' Tiran said sourly. "Selwin and his group are sorry for the misunderstanding, and want to come back and swear loyalty to the Crown.''

"Yeah, right,'' Damis said with a snort, one echoed by

Cadry from her own chair. "What they want is Pavar released immediately, and the throne vacated by all 'interlopers.' If you don't answer them in two more days, assuring them of your agreement to their demands, they'll have no choice but to assume a refusal on your part. That, in turn, will leave them no option but to remove the pretenders by force."

"Reluctantly and regretfully, but with Right completely on their side," Tiran muttered, much too familiar with the attitude. Almost a quarter of his former clients had had the same attitude, but since it was their realms and they were paying in large amounts of gold, Tiran hadn't cared. He cared now, though, more than a little.

"Are you going to give them a straight answer, or stall for time?" Damis asked, getting up to hand over the roll of parchment he'd just summarized for Tiran. "Gann tells me that the army is growing daily, but too many of the newest recruits have had little or no training. The more time you can give him, the better an army he'll have for you."

"If Selwin and the others have found professionals to hire, even extra weeks won't help," Tiran told him with a headshake. "Since the most stalling would gain us is days, we won't lower ourselves to such shabby tricks. Instead we'll give them an answer that's completely unambiguous: set out the proclamations that tomorrow at noon Pavar dies. If he begs his rights as a former noble of this realm, I'll face him in individual combat. If he has no stomach for facing the man he plotted treason against, he'll simply be executed."

"Do you want to send a private communication to Selwin?" Damis asked after nodding. "Something to tell him what to do with his demands and ultimata?"

"A real ruler ignores the mewling of disappointed malcontents," Tiran said, tossing the parchment away in the general direction of the room's hearth. "But I do want you to set small patrols on the road leading to Selwin's estates before that proclamation goes up. If they find anyone racing out of the city, as if hurrying with the latest news, I want that someone stopped and detained. And warn them there's likely to be more than one someone, so they're to stay alert even if they catch one. Keep them at it until noon tomorrow, and then bring them back.''

"What about the scouts you sent to keep an eye on Selwin's manor house?" Damis asked as he stood. "Do you think it's time to send them support?"

"Send out their next reliefs with orders to check first with Rhodris," Tiran decided after a moment's thought. "Rhodris is there on the spot, working with the villagers, so he'll know what's necessary. If they need more support because Selwin *has* hired a fighting company, the returning scouts can tell us so."

"I'll get right on it," Damis said, but rather than leave he glanced around. "I've been wondering where Alex is. Cadry said she's healed and everything, and I expected to see her here with you. She *is* all right, isn't she?"

"She decided she could use a little *unforced* rest," Tiran answered, suddenly wishing his cup held something stronger than coffee. "Since she almost went face first into her breakfast eggs, I was forced to agree with her."

"That's all right, then," Damis said, his grin returned. "I'll go and get the fireworks started, and pass on all the good wishes I've been given for her later."

He strode toward the door, but once it closed behind him it was Cadry's turn to stir.

"Won't push it if you don't want me to, Boss, but I ain't Damis," she said quietly. "Somethin's wrong, and you can't tell me different."

"You've been closer to it than he has, Cadry," Tiran admitted with a sigh as he closed his eyes and rubbed them. "Something *is* wrong, but even Brandis can't figure out what. Alex is ... not herself, and she refuses to have any guards at all around her. She also wants me to reassign *you*."

"Blamin' herself for the six who died," Cadry said with a weary, pained nod. "That was just about the first thing she asked me when she finally woke up: were they really dead. She hated the idea of anybody standin' in front of her even before this; now it's gotta turn her soulsick. Is that the only thing botherin' her?"

"It's the only thing she's talked about," Tiran answered, then finished his coffee and stood to replace his cup on the table. "We also figured out that she wasn't killed because our enemies expect her to seriously interfere with *me* in some way, which means they have to be responsible for whatever's affecting her. The only thing we can't figure out is what they did—and how to undo it."

"You want me to stay here in case she needs somethin'?" Cadry asked, also on her feet. "I don't have to go in where she can see me and get upset, but there oughta be somebody here for her."

"I can't afford to take the chance," Tiran said with a firm headshake, already having considered the point. "Alex told me that if anyone else died for her *she* would also die, even if not a single weapon touched her. I believe that, at least as far as her mind is concerned, and it isn't possible that our enemies don't know what close friends you two are. For that reason I'm keeping you with me. If Alex needs anything, she can ring for a servant."

Cadry nodded with a sigh, understanding the point Tiran had made. If Cadry was marked as a target in order to take even more of Alex's sanity, it would be stupid to play into their hands. Tiran had a lot of things to see to, but he fully intended to be back in the apartment for lunch. Maybe Alex would be better by then, he prayed as he walked to the door. Maybe even a little of the usual life would be back in her . . .

But it wasn't. After a busy morning Tiran went back to the apartment for lunch, but Alex seemed worse rather than better. He had to gently insist that she join him before she would even leave the bed, and then she sat silently at the table as though deep in thought. At one point she cocked her head slightly, as if listening to something he couldn't hear, but when he asked her what was wrong there was no answer but a headshake. Granted she'd hesitated first, as if *about* to tell him, but then obviously changed her mind.

It was late afternoon before he got back to the apartment the next time, and again there was no sign of Alex in the reception room. This time Cadry was with him, and they were discussing the wisdom of her paying Alex a brief visit. Tiran had arranged for coffee to be waiting for them, and he was on his way to pour a cup when Brandis was admitted.

"Either your timing is excellent, or you were watching for me," Tiran told him, pausing to study the magic user's face. "From your expression, I'd say you were watching."

"Yes, I was," Brandis admitted. "I thought you'd like to know that your people working with the villagers are doing very well. They split up to go into Duke Selwin's villages, and although there was more opposition than they'd expected, all three of the villages are now liberated. The rest of the nobility have at most two villages on their estates, and with the reinforcements you sent, your man expects to have every one of them cleared tomorrow."

"Now *that's* what I call excellent timing," Tiran said, wishing he could enjoy the news more. "Selwin should find out about losing Pavar and all the villages at about the same time. Too bad we can't do as well against our other set of enemies."

"You're sure there *are* others?" Brandis asked, a faint, odd expression behind his otherwise neutral look. "I thought it was possible that it was simply Duke Selwin and his group working secretly as well as overtly."

"That was never possible," Tiran replied, giving the man a quizzical look before turning to the coffee. "Selwin may consider himself a great plotter and manipulator, but he's actually small-time and obvious. The subtlety and strategy behind our major troubles means there's someone else involved."

"I should have listened more closely during our conversation the other night," Brandis said with a faint smile. "You kept demanding to know who might be responsible for going after the queen, but I thought you meant some unknown in Selwin's group. Are you sure there *is* no unknown associated with him?"

"Absolutely sure? No." Tiran handed Brandis a cup of coffee, then matched the other man's faint smile. "It's possible, of course, but I don't believe it. Whoever is opposing us doesn't *need* Selwin, no more than Alex and I need him and his friends. The nobility weren't able to do anything to dislodge our predecessors, but *we* were able to defeat them. That makes our takeover legitimate no matter *how* annoyed Selwin is, and—''

Tiran's words stopped dead as a thought occurred to him, one that should have come a lot sooner. That *had* to be what it was all about, it couldn't be anything else.

''Your Majesty, are you all right?'' Brandis asked, faintly concerned. ''You look . . .''

''As if I'd just been struck by lightning?'' Tiran supplied after a moment. ''I'm not surprised, since I think I just figured out what those unknown enemies are after. They want to take over *legitimately,* so eventually they mean to face Alex and me. That would give them a legitimacy *no* one could argue with, especially if we first do them the favor of seeing to Selwin and company.''

''And that would explain why they tried to sabotage your new programs,'' Cadry said, also sounding as if revelation had struck. ''They'd want people thinkin' you were just another gold-grabbin' thief, so when *they* took over nobody would be particularly bothered. You think they do mean to wait to make their move until after Selwin makes his?''

''It's possible, but there's no way of knowing for sure,'' Tiran answered, abandoning the coffee to begin pacing. ''For all we know, we've already crippled Selwin's efforts to the point where even a group of children could defeat him. If that's true then the others could come at Alex and me at any time—and there's no way Alex is up to it. I'd refuse to let her fight even if she insisted, but very frankly I can't picture her insisting.''

''She's changed *that* much?'' Brandis asked, now looking shaken. ''But even this morning it wasn't quite that bad . . . Your Majesty, *can* you refuse to let her fight? It was the two of you who defeated your predecessors, so it can be argued that no subsequent claim to the throne can be completely legitimate unless the *two* of you are defeated.''

''And we gotta assume the others are damned good fighters, otherwise they'd know they wouldn't stand a chance in a one-on-one,'' Cadry contributed, almost biting her lip. ''If they suddenly show up in a place where you

and Alex *have* to face them, right now you'd be fightin'
alone. And if you happen to go down . . .''

"Then she'd go down right after me even if she never
lifted a finger against them," Tiran finished when Cadry
didn't, hating the idea but needing to accept it as a possibility. "And I've got to assume they *will* find some way
to face us, otherwise I'm kidding myself. So what can I
possibly do to get around this?''

Tiran was primarily talking to himself, thinking out loud
the way he'd gotten into the habit of doing with Alex
there. Half the time she saw the answer to a problem
before he did, and it was wonderful to have someone that
sharp to confide in. And to share things with, and to love.
Now . . .

"Your Majesty, something has to be done," Brandis
announced as if the thought had only just occurred to him.
"I've spent hours thinking about the problem and getting
nowhere, and I've come to the conclusion that I must be
missing part of the story. I'd like to go over everything
that happened again, with both Cadry and the queen present. Will you let me do that?''

Tiran exchanged a glance with Cadry, the two of them
apparently thinking the same thing: was Alex strong
enough to stand going through it yet again? It felt strange
thinking of Alex as frail and needing protection, but that
showed how strongly she'd been affected. If something
wasn't done, they might not have to worry about challengers coming forward to cut her down. She'd fade away
into shadow first . . .

"I can't see that I have a choice," Tiran said to Brandis
after taking a deep breath and letting it out slowly. "If
Alex or Cadry have whatever information you're missing,
keeping them from giving it to you won't help anything
or anyone at all. I'll get Alex and bring her in.''

Brandis nodded with grim intent, but Cadry just looked
worried. Tiran was also worried, but tried not to let it
show as he headed toward the bedchamber. Something had
to be done, all right, and the stakes were no longer just the
possibility of losing the kingdom. His Alex could lose her
life, even if no one reached her with a weapon. And wasn't
that what *she'd* said . . . ? Now, that was strange . . .

*   *   *

I saw the door open and Tiran come in, and couldn't decide how I felt about his being back. I still had to tell him that he no longer had a partner he could count on, but saying the words hadn't turned out to be easy. I'd already tried once and hadn't been able to do it, mostly because I knew how badly I'd be letting him down. But there was also something inside me that felt it wasn't true, that I *could* do whatever was necessary just the way I always had. The whispers told me differently and for the most part I believed them, but there was still this tiny little battle going on . . .

"Alex, I'd like you to get up and come into the reception room with me," Tiran said gently, drawing my attention back. I'd actually forgotten he was there, so insistent had the whispers become. I'd noticed they did that whenever the tiny battle started up, trying to drown out all opposing opinion.

"Alex, Brandis needs to ask you some questions," Tiran insisted, bending down to brush the hair back from my face. "It won't take long, and then you can lie down again. Come on, I'll help you."

I didn't want to leave the place where I could hide under the covers when the memories became too overwhelming, but Tiran was too strong to resist. He got me sitting up and then onto my feet, and the world tilted a little for a moment and then settled down. I was able to walk with him, but the whispers weren't happy about it. They'd been insisting I couldn't do more than lie in one place, remembering . . .

"Good afternoon, Your Majesty," Brandis said when Tiran and I got close enough, his face trying to smile. "I appreciate having your help with this, since I've discovered I can't do it alone. I'm afraid it won't be pleasant for you, but we'll try to get through it as quickly as possible."

As Tiran helped me to sit in a chair, I noticed that Cadry was also there. That bothered me badly for a moment, but then I realized it was all right. Tiran and Brandis were both there, so if another attack came I would not have to just stand there and watch her die. Which certainly would have happened if she and I had been alone.

"Now, Your Majesty, I'm going to have Cadry tell me again about the day of the ambush," Brandis said, still trying to sound pleasant and unconcerned. "If you find that she's leaving anything out or telling something wrong, I'd like you to make the addition or correction. All right?"

I nodded to show that I knew what he wanted, but privately I wondered if I'd be able to do it. The whispers didn't like me listening to anything but them, and tended to take my attention and hold it.

"Okay, Cadry, I want you to start from when those two people came over to tell you about the ex-guardsmen," Brandis said. "Give it to me in detail and just a little bit at a time, and we'll see if the queen agrees."

"Don't see why she wouldn't," Cadry answered with a sigh. "We both saw the same thing. Well, the man and woman came up last behind the others wantin' to say somethin', and the woman wasn't as nervous as the man. He started to talk, but she took over when he was too long gettin' to the point."

"Is that true so far, Your Majesty?" Brandis interrupted to ask me. "The woman wasn't as nervous as the man, and she did most of the talking?"

"She was so not-nervous that she almost touched me," I said, determined to try to help him the way he'd asked me to. "She reached out without thinking, then realized what she was doing and quickly pulled her hand back. He just turned his hat, around and around and around, the whole time he stood there. Around and around and around . . ."

The whispers tried to carry me away then, but suddenly Brandis was crouched in front of me, shaking my folded hands to get my attention.

"Did you hear that, Your Majesty?" he asked, as if he'd repeated the same words more than once. "Cadry says *you're* wrong, and it didn't happen like that. She said the woman did no more than gesture once, and the man turned his hat only a minute or two."

"No, it wasn't like that," I protested with a frown. "She almost touched me and he kept turning his hat, and the way they spoke was wrong. They were trying to sound uneducated, but they changed only their words, not their sentence structure. And *he* whispered while she was talking.''

I hadn't remembered that last, that he was whispering while the woman talked, probably because I hadn't heard his words. There had *been* words, I was sure of it, but I hadn't noticed at the time and hadn't remembered.

"What was his whispering about?" Brandis asked after shaking my hands again. "Alex, you have to try to pay attention instead of constantly drifting off. Cadry says she didn't hear any whispering, but she was busy listening to the woman. Can you tell me what the man said?"

"I didn't hear him," I answered, bothered that I'd twice missed Cadry speaking. I did have to pay closer attention . . . "I have the impression he whispered the same things over and over, and all the while he kept turning that hat . . . and he did keep turning it, because it had something to do with the whispering.''

"Something to do with it how?" Brandis pressed, holding to my hands with a grip just short of pain. "Don't try to remember the exact words if you think you can't, but see if you can give me the *impression* you got from the whispering."

"It was . . . *around,*" I managed to get out, struggling so hard that the memory of fear and pain came blazing back. I started to tremble so hard that I thought I'd be sick, but then Cadry distracted me just a little.

"Wait a minute," she said, sounding excited. "I just found somethin' that makes more sense now. When I broke into that house I thought Alex was right there with me, and later, when I found out she wasn't, I blamed her need to do things herself for the way she'd taken off. But she and I both expected those ex-guardsmen to be *inside,* so she *wouldn't* have taken off—unless somebody told her to go *around* to the side!"

"That's got to be it," Brandis said, holding my hands tight while Tiran hugged me to him in an effort to stop the shivering. Tiran was now sitting on the arm of my chair, and I really didn't want him to let me go again.

"Alex, you're doing wonderfully," Brandis enthused, moving my hands in time with his words. "The woman might have thrown something at you, like a specially prepared powder, and then the man began to give you orders that you *did* hear on another level. Part of the orders was to go *around*, which certainly meant to go around to the side of the house where the trap was waiting. Now you have to try to tell me what else you were ordered to do."

"I . . . can't," I whispered, trying to stop my teeth from chattering. "When I ignore the whispers the memories come back . . . the fear and the pain . . . ten times worse than I've ever felt . . ."

And then I screamed as the memories drowned me, for I'd done what the whispers said I mustn't ever do: I'd told someone about them and what they were saying, both the loud whispers and the faint ones. The pain was agony again and worse than ever . . . the fear was terror, and threatened to make my heart explode . . . I begged for darkness and death to make an end to them, and finally, after an eternity, the blackness came—

"All right, I've put her out," Brandis said, but Tiran couldn't quite let Alex go. She was limp in his arms now, but the way she'd screamed . . . ! He'd been present once while a man was being tortured to death, and even the sound of *his* screams hadn't been so blood-chillingly horrible.

"Why?" Tiran demanded, holding Alex and rocking her back and forth. "Why did she scream like that?"

"I imagine it's because she disobeyed orders," Brandis said, now looking pale and haunted. "She must have been forbidden to discuss what was happening to her, and when she did it anyway the attack was intensified. She *is* under attack, you know, and has been the entire time."

"No, I don't know," Tiran denied, fury trying to rise up and choke him. "I don't know any damned thing about what's going on, so you're going to have to explain it. And while you're at it, you can explain why you understand everything now when you didn't before."

"I understand now because I have all the pieces to the puzzle," Brandis answered, and surprisingly he was even angrier than Tiran. "I couldn't imagine how one would create a Mist of Fear and add anything to it, since a Mist of Fear is very unstable. It also can't be used *with* anything else, otherwise the two compounds fight and effectively cancel each other out. If I'd known sooner about the woman throwing something I would have known at once what was being done, but they were very careful, curse them. At least we know now, so I'll be able to do *something*."

"I still don't understand what it is that we know," Tiran repeated, actually surprised over Brandis's vehemence. The man was usually so calm and even-tempered ... "Cadry said she didn't see anything being thrown, and at the moment I trust *her* observations more than Alex's."

"At the moment, maybe, but this was back then," Brandis reminded him with a frown of concentration. "The woman probably positioned herself so that her movements were mostly hidden from everyone close enough, and also surely moved only when the man was speaking. You tend to give your attention to the speaker, and notice others only partially. And what she threw—it could only have been what's known as Slave Powder. Most magic users won't produce the filthy stuff under any circumstances, and I couldn't believe—"

His words choked off as he apparently swallowed the next few, then he looked at Tiran bleakly.

"I couldn't believe any Sighted could be so twisted as to produce the powder," he finished, his tone bitter. "I feel betrayed and dirtied, just from being Sighted myself. The woman threw it at Alex, the man ordered her to go around to the side of the house and then into the areaway, and the five in uniform waiting for her didn't attack just with swords. They also must have given her detailed orders, as well as directions on what was to happen if she disobeyed."

"But she still *did* disobey," Cadry pointed out from where she stood, looking as if she really wanted to spill blood. "If all that stuff is so strong and effective, how come she was able to ignore it?"

"I think ... it was because Brandis asked for her help," Tiran answered slowly when the magic user remained silent. "She tends to ignore consequences when someone needs her, a reaction that's part of her basic character. But what I want to know is how soon—and how completely—

she can be freed from whatever it is that's holding her. Brandis?''

''At a guess, I'd say she's still hearing whatever she was told,'' Brandis answered even more slowly, avoiding Tiran's eyes. ''The way she cocks her head when she loses awareness of the world makes that a virtual certainty. I should be able to still those voices and counter the orders about 'ten times the pain and fear' she mentioned, but— but I don't know what else she might have been told, and if there *is* something, even she won't know what it is.''

''What are you talking about now?'' Tiran demanded, back to feeling a sense of dread. ''If she was told something, how could she *not* know?''

''You have to keep in mind what your enemies are after,'' Brandis answered obliquely, then clearly forced himself to look directly at Tiran. ''They want to *defeat* the two of you, not just kill you, and if they thought they could do that fairly and honestly they probably would have already challenged you. At the very least they wouldn't have set such an elaborate trap for Alex ... They could have told her to stop fighting at a particular point, and if they did she'll do it.''

Tiran was absolutely appalled, and Cadry's expression said she felt the same. And then Tiran realized that even if Brandis pulled Alex out of whatever now held her, she'd still refuse to be guarded. As Cadry had mentioned, *that* attitude came from her own beliefs and opinions. They'd been outmaneuvered all the way down the line, and it could well be too late to do anything about it.

''Let's take first things first,'' Tiran finally decided. ''We need to get Alex back, and then we can worry about the rest. Do you want her in here, Brandis, or in the bedchamber?''

''The bedchamber, if you please,'' the magic user replied, pulling himself together with a deep breath. ''She's already been through more than most people would have been able to stand, and when I'm through with this latest I'll want her to sleep.''

Tiran nodded, then picked Alex up in his arms. She felt lighter than usual, but considering how little she'd eaten over the past few days, that wasn't surprising. His love for her flowed out in all directions as he carried her toward their bedchamber, and he couldn't keep from making a silent vow.

They won't get away with doing this to you, beloved, he swore mind to mind. *I'll find a way to make sure they never do it to anyone else, but not until I make them regret having done it this time. You have my word, my love, my solemn word . . .*

Alex stirred not at all, but that was all right. He'd take care of things, and everything would be fine. It *would* . . .

CHAPTER ELEVEN

It was something of an effort to wake up, and I felt really strange. As if I'd been sleeping for a very long time, and was only now able to escape out of it. I forced myself into sitting and looked around, but I was alone in the room. Now that was also strange. Why did I think there would be female fighters stationed all over . . . ?

That was when everything started to come back, like an old memory of something that had happened years earlier. Only it hadn't happened years ago, but a matter of days. And I felt as if I'd been through hellfire after being run down by a wagon, but that was perfectly all right. The whispers had stopped, the pain was gone, and the fear was only a small, sickening memory.

I took a deep breath for what felt like the first time in years, then let myself admit that the memory of fear wasn't quite that small. For a while it had filled my entire world, but not only the fear itself. One part of me had hated being so afraid, had hated the rest of me for letting the fear rule me. Hatred and self-loathing all mixed up with terror and the too-vivid memory of pain, pain made worse by the presence of the fear.

Remembering it together was more than I could handle at the moment, so I pushed it away and thought instead about the short time I'd awakened the night before. Tiran's coming into the room had brought me out of sleep, and all those terrible memories had been hidden somewhere behind a wall I couldn't see through. All I knew was that the man I loved was back, and I hadn't even given him a proper greeting.

"I don't believe we're finally alone," I commented, stopping him on his way toward the bathing room. "I'm starting to wonder if all the guardsmen were there for my protection or for yours. You haven't decided I'm too dangerous to associate with, have you?"

"Alex, you're awake!" he'd exclaimed, hurrying over to the bed to bend toward me. "Are you all right? Are you still hearing all those things Brandis said you were?"

"All what things?" I'd asked in turn, but not because I really wanted an answer. He was now sitting on the edge of the bed and leaning over me, and having him that close was beautifully distracting. "I think we should pass a law against wearing too many clothes in a bedchamber," I went on in a murmur, starting to slide my hands under his tunic. "Since I'm naked under these covers I'm already setting a good example, but you aren't. Don't you believe a king should be the first to follow whatever new laws he comes up with?"

"Alex, I'm so glad to have you back," he murmured in return, taking my face in his hands. "I can only hope that this time you don't fade out again, especially not the way you did the first time. But as far as right now goes . . ."

He leaned all the way down and kissed me then, giving me no chance to ask what he was talking about, and then I no longer cared. His lips were more demanding than they'd been in quite some time, showing that he felt the same way I did. As if that had ever been in doubt. We'd both discovered that our feelings were more than simple passing lust, and that made a *lot* of difference in a relationship. As did the use of a little bit of imagination, which that occasion seemed to call for.

So I waited until his hands left my face and reached to the covers over me, and then I Shifted my skin into the soft, furry pelt of a mink. When those hands came to caress me they found fur instead of skin, and Tiran was so startled he pulled back from the kiss.

"What's wrong?" I asked innocently while he pulled

the covers completely away to get a good look at me. "I thought men *liked* to be surprised in bed."

"There are surprises and then there are surprises," he countered dryly as he stood to begin getting out of his clothes. "I was expecting to find skin, not fur, so why don't you put it back the way it was."

"Oh, you're a *skin* man," I said with what should have looked like sudden revelation. "Why didn't you say so? How's this?"

"This" was the lizard skin I Shifted to next, smooth and sleek and beautifully colored. Tiran narrowed his eyes and pretended to growl while he fought his boots off, so I shrugged and Shifted again—to alligator skin.

"This has to be what you were after all along, right?" I asked, struggling not to laugh. "It's a great texture, so I can't really blame you—Hey!"

"Hey yourself," he said from his place on top of me, holding me down with both his body and his hands. "You do know what kind of skin I want, but I wouldn't *dream* of demanding that you give it to me. I'll just wait until you're in the mood to Shift back to it, and until that happens I'll simply amuse myself a little."

His kiss cut off my question about how he meant to amuse himself, and in another minute I didn't need to ask. Even alligators have soft underbellies, and that was what Tiran went after on me. One of his hands found its way between my thighs, and three breaths later I discovered I couldn't dislodge it. He just kept touching me in that very special way he had while he also continued to kiss me, and it wasn't long before I had to admit that I didn't *want* him to stop touching or kissing me. I loved him very much, and I wanted everything he could give.

At that point the alligator skin was no longer the funny joke I'd been considering it, so I quickly Shifted back to natural. Tiran would make me wait, of course, to get even for the trick I'd played on him, but—

But he *didn't* make me wait. He briefly interrupted our kiss to murmur, "Thank you, love," ran his hand slowly and gently over my body, then came to me with as much raging desire as I had for him. His thrust inside me was heaven attained, and I locked my legs around him and joined him in the sweet battle of trying to merge ourselves into a single being. We actually came close as it went on and on, healing our loneliness and separation in the best way ever. We were now together again, and once again each of us was whole.

Our lovemaking lasted a very long time, and once it was over I fell asleep in Tiran's arms. Now I was awake again and his arms were gone, so I sighed and just got out of bed. The daylight outside the windows seemed to be the morning variety, which meant a bath and dressing were in order. Things had been happening while I'd been so wrapped up in listening to whispers, and I needed to find out what. And even more I needed to see Tiran again, now that I realized how drawn he'd looked. He must have been going through worse hellfire than I had . . .

Getting ready took its usual length of time despite an urge to sit and soak in the hot bathwater, and walking out into the reception room brought a surprise. Not only was Tiran out there but Brandis and Cadry as well, and they all got to their feet when they saw me.

"Why are you all staring so hard?" I asked, trying to break the tension pouring out of all three of them. "Do I have a smudge on my face I somehow missed?"

Brandis and Cadry laughed with relief, but Tiran let out a whoop and came charging toward me. I did some charging myself, and our lips came together the instant we were folded in each other's arms. I could have stayed like that for an hour or a day or a year, but seconds later the doors burst open and armed fighters came storming through. Tiran turned to them immediately with a rueful expression, one hand raised with palm out.

"Okay, hold it, I apologize," he said while the fighters looked around in all directions. "I shouldn't have been so loud that you thought I was being attacked, but I didn't stop to think. Everything's all right, so you can return to your post."

Some of the fighters looked around again as if they didn't quite believe him, but the rest saw the way we held each other and left wearing small smiles. When the last of them closed the doors again I thought we'd go back to deliberately repeating last night's performance, but Tiran had other ideas.

"We'd better save the rest for later," he told me with very obvious regret and a brief kiss. "There's a lot you have to be told, and not much time to do it. In three hours I have a date with the former Duke Pavar. We can fill you in on what you've missed while *you* fill up all that hollowness I know you collected."

He pointed to a tray of covered dishes that had to be breakfast, and suddenly I felt hungry enough to eat a whale. I lost no time getting to the table and helping myself, and while I ate I heard all about the speculation the three of them had been doing, as well as what Brandis had revealed about what was done to me. Once they'd finished I had tons of questions, but one set clamored to go first.

"Brandis, there's something I don't understand," I said, putting it *very* mildly. "If a magic user wanted to ... frighten and enslave someone, why would they need powders and mists? Why not just cast a spell and do it the easy way?"

"The powder and mist aren't created to be used by a Sighted," he answered with a sigh, not quite looking at me. "They're created *by* a Sighted to be used by the untalented. It's basically very simple so we all know how to do it, but most of us would never even consider it. For those who do more than consider it, the penalties are very severe."

"So that means two things," I concluded, leaning back with my coffee. "Number one, our enemies have a very unethical magic user working with them, and number two, *none* of us will survive their takeover attempt if they manage to gain the upper hand. If the penalties for making the stuff are that severe, their magic user won't want anyone left around who can talk about what he's done."

"Now *that* point is so obvious it escaped me entirely," Brandis said with a frown, no longer looking so diffident and embarrassed. "It's completely outrageous, of course, and that's why I didn't think of it. I'd better stop seeing myself as little more than an observer, or I won't live long enough to learn better."

"What about the ones he made the powder and mist *for?*" Cadry asked, also looking disturbed. "I mean, how can he trust *them* not to say anythin'?"

"I doubt if trust is involved in any way at all," Brandis said with a small headshake. "He's probably already put them under a compulsion not to speak, and ordered them to arrange things so no one would find out what was done. He may already know that they weren't quite as successful as possible with that, but if not he'll certainly find out when Alex appears in public. I'm sure they counted on her to be strong enough to survive until they issued their challenge, but even a blind man would know she's doing more than surviving."

"And the time for her next public appearance is only a couple of hours from now," Tiran mused, no happier than the rest of us. "It's come to me that it's essential for her to be there when I face Pavar or have him executed, otherwise people may think she isn't backing me on the point. That in turn will cast doubt on the whole situation, both the question of whether what I'm doing is right, and even whether I'm entitled to do anything to him at all. Kingdoms have fallen over smaller questions, and we all know what's in store for us if *this* kingdom falls."

"So that means I can't swagger out there with head held high and palm to pommel," I summed up dryly. "I have to go back to barely surviving, but at least we now know when that challenge will come at us: either before or after our appointment with Pavar, depending on whether or not they want us to get rid of him for them."

"But Alex, we can't accept their challenge," Tiran said in a more than weary voice. "You heard what Brandis told you, that they may have given you crippling orders that you're not aware of. You can't win with something like that hanging over you, and if *you* don't win then I don't want to either. I've been thinking about this, and we've been left with only a single choice: we get Brandis to take us to Conclave, and once there we lodge a complaint of unfair intervention. They'll take care of that magic user, and then—"

His words broke off so suddenly that I hurt for him,

but there was no sense in pretending I didn't know why it had happened.

"It's hell when your mind's too logical to let you fool yourself for long, love," I said as I put my hand over the fist he'd made. "Even if wizards came here, found him, and carted him away, the ones he did all that for would still be seated firmly on our thrones. The only way we'd get them back would be to face our enemies in challenge, which brings us in a circle that returns to the point you're trying to avoid."

"What if we just pick up and walk away?" he countered, then immediately shook his head. "Okay, never mind, that one's even worse. Even if that magic user lets us survive after walking away, our direct enemies can't afford to let us live. We'd be able to come back and challenge them at any time, especially if we found a way around whatever they've done to you. So what *can* we do?"

"What else but keep going as if we still don't understand what's happening?" I said, not nearly as confident as I was trying to sound. "And maybe Brandis will be able to come up with something useful, like a compulsion for me to do the exact opposite of anything our enemies may say to me. How about it, Brandis?"

"It wouldn't be practical even if setting a compulsion was ethical," he returned immediately with a headshake. "They don't have to give you any buried orders right away, you know. They could say something like, 'Let's all relax and enjoy this,' and you'd do the exact opposite. I also can't make you 'not-hear' any orders, because you'd have to hear them in order to know that you don't want to hear them. Do you understand?"

"Unfortunately, yes," I muttered, beginning to feel frustrated, then I suddenly had a thought. "Wait a minute. I'm noticing a serious breakdown in logic here. If our enemies expected me to be a basket case from the treatment they gave me, why would they have added any hidden orders? And if they *didn't* expect me to be a basket case, how did they think I'd get around it?"

No one jumped forward with any easy answers, but after a moment Brandis took a stab at it.

"They could have been expecting you to get help from your Sighted friends in the next kingdom," he suggested slowly, then got more enthusiastic. "Yes, that's an excellent possibility, or they simply may have assumed that you'd find someone like me. Of course, they may have just been trying to play it safe, something they seem to like to do."

"Something they like too well to suit *me*," Tiran said as he reached for the coffee pot. "So we're left with just forging ahead with it, having nothing going for our side but Alex pretending to still be in bad shape. As strategy goes, it wouldn't even win a game of checkers."

"But we'll also have *you* pretending to be worried sick about *me*," I reminded him, then thought of something else. "Ti, if Pavar decides to face you, you might also want to think about showing less than your usual ability. Not so much less that you'd get hurt or lose, of course, but if we're not challenged before you see to Pavar it might also be because they want to watch you in action."

"Which would give them a definite edge," he said with a thoughtful nod. "You're right, Alex, and you'll have to remind me later to thank Brandis in some special way for bringing you back to yourself. I've lost the habit of thinking clearly when you're not around to help me."

We spent a couple of minutes holding hands and smiling at each other, and I didn't feel silly in the least. When a man still hands you compliments even after you've married him, he has to be at least a small bit sincere.

"Hate to be a wet blanket here, but I need to know about your guard escort," Cadry said much too soon, drawing us back to reality. "You gonna give me a hard time about it, Alex, or are you over that part of it, too?"

"I'm not over anything, and *you* can't be in charge of our guard escort," I said, turning my head to look at her. "If they decide to push me all the way over the edge at the same time they issue their challenge, they'll do it by taking you out where I can see it and feel guilty about it. Am I wrong, Ti?"

"Not that I can see," he answered, now inspecting Cadry. "Since everyone knows what good friends you two have become, Cadry's been put in the middle of this. I'd say she needs to be a good distance away from us, with an escort of her own. And one that's been warned to hold their collective breath at the first sign of *any* kind of smoke or mist."

Cadry had been looking rebellious, but when Tiran made his final point she gave it up with a sigh.

"Okay, okay, I know when I'm overmatched," she grudged, then got to her feet. "Somebody around here's got to be reasonable, so it might as well be me. Who do you want in my place?"

"Not Damis and not Gann," Tiran told her immediately. "Those two have their own jobs to do, and as secondary targets they're absolutely prime. Make sure you warn them about their danger, but don't say anything about Alex being recovered. Assure everybody that she's just fine, but do it in a way that anybody listening from cover will be sure she's not."

"Got it, Boss," she acknowledged, then she left the apartment. It felt odd not to have her right there ready to jump into things with me, but it also came as a great relief. Tiran's people deserved to survive this even if he and I didn't.

"Now let's get down to *our* part of this," Tiran said to me. "I'd intended to have the business with Pavar done in that large courtyard off the west wing, but what we've found out from Brandis has made me change my mind. Beyond the back gardens is an acre or so of grass meadow, and I've shifted the show to there. What do you think?"

He included Brandis in on the question, and the magic user nodded with a smile.

"That should help considerably," he agreed. "The Mist of Fear needs a closed-in place to be effective, but the same doesn't apply to the Slave Powder. You'll have to make sure everyone is kept back from you including your guard, but you can rest assured that I'll be right there beside the queen."

"Which may be exactly what they want," I pointed out, suddenly suspicious of all easy solutions. "They come at *me* the first two times, but that's just to make sure Tiran's unprotected when they go after *him* the third time. And we've also been maneuvered into changing the location of

Pavar's execution. Can that be the real reason they used the mist, to force us out into an open meadow with no guards closer than ten or so feet away? I keep getting the feeling that everything's been done for a double purpose at the very least, and all our very clever precautions are exactly what they want.''

"So how do we counter them?" Tiran asked, but not in an argumentative way. "If we change the location back to the courtyard, they can use that mist on us. If we set guards around ourselves six deep, any one or more of those guards could be in our enemies' pay or under their control. If we have Brandis guard me instead of you, they could decide to go after *you* again. We're trapped in place with limited options, so what do you suggest? Postpone Pavar's execution?''

"That we *can't* do," I said with a headshake, the frustration rising again. "Not only would it look bad to the people, it would give Selwin and his bunch a chance to break Pavar loose. We have to do something else, but I can't—''

When my words broke off, Tiran looked at me with sudden hope, and he wasn't wrong. I *had* gotten an idea, and at the very least it ought to mess up some of our enemies' carefully laid plans.

"I think I understand now why they went after *you* first," Tiran said with a grin. "I'm a better than average strategist, but you've got me beat by a mile. What have you come up with?''

"Well, it suddenly came to me that our deaths would mean that our enemies could take over because we have no heirs," I said, enjoying that second compliment. "But what would happen if we designated heirs—like Bariden and Chalaine, for instance? Killing us would simply put two powerful magic users in the position of legitimacy, leaving those backstabbing sneaks out in the cold. They'd have their thrones only until Bariden and Chalaine freed up the time to come after them.''

"Now *that's* what I call an idea," Tiran said with a soft laugh, his grin having widened. "We let them maneuver us in any direction they like—after making *every* direction a dead end. We'll still be at a serious disadvantage when we face them, but that's something we can't change. If legitimacy is as important to them as it seems to be, our losing won't give it to them.''

"But I strongly suggest that you make that announcement *before* you begin with Duke Pavar," Brandis said with a gleam in his dark eyes. "That way you won't lose the opportunity by having something interrupt you, and you can make it sound like a simple precaution taken to insure an orderly succession in case of accident. Once the words are spoken it will be too late for anyone to change matters."

That made the decision unanimous, and we toasted its success and ours with coffee cups raised high. Attitude is absolutely essential in every phase of life, a good one usually bringing success and a bad one usually bringing failure. If our ploy ruined our enemies' attitude to the point of helpless frustration, it might cancel some of the edge they had. If it didn't, we'd be no worse off than we already were.

After a little more conversation Tiran and I left Brandis in the reception room, and went to dress for the execution—which it would be even if Pavar chose to face Tiran. I also needed to hear in detail what I had looked like while the powder and mist had me in their power, and then I practiced a little. The way Tiran got upset said I was doing it right, but the act was more than a little painful for me as well. Fear is one of the worst opponents you can have, especially when you're helpless . . .

Brandis stood up when we came back out into the reception room, undoubtedly a reaction to the fur-trimmed and jeweled robes we wore, not to mention our crowns. By rights we should have had lots of servants to help deck us out, but we hadn't really needed them. Underneath the robes I wore ordinary exercise clothes and my sword, while Tiran wore all black leather. If Pavar decided to face him, one glance would give the former duke the proper message.

Outside in the anteroom our escort waited, and I had to swallow down the urge to order them all away from me. If I hadn't known they would probably be safe I would have done it anyway, even in spite of the act. I *hadn't* changed my mind about letting people die for me, but that wasn't the time to go into the matter.

Instead I concentrated on the act I had to put on, and it wasn't easy. I was pretending to be someone who was distracted and terrified, but who was also trying to pretend that nothing was wrong. I smiled around woodenly from my place between Tiran and Brandis, meeting no one's eyes, showing nothing of recognition for anyone there. If my hand tried to tremble where it rested on Tiran's arm, that was more memory than acting. It had come to me that if there *was* a buried command somewhere in my mind, the fear and pain and whispering voices could return to tear me apart again.

So I spent the walk downstairs and out to the meadow thinking about that, a very effective distraction under the circumstances. Brandis must have done something to make the memories easier to handle, but there's only a small difference between boiling hot and red hot. Both temperatures will burn you badly if you try to touch them; the lesser heat just takes a little longer to do the job.

"Alex, love, you can sit down now," Tiran's voice came suddenly but very gently. "There's a seat right behind you, so you can sit down."

Tiran was looking properly worried, but I glanced around before doing as he'd asked. Someone had actually put down part of a wooden floor in the middle of the meadow, and on the floor they'd set two throne-like chairs. That raised the chairs only a couple of inches off the ground, no more than a token of the distance royalty was supposed to be above the common. I would have bet that that had been Tiran's idea, and needless to say, I agreed completely.

And the people in the crowds all around, about thirty feet away, also seemed to approve. There was a much larger audience than I'd been expecting, as if everyone in the city had showed up, and here and there someone looked at our dais-without-height and frowned in scandalized disapproval. But for the most part everyone else smiled and nodded happily to the people around them, as if we'd proven some sort of point for them.

Over to the left, about ten feet beyond what would be

Tiran's throne, six smaller chairs had been arranged for the members of what was left of our nobility. Count Nomilt and Countess Leestin, Baron Obrif and Baroness Iltaina, and Baron Sandor and Baroness Tovail stood lined up in front of the chairs, Leestin and Tovail looking really worried. The rest simply looked disturbed, but whether it was my act or the occasion causing the disturbance, I couldn't tell.

"Alex, please sit down," Tiran said, and now his worry had visibly increased. "It's almost noon, and we have to get started."

I'd been clutching my robe to me with one hand, mostly to keep it from opening and showing what I wore underneath, so without speaking I changed clutching hands and sat down somewhat unsteadily. The unsteadiness was absolutely necessary, as I had to jiggle my sword and a fold of the robe into the sword slot of the chair. If I hadn't, the game could have been up on the spot.

Tiran waited until his problem-queen was settled, and then he stepped forward a couple of feet to the end of the floor. He'd also nodded to Brandis, and the spell the magic user muttered manifested as soon as Tiran spoke.

"My friends, I appreciate your support in being here today," he said, and the amplified words rang out clearly for all to hear. "I haven't been your king long, so I've decided not to use the royal 'We.' Once I earn it, if I do, we'll see how it goes.

"We've gathered here today to see the end of a self-professed traitor both to me and this kingdom, but first I have an announcement to make. My queen and I have discussed the matter, and we've decided that leaving this kingdom vulnerable to conflict and upheaval in case of an unexpected tragedy involving the two of us would be unconscionable. For that reason we now designate King Bariden and Queen Chalaine, our neighbors to the west, as our sole heirs if we should die without issue. I ask you all now to be witnesses to this designation."

A muttering roar of comments erupted all around, and while pretending to be staring at nothing I was able to study our group of nobility. Thunderstruck would have been a good description of the men, while the women simply looked confused.

Tiran stood and waited for the noise to die down, and the way his head moved just an inch or so at a time said he was also inspecting our guard escort, who now stood at intervals in front of the crowd. They'd added themselves to a detachment already there when we arrived, and were supposed to keep the crowd back if Pavar decided to fight. When the crowd finally quieted, Tiran concluded, "That's all I have to say for the moment. Now let's get on with our reason for being here."

With that he came back to the seats and took his place next to me, the signal that Pavar was to be brought out. Brandis stood silently behind our chairs, and all of us watched as the central figure of that occasion was brought. Two guards marched Pavar between them, and despite all the time the man had spent in a cell, he still hadn't learned not to let himself be enraged.

"Pavar, formerly a duke of this realm, you stand condemned by your own words," Tiran said when the tall, lean, and furious man had been stopped about six feet away. "Have you anything else to say before final judgment is handed down?"

"How *dare* you have me dragged out in public looking like a commoner?" the damned fool raged, and his voice, too, had been amplified to reach everyone in the crowd. "I am a *noble,* you mindless upstart, something you'll never understand the true meaning of! If you intend to proceed with this farce before releasing me, you'll first have them let me clean up and change clothes!"

"You know, Pavar, you really are too stupid to live," Tiran commented, looking the rumpled, filthy man up and down. "You look considerably better than the people of your villages did in the slavery *you* condemned them to, so don't expect any sympathy from me. And whoever told you you would be released lied, so you can forget about your precious image. I was prepared to just have you executed, but it was pointed out to me that as a *former* noble of this kingdom you should have the right to personal combat. You're going to die today, man, and the only choice you have is in how."

Pavar's face had reddened even more with his increased rage, and he paid no attention to the muttering of the crowd when they heard what he'd done to his villagers. But his rage turned to vicious anticipation when he heard Tiran's offer, and he laughed aloud.

"You've overstepped yourself for the last time, you common dirt," he sneered, shaking free of the two guards who held his arms loosely. "This is the way I *wanted* to take the throne, and in a few minutes it will be done. Give your last order and have them bring me my sword."

Tiran tried not to show how pleased he was as he gestured for Pavar's sword to be brought, but even though I wasn't looking directly at him I could still tell. He must have been afraid that Pavar would beg or apologize or do something else to make killing him virtually impossible, but the fool had acted true to form. The others had obviously talked him out of challenging Tiran immediately, but now he was about to get his way.

And thinking about challenges, it looked like the expected one would be held off until Tiran saw to Pavar. Our major enemies weren't likely to want it to go the other way and help Pavar to win, not when that would muddy the waters even more. Pavar had heirs of his own which, added to the ones Tiran and I had just named, would put anyone then besting Pavar at the end of a very long line.

The crowd's muttering continued until Pavar's sword was brought, and then a hush fell as everyone gave the confrontation their undivided attention. Tiran stood up and took his crown off, setting it carefully on his chair, then let the robe drop from his shoulders without trying to catch it. That brought the black leather abruptly into view, along with the plain, workmanlike sword he preferred for serious fights.

Pavar lost part of his sneer when he first saw Tiran walking slowly toward him, but then his obnoxious conceit reasserted itself and the sneer came back stronger than ever. He'd probably decided Tiran was just putting on a show, and Tiran was doing exactly that—but not for Pavar's sake. Tiran wanted people to be reluctant to face

him, which they certainly ought to be once he finished
with Pavar.

The former duke already had his sword in his hand so
Tiran drew as well, before he had quite reached Pavar. I
saw a flash of anger in Pavar's eyes at that, but whether
it was from frustration or insult I couldn't tell. Tiran had
all but said he didn't trust Pavar to be honorable enough
not to attack before his opponent was ready, which may
have been the truth of Pavar's intentions. In any event,
Pavar didn't hesitate to let himself get angry.

Which proved all over again what a fool the man was.
Losing his temper made him lunge viciously at Tiran,
which by rights should have killed him right then and
there. I was pretending to stare at the ground somewhere
in front of the two combatants, but even so the opening
Pavar gave Tiran was too obvious to miss. But Tiran ignored it as he stepped quickly aside, leaving Pavar ex-
tended in a lunge at empty air. Most of the crowd laughed
and some even applauded, and I thought Pavar would explode with rage.

But then he must have realized that he was giving the
fight—and his life—away for free by letting the anger
control him. He stepped back and went through a minute's
worth of silent struggle, and then stepped forward again
with what he must have considered as having his temper
under control. At least his teeth were clenched, vindic-
tiveness stared out of his ice cold eyes, and he'd taken
the standard en garde posture.

Tiran matched Pavar's stance, and then the two of them
began to fence. It was a lovely demonstration of the proper
use of a sword and Pavar's form was flawless, which
slowly let his aggressive confidence return. Tiran wasn't
quite as perfect in form, and that obviously made Pavar
feel superior. What he didn't seem to know was that there
are as many different proper forms as there are swords of
different shapes and sizes, and when you happen to know
most of them you tend to develop your own version of
proper.

But Pavar got happier and happier thinking he was better than Tiran, which in turn made him begin to press his
attacks. From the way he behaved I began to believe he'd

never had a serious fight, that is, one against someone with real skill who wasn't impressed by his position in life or his reputation. A lot of people were afraid of Pavar on general principles, but Tiran wasn't one of them. He let Pavar attack for a minute or two, and then he went on the offensive.

And even with Tiran using little more than half his ability, Pavar was immediately forced to give ground. It was completely clear that the former duke had no experience with defense and counter, only with attack. The spoiled brat of a man had never faced any sort of real challenge from the people in that small backwater of a kingdom, and so had decided he was the best swordsman in the universe. A fool's decision deserving a fool's reward, which came rather quickly.

Tiran backed Pavar all over the meadow, obviously to show that he could, and then he went after him seriously. Pavar's perfect form disappeared behind frantic attempts at defense almost at once, and Tiran gave him just enough time to sweat and worry before he knocked the other man's blade aside and ran him through the chest. Pavar screamed at the thrust, but was dead even before Tiran withdrew his steel. He'd deserved a slower and more agonizing death, one to match the agony he'd caused for so many others, but this way he'd never be able to do it again.

A couple of people in the crowd began to applaud, but the rest stood silently as Pavar's body folded lifelessly to the ground. Everyone there seemed to know that the man had earned his death, and you don't celebrate something like that. Too many people had been hurt in order to bring it about, and only the insane celebrate other people's pain. Tiran turned away from the body and raised his arm as if getting ready to say something, but he never got the chance.

A man suddenly appeared inside the semicircle of people, about fifteen feet away from Tiran. Before anyone had the chance to react to his presence, he took what looked like a small glass ball and threw it to the ground in front of one section of the crowd. The ball shattered on impact, releasing an odd-looking cloud of smoke, but no one near it screamed and ran. Instead they stood silent and frozen, and the stranger laughed harshly.

"They don't get released until *I* release them," he said in an amplified voice to Tiran. "Keeping in mind that the lives of all those people are on the line, do you think we might discuss the matter of challenge?"

His tone might have been mocking, but he certainly wasn't joking. Our real enemies had finally made an appearance.

CHAPTER TWELVE

Tiran stepped back from Pavar's body, glad the man was dead but not enjoying the role of executioner. Because that's what it had been, not a fight but an execution. Pavar's reputation hadn't been based on much beyond blind arrogance and the unearned deference paid by the people around him. When would people learn the difference between looking pretty and really being able to fight?

Well, he could complain about that later. Right now it was time to announce that Pavar's estates were forfeit, along with the rest of his possessions. If his widow decided to argue the point and dig in, it would be annoying, but nothing they couldn't—Tiran's thoughts broke off at the sudden appearance of a stranger, who wasted no time letting them know why he was there.

"They don't get released until *I* release them," he said, referring to the section of crowd he'd frozen with some kind of cloud or mist. "Keeping in mind that the lives of all those people are on the line, do you think we might discuss the matter of challenge?"

He stared directly at Tiran as he spoke, and his attitude made Pavar's former one look unassuming and courteous by comparison. His grin couldn't be described as anything but shit-eating, the kind that makes you want to wipe it away with a fist or foot, but Tiran wasn't impressed. People had tried to force him into losing his temper that way before, and it hadn't worked then either.

"You know we can," he answered calmly, his voice as amplified as the intruder's. "You obviously don't care about anyone but yourself, but you know I do. That means we can go at it right here and now, just the two of us. As soon as I have this body removed, we'll—''

"Not so fast," the intruder interrupted, briefly annoyed. "I happen to care about these people a lot more than you do, and you know it. Putting their lives in jeopardy in front of witnesses was the only way to force you to face me, since I know you can't afford to ignore the false reputation for concern you've been building to fool everyone. You expect to get them to trust you and then you'll kick them in the teeth—unless someone stops you first. But that means you *and* your partner in deception, so get her out here. Everyone else might be afraid of you two, but my wife and I aren't.''

Now the man projected bravery and dedication, but Tiran could see the ridiculing gleam in his eyes. He hadn't meant a word he'd said—except for the part about how unafraid he and his female accomplice were. Considering what they thought they'd done to Alex, of course they weren't worried.

"I'll need just a minute, and then we'll be with you," Tiran answered simply, making no effort to argue the man's claims. At that point there was really no way for the listening crowd to know which of them was telling the truth, and they'd have to fight eventually anyway. There was no sense in putting it off, but as he turned and headed back toward Alex, he suddenly had someone unexpected hurrying along at his side—Caldai Moyan.

He'd run into the woman half a dozen times over the last couple of days, and the first time she'd pretended to be annoyed with him for not having told her who he was. Then she'd graciously forgiven him, and had spent the few minutes each time they'd met simply chatting. She'd told him she liked his company and the people in it, and had decided to hang around for a while. She hadn't done anything really overt, but after the second or third time they spoke Tiran had had the impression she was waiting for *him* to offer something more than casual conversation. He hadn't, of course, but the incidents had made him faintly uncomfortable . . .

"That guy has a lot of nerve," Caldai now said breathlessly as she hurried along with him. "I know I shouldn't have left my post, but this is my chance to pay back what I owe you. I happen to also know you need me, and I don't want you to be afraid to ask."

"Afraid to ask what?" Tiran put, glancing at her but not stopping. "What do you think I need you for?"

"What else but a fighting partner?" she returned in annoyance, then gestured to Alex. "I may not have been around here long, but from the things you and other people have said about your wife, I can see that the rumors are true and something serious is wrong with her. There isn't anything left of the topnotch fighter about her, and if you go out there with *her* as your partner you'll lose. Take me instead, and together we'll win."

Caldai's eagerness seemed to contain a solemn promise, and for the briefest instant Tiran considered the suggestion. It would have meant keeping Alex safely out of the fight, but then he realized there would be no safety for Alex anywhere if these new intruders weren't defeated. Not to mention that the only one who could make Alex really safe was Alex herself.

"I appreciate your offer, Caldai, but I have to decline," Tiran said after the very short hesitation. "Alex and I started this together, and that has to be the way we finish it. You'd better go back to your post in front of the crowd now."

"You're a damned fool," the woman growled, and now bitterness mixed with heavy frustration in her expression. "Fools always do things to ruin themselves, but that's all right. I have someone waiting who *isn't* a fool, so you can do as you please. It will just look better this way."

With that she turned and walked away, but not to go back to the post she'd been given in front of the crowd. She headed straight for the intruder where he stood alone in the grass, and his expression said he knew her and was waiting to hear what she had to say.

"What a surprise," Tiran muttered as he bent with supposed concern to Alex. "The woman who was so conveniently around for me to rescue turns out to be one of the enemy. No wonder she wanted me to choose *her* to fight with me instead of you."

"That would have made her your temporary queen," Alex murmured back, not quite looking at him. "If the two of them then turned on you, she would be *left* as queen in fact once you were dead. What *is* this thing they have about legitimate succession?"

"I don't know, but since it makes things easier for *us,* I'm glad they do," Tiran answered. "And in another minute they'll see how you're dressed, so is there any point in keeping up your act?"

"There's always a point in keeping people off-balance," Alex murmured as she let Tiran remove her crown, push her robe back, and help her to her feet. "They might think you got me to dress this way as a bluff, just to make them unsure. Not knowing *will* make them unsure, at least until the fight starts."

Tiran murmured agreement and began to urge Alex away from the chairs, while she in turn pretended she didn't want to go. She clung to him piteously, begging in a small voice to be allowed to cover up again with the robe and huddle into the chair, and she did *too* good a job. It wasn't hard for Tiran to believe she was back to being as she had been, and that let him glance at the waiting intruders with all the desire to maim and destroy that he'd felt from the very first.

The two stood together watching what he and Alex were doing, and the triumphant enjoyment in the man's eyes was echoed in Caldai's along with grim satisfaction. They were looking forward to slaughtering him and Alex, Tiran saw, and then they would start to wring the kingdom dry. It was all Tiran could do not to fall screaming into a sickened rage ...

"I think he's the one who was in charge of the original kidnapping attempt against me," Alex murmured as she held to Tiran's arm even more tightly. "He has golden eyes now rather than brown or whatever they were then, but I'm sure it's the same man. That means he's a Shapeshifter, so watch yourself when you face him."

"Since Caldai's probably the same despite those dark eyes, make sure you take your own advice," Tiran returned in his own mutter, patting her hand as though in comfort. "And we're almost there, so get ready."

Alex's nod was all but imperceptible, but it was more than enough for Tiran. They'd been moving slowly and with small steps, something forced on them by Alex's pretense, but there were only about ten feet now between them and the waiting two. Another step and another, paying more attention to Alex than to them, and then—

And then there was a blinding flash and a great roaring, and everything in the normal world disappeared . . .

". . . right through that entry, sir," the young man said jovially, gesturing toward the faintly glittering doorway. "The reservations for you and the lady are completely in order, and we do hope you both enjoy your vacation with us. If there's anything you need, just stop by one of the large glowing boulders and say, 'Service, please.' In just a few minutes someone will come through to help you."

"Thank you," Tiran said, then went to join Alex, who was already peering through the entry, trying to see what lay on the other side. "Patience, woman," he ordered with a grin for her eagerness. "You'll like what's there, you have my word on it."

"I know I'll like it, that's why I can't wait to go through," she answered with a happy laugh. "How did you find out about this place?"

"When you do as much traveling as I've done, you see or hear about almost everything there is," he answered, putting an arm around her. "This place was put together by magic users, but designed by Shapeshifters. You don't have to be able to use magic or Shift to enjoy it, all you have to do is afford it. Shall we?"

She glanced at him before stepping through the entry, and he was right with her. On the other side lay what seemed to be an open cavern with small boulders scattered all around, along with giant ones here and there. The cavern ceiling was high and there were a number of openings spaced along the outer rim at irregular intervals, most of them letting in bright sunshine and fresh air.

"Why is that opening darker than the others?" Alex asked, leaving him to walk toward it and then peer out. "Hey, Ti, it's raining outside this one, raining hard! How can it be raining out here when there seems to be sunshine outside all the other openings?''

"That's because each opening leads to a different kind of playground," he answered, walking toward a medium-sized boulder on the right. "There's even one that lets you out in a common-area sort of place open to all guests, where you can do ordinary things like swim, or have dinner with dancing, or just have the company of other people. The rest of it is private and for the sole use of the occupant or occupants of this room."

"Room?" she echoed, glancing at him as she stopped at another opening to peer out. "This isn't like any room *I've* ever seen."

"There are a lot of fascinating things you've never seen, and it's going to be my pleasure to show them to you," he responded, touching the thigh-high boulder he'd stopped near. "Like this, for instance. We haven't had lunch yet, so why don't we take a meal before getting down to serious playing."

Touching the boulder in its middle had caused it to turn into a square table, and two comfortable chairs had appeared on either side of it. Alex made a sound of interest and came over to examine the transformation, and Tiran pointed to the two small booklets that had also appeared.

"Those are the menus," he said, flipping one open to show it to her. "When you decide what you want you run your finger across the items, and they'll appear on the table in front of you. A lot of the arrangements here let you feel as if you're doing magic, an experience most people never get to have."

"But we'll have it because between the two of us, we have enough gold to last us for three or four lifetimes," she said, suddenly coming close to put her arms around his waist and smile up at him. "I'm sure traveling around and seeing things will eventually get boring, but right now I'm awfully glad you talked me into marrying you. I love you very much, Tiran, and seeing things like this means a lot more because you're here to show them to me."

Since his arms had gone around her as soon as she came close enough, he only had to lower his head to kiss her. Her own kiss was already waiting, and the passion immediately flared into life from the merging of their lips and love. He'd never imagined how *complete* it was possible to feel until he'd met Alex, and now they belonged to each other forever.

Tiran stood and shared a kiss with his beloved for as long as he could bear it, and then he picked her up and carried her to the boulder that had turned itself into a large bed. Much of that "room" was attuned to them by magic, like the appearance of the bed when it was wanted. They spent quite a long time making wonderful, glorious love, and when it was finally over they returned to the table for their meal.

Alex enjoyed the way her food choices appeared as soon as she ran her finger across an item, but the way the wine behaved absolutely delighted her. Tiran showed her how it worked by pointing to the decanter he'd ordered, and then watched with her as his glass filled. She laughed like a small girl and filled her own glass in the same way, and then they settled down to eat.

After all the magic the food should have been disappointing, but it wasn't. They ate every last scrap and crumb and refilled their wine glasses a number of times, but the wine didn't affect them at all. The magic around them knew they wanted to go out after eating, and so it neutralized the alcohol in them.

"You can't mean we're going out like *this*," Alex asked with a grin when he took her hand and headed them toward an opening on the far left. "We're stark naked, Ti, and some people object to terrible things like the sight of skin."

"Ah, but there won't be anyone else around, and we won't be wearing plain skin for long," he told her with his own grin. "Come and see what *this* opening offers."

She followed him with very obvious curiosity, and when she looked out she gasped.

"Ti, there's nothing here but a narrow ledge," she exclaimed. "Beyond it is just open air, miles of it in all directions."

"That's because open air is what *birds* fly in," he answered, still enjoying himself immensely. "You know we can Shift to bird form, Alex, but by ourselves we can't fly. Here it's magic that does the Shifting, and the resultant birds *can* fly. Are you ready to share the freedom of the skies with me, my love?''

"But Ti, you don't *like* flying," Alex answered with a confused frown. "I know you don't, so why—"

Tiran knew she was about to ask why he intended to do something he feared and hated, and that was a very good question. He'd feared soaring ever since childhood, so why—

There was a blinding flash that also numbed, and then—

"You can't mean we're going out like *this*," Alex asked with a grin when he took her hand and headed them toward an opening on the far right. "We're stark naked, Ti, and some people object to terrible things like the sight of skin."

"Ah, but there won't be anyone else around, and we won't be wearing plain skin for long," he told her with his own grin. "Come and see what *this* opening offers."

She followed him with very obvious curiosity, and when she looked out she gasped.

"It's not only snowing out there, it's *cold*," she exclaimed. "And look at the crazy way the terrain is arranged. That long stretch of snow-covered hillside looks like a slide."

"It *is* a slide," Tiran confirmed, still enjoying himself immensely. "It's made for playing in the snow, along with other things you can't see from here. We can Shift into any cold-weather animal we care to, and the magic in this place will take care of annoying problems like too much mass. We'll *be* the animals we Shift into, for as long as we care to stay in the forms."

Rather than answering in words, Alex began to blur. In a moment she'd Shifted to polar bear form, and was lumbering out into the snow. Tiran quickly Shifted to the same form and followed after her, and they had a marvelous time. At the bottom of the snow slide was an ice pool, one that contained fish for them to catch when they got hungry again from playing. When it began to snow hard they enjoyed that too, although Tiran was briefly reminded of playing in a snowstorm when it *wasn't* cold. The memory was odd and he tried to recapture it, but a small flash of light came and he forgot all about it.

That night they returned to their cavern, dressed in fancy clothes, and went through another opening to find dinner and dancing. There were a lot of other people there and some of them were friendly and amusing, and they all had a marvelous time.

The next day they met three other couples before venturing out onto sand and heavy heat as lizards, and that was even more fun. One of them was a Shapeshifting couple like themselves, but the other two were ordinary people who had never changed anything but their minds and their clothes. Watching them bounce around in delight was a riot, especially when Alex Shifted to camel form. They had to do the same, of course, and hearing camels laugh was even funnier.

That time two flashes of light came to distract Tiran from whatever he'd been thinking, and the next day, when they went underwater and took fish form, the same thing happened again. Tiran didn't remember the incidents long enough for them to become annoying, but when they left the resort there was a formless feeling of relief.

"So where are we going now?" Alex asked as she watched some men come through a brand new entry and begin to pick up their luggage. "I didn't hear what you told the magic user who called that entry into being."

"I didn't want you to hear what I told her," Tiran answered with a deliberate smirk. "I want to surprise you again, but you'll probably guess our destination as soon as we pass through the entry. I doubt if you've ever been there, but you certainly must have heard of it."

Strong curiosity grabbed her again, which means she headed straight for the entry. Tiran was right behind her when she stepped through, and her laugh of delight came even before her second step.

"Tiran, this has to be The Battleground," she said as soon as she saw the giant arena rising a good twenty levels in the distance—not to mention the purplish-blue sky with black clouds. "This is where fighters come to show just how skilled they are, and you're right that I've heard about it but have never been here. How do we sign up for the competitions?''

"First we'll look around a little and do some practicing, and *then* we'll see about signing up," he told her before gesturing toward the area around them. "These guest accommodations are for those who might want to enter the competitions, and they all have practice rooms. The accommodations for those who just want to watch are on the other side of the arena."

She nodded with understanding, then they both followed the men carrying their luggage to the nearest inn. It was also the largest inn, boasting four floors and an eight-window width. Tiran had reserved a small suite on the second floor, which put them above the noise from the common room and two floors below the thuds and vibrations from the practice area on the top floor.

"I once stayed here on the next floor up," Tiran told Alex when they stood in their tiny sitting room after the men who brought up their luggage had left. "I didn't have much money then, so I took one of the tiny cubbies they call rooms up there. It's cheap because the sounds of practicing come right through the ceiling in spite of the heavy padding and insulation between floors, and that practicing goes on at all hours. But once you've gone through a couple of the rougher competitions, you're tired enough to sleep through anything."

"Why would there be that much practicing?" Alex asked, just glancing around before sitting in one of the only two comfortable chairs in the room. "What's the sense in coming here, if you spend all your time practicing and none of it competing?"

"You'll see it for yourself," Tiran promised, taking the other chair. "There are hundreds of fighters competing in that arena, and most of them are really good. All the bouts are supposed to be with practice weapons, which is why all comers pay an entrance fee. If a fighting company happens to take large, unexpected losses during an engagement, it will send a recruiter here to hire fighters who won't start out green. That's the way it worked out for me."

"So for anyone who wants the same, the entrance fee

is an investment," Alex said with a nod of understanding. "But that still doesn't explain why some people practice rather than compete."

"Some of them are talkers rather than fighters," Tiran explained, wishing the coffee they'd ordered would arrive. "They like strutting around pretending to be important, and some of *those* men earn a living at it. There are a lot of women in that arena on any given day, and for the most part they can't tell the fighters apart. Once the competitions are over a large number of those women offer silver and gold for a night with a 'real fighter,' and if the men *look* like fighters the women never know the difference. But the biggest reason some fighters practice rather than compete is that they're trying to decide whether or not to go for the heavy gold."

"Now *that* I want to hear about," Alex said, and then a knock came at the door. It was their coffee being delivered, and once they had full cups in front of them and the kitchen maid was gone, Tiran went on.

"As I said, most of the competitions are with practice weapons, and most people don't hear of any other kind. But fighters who compete and show better than average skill are offered an opportunity to earn a large amount of gold. All they have to do is participate in the small, very private competitions held for the pleasure of a certain select few."

"And those competitions are with real weapons," Alex said with a sour nod. "I'd heard rumors about that, but not from anyone who knew it by personal experience. It's fairly clear they made the offer to *you*, but you haven't said whether or not you accepted."

"I almost accepted," Tiran admitted with a sigh. "I was close to being flat broke, and still hadn't been offered hire. One more day and I probably would have *had* to agree, but I got lucky. One of the men I practiced and entered with didn't wait that day, and he died. I Shifted form and slipped in to watch his match, and as good as he was, he didn't stand a chance. He was skilled but not experienced, and his opponent turned out to be someone who'd fought in those matches a long time. I was bothered by that for a lot of years, but there's nothing you can do about it. As long as there are people who offer gold, those without it will turn up to accommodate them.''

"And if everyone had enough gold, there would be other reasons for people to compete," Alex agreed distantly. "There's always someone with something to prove, and the worst of that group *have* to win. It's a need stronger even than food or drugs, and they—''

A silent white flash came, making Tiran think he'd seen the same before, but then he forgot about it since the wagon they rode in now approached the arena.

"This should be fun," Alex enthused from her place to his right, toward the front of the wagon. "I hadn't realized there were professionals-only competitions where it's possible to show off for and with your equals. I probably would have decided against competing with newcomers.''

"Alex, for all intents and purposes *you're* a newcomer," Tiran said with tender amusement. "You've only had a small number of serious fights, and you've never been in battle. Facing someone with experience is never easy no matter how good you are, and that's the main reason I brought you here. I think that's something you need to learn, and I'd like you to watch for a while before deciding to enter.''

"And then maybe not enter at all?" she said, looking disturbed rather than annoyed or insulted. "All right, Ti, I'll take your advice.''

Tiran hugged her with a great deal of relief, delighted that she was going to be sensible. The men and women who competed here were better than good, having proved their expertise in the hardest way possible: by surviving real battle. The Battleground was just a place to play, but that didn't mean the entrants took matters less than seriously. If Alex decided to compete after all she couldn't really be hurt, and she might well learn something.

The wagon pulled up to a modest side entrance of the arena, and everyone got out slowly and walked through a small crowd to the door. The people in the crowd stared intently at each of them in turn, trying to judge who looked good enough to bet on. Almost everyone in the arena audience would place at least one bet, the standard way of trying to win back your admission fee. Or just supporting someone whose looks you liked. It was all part of the entertainment and made the events more enjoyable.

Inside the door was a wide hall with a long table, and on one wall was a schedule of events. All but two of the people who had come in the wagons with them headed for the table, while those two joined Tiran and Alex at the schedule.

"Look, Ti, there's a tandem competition later today," Alex pointed out. "I used to do tandem fighting with Gromal as my partner. We should have tried that during practice instead of simply loosening up."

"You should know how long you have to partner with someone before you can fight in tandem with them, Alex," Tiran had to point out. "You trained with Gromal so long that you knew every move he would make before he made it. Do you really think you could do the same with me after only a few minutes of practice?"

She glanced at him without answering, but the look in her eyes was an answer itself. She hadn't stopped to think before speaking, and was now regretting it. There was more to being a fighter than just having skill, something people needed to know if they were going to live. Tiran was pleased with Alex's progress, so he read the schedule again, chose a competition, then took Alex with him when he went to register for it.

There were really a lot of people around, some fresh from having just competed, some waiting their turn, some simply looking at everyone else. It was dim there inside the corridors of the arena, and the hum of the crowd above our heads was an everpresent rumble we felt as well as heard. It stayed a hum in between events, rose slowly or quickly to a roar depending on the events being watched, and usually rose to a deafening, shudder-making scream at every climax. Usually there were multiple events going on out on the gray sand of the arena floor, but when the professionals competed there was only one, right smack in the middle of the floor.

And in just a few minutes Tiran would be one of those professionals. I stood to one side of the corridor, watching him chat with a couple of men he knew, big, easy-going men with ready smiles and the look of death in their eyes. They were experienced professionals just like Tiran, and I was fairly sure one of the two would be his opponent. They all wore exercise clothes but no swordbelts or other weapons, and that made no difference at all. What they were was easy to see.

What they were and what I *wasn't*. At one time I would have argued the point bitterly, but I couldn't argue the things Tiran had been trying to tell me. Experience did make a difference in fighting, and I'd been lucky until now in that the few people I'd faced seriously hadn't been anywhere near my level of skill. When we'd first gotten there I'd really wanted to measure my ability against those who had spent years developing their own, but now . . .

Now I'd had second thoughts, and maybe even third and fourth ones. Since everyone was using practice weapons I couldn't have gotten seriously hurt, but I didn't like the idea of getting hurt at all. Once that wouldn't have bothered me, and certainly wouldn't have kept me from entering a competition. I'd been hurt any number of times during my life, but that hadn't—

There was suddenly a noiseless but blinding flash of light, interrupting my train of thought. I tried to remember what I'd been thinking about, and then it came back: getting hurt, and how much pain there was when it happened. The thought of that much pain turned my mouth dry and twisted my insides, and I knew I couldn't face that again— or any part of it. I suddenly wished we'd stayed at the resort, having a marvelous time doing nothing more than playing and making love.

"Okay, Alex, it's just about time for my event," Tiran said, showing that he'd walked over without my noticing. "Why don't you come along to the outer section, and you can watch from there."

I nodded and he put his arm around me, and then we went with a number of other men and women through a section of wall that had been slid aside. Beyond was a much smaller tunnel-like area with open doorways at intervals around the outer part of it, and Tiran left me to join the others in going through one of the doorways.

When they were all outside I followed to stand beside

the doorway, and was able to see the gray sand of the arena and a large portion of the seating on the side, opposite to where I stood. The place looked jam-packed, and the noise was a lot worse out here. Tiran and the others were greeted with yells of excitement, a deafening anticipation of the skill they were about to display.

And skill it would be. I leaned a shoulder against the side of the doorway and watched practice swords being handed out, but not ordinary practice weapons. These swords had blades produced by magic just as the ordinary sort did, and would also pass harmlessly through a living body. The difference was that these weapons took their users one step closer to reality by making anyone they passed through unable to move for a while. That rendered them "dead" for the purposes of the competition, eliminating people in a way that no referee or judge could.

As each person got his or her weapon they continued on into the middle of the arena, and I saw I'd been partially right. One of the men Tiran had been talking to *was* his opponent, the first one he would start against. Everyone out there was paired off, and each pair would fight until one of the two was frozen in place. The winner would then turn to face another opponent, but the trick of the thing was timing. If you took too long besting the fighter in front of you, chances were good that someone else would get you from behind before you could turn.

The event was called a melee, and the winner would be the last fighter still unfrozen. The excitement-noise of the crowd rose as the event began, especially since no one was eliminated quickly. Those were all experienced professionals out there, and none of them was easy to take. Everywhere you looked was an incredible exhibition of fighting skill, but even so it seemed that a lot of them weren't as good as I'd been expecting—

Another flash and a pause to remember what I'd been thinking, and after rubbing my eyes I had it. All those fighters out there were incredibly good, and I was lucky I wasn't out there with them. I wouldn't have stood a chance, and would have been eliminated even sooner than those who now stood motionless here and there on the sand.

One of them was Tiran's opponent, and even as I watched he ducked someone's slash, took that someone out with a backhanded stroke, then engaged a third fighter. Tiran was so *good,* so very much more experienced than me, the best fighter in his company. I really expected him to win the melee, but even though he came close it didn't happen. That third opponent got in under his guard and "ran him through," and that was the end of his participation. The man who had bested him then turned to the two remaining contestants, and took them both to win the event.

Once the winner was declared, Tiran and the others came out of it. There was a lot of laughing and joking as they came in from the sand, but I couldn't quite join in the festive atmosphere. We took another wagon ride back to our inn, and I waited in our rooms while Tiran partied a while with the other professionals. When he got back, we paid our bill and went on to another resort. That made me a lot happier, and I enjoyed myself very much. Then everything changed—

CHAPTER THIRTEEN

Tiran sat behind his desk and brooded, using the dark mood to help him make up his mind. He'd been playing king for years now, and it was time he exercised some royal prerogative. He was sick and tired of listening to everyone's problems and complaints every time he held an audience, so there would *be* no more audiences. He'd thought cutting them down to once a month would help, but it hadn't. He was as bored as ever, so the audiences were finished completely.

But that wasn't the only thing about his life boring him. Now that he thought about it, everything else was just as bad. People were constantly coming to him to make routine decisions, a process he hated but had no choice about sticking to. The couple of times he'd tried to let others make those decisions they'd screwed everything up, and he'd even had to throw some of those screw-ups out of the kingdom. Not that they were worth anything to begin with. All the really competent people from his former company had left years ago, with Damis and Gann.

Thinking about that time got Tiran angry all over again, even though it had been years earlier. Once everything had settled down in the kingdom to everyday routine, Tiran had been able to look around at his organization with an eye toward practicality. He'd noticed that Damis and Gann had an awful lot of power between them—so much, in fact, that it had made Tiran uncomfortable. So he'd rearranged things to put the power back in his own hands, using some of the new people who had come to his court.

And Damis and Gann had had the nerve to resent what he'd done! They'd accused him of sneaking around behind their backs, and had even claimed they would have given up their places voluntarily if he'd bothered to ask. He hadn't believed that for a minute and was making plans to have the two men arrested, when he'd learned they'd picked up and left—taking many of the old company members with them.

Tiran left his chair and went to pace around the very large room that was his private office. The ingrates who had gone with Damis and Gann had been troublemakers, spreading rumors that he hadn't kept his word about rewarding them properly, which just wasn't so. There were political considerations which had had to take priority, but he would have given them their silly little rewards eventually. He was well rid of them, but the *way* they'd left still grated.

Just as much as some of those who *hadn't* left grated. Tiran paused to look up at the large painting of Alexia which hung on the wall, one where she was dressed to the teeth and holding their first son and his heir. Alexia looked radiantly beautiful and the boy was a lovely baby, but neither of them had looked like that in quite some time. Alexia had done her duty and had had his children, but after that had paid not the slightest attention to them. And the boy had grown into a whiny, weepy brat who screamed bloody murder at the first mention of beginning to learn weapons skill . . .

And now that he thought about it, he wondered if the boy really was his. Or if any of the children were. After the first year Alexia had started to take "trips," claiming the boredom of sitting around and doing nothing was more than she could stand. She acted as if it hadn't been *her* idea for him to do all the ruling, that he should have ignored her wishes and given her some power anyway. Which was perfectly ridiculous, since there was only so much power to go around.

So Tiran couldn't understand why she refused to see that. Instead of being reasonable she'd taken more and more trips, until now she came back for no more than a few days before leaving again. And the last two times she'd even refused to sleep with him, which was *not* going to happen again. He'd long since grown bored with serving girls, and even the female fighters in the army lost his interest after the first couple or three times. None of them made him feel as good as he did when he had a woman in his bed who had once been a princess. *She* meant something, or at least having her did . . .

Tiran cursed under his breath, then went to pour himself another drink. What he really wanted was to pack up and leave that backwoods kingdom, walk out and never look back again, but how could he do that? In the place where he was king he could do anything he pleased, so how could he just leave all that? Even if he was going out of his mind with boredom, he couldn't just toss it all away.

And even taking a vacation was out of the question. He knew well enough that the kingdom would fall apart without him, and a vacation would lose its attraction if he knew he was coming back to chaos. Or the plotting of his so-called nobles. He hadn't let any of the old ones keep their positions, not even the three who had pretended to be loyal to him, but the new crop was no better than the old. They complained constantly about taxes and conscription, forgetting who they had to thank that they were in a position to *pay* high taxes to begin with.

"Maybe it would relieve the boredom if I had a couple of them executed for treason," Tiran muttered after finishing his drink in one swallow, then started to pour another. "That would keep the rest quiet for a while, and maybe then I'd be able to figure out what to do about everything else. I'm really beginning to hate it here, but giving it all up is out of the question. I wish I'd never won the damn throne to begin with . . ."

The second drink—or tenth, or twentieth, he'd lost count—went down as fast as the one before it, but he wasn't given the time to pour another. A knock came at the door, and then a servant entered and immediately knelt.

"Your Majesty, word has been sent from the queen's apartments just as you ordered," the servant said with head bowed. "Her Majesty has just told her maids to pack again, as she means to leave tomorrow morning."

Even though she'd only been back two days, Tiran realized with sudden anger. She'd sent a servant to tell him when she'd gotten back, but had made no effort to come to him in person. It was almost as if she expected *him* to go to *her*, which only showed how far out of touch she was with reality. *He* was the king, which meant it was her place to come to *him*. That she hadn't had made him furious, but now he was well beyond fury. If *he* had to be stuck here like a prisoner, she would be the same. He should never have let her go traipsing off in the first place.

Tiran stalked out of his office past the still-kneeling servant, who knew better than to straighten up again without express permission. Alexia's traveling days were over, and so was having others take her place in his bed. It was time he got himself a *real* heir, one he was certain was his. By locking her up for a month or so he'd be sure she wasn't carrying someone else's bastard, and then he'd put a real son in her. Yes, that's what he'd do, but first he would have a princess in his bed again for a while, just the way he used to.

I retreated to the sitting room to get out of the way of the maids who were packing my things, but went to the tray with the coffee service rather than to the bar. Every time I came back to this place I started to drink again, which should have told me a long time ago that I was being a fool. This time I'd decided to leave rather than drink, and not coming back again would settle the problem permanently.

My hands weren't quite shaking as I poured coffee into a cup, but only because I refused to *let* them shake. I'd come back for the same reason I always did—to see my children—but I just couldn't stand it any longer. Not only were they complete strangers to me, I didn't even like them. If only I hadn't let Tiran talk me into allowing them to be taken care of by "those more suited to raising children."

But I *had* let him talk me into it, and those wonderful professional child-raisers had ruined them all. Even the youngest thought—no, *knew*—she was much better than everyone else, simply because she was a princess. She demanded things and was given them, insulted people and then made *them* apologize, and everyone around her told her how wonderful she was. And my eldest son—! He cringed if anyone so much as looked at him, and whimpered like the thin, hurt little animal he'd become. And they still hadn't let me do more than watch the children for a while from a distance . . .

I gulped the hot coffee in an effort to regain control of myself, but that little trick had been beyond me for years. It was all Tiran's fault, every bit of the horror of my life, floating from place to place like a ghost because I couldn't bear to go back to what was supposed to be home. And every time I forced myself to go back, deluding myself into thinking things might have changed, I found that they *had* changed, but only for the worse.

So this time, after only two days of being back, I'd finally decided to leave again and never repeat the mistake of returning. Everyone I'd known and liked was gone anyway, from the members of the company to the old nobility to the lowliest of the palace staff. Everyone decent had turned and walked away after Tiran decided doing things the right way was too much trouble, but I'd stuck it out. I'd made a deal to do certain things, and now that they were done *I* could turn and walk away.

But to where, exactly, I still didn't know. It was lonely out there in the worlds in spite of all the men who were downright eager to be nice to a rich and beautiful woman. I hadn't wanted any part of them, but maybe I should have. There's more to loneliness than just being by yourself, and one of them might have been able to reach to the heart of the problem.

Then I laughed bitterly at that thought, knowing well enough that no one could have solved *my* problem. It had all started when I'd agreed to fight for a kingdom, to win a place I now wished I'd never heard of. When you think that the worst thing ahead of you is the possibility of death, you obviously don't know anything about life. When it comes to unbearable agony, being forced to continue living beats death in every way there is.

I'd gulped down one cup of coffee and was pouring a second when the hall doors were suddenly thrown open. I was so startled I dropped the pitcher, and when I saw who it was I felt even worse. Tiran had decided to come calling, and from the way he moved I knew he'd been drinking.

"Ah, welcome home, wife," he said, stopping when he saw me. "We've missed you in your absences, but now you've returned to Us. You may show Us your respect and affection with a curtsey and then a kiss."

"I'm supposed to be your co-ruler, so I don't owe you any acts of fealty," I reminded him, rescuing what I could of the dropped pitcher and spilled coffee. "And as for acts of affection, that feeling died out a long time ago. What are you doing here? You've always said you hate this tiny apartment and its pathetic memories."

"I do," he answered, looking through the far doors into my bedchamber. "Which is why I'm glad your maids are packing all your things. You're moving out of here and upstairs with me, where you belong. It's been much too long since you've been a real queen to me, but that's about to change."

"No, it's not," I said after taking a deep breath, turning to look straight at him. "Any obligations I had to you are long satisfied, so don't waste your time trying to claim they aren't. Now I'm leaving here for good, so you'll never again have to worry about someone trying to steal your 'power.' "

"But you *were* trying to steal it," he insisted before I could turn away again. "You were wrong, Alexia, and I want you to admit it."

"You sound like your daughter," I commented, looking him up and down. "If you want me to say I was wrong, I'll be glad to. I was wrong to help you win this kingdom, I was wrong to marry you, and I was wrong to let you take my children away. I was even more wrong to come back here again, because if I hadn't I would have been saved this scene. Now please leave me alone."

"Alone," he echoed, his face twisted as he took two unsteady steps toward me. "That's all I've been these last years, completely alone. I miss you, Alex, more than I can say, and I love you. Please don't—''

I felt something stir in me that hadn't stirred in years, but then there was a silent flash of light that interrupted him, and—

''Alone,'' he echoed, his face twisted as he took two unsteady steps toward me. ''That's all I've been these last years, and it's all your fault. You abandoned me as if I were a nobody, but you won't get away with it. And you'll never abandon me again . . .''

He reached for the jeweled dagger he wore, unsheathing it half way to show sharp-edged steel. The look in his eyes told me what he intended to do, but somehow I couldn't believe it. Tiran, threatening to hurt me? It just wasn't possible. A flash of light came, trying to erase that absolute doubt, but it couldn't. And Tiran still stood where he was, the dagger only half drawn, his eyes narrowed and blinking as though against a very bright light. It was crazy, absolutely insane, and then—

One minute Tiran struggled against drawing a dagger that was meant to do harm to his beloved, every fiber of his being set in refusal, and the next minute everything changed. Alex and his apartment in the palace was gone, and they stood in a meadow not far from two people who were obviously waiting for them.

''Well?'' the man said, looking faintly curious. ''Why did you two just stop like that? We're right here and waiting, so just come ahead and—''

His words broke off when something that looked like a big soap bubble appeared in front of him, then floated up to his face and seemed to *soak* into him. His expression went blank for a moment, and then he came back to himself with a look of frustration.

''It seems our encounter might have to be postponed for a short while,'' he said, looking between Tiran and Alex. ''I've just been told that an army has started to march on this city, and if you don't do something fast then the city will fall. But my wife and I refuse to give up our legitimate challenge. If we release those people now and let you take care of the threat to the city, do we have your word that you'll face us once the threat is over?''

Tiran realized the man must have been sent a message-sphere by their magic user, and that was what the giant soap-bubble had been. He glanced at Alex, who looked drawn and worried, and then he nodded in answer to the intruder's question.

"No, you have to say it out loud," the intruder insisted, gesturing aside the nod. "Do we have the word of both of you that you'll face us in challenge once the attack is over? Without our having to force you into it again?"

"You have our word," Tiran obliged after Alex's tenta-tive nod to him. "We'll face you once the city is safe."

"In public," the intruder pressed, still looking back and forth between them. "Say it."

"In public," Tiran agreed, which finally seemed to sat-isfy the man. He and Caldai Moyan—if that was her real name—exchanged glances, and then the intruder took her hand. A moment later there was a swirl of smoke, and when the cloud cleared away it was possible to see that they were gone.

"That's almost the same thing that happened at the end of the kidnapping attempt," Alex commented in an un-steady voice. "And all those people are free of whatever was used to freeze them in place. What kind of magic user do they have anyway? A wizard?"

"Beats me," Tiran muttered, trying to pull himself to-gether. "Whatever he or she is, I don't like his or her methods. Was I dreaming alone, or did you go through that too?"

"Unfortunately I was right with you," Alex replied, her beautiful eyes looking haunted. "That last part of it—I felt that someone was trying to change my mind, but I refused to believe that you would hurt me."

"And I refused to *try* to hurt you," Tiran agreed, put-ting a gentle hand to her face. "That something tried to force me into doing it, but for me it just isn't possible. It must have been our double refusal that broke us out of whatever spell they had us under."

"And now we still have facing their challenge to look forward to," Alex said with a wan, bitter smile. "They must have been really disappointed, having to give up the kind of great edge they *would* have had. I mean, if we'd had to face them now, after going through all that.''

"The first part of it was pleasant," Tiran reminded her, then looked around at the milling people and guardsmen. "No one knows what's going on, so we'd better tell them—and then find out what sort of army is coming. It's a good thing those intruders understood that *our* people would not have fought for *them* if they'd defeated us now."

"Tiran, something isn't right here," Alex said, shaking her head hard as if to throw off an unacceptable idea. "While we're seeing about that army, let's also think about what went on. I have the feeling we're missing something important."

Tiran had the same feeling, but there really wasn't time now. He called over one of his fighters and sent the man to alert Damis and Gann, then went looking for his own magic user. Brandis still stood behind the two chairs Tiran and Alex had used, and by the time Tiran reached him he was frowning.

"What's wrong?" he asked at once, stepping out to meet Tiran. "What did he say to you?"

"He said there's an army on its way to attack the city," Tiran answered, studying the other man. "Weren't you listening in with magic? Didn't you notice anything strange even before that?"

"No, I didn't expect to *need* to listen in with magic," Brandis denied with a headshake. "And what do you mean by strange? You and Alex simply walked toward them, and then you paused for a moment before the man spoke to you. That *is* what happened, isn't it?"

"Not all of it by half," Tiran replied flatly, to keep the agitation out of his voice. "We'll talk about it later, after we find out what kind of forces are being sent against us and decide what to do about it. My people will meet us in that ground floor conference room I use, so let's get there first and find something to tell them."

He nodded and started back toward the palace, and after collecting Alex, Tiran followed. Their robes and crowns could be gathered up and returned to their apartment by members of the guard; at the moment, he and Alex had more important things to worry about. They reached the conference room only a minute or so behind Brandis, but the magic user was already seated in a chair and staring off into space.

"Looking for that information we need," Tiran murmured to Alex, nodding toward Brandis as he closed the door quietly. "I'm glad he's on it this fast, but I thought scrying required something to look into."

"So did I, but maybe not all magic users need it," Alex murmured back, rubbing at her neck with one hand. "I feel absolutely lousy, and my mind doesn't seem to want to do anything but remember those—*visions*. If I could get my hands on that magic user without his being able to *use* his magic . . ."

"I know, and I feel the same way," Tiran agreed, hesitating only a moment before putting an arm around her and drawing her close. "I became the sort of man I loathe and despise, and it didn't even bother me. Nothing is worth that high a price, not even being a king. Once we take care of this attack, we'll have to talk."

"About whether or not to stay here," Alex said with a nod. "I know we weren't shown what *will* happen, only what might, but that doesn't seem to make a difference. As long as it's even remotely possible, I'd rather not take the chance. But there's still something wrong."

Tiran found it really hard to push through his emotional reactions to reach objectivity, an effort he wasn't used to considering a chore. He was ready to be as logical as necessary where the coming attack was concerned, but as far as the rest of it went he couldn't seem to think straight. Just what Alex said *she* felt, and obviously for the same reason . . .

"We've been manipulated into wanting to give up the kingdom," Tiran said, struggling to put the conclusion into words. "That much is perfectly clear, but now that I've fought my way through to an understanding of what was done, the conviction is starting to fade. Is the same thing happening with you?"

"As a matter of fact it is, and that bothers me more than the conviction did," she answered, looking up at him with a frown. "If it was that easy to get rid of the implanted suggestion, why did they take the trouble to implant it in the first place? It can't possibly be this easy, Ti, so there's something we're not seeing."

"Maybe we're supposed to *think* there's something more when there really isn't" he suggested, letting her go so that he could reach to a bell cord and pull it three times for coffee. "That way we'll be so busy looking for what isn't there, we'll mess up everything else."

"Like defending against the attack?" she asked, considering the point, then she shook her head. "No, they want us to stop the attack, otherwise they wouldn't have warned us about it. We were so disoriented that they probably could have won against us easily, but they backed off to let us do what had to be done. If they were the ones behind the attack, they wouldn't have backed off and they wouldn't have warned us."

"Unless for some reason they thought they *couldn't* win, either against us in individual combat or against our people directing our army. Or maybe even both." Tiran shut his eyes and rubbed them, but that didn't erase his growing anger. "Damn it, all they do is jump out at us from the shadows, daring us to figure out where the real attack is coming from. I never knew it was possible to be this sick and tired of a situation. I wish—"

He cut his words off before he said the wrong thing, but glancing again at Alex showed *her* looking at *him.*

"You wish we'd never started this," she said rather than asked, her expression strange. "That's a holdover from whatever they did to us, and although it's fading, I also feel the same. Ti, what would happen if the two of us picked up right now and walked away? We'd take the company with us, of course, so what would happen?"

"The attacking army would take this city without a fight," Tiran answered slowly, trying to see what she was leading up to. "If it's Selwin's army he'd then declare himself king, but I doubt if he would live long enough to enjoy the victory. Those two who wanted to face *us* are Shapeshifters, so they'd reach Selwin no matter what kind of guard he had. After that ... Well, either they'd pretend to be Selwin and his wife for a while until things settled down, or they'd declare themselves the new king and queen by displaying Selwin's head. Either way they'd have what they want, and we'd be out of it.''

"Part of me wants to agree with that, but it just isn't true," Alex replied with an impatient headshake. "To begin with, Selwin's claim to the throne could be challenged by just about anybody if he simply walks in. He won't be defeating anyone to establish his legitimacy, so defeating *him* won't establish it either. You do remember how concerned those people are with legitimacy?''

"Yes, I do," Tiran muttered, beginning to see the light. "If we walked away they might take over, but they could never claim full legitimacy as rulers. For that they need us dead, so either we'd never be allowed to leave, or they'd have that magic user of theirs bring us back somehow. But I thought we messed up that particular plan by naming Bariden and Chalaine as our heirs. What happened to *that?*''

"I think what happened is that Bariden and Chalaine have their own troubles," Alex said slowly. "I just remembered that we're still supposed to be warded by them, but this enemy magic user has been wiping the floor with us. That has to mean they do have a wizard on their side, so we're definitely hip-deep in you know what as well as on our own. But none of that completely explains why we both want out of here, right now if not sooner. One way or another we *can't* leave, so what good does it do them?''

Tiran began to say he didn't know, but suddenly that wasn't the truth. He settled for saying certain select words and phrases under his breath instead, then turned to look at Alex.

"Attitude," he said, using it as the curse word it had become. "That's what makes the difference between winning and losing in a fight, *any* kind of fight. So what has *our* attitude become?''

"That we don't *want* to win," Alex groaned, turning away to run her hands through her hair. "Winning means we'd have to stay here, and we don't want to do that. Right now I'm trying to tell myself that we could always give up the throne once we won the fight, but who would we give it up *to?* We don't have eager heirs to dump it on, and there isn't even anyone around competent enough to *name* as heir.''

Tiran was about to add his own point when a knock at the door announced the arrival of the coffee. Two servants brought in trays with the service and cups, and once they were gone Tiran poured two cups and handed one to Alex.

''We also can't decide to just hand over the kingdom to the intruders in a ceremony that *would* legitimize their takeover,'' he said after glancing at Brandis to see that the magic user hadn't changed position. ''Considering the methods those two have been using against *us,* I can just imagine what they'd do to a bunch of helpless people under their rule. No matter how much I want out of here, I can't see getting it by throwing everyone to those conscienceless wolves.''

''And we really have to remember that we're supposedly the ones destined to rule this place,'' Alex said with a frown as she rubbed at her forehead. ''That point keeps trying to get away from me, but we can't afford to forget it. It means that even if we gave the kingdom to those two, they still couldn't afford to let us live. As long as we're alive, we can always decide to come back and challenge them.''

''And then it would be *us* coming out of the shadows without warning instead of them,'' Tiran agreed, also finding it hard to hang onto the thought. ''But we're not supposed to remember that, because it works against the attitude they want us to have. When you know your life is on the line, you tend to fight harder.''

''But I still don't really *want* to fight,'' Alex said after sipping at her coffee, looking up at him with quiet desperation. ''My mind just wants us to be out of here, and winning against those intruders won't accomplish that. What are we going to do, Ti?''

''I don't know,'' he admitted heavily, leaning against the edge of the table holding the coffee service. ''Reason isn't working too well with me either, so we'll just have to hope that Brandis has an idea. Or somebody.''

She nodded without much hope, and they each took a chair to wait for Brandis to come out of it. A few minutes later Gann arrived, and by the time he had coffee it was

Damis coming in. Tiran gave the two men a brief rundown on what was happening—including the problem he and Alex had—and then all four of them waited for Brandis to return to himself.

Which took a while. Damis was getting his second cup of coffee when Brandis suddenly stirred and took a deep breath. He then looked around at all of them and smiled faintly.

"Sorry that took so long, but I wanted to be sure," he said, then got up to stretch. "That 'army' is supposed to be impressive, but something seemed odd so I looked at it more closely. It's fairly large, but there's no middle to it. What I mean is, its formation suggests a lot more fighters than there are, with men spread very thinly toward the center. It's as if five or six hundred troops are missing."

"The villagers we freed," Tiran said at once, knowing he was right. "They meant to stuff them into the formation to fill out their numbers, but we spoiled the plan. Or at least we spoiled most of it. The last word I had from Rhodris yesterday was that the villages have now all been freed, but the men were missing from at least two of them, which means a good couple of hundred extra 'fighters' for our enemy. Did you see who's leading the attack?"

"Duke Selwin is there along with one other of the nobles," Brandis answered, going toward the table with the coffee. "I recognize the man, but don't remember his name. There's also someone in rust-colored leather, a very hard man to describe. He has medium brown hair and brown eyes, a face with no distinguishing marks, of average height and build ... If he hadn't been in rust leather, I might well have looked right past him."

"Jend Oblin," Gann and Damis said almost together, beating Tiran to it by no more than seconds.

"Who's Jend Oblin?" Alex asked, looking at the two. "Have any of you ever mentioned him? And even more importantly, is he any good?"

"He's—obsessed, I guess you could call it," Damis answered with a vague wave of his hand, Gann letting someone else do the talking as usual. "The man is one of the most average, ordinary people you've ever met, and that's what his obsession is based on. He hates being ordinary and wants more than anything else to be special, but he's never been able to manage it."

"And he detests Tiran," Gann added, his serious face even more concerned. "He's convinced himself that Tiran has systematically stolen commissions from him, and that's why Tiran's company prospered and was so much in demand—and his has barely scraped by and is unknown and unwanted. He's neither a good fighter nor a decent tactician, and if he hadn't bought his company with inherited gold, he'd be working as a clerk somewhere."

"So that means we won't have any trouble stopping him, right?" Alex said, looking around again. "If he's that pitifully bad, he might even take a wrong turn and end up in another kingdom instead of here."

"*He's* that bad, but his new assistant isn't," Tiran admitted when the other two men just glanced at each other and remained silent. "He took the man on about a year ago, and although Oblin *pretends* he still makes all the decisions, they really come from the new man. No one knows who he is, but he's damned good, which we found out the hard way. Five months ago they and we were on opposite sides of a commission, and if not for a lucky break they might well have taken us. They outnumbered us at least two to one."

"But we won instead, and Oblin almost started to foam at the mouth," Damis contributed with a sigh. "He actually came riding into our camp after everything was over, and stood there screaming at Tiran like a madman. It had been seven months since anyone had found it possible to best his company, but as soon as he came up against us he was stopped."

"Which fed his obsession even more, and now he has the chance to teach a final lesson to the man he hates most," Alex said with a weary nod. "That means he won't back off for any reason, and whether or not Selwin can pay him enough doesn't enter into it. He'd probably do it even if *he* had to pay."

"So we can expect some heavy fighting," Tiran summed up, then looked at Brandis. "Gann has a map of the kingdom, and we'll need you to mark it to show where the army is and tell us how quickly they're moving. I'll also need to know about Rhodris and the reinforcements I sent to him. If they ran into any part of Oblin's force, they could be taken or dead.''

"That was one of the first things I checked on, and they're neither,'' Brandis quickly assured him, coffee cup now in hand. ''My guess would be that they discovered the presence of the very large force and knew they were outnumbered, because they've evacuated the villages and have moved all the people well out of harm's way. And the army *isn't* moving yet. They've only just started to deploy in marching order.''

"That isn't what the intruder said, so this has to be a shadow move against us as well as an open attack,'' Tiran decided after a moment. ''But knowing Rhodris and his fighters are safe gives us additional options on what moves we can make. Let's see how that army is deployed, and then we can discuss the possibilities.''

"*I've* got a couple of ideas I'd like to present,'' Alex said slowly while Gann got up to spread out the map on a table. ''Selwin must have been delighted to have found someone obsessed with destroying you, Ti, but I think we can make that singlemindedness work against them.''

Tiran sincerely hoped she was right, but that didn't change the fact that they had a real fight ahead of them. Selwin couldn't yet know about Pavar, but he must have found out about the villagers being freed and that was why he was now beginning to move. He probably expected to be arrested as soon as word got out about what he'd done to his villagers, and under normal circumstances he would have been right.

But nothing was normal these days, not even Alex and himself. For a couple of people who were supposed to be better than almost everyone else, he and Alex weren't doing very well at all . . .

CHAPTER FOURTEEN

It wasn't quite dark yet, and we weren't going to be moving out until it was. Cadry and her entire group waited in the trees with me, our horses left much deeper in the wood. What we were going to do would be done on foot, and hopefully as quietly as the slowly falling dark.

In the meantime, I tried to think about what lay ahead in general, not in detail, since I felt strangely unsettled. The enemy forces had camped in their order of march, spread out to make it look as if there were a lot more of them, and strategically that was a good idea. But tactically it left them vulnerable to being taken on piecemeal, a small number of theirs by a larger number of ours. We would be hitting them all night all over their perimeter, and by morning there should be very little left. That little would be Oblin's core group, which would then, hopefully, decide that withdrawing was the smartest thing they could do. When Oblin refused, which he was almost certain to do, they would pull out without him, leaving him where Tiran could settle the problem he represented finally and completely. But before that . . .

"You wanna talk about it?" Cadry asked very softly from right next to me. "What you haven't been sayin' says a lot more than what you have."

"That doesn't make any sense," I decided after a moment, still staring out into the almost-dark nearly-night. "If it did, you'd want me to continue keeping quiet so you could find out everything."

"It makes more sense than you worryin' at somethin'

alone,'' she declared firmly, refusing to drop it. "If it's somethin' I don't know nothin' about, I'll say so.''

I hesitated, wondering if I *should* discuss it, then decided I might as well. I certainly wasn't getting anywhere thinking about it alone.

"You know that what we're about to do was my idea?" I asked, finally turning to see her nod. "Well, strategically and tactically it's one of the best things we *can* do, but when you get to the reality of it I'm not sure if it's *right*. People are going to be dying in large numbers, but it won't be fighting, it'll be slaughter. If we're the good guys, should we be indulging in slaughter?''

"You'd rather have us go out and take on a larger, mostly experienced group face to face?" she said, then immediately waved a hand to erase the question. "No, scratch that, 'cause that *is* the way we usually do it, more or less. If we'd started this fight, I'd have the same trouble with sneakin' up on people in the dark while they were sleepin' and takin' them out. But did we start this fight? Did we invite them to come after us?''

"Selwin probably thinks we did," I couldn't help pointing out. "If we'd stepped aside and let him take over, he wouldn't be out here with an army now.''

"No, he'd probably be makin' plans to enslave the rest of the kingdom the way he did with those villages," Cadry countered, watching me closely. "Did those village men *ask* to be trained as fighters while their women and kids were forced into the fields? And these fighters we'll be goin' after in a little while . . . were any of 'em *forced* to go along with this?''

"Okay, the answer is no to both questions," I allowed sourly, "but that still doesn't mean we're doing right. We're doing what we have to to keep Selwin out of power, but that means we're using the end to justify *our* means. Most people don't think much of that sort of thing.''

"Most people don't think much, *period*," Cadry said with a snort. "Sayin' that the end don't justify the means is usin' fancy-soundin' words that don't mean anythin' in real life. We could play this fair and keep our consciences clear, and we might even win. But a lot of our people would die makin' it happen, and since we didn't start this I don't consider *that* fair. Do you?''

I had to shake my head, because I really didn't. If you're just standing there minding your own business and someone starts a fight with you, it's not only your right to finish it, it's also your duty. The next person who gets picked on might not be *able* to finish it—or even to hold his or her own—so if you *can* stop what's happening but don't, you're directly responsible for what's done to those attacked after you.

"Or we could lose," Cadry continued grimly. "People would still be dead, theirs and ours both, but then even worse would happen. Selwin would be in charge, and he'd start right in to make sure he stayed in charge. Would the people who had to live their lives under his rule thank us for playin' fair and keepin' our consciences clear? Would people watch their families bein' torn apart and their lives destroyed and be *glad* we didn't use ugly means to bring about the end of allowin' them freedom and the chance at happiness? *You* tell *me*, Alex.''

"No, only damned fools worry about ideals when reality means the misery of actual people," I answered after letting out a deep breath. "Everyone should have his or her own set of standards, but when you put your own idea of what's right above the obvious misery of others, you've stepped over the line. So we do what we have to, even if it turns our stomach.''

"Stomach-turnin's easier to take than watchin' little kids fall over dead in a field from bein' worked too hard," Cadry said more gently but just as flatly. "The fighters in this army had a choice about bein' here, so they've got no kick comin'. You can't complain when you get what you asked for.''

I nodded firmly to show I really did agree, at the same time wondering what was wrong with me *this* time. Cadry had sounded the way I usually did, since these were all things I'd considered while growing up. But suddenly everything seemed to have changed, not to different ideas and outlooks but to a muddle of confusion and uncertainty. I didn't know where I was coming from or going, and wasn't sure I *wanted* to know.

"I just got an idea, so I think it's a good thing we had that little discussion," Cadry said, distracting me from personal chaos. "How sure are we that Rhodris got to free *all* the villages Selwin took over? What about the ones belongin' to the other nobles with him?"

I cursed briefly under my breath, because I already had the answer to that—and Cadry should have known the same.

"We found out yesterday that Rhodris freed all the villages, but the men were missing from a couple of them," I told her with a frown. "Wasn't the word on that passed to you? We're supposed to be watching for those villagers, to make sure they don't accidently end up dead."

"Never heard anythin' about it," Cadry said with her own frown. "Somewhere along the line somebody forgot to pass the word, and that ain't gonna help those village men."

That was an understatement if I'd ever heard one, but rather than waste any more time we took care of repairing the omission. While Cadry called her people together, I went to the group of six messengers that had been assigned to me. I picked out two of them, told them to pass the word to be on the alert for the presence of any impressed troops, then sent them off to the other groups on either side of us. Since there was still time before we were scheduled to move, the word should reach everyone involved; but even if it didn't there was more than a little cause to hope for the best. Impressed troops were more likely to be toward the center of the formation than toward the perimeter, so hopefully they would be all right.

The rest of that night wasn't something any of us was proud of, but we still got the job done. Those of us who could Shapeshift took out the sentries, and then the rest of our group went after the sleeping troops in that area of the camp. We'd gone on to the third section before we found an indication that there *were* impressed fighters on the perimeter: a tentful of men who were chained to stakes driven into the ground. After we took care of the troops all around them we woke them, got them free of the chains, then got them safely into the woods. Some of them actually cried with relief, which did a lot to quiet the clamoring in my head.

After that I simply remembered that the fighters must have known there were literal slaves among them and hadn't done anything to change the situation or walk away from it, and had less trouble with putting them down. Simply standing by and letting something wrong continue to go on doesn't make you innocent of actually doing the something wrong. I'd learned that from my father years earlier, and swore not to forget it again. No matter what happened.

Every now and then the targeted troops woke up and we had to fight rather than slaughter, but that was perfectly all right with us. The groups were spread out much too far from each other, which meant no one heard the minimal amount of noise. I couldn't understand *why* they were so spread out, unless it had been Oblin's idea that he could simply scare Tiran into running from what looked like a really large army. That would have brought him an incredible amount of satisfaction, but it just proved the man wasn't in touch with reality in any way at all.

When we reached a section of the camp that had no one alive left in it, we knew we'd come to the end of our own section and were finished for the night. We hadn't lost any of our own people and had freed three sets of chained villagers, and now *we* were free to meet the rest of our people at the rendezvous point. We headed back to the woods with a lot of relief but also with caution, and retraced our steps to the horses we'd left hours earlier.

Only to find the horses surrounded, but not by enemy troops. The villagers we'd freed were sitting all around the horses, apparently waiting for us to get back. When we appeared they got quickly to their feet, and one of them stepped forward with nervous determination.

"Need t'talk t'whoever's in charge," the man said, looking around at each of us he could see. It was dark there in the woods, all of us shadows to one another where the moonlight failed to reach through the branches, but that man had carefully placed himself right in a stream of moonlight.

"Makin' sure we see he's weaponless," Cadry murmured to me, the rest of her attention on the man as well as on the ones behind him. "You gonna talk to him?"

I was about to say of course I would, when the suspicion of a certain line of logic forced its way into my mind. I considered the thought for a moment, and then I quickly whistled the signal for separate-and-get-to-cover. Happily, Tiran's people are well trained. No one hesitated to obey the signal, so in little more than an instant we had all melted back into the darkness and out of sight of our reception committee. They all made sounds of surprise, but some of them also began to curse.

"No, wait, we gotta talk t'ya!" the spokesman called desperately, trying to search the dark with his eyes. The rest of my people were putting some distance between them and their location, but I'd just moved back a little and Shifted. A handy bush hid my fox body from easy sight, but *I* had to see what went on to know if I'd been right. Everyone stood where they were for another moment or two, and then one of the "villagers" came forward with three other men at his back.

"They didn't listen to you, boy," the man who had come forward said to the one who had spoken, his tone flat and accusing. "You were supposed to *make* them listen, but you failed. You do know what that means, don't you?"

"Please, it waren't my fault!" the first man begged, pure terror in his own tone. "I tried, you seen I tried, but they still run off! They cain't do nuthin' t'our famlies, not when it waren't our fault!"

"But our people with your wives and children won't see it like that," the second man said, clearly enjoying the first man's terror. "Even if the bunch of you here somehow manage to stay alive, your families won't—not unless we send word to say you've done what you were told to. Now I want half of you to spread out and find those fighters, and then convince them to take all of us along to wherever they're going. And in case you were wondering, this is your last chance to get it right."

The first man began to babble assurances that they *would* get it right no matter what, but I'd heard enough. While I'd been listening I'd been joined by a badger and a porcupine, the two other Shapeshifters I'd been working with. I Shifted back to natural just long enough to whisper, "The one on the right and the three behind him," and then I Shifted to my fighting form.

For some reason it seemed like years rather than weeks since I'd last been in fighting form, and it felt unexpectedly good. Fighting form seems to have a stronger link to natural form than any other for Shapeshifters, almost like a second, *nearly* natural, personality. No one seems to know exactly why that is, but it's certainly related to the fact that your fighting form does have a direct connection to the basic *you* inside. Shifting to fighting form felt like "coming home," but I didn't have the time to just stand there and enjoy it.

My two companions followed my example and Shifted to their own fighting forms, and once they were ready I led the attack. My puma form covered the distance between me and the man who had spoken in two bounding strides, and a swipe of my paw opened the man's throat and cut short his scream of terror. The third man behind him, on the extreme left, came into clear sight when the first collapsed, and he was in the midst of digging frantically inside his tunic. It wasn't hard to guess that he was digging for a hidden weapon, but there was no reason to let him reach it. Another, shorter, bound let me knock him down, and an instant later his throat was also open.

With all that blood around, the urge to go feral was almost overwhelming. But I was used to having a problem with that, so I forced myself to Shift back to natural. Once I did I saw that my brother Shapeshifters had also seen to their targets, and were again following my example by Shifting back to natural.

"No," a voice moaned, and I looked up to see the real village man standing with one hand to his head and one to his middle. "No! You kilt 'em, an' now our famlies'll be done th' same! Our wimmin 'n little 'uns—!"

"Stop it!" I snapped, trying to bring him out of it before he went crazy from grief. "Your families are safe. Do you hear me? These men were lying to you or maybe just hoping, but they were wrong. Your families are safe!"

"How c'n thet be?" the man demanded after something

of a hesitation, the others happily following his example and listening rather than working themselves up. "They left some uv theirs with our wimminfolk 'n kids, swearin' they'd die if'n any a us gave 'em trouble. Then they said—how c'n our famlies be safe?"

"They're safe because by now we've cleared the intruders out of *every* village," I told them slowly and clearly, trying to make the words sink in. "You may have noticed that they don't have as many men in this army as they expected to, and that's because we were able to free some of the villages *before* the men were taken away from them. Those men have been helping us with the rest of the villages, and earlier today we got word that all villages involved in this mess are now clear. Your families are *safe!*"

They all hesitated for a moment, as if afraid to believe me, but then they realized they had to. If I were lying to them their families were already lost, and they couldn't bear the thought of that. When they began to move together to reassure one another, Cadry and the rest of her fighters appeared around us out of the dark.

"Thought for a minute we'd have more slaughterin' to do," Cadry murmured with relief when she stopped next to me. "Glad we didn't, since their families *are* okay. How'd you know there was somethin' wrong?"

"I didn't *know,* I only guessed," I told her, watching the dark shadows who were the villagers. None of them held back from joining the others, and none of them was being avoided or drawn away from. That should mean we'd gotten all the pretenders, but there was only one way to be certain.

"I think you men ought to head for home now," I said, loudly enough to break through their low-voiced discussions. "Your families have to be desperately worried about you, and we ourselves have things to do."

They all agreed with that with enthusiasm, and a couple of them apparently knew where they were. Those men pointed in the right direction and began to lead the way, and a minute later they were all gone from sight.

"Now we have to ride fast and hard," I said to Cadry, then held up a hand. "And before you ask me again, the very fact that these men did *not* immediately head for home was what made me suspicious. Guards had been left in their village to guarantee their good behavior, something they *had* to know, but not one of them had taken off for home to help the women and children. That made no sense at all, not unless they were being forced to stay.''

"But why were those four in with 'em?'' Cadry demanded with confusion. "To catch us in a trap? If so, then why didn't they give the alarm and bring over a bigger force than we'd be able to handle?''

"Because that's not what they were put in with the villagers to do,'' I explained as I led the way closer to the horses. "They were there to make the villagers ask us to let them go to the rendezvous with us, probably under the pretext of wanting to fight the people who had enslaved them. That would have brought them right to where Tiran was, and who would have wasted time keeping a group of freed slaves under observation?''

"Damn that Oblin,'' Cadry growled, her voice sounding more than angry. "He spread his forces out so we'd be able to come in and take 'em, sacrificin' those fighters just to sneak assassins in close to the boss. What the hell kind of thing is *that* to do?''

"A potentially war-winning kind of thing,'' I answered, swinging up into my saddle. "If the other groups also found 'slaves' and freed them, there have to be other assassins in among them. I've got to find Tiran and warn him. You take your people and try to locate any other 'freed villagers.' ''

I know she said something in acknowledgement, but I didn't wait around to hear it. I headed my horse through the trees at the fastest pace possible, and once we reached the road that had brought us to that area I kicked him into a gallop. Tiran was out with another group, doing the same thing I'd been doing, which meant he also must have freed some "slaves.'' My only hope was that none of the assassins would recognize him, and therefore would have to wait until everyone reached the rendezvous.

But it was a very slim hope, and one I couldn't quite bring myself to count on. Most experienced mercenary fighters knew Tiran by sight as well as reputation, and they could have decided *not* to wait. They might have already attacked him, already completed the mission Oblin had sacrificed hundreds of lives to pull off . . .

I was so torn apart by that thought that I almost missed the way I reacted to the concept of "experienced mercenary fighters." If the sudden chill and touch of terror over the phrase hadn't been really extreme I *would* have missed it, losing it in my fear for Tiran's life. But when your blood runs even colder than you expected it to, when your mouth turns dry, your hands tremble, and your knees try to turn weak . . . Something was definitely wrong, but I didn't have the *time* to think about it, not when Tiran's life was being threatened.

By the time I reached our rendezvous point, I'd forced away most of those unexplained feelings of fear and illness. Or at least I'd set them aside for a time. I could feel them hanging on and waiting to take me over again as soon as I quit fighting them, like an unstoppable ocean waiting to drown a tiring swimmer. But first I had to make sure Tiran was all right; that *had* to come before anything else.

The rendezvous point was a tent hidden in the woods just off the road from a giant oak, and in the tent Brandis waited. He'd put a spell on the tent so that no one who wasn't supposed to see it *would* see it, and he was there to help us know what effect our night's work had on the leaders of the invading army. Once everyone got back he was supposed to set up a scrying pool in a basin so we could watch what went on, but right now there was something more important for him to look for.

I pulled my horse to a stop, jumped off, and ran into the tent. In the light of the single lamp Brandis looked up in surprise, but before he could say anything I beat him to it.

"Brandis, quick, you have to tell me where Tiran is!" I panted out. "They've set a trap for him, assassins among the impressed villagers. I have to get to him before one of the assassins does!"

"Calm down, Alex," he soothed immediately. "I'll find Tiran and send a message sphere, which will be much faster than you riding after him. Now tell me again, but in detail."

So I told him again, more slowly than the first time but not much. Brandis listened carefully, nodded, then spoke a spell, which apparently satisfied *him* but didn't do much for me. He must have seen that, since he spoke another spell which produced a second comfortable chair like the one he sat in, a small table next to it with a cup of coffee on it, and a large, water-filled basin between the two chairs.

"Why don't you make yourself comfortable, and we'll watch what Tiran does together," he suggested, gesturing toward the chair. I hesitated briefly, wishing I could *be* with Tiran rather than just watch him, but Brandis's way was much more practical. So I took the chair and reached for the coffee, and by the time I did Brandis had already moved his hands over the basin and muttered something.

At first there was nothing in the basin but motionless water, then suddenly the water began to move. It looked as if it were *clearing,* the way heavy fog does when the sun comes up, slowly and in patches. I saw the area first, a part of the army camp that looked just like the parts I'd seen personally, and then people began to appear. I recognized members of the group Tiran had gone out with, and then, finally, I saw Tiran himself. He still seemed to be all right and was apparently ready to leave the area, but then he stopped short and just stared.

"The message sphere just reached him," Brandis interpreted, relieving my instant worry. "Apparently he took a larger part of the camp than he gave to you and the others, so he hasn't quite finished. Which turns out to be a lucky thing."

"I'll say," I muttered, watching the tiny Tiran come out of it and look around. Then he gestured over some of his people, and began to speak to them in a whisper. After a moment they nodded and moved off again, obviously heading for other members of the group. Tiran himself seemed to be thinking about something, but not something easily decided. When he finally moved off, he didn't look as if he'd made up his mind.

"And that should be that," Brandis said, moving his hand across the basin and clearing the picture from it. "It won't be long before the king is here to join us, and then we can establish a watch on this Jend Oblin and Duke Selwin and the others. Is there anything I can do for you until then?''

I was about to say yes, I did have another problem, but when I stopped to think about it I couldn't remember what it was. I wracked my brain for a minute, feeling stupid, but whatever I'd meant to talk to him about was simply gone.

"I think there *was* something, but it couldn't have been very important," I decided aloud after taking another sip of coffee, delighted that the cup seemed to be refilling automatically. "Are you ready for your part of this if Oblin's people don't decide to pick up and walk away?"

"You mean healing the wounded of the battle that will come?" he asked with a sigh. "I'm prepared, of course, but I don't think I'll ever be 'ready.' Setting large groups of men and women against each other seems like a horrible thing to do, and I wish it didn't have to be."

"We all wish that, but it happens to be reality," I told him gently, almost feeling his upset. "As long as there are people around who are willing to take what they want by force, others have to be ready to resist them. Giving them what they want is no solution, since giving in only encourages that sort to want more and more. And makes others think they can get what *they* want in the same way. Being ready and willing to fight usually means you won't have to, but when the time comes for doing it, all you can do is make it as brief and decisive as possible."

"I'll have to take your word for that," Brandis said with a faint smile. "I'm not qualified to have an opinion on these things. My bias against confrontations and violence, you understand . . . How about something to eat?"

"Maybe later," I said with a headshake and as much of a smile as I could manage. I might be what Brandis wasn't, but there had been too much slaughter that night for anyone claiming to be sane. Even if those who had been killed had deserved it. Doing what's necessary doesn't also mean enjoying it.

And while I waited, maybe I'd manage to remember what in hell I'd wanted to talk to Brandis about . . .

CHAPTER FIFTEEN

Tiran stopped short in shocked surprise when the large bubble appeared suddenly in front of him, and he almost tried to avoid letting it touch him. He couldn't help remembering the message sphere that had been sent to the male intruder by his wizard-accomplice, and for an instant thought that *this* message sphere had the same source. But before he could move it had melted into him, and he had the message from Brandis.

Or, rather, the message from Alex. The woman's instincts were incredible, and every time she did something like this he found himself delighted. Putting something past her *would* take more than most people had, and he'd have to remember to tell her again how much he appreciated her. But first he had other things to tell other people. Fasin Wohl and some of his fighters stood not far away, so Tiran called over the group chief and squad leaders.

"Fasin, I've just gotten a message sphere from Brandis, sent because Alex learned something important," Tiran told them in a very low voice. "Do you remember those two groups of villagers we freed from the shackles, and how we wondered why they were here on the perimeter? Well, Alex found out why."

He told them quickly about the assassins, and that both groups of villagers which had been freed would probably be waiting for them near the horses.

"So we'll have to prepare a decent response before we go back," Fasin whispered with a shrug, then grinned.

231

"Too bad for them it was too dark for them to recognize you when they were near you the first time."

"They have all my sympathy," Tiran returned dryly before shaking his head. "But it won't be as easy as you're picturing. We first have to separate out the assassins from the innocent villagers, and then we have to keep the villagers out of the fight without hurting them. When a man thinks his family's lives depend on what he does, you can't expect him to act rationally. Get the rest of your fighters together, and we'll have a short discussion about it once we're back in among the trees."

Fasin and his squad leaders nodded and went off to get the rest of the group together, but Tiran stood there for another moment to think. It followed logically that the assassins would know where Oblin was waiting to hear that his trick had worked, so Tiran had to decide whether or not to try to get that information. It would make things easier—and save lives—if he took Oblin out tonight, but he found himself suspicious of easy solutions. They'd anticipated having their perimeter raided, and had planned accordingly by having assassins planted in the safest of places. Didn't it also stand to reason that they would expect him to capture an assassin and force the man to talk?

It certainly did, so he'd have to consider the wisdom of springing the trap anyway. But there was time for thinking about that and the assembled group was waiting, so he joined them and they all went back to the woods. Tiran had started out that night wondering why it seemed too easy to take apart the army that was supposed to have such a good tactician. Now he knew the answer, which meant he and Alex and their fighters just might pull it off after all.

"So how are we going to handle this?" Fasin asked once they were far enough into the trees. "Our sector of perimeter is all taken care of, so it's time to get the horses. Suppose I sent half the group to collect them, and they tell the farmers they don't have the authority to let them come along? That might flush out the assassins, making them come forward with complaints if nothing else."

"Alex said it was a real villager who was made to do all the talking," Tiran told him with a headshake. "They

think the safety of their families is at stake, remember, so
they'll be the ones who do the insisting. What we need is
a way to separate the sheep from the wolves without putting the sheep in danger, and that means a decoy. We have
to—"

"I volunteer to play decoy," Fasin interrupted at once,
then he grinned wolfishly. "And since we all know *you*
can't be risked, Captain, you have to accept my offer."

"Guess again," Tiran countered with his own feral grin,
deflating Fasin's. "We're all risking everything here, so
no one is more important than anyone else. But in a way
I'll still be taking you up on your offer, so you can stop
looking so worried. The decoys will be you and me and
one of your squad leaders."

"*One?*" all three of the squad leaders squawked, almost
in unison. Then each of them started a low-voiced lecture
as to why *he* should be the one, or a second if someone
else was chosen first. They knew better than to be really
loud, but Fasin still held up a hand to silence them.

"You heard the captain. Just one," he stated, ending
the argument. "Once we hear the plan, we'll toss a coin
to see which of you gets to go. What'll we be doing,
Captain?"

"Once we reach the horses, we three will move off to
one side to discuss 'something important,' " Tiran answered with swallowed amusement. "When the villager
comes forward to ask about coming along with us, whoever he talks to will answer very casually that the man
can ask *the king* when he finishes conferring with his men.
He'll then gesture in our direction, and go back to paying
attention only to what he'd been doing before being
interrupted."

"You men hear that?" Fasin asked, looking around at
everyone. "We don't know which of you will be approached, so you all have to be ready to look and sound
casual. And if you're the one, *don't* try to watch what the
farmer will do next. You just play uninterested, and leave
the watching to those assigned to do it."

"And that will be the two squad leaders who aren't
with the rest of us," Tiran continued, watching the men
nod with understanding. "They'll make sure they're hid-

den by the rest of you men, so they'll be able to watch without being seen. When the assassins find out that I'm right there they should decide to attack, using their entire force in an effort to reach me. But they *may* keep one of their number in reserve, just in case their open attack fails. That's what I want our two watchers to watch for.''

"And even though everybody else'll be playing casual, you'd all better be ready," Fasin added again. "If the assassins decide to cover their try by having the farmers attack the rest of you, I want those farmers laid out fast. You shouldn't have to kill them, but keep in mind that there could be an assassin left behind to continue playing farmer. If it comes down to it, I'd rather have one of them dead than one of you.''

Tiran couldn't argue with that, and didn't even try. He felt sorry for the position the village men had been put in, but not sorry enough to sacrifice his people in an effort that might not even save them. All he could do was hope, and that he'd already started.

Fasin took his three squad leaders aside, and in a moment the one who would play decoy was chosen. The other two were disappointed, but having special assignments soothed them a little. It wasn't too dark where they currently stood, not with the moon shining down through the trees, and it ought to be just the same where the horses were tied. When the fight started, everyone should be able to see what they were doing.

They made their way toward the horses, and Tiran spent the time reviewing his plan. Having only two men standing with him ought to encourage the assassins to make a try for him right there, getting them out from the middle of the villagers the easy way. If they didn't make their move he'd have to let the villagers know that their families were safe, which ought to get the assassins *pointed* out. One way or the other he wanted them taken care of right here, before they went to rendezvous with everyone else. The other groups would certainly have been given villagers and assassins of their own, and there was no sense in adding to his enemies' strength.

When they reached the vicinity of the horses, there was no opportunity to wonder if the plans would go to waste.

The moonlight clearly showed the men sitting on the ground waiting for them, so Tiran took Fasin and his squad leader to one side and pretended to get into an intense conversation with them. He stood with his back to the villagers, so it was Fasin, pretending to look at him, who actually watched what was going on.

"One of them just got up and stopped one of the men," Fasin reported in a murmur. "I can't make out who it is, but it looks like he's doing it right. He threw a thumb over his shoulder in our direction, then went on to the horses . . . And the farmer went back to the others after looking in our direction."

"If this works, don't pay any attention to whoever comes over until they're almost on top of us," Tiran murmured back. "But keep an eye on the man who first did the talking. If he's one of the ones who come over, I want to know about it."

"No problem," Fasin returned. "He's crouched down talking to somebody now, and if there isn't a ripple of some kind going through that group, I've never seen hidden excitement. Or nervousness, more likely. The one he's talking to isn't saying anything, probably thinking about it . . . and now he's got his mind made up. He's saying some things . . . the farmer's sitting down while the one he talked to and two others are getting up. Looks like they're going to try it without a diversion."

Tiran felt exposed and vulnerable with his back to the assassins, but turning around now would ruin everything. He'd have to wait until they got close enough, but then . . .

"They're on their way," Fasin reported, only the faint tightening in his tone showing his reaction to that news. "They're trying to play farmer, but they're not moving slow and cautious enough, and their shoulders are too straight. Even a farmer volunteering to help would be more nervous about coming over . . . They're glancing around, but only to see if anybody intends to stop them . . . Nobody's paying attention, so they're going for it . . . Now!"

Tiran took that as his cue to turn quickly, and the timing was perfect. Three men stood about four or five feet away, and they stopped abruptly when Tiran faced them.

"Was there something you wanted?" he drawled to the

three, seeing the casual way two of them had a hand under their tunics. The third had his right hand hanging down straight at his side, and it didn't look empty.

"We—ah—wanted t'ask somethin'," the one in the middle, with something in his hand, responded hesitantly. "It's real important, but it won't take no more 'n a—"

He'd been drifting forward as he spoke, and as soon as he was close enough he forgot about making excuses and simply attacked. Tiran was aware of the other two also trying to close with him, and now all three held daggers out in plain sight. He grabbed the wrist of the one in the middle even as he kicked the one on his right, leaving the one on his left to be intercepted by Fasin.

But the one whose wrist he held wasn't accounted for quite that easily. He kicked hard into Tiran's middle, freeing his wrist, and then that dagger was coming back at him again. Tiran ducked out of the way while he recovered his breath, then blocked another kick from the assassin. The kick was accompanied by a slash of the dagger, as if the assassin didn't care where he reached Tiran as long as he reached him *somewhere*.

"The blades are poisoned!" Tiran called out as soon as he realized that, hoping neither of his men had already been touched. Fasin's squad leader had engaged the third assassin, and the triple fight was fast and furious.

But not for long. The rest of the fighters in the group hadn't been asleep, and three of them had gotten their bows. When Tiran shouted his warning they took it as a signal, and a moment later there was the hum-thud! of arrows flying and hitting. The assassin in front of Tiran, who had been trying doggedly to reach him with that dagger, stiffened suddenly, tried to make one last effort, then collapsed to the ground.

A glance around showed Tiran that the other two were down as well, and little wonder. The three fighters who had loosed were primarily bowmen, whose training included letting fly at targets in deeper dark than what was around them. The villagers had all come to their feet, but since none of them was rushing forward in solitary attack, Tiran was able to turn to his nearest companions.

"Are you two all right?" he asked. "You weren't scratched even once, were you?"

"No," Fasin answered while the squad leader simply shook his head. They were in the midst of kicking away the daggers before making sure the assassins were dead, and one of the other fighters had come forward to do the same with Tiran's late opponent. That gave Tiran the chance to notice how the villagers were stirring in agitation, so he stepped toward them before they lost their heads and did something stupid.

"Listen to me, you men," he said loudly enough for all of them to hear. "You were probably forced into cooperating with those three because they threatened your families, but they were lying to you. Your families aren't in their power any longer, not since we finished clearing the last village yesterday. Your families are safe, and if I have anything to say about it, they'll never be threatened again."

A different kind of stirring and murmuring began, this time one filled with hope, and then they were being bombarded with questions. Everyone in the group did his best to reassure the men, but it took a while before they really believed what they were told. When they also found out that they weren't being detained, they hurried off in what must have been the direction of their village.

"My men tell me that they don't believe any assassins were left among the farmers, and I tend to agree," Fasin said once the villagers had disappeared into what was left of the night. "If any outsider had still been among them, those farmers probably would have torn him apart."

"That's too bad," Tiran said with a sigh. "I would have enjoyed having one of them to question. Ah, well, I'll just have to try again with the ones who'll be taken to the rendezvous point."

Fasin frowned at that, as if he'd forgotten there would be more assassins, but he followed Tiran to the horses without comment. Logic said they would probably play the same decoy game again, and he probably had no desire to gamble his place in the game by pestering Tiran.

They were cautious in making their way to where Brandis waited, and they got there without incident. The moon was beginning to set, but there was still enough light to see that everyone else had apparently gotten there before them. Tiran looked around for the villagers who should also have been there, and when he didn't see any he went straight to Brandis's tent for an explanation.

Alex was in his arms almost before he stepped inside, so for a moment he was happily distracted. When they'd each made sure the other was all right and had exchanged a brief kiss, Tiran forced himself back to business.

"So what happened to the villagers the other groups should have brought back?" he asked Alex and Brandis both, one arm still around Alex. "I was hoping to take one of those assassins alive for questioning."

"It didn't work out that way," Alex answered with a shrug. "I sent Cadry and her people to the other groups while I came here to get a warning to *you*, and one way or another they all flushed the assassins from among the villagers. And once the village men found out their families and homes were safe again, they headed back as fast as their legs could take them."

"What questions did you intend to ask the assassins, Your Majesty?" Brandis put in from where he stood. He'd risen when Tiran had walked in, and had quickly produced another chair together with a small table and coffee cup.

"I wanted to know where Oblin is right now, and if he's waiting for me to come after him," Tiran replied as he headed toward the waiting coffee. "My finding out where he is and going after him is probably part of his strategist's overall plan, but that kind of thing can sometimes be turned around to bite the planner rather than the one being planned against."

"Not if the planner knows that the one being planned against is all but guaranteed to see that part of the trap," Alex disagreed from where she'd stopped, near her own coffee. "They have to be expecting the possibility of you trying to spring the trap without getting caught, Ti, and that means they're ready and waiting with more than they believe you can handle. The only way you'd have a chance against that would be to take our entire army with you, but that's what we were supposed to be trying to avoid by going out tonight. Have you changed your mind about not wanting an all-out engagement?''

"No," Tiran granted, after taking a long, satisfying swallow of coffee. "I haven't changed my mind, but I can't help thinking that we might be passing up a chance to end this right now, tonight. If I can take Oblin out of the picture, Selwin and his friends will be caught with their backs to a wall that isn't there any longer. When they tried to lean on it, they'd just fall over. But there's no sense in wishful thinking, not when there aren't any assassins to question.''

"Excuse me, Your Majesty, but you don't really *need* any assassins to question," Brandis put in diffidently. "I can find the man Oblin, and we can also learn whether or not he's set a trap that you would have trouble getting out of.''

"Of course, by scrying," Alex exclaimed, then turned toward Tiran again. "That's how we found *you,* so Brandis would know where to send my message.''

"Then let's take a look," Tiran said, much of the disturbance he'd felt disappearing. Maybe it *would* be possible to finish this tonight ... "What do we have to do, Brandis?''

"Nothing but get comfortable in your chair," the magic user answered with a smile. "The rest is up to me.''

And it certainly was. As soon as Tiran was seated and Alex had taken her own chair, Brandis raised his arms and spoke a spell. A large basin of water appeared in the loose circle of their three chairs, but the water was both cloudy and misty. Almost at once the mist and clouds began to clear, and by the time Brandis was also seated Tiran could see a picture in the water.

The picture was of Jend Oblin, but it wasn't anything like a portrait. This picture moved as Oblin paced back and forth in what looked like a field tent, his very ordinary face now showing extreme impatience. He strode back and forth another half dozen times, then suddenly paused in mid step when someone else entered the tent.

"The scout came back to report that it's done, Jend," a boyish voice said, then the boy himself, about sixteen or seventeen years old, came forward to join Oblin in the picture. "The perimeter is devastated, but d'Iste took the bait. It may soon be over, brother."

"Where d'Iste is concerned, you can always expect the worst, little brother," Oblin said to the boy, not very kindly. "If my fighters don't get him, how do you know he won't attack in strength? I know he'll come, but why not with most of his company?"

"I've already explained that, Jend," the boy said with a sigh. "From what you and others have told me about the man, he's most likely to try to find you tonight, when you shouldn't be expecting him, which means he'll try to sneak up on you. It isn't possible to sneak up on someone with a full company when they're in the middle of a camp, so he'll come with only a squad at most. He may decide you *might* be expecting him, but I'm betting he's too arrogant to believe you'll have anything he can't handle."

Arrogant. Tiran glanced at Alex when he heard that, and she met his glance with a shrug and faint smile. He could have wasted his breath trying to deny the charge, but the conversation in the water basin was continuing.

"But I *do* have more than he can handle," Oblin said with grim satisfaction. "Three groups of my best fighters, two sleeping in shifts while the third group stands hidden sentry posts. When d'Iste shows up he'll find himself surrounded in a moment, helpless no matter what he tries. He'll only have that squad with him, so he'll be *mine*."

"And you'll have to put him down fast, before he says the wrong thing," the boy advised nervously. "You told the others that you sent volunteers for him to capture and question, and that's why you expect him to be here. If they ever found out we sacrificed members of the company along with all those new recruits out on the perimeter ... I don't think knowing that would sit well with them."

"What difference does it really make?" Oblin demanded with a gesture of dismissal. "Once d'Iste is dead it will all have been worth it, especially since most of those recruits would have died in the first real battle anyway. As for the members of the company, they were the worst and newest we had—except for the ones put in among the villagers. I'll need to recruit a new personal squad, which won't be easy, but with d'Iste finally gone even that will be worth it.''

"Jend . . . I've already told you why I think d'Iste will be here," the boy said hesitantly. "That does happen to be the most likely result of the planning, but you don't seem to be considering that the least likely can also happen. You have to be ready for the possibility that he may *not* come.''

"That can't happen," Oblin denied with a violent shake of his head, his expression now savage. "No one has ever gotten around your planning, and no one ever will—especially not d'Iste! He'll come and we'll take him, and no one will ever find out what we did! And tomorrow it won't matter that we no longer have an actual army. Theirs won't have a leader, so they'll have no choice but to surrender.''

"And then we can collect the gold that duke promised us, and use it to build up the company again," the boy said with a distracted nod. "We'll blame the massacre at the perimeter on a dead man, and we'll be innocent as well as victorious. It ought to work—as long as d'Iste actually shows up.''

"He will!" Oblin said like a litany. "He *will* show up, he *will!* All we have to do now is wait.''

And with that, Oblin went back to pacing. The boy, looking the least bit less sure, went to sit down on the tent floor next to a large water skin which probably didn't contain water. They waited a short while, but nothing else was said.

"What do you think they'll do when you *don't* show up?" Alex finally asked as she leaned back in her chair. "Oblin obviously isn't sane when it comes to you, and his younger brother seems to be the sort willing to do anything to please him. Do you know Oblin well enough to make a guess?''

"It isn't possible to know a crazy man well enough for that," Tiran said with a sigh and a headshake. "But they almost know *me* well enough to end my career *and* my life. It isn't always arrogance when you think you can do anything; sometimes it's stupidity. The trick seems to be to learn which is which . . . Well, that's beside the point.

Now I think we need to modify our plans for the morning.''

"By countering Oblin's storytelling to his fighters with the truth," Alex agreed with a nod. "So how do we let them know that their own captain betrayed them? It has to be in a way they'll believe, otherwise we'll be wasting the effort.''

Tiran thought about that while he sipped his coffee, but there was really only a single choice. He would have been happier if he could have done something personally—but that would have been pure stupidity.

"We'll have to send somebody from the company in to talk to them," Tiran said at last. "It will have to be someone Oblin's fighters know and respect, and we'll have to get the man into their camp unseen, just before dawn. By sunup Oblin will have to admit to himself that I'm not coming, and then he'll be on the alert against someone betraying what he did.''

"I have the feeling you've got someone specific in mind," Alex said, studying him. "But you also seem to be reluctant about the choice. Would you like to explain?''

"There's a fighter in the company named Limos Zin," Tiran told her, faintly amused over how well she'd gotten to know him. "The man has been around almost forever, and everyone knows him as someone who won't lie about important things. The reason I'm hesitating is because he'd finally decided to retire—until he heard what I meant to do in this kingdom. Then he decided to save retiring until after we won, which should have happened by now.''

"And since carrying word to our enemies will be dangerous, you're not sure you should ask him to do it," Alex finished for him. "I see your problem, Ti, and there's only one thing I can suggest: call everyone together and tell them what has to be done, then ask for volunteers. If you don't stress the part about needing someone who'll be believed, he won't feel that he *has* to volunteer.''

"But if he does it anyway, I'll send him out," Tiran said, fighting off familiar pangs of guilty conscience. That had always been the hardest part of leading the company for him: sending men and women out to risk their lives when he wouldn't be doing the same himself. He'd learned that it was sometimes necessary, but he'd never learned to do it easily. "Well, no sense in wasting time our volunteer will need. I'll be back in a few minutes."

Both Alex and Brandis nodded with expressions of sympathy and support, then sat silently as he left. There wasn't anything they could have said to help him, no more than he was able to tell himself. He had Fasin get everyone together, explained why he needed a volunteer, then had to exclude group chiefs and squad leaders. That brought the number of volunteers down only a little, but then Limos Zin himself pushed through the clamoring crowd.

"This job's mine, Cap'n," he announced firmly in his gravelly voice, flames from a nearby campfire speckling his face with uneven shadows. "You gotta know it's me 'r nobody, an' I'm real glad. With th' trouble I had keepin' up t'night, I wus thinkin' I'd waited a little too long t'get outta people's way. Now I know I din't, so let's get on with 'er."

Tiran clapped Limos on the shoulder, then took him back to the tent. Alex had gotten Brandis to come up with a spell that would keep Limos invisible until he deliberately showed himself, but that only reduced the danger a little. The grizzled fighter didn't seem to care. He listened to the directions Brandis gave him on the best way to penetrate what was left of the enemy camp, waited patiently while Tiran repeated what he was to tell Oblin's fighters, and then he left.

Brandis recreated the basin and its water, and they watched Limos's progress. The man made it all the way through and almost to where Oblin waited, but made no effort to reveal himself to any of the fighters he passed. He did no more than glance at them before continuing on, and Tiran suddenly began to worry. Limos knew he was invisible; would he decide to use that and go for Oblin's tent? Killing the man could well stop the war, he would believe, even if doing it that way was dishonorable. But he didn't know about Oblin's younger brother, who would turn such a sacrifice into wasted effort . . .

But Tiran needn't have worried. Limos had been searching for someone in particular, something he proved when he found the man. He'd started with looking around at those fighters who were still awake, and luckily hadn't had to go on to searching the tents of those who were asleep. He came up behind the man and whispered something, causing his listener to turn with a frown. When the man saw who it was he glanced around quickly to make sure no one was watching, then pulled Limos behind a tent with him.

Limos spoke to the man very softly, and at first the man didn't seem prepared to believe anything he heard. Someone else might have become upset at having his word doubted, but Limos just kept murmuring things too low to be easily overheard. After what seemed like a very long while the fighter stopped arguing with Limos, his shadowed face somehow looking more pale than it had. When the man turned abruptly and strode away, Limos stood in the silent shadows for a moment before beginning to retrace his steps.

Tiran wanted to follow the man Limos had spoken to and find out what he would do, but the picture in the water suddenly flickered, then changed to a different scene. Alex looked up with the same confusion Tiran felt, but Brandis was quick to explain.

"I didn't think you wanted to miss Selwin's arrival, so I set my spell to switch over to him whenever he showed up," Brandis said apologetically. "I think you were about to suggest that we follow the man Limos spoke to, and if you'd rather do that, we can."

"No, watching the man won't change whatever he's decided to do about what he was told," Tiran said, keeping his eyes on Selwin's approach to what must certainly be Oblin's tent. "I wasn't expecting our main conspirator to show up so early, or with such a small escort. Either he's very sure of himself, or he has a problem."

"If it's a problem, I hope it's a bad one," Alex muttered, looking at Selwin's image with no friendliness at all. "Oblin may be obsessed with you, Ti, but if Selwin hadn't brought him here we wouldn't have had to do all that butchering. I think we owe the man for that, and I hate not paying my debts."

"I agree with you, but Oblin's the one at the top of *my* list," Tiran told her. "He knows damned well I would have accepted any personal challenge he cared to give, but hating me is easier than facing me. He threw away the lives of hundreds of men just for the chance to get at me, and that's something I can't forgive. If I'd known what he was up to, we might have been able to take them captive instead—''

Tiran broke off that thought, and not only because it was much too late to consider the option. The butchering had bothered him as much as it had Alex, but he'd still gone ahead with it. That made him guilty of murder no matter how anyone looked at it, but he wasn't going to accept the blame alone. Oblin had no conscience to be troubled, so it was up to Tiran to avenge all that needlessly spilled blood in another way.

Selwin and his escort of five dismounted in front of the tent, then Selwin and one other man went inside. Once they were in the tent Tiran could see that the other man was Viscount Yellin, a man close to Selwin's age. They both looked really agitated, and it wasn't long before Tiran found out why.

"What are you doing here?" Oblin demanded harshly, needing to resheathe the sword he'd drawn at their abrupt entrance. "I said I wanted you here early, but I didn't mean in the middle of the night.''

"It's less than an hour to sunrise, you fool,'' Selwin snapped, all his smoothness having disappeared. "And I was given some very bad news a little while ago. Yesterday that gutter peasant killed Pavar in front of the entire city, but no one brought word to me. Now what do we do?''

"He was your friend, so *I* don't have to do anything,'' Oblin retorted, nervousness making his motions short and choppy. "And it can't be that close to sunup, not when *he* hasn't gotten here yet. I know he'll come, I'm counting on it—''

"Of course this concerns you as much as it does me!'' Selwin snapped, apparently very short of patience. "Half of the men supporting me did so because of their fear of Pavar. With him dead they may well back out of our deal, and if they do they'll be taking half of *your* gold with them! *Now* do you see why this concerns you?''

"That gold was guaranteed by all of you," Oblin growled in return, his skin darkening with rage. "For personal reasons, I let you get away with paying only half in advance, but I've already taken losses so I'll need the rest as well. Or don't you and those other fools understand that if I'm not paid, *you* don't go on living?"

"If you don't win, we won't have to worry about that," Selwin countered harshly while Yellin paled. "The peasant will probably try to see us dead even if you don't, so what are your plans? A quick victory will save everything, including your gold."

Oblin hesitated then looked at his brother, who got to his feet and cleared his throat nervously.

"We've set a trap for d'Iste which may or may not work," he said, his voice higher than it had been. "For all we know it *has* worked, and that's why he hasn't come. But assuming he's escaped the trap, at first light we set the army moving again.

"We'll pretend we mean to engage in open battle, but in reality we'll break up into small groups that are able to melt into the forest. From there everyone heads for the city, and once in it we begin to burn and destroy everything we can reach. The people will panic and stampede *out* of the city, and our fighters will be hidden among them. That way we'll be able to get behind segments of d'Iste's army, and destroy it piecemeal."

"But—you never said anything about burning the city!" Selwin blurted to Oblin, obviously horrified. "That's going to be *my* city, and rebuilding it will cost a fortune!"

"If we lose, *you* won't have to worry about the cost of rebuilding," Oblin pointed out impatiently. "And it hadn't occurred to me that one of my fighters might have already succeeded in ending d'Iste. That *must* be why he didn't show up: he's already dead! When the one who did it reports back, I'll have to find a really excellent reward for him. Assuming d'Iste's men didn't kill him as soon as he did his job . . ."

Oblin's voice trailed off as he happily contemplated possibilities, and Tiran glanced up to see that Alex was looking very pained.

"He really is insane," she said with a headshake. "He

goes from depression to elation on nothing but guesswork, and rambles on in a daydream.''

"I think Selwin and Yellin have just noticed that," Tiran pointed out, gesturing at the picture. "From their expressions I'd guess they're sorry they ever got involved with him, but that decision comes a little late. And speaking of late, we're going to have to join the rest of the army soon."

"Let's see what *this* is about first," Alex said, frowning at the picture again. "It looks like Oblin has made up his mind about something."

Oblin *had* made up his mind, but when Tiran listened for a moment he discovered it was to have breakfast with his group chiefs and squad leaders. He sent his brother out to arrange it, then engaged a nervously distracted Selwin in conversation. Nothing of any importance was discussed, and Tiran was about to tell Alex again that it was time to leave, when Oblin's brother came running back into the tent.

"Jend, they're gone!" he gasped out, his young face a good deal more pale than it had been. "They're *all* gone, along with their equipment and mounts!"

"Who are you talking about, little brother?" Oblin asked with amusement, obviously in too good a mood to be easily bothered. "Do you mean Duke Selwin's escort? Well, that doesn't matter, not now. We can always—"

"Jend, I'm talking about *our* men, the rest of our *company!*" the boy interrupted wildly. "Every one of our regulars is gone, along with most of the new recruits! The only ones left are the men supplied by Duke Selwin and the others, which means no more than a handful, and the six remaining members of your personal guard!"

Tiran could see the blood drain out of Oblin's face, leaving him looking like a ghost. If all the remaining members of his company had left, that meant Limos Zin's assignment had been a success. Whoever he'd spoken to had spread the word to everyone else, and they'd proven how quickly and quietly a large group of men could move when they wanted to. Oblin had betrayed them, so they'd returned the favor.

"That can't be possible," Oblin whispered, then he

broke into a staggering run outside. The others followed, and when they were all outside it was possible to see, in the shadowed gray of predawn, an emptied meadow. Where there had been hundreds of tents there were now only a handful nearby—as well as the permanently silent ones on the perimeter—and the picture showed the end of a large group of riders moving slowly off into the distance—away from the city.

"Where are you all going?" Oblin screamed to the departing men, although they couldn't possibly have heard him. "You can't desert me like this! Get back here this minute!"

The man was all but foaming at the mouth, and it took a few minutes before he realized that there were six fighters standing just a few feet away. When he did he took a step in their direction, gesturing wildly at those who were leaving.

"Why?" he demanded of the six. "Why did they do that? How can they just pick up and leave in the middle of a campaign?"

"Somebody spread the word that you set up everybody on the perimeter to die," one of the six answered with a shrug. "Couple of 'em went to look and see if it was true, and the way them camps is set up—along with the bodies—gave 'em the answer. Once they had it, they packed up and left."

"They'll regret that, every single one of them," Oblin snarled, no longer looking as pale. "We're still going to win here, and when we do I'll build another company, then hunt down those deserters. I'll take a minute to confer with my brother, and then I'll tell you what we'll do first."

"We don't need the boy's knack with tactics to know what comes first," the man interrupted, bringing a shocked expression to Oblin's face. Tiran had the feeling Oblin had actually believed that no one knew the company's string of successful campaigns was due to his younger brother's ability. It was a measure of how far out of touch with reality the man was, but the fighter speaking to him didn't seem to care.

"What comes first for *us* is the payin' over of the gold you promised us," the man continued evenly. "It don't look like any of the others is comin' back, so you got it easy. You pay the six of us here, and we don't ride after everybody else.''

"That's—that's no problem," Oblin responded, his voice quavering. "I used all of my own gold to hire all those new recruits, but Duke Selwin here still owes me a large sum. He'll pay me now, and then I'll—''

Oblin's words broke off when he looked toward Selwin—only to find that he and Yellin had remounted their horses in the midst of their escort. Selwin looked ill, and the glare he sent toward Oblin was filled with hatred.

"We've lost, and it's all because of *you*," he snarled at Oblin as he gathered up his reins. "Now I'll have to crawl to that peasant, beg his forgiveness, and swear future loyalty to him. He said he'd refuse to pardon any of us, but that was just talk. As long as we don't insult him openly the way Pavar did, he'll feel superior when he forgives us. As for you—even a handful of coppers would be too much to pay—even if you still had your company. You're a fool as well as insane, and you're never to return to this kingdom again.''

With that, Selwin and the others turned and rode away, leaving Oblin to stare after them for a moment with the most terrible stricken expression. It worsened when he finally looked away from them to discover that the six men had also gone to their horses, and were obviously preparing to leave.

"But you *can't* leave me!" Oblin whispered intensely to the six, much too softly for them to hear him. "D'Iste can take five men, so I need six to protect me! If you leave, who will I have to protect me?''

Naturally there was no answer to that, and Oblin began to cry. His brother hurried over and tried to comfort him, but he seemed to be inconsolable. He let himself be helped back into the tent, but his sobbing sounded as if it would never end.

"And that seems to be that," Alex said with a sigh, leaning back in her chair. "The war is over and the people in the city are safe—unless you do decide to pardon Selwin. He'll swear to anything he has to in order to give himself the time to put together enough gold to hire another army.''

"Tell me about it," Tiran answered sourly as he did his own leaning back. "I'll have a squad pick up Oblin and his brother while a couple of groups get the rest of those fighters on their way out of the kingdom, but Selwin I intend to leave alone until he comes to *me*. It shouldn't take long at all, and then I can show him the surprise I'll have for him."

Tiran sipped his coffee as he thought about it, but Selwin was no longer his biggest problem. Oblin was, along with what it would be possible to do with the man. He seemed to be hopelessly insane, which meant he ought to be put down. But he was also pathetically helpless right now, and it was more than difficult to do the necessary thing with someone like that.

Tiran stood up and stretched, promising himself he'd think about it again once he got some sleep. And after he slept he'd most likely have Selwin to deal with, and that surprise he meant to have waiting. After that . . .

After that those intruders would certainly be back, and as far as he could tell his attitudes hadn't changed much. He still had the vague feeling that he would be best off with someone taking over the throne, and if he didn't find a way to change that conviction it could mean his life. But his "arrogance," his belief in himself, wasn't letting him take the threat to his life seriously.

He joined Alex and Brandis in heading for the way out of the tent, but the satisfaction he'd felt just a couple of minutes ago had disappeared completely.

CHAPTER SIXTEEN

The day was already well begun by the time we got back to the city, so we had something to eat before falling into bed. I know I slept deeply, but there were also dreams that I couldn't quite remember when I woke up. I did know they weren't pleasant and that, combined with the fact that Tiran was already up and gone, convinced me not to try to go back to sleep.

It didn't take long to bathe and dress, and by then I knew it was late afternoon. I had a quick meal of something I didn't notice because of the dark mood that had wrapped itself around me, one caused by the situation that Tiran and I hadn't even mentioned aloud to each other. With the war finished even before it had really gotten started, those two people who had challenged us would be back. And before, I was certain, I could do anything about my attitudes.

I pushed my plate away and sat back with my coffee, probing at my feelings in an effort to get some control over them. The desire to pick up and leave that kingdom for good wasn't anywhere near the level of compulsion, but I still couldn't seem to dismiss it. It hung on stubbornly, the picture of lost and ruined children a faint bracing behind it, along with the fun Tiran and I had had traveling around together. I'd never before had the urge for children, and didn't really have it now; what I did have was a vague fear of losing something infinitely precious, a loss I'd never be able to bear.

"Excuse me, Your Majesty," a voice came, pulling me

out of deeply disturbing thought. A servant stood not far away, and when I nodded he continued, "His Majesty has asked that you join him in the throne room. He said to tell you that callers have arrived, and he would appreciate it if you *didn't* change your clothes."

It had to be Selwin who had arrived, but I didn't understand that part about not changing my clothes. Tiran must have known I'd be in something comfortable rather than something fancy, but if that was what he wanted, that's what he would get. So I dismissed the servant, finished my coffee, then headed for the throne room. There were fighters waiting in the anteroom to act as my escort, but I barely noticed them. There were too many other things to think about, including the fact that if I were no longer queen, I'd never again have to worry about someone dying in an effort to save my life.

The palace's throne room was even a little larger than my father's, with two thrones up on their dais above five broad steps, and not another place to sit in the whole oversized room. The walls were draped with red silk to match the cushions on the thrones, which themselves were supposed to have been cast from pure gold. The candle sconces along the walls looked to be the same as well as jeweled, and the calculated emptiness with its narrow red carpet leading to and up the stairs of the dais was supposed to be very impressive.

Possibly I just wasn't in the mood to be impressed, or maybe the room looked better when it was full of people in beautiful clothes. Right now there was only a group of fighters along with Tiran, and he was busy talking to their group chief. As I approached he finished with the man, then turned to me.

"Selwin and half his bunch have come 'begging' an audience, so I'm going to give them one," he told me after sharing a brief kiss. "You should enjoy the show, but I doubt if they will. Let's get up to the thrones and get this started."

"Where's Brandis?" I asked, looking around as I walked with Tiran to the dais. "I had the feeling he would be here."

"He *is* here, but don't expect to see him," Tiran answered with grim satisfaction. "He won't be seen until just the right moment, and by then it will be too late."

I felt tempted to ask him what he was talking about, then decided not to ruin his surprise. He couldn't have enjoyed what Selwin had called him when speaking to Oblin, and I was certain Selwin would regret every word.

"By the way, Oblin seems to have disappeared," Tiran said as we took our places on the thrones. "The squad I sent after him couldn't find him or his brother—but crazy men like him are dangerous, if not to me then to some innocent bystander he's bound to come across. I have people out looking for him, and they won't stop until they've found out where he's gone."

I nodded as he gestured to one of the fighters to get things started, but I suddenly felt really disturbed. Jend Oblin wasn't likely to have left the kingdom, not when he would be blaming Tiran for his latest defeat as well as all the rest of his troubles. He'd most likely try to get revenge, and with his brother's help the try probably wouldn't be lame. We'd have to think about it once that business with Selwin was taken care of.

But right now a set of doors was being opened, and people began to stream into the throne room. They weren't beautifully dressed and highly placed people, any more than Tiran or I was prettied up. He wore black leather trousers and boots, a lemon-yellow shirt, and his sword-belt. I wore an outfit in blue that was basically exercise clothes, but white embroidery and white boots did quite a lot to disguise that fact. The people coming in were even more plainly dressed, obviously ordinary citizens who had come to witness the goings on.

Our six resident nobles came in after the crowd to stand themselves to Tiran's left, down on the floor but close to the dais, and even they were rather plainly dressed. They also looked curious and confused, which probably meant they'd been told to show up and what to wear, but not why. I thought I knew why Tiran was obviously pushing the plain clothes, so I sat back and waited to see if I were right.

After everyone had found places in the large room, the double doors directly opposite our thrones were opened.

Beyond them were Selwin and his wife Tiraya, Viscount Yellin and his wife Bonnea, and Pavar's widow Ravina. I hadn't expected to see Ravina again, and the surprise was something less than delightful.

"They've been waiting almost three hours," Tiran murmured from his throne to my left. "If they're not worried sick, they're frothing with rage. Care to make a bet on which?"

I made a low, rude sound instead, having no interest in betting on or against a sure thing. Selwin wouldn't be worried, not when he *knew* the peasant king would rather humiliate him than kill him. He would be hopping mad for having been made to wait so long, and certainly without any of the amenities. It was even possible that Tiran had ordered Selwin and his allies to be put in a place where there was nothing to sit on but the floor.

I got that idea about lack of chairs—and the reason why the rest of us were dressed the way we were—when I saw the finery being displayed by the five people walking slowly toward us. They were dressed to the teeth in what had to be the absolute best they owned, clothing as well as jewelry. Ravina walked alone behind Selwin and Tiraya and in front of Yellin and Bonnea, looking more like a sullen and displeased child than a woman who had only recently found out she was a widow. I wondered why they'd brought her, then dismissed the thought. I'd certainly find out before very long.

Their procession was slow and stately and extremely dignified, but I was willing to bet Selwin was getting increasingly angry during the walk. He couldn't possibly have missed the fact that no one else in the room was wearing formal dress, and rather than looking elegant and noble, he and his friends looked ridiculously overdressed. I saw the man's complexion darken when snickers broke out here and there, but by the time he reached the foot of the dais he seemed to be back in control of himself.

"Your Majesties," he said in a deeply solemn voice, bowing almost double while his wife curtsied low. The others did just the same, but they gave the impression that they were offering the courtesy voluntarily rather than being required to give it. They were all doing *us* the favor, their attitudes said.

"I know you've come for a reason, Selwin, so you might as well get to it," Tiran responded in a bored voice. "I have *important* things to do today."

"I deserved that comment, Your Majesty," Selwin said wryly once he'd straightened up. "I was a fool to let Pavar talk me into going along with his plans, and I deserve whatever happens because of that. I may have been—wary—of his influence with the others, but I should have quietly stepped out of the mess if nothing else. Now that he's dead, I've come to beg the royal pardon."

Selwin sounded like a proud man being forced to publicly admit a stupidity, one whose bearing let everyone know he was suffering. He did such a good job of it that our resident nobles, Nomilt, Obrif, and Sandor, all began to look very worried. Behind Ravina, Yellin also appeared contrite—or as close to the feeling as he could come. The three women tried to keep all emotions from showing, but only the two older women succeeded. Ravina still looked sullen, not to mention put-upon.

"Why did you wait until Pavar was dead?" Tiran asked casually, making no effort to sit straight and stiff on his throne. "Why didn't you come to your senses when I had him arrested?"

"Frankly, Your Majesty, because I expected him to be released again almost immediately," Selwin replied without hesitation. "He had a way about him that—affected—most people, and even the old king hadn't dared to move against him. If you must hear me say it out loud, very well: I feared the man, and my courage has returned only now that he's dead. Others may, out of spite, tell you differently, but that happens to be the truth."

"And if I *should* happen to pardon you?" Tiran pursued, still sounding only faintly interested. "What then? What plans do you have?"

"My plans include nothing more than retiring to my estates, Your Majesty," Selwin answered with a sigh. "I'm no longer a young man, and I'd like to spend my remaining days tending my own personal garden. I will, of course, swear fealty to the Crown, and will also swear to stay uninvolved in whatever court politics develop. I seem to have lost my taste for involvement."

His words were dry as well as bitter, and from the expressions on most of the people listening to him, they believed every word he said. That didn't include Baron Sandor and the other two, of course, but they knew Selwin a lot better than the ones who believed.

"I've been curious as to why you've brought Pavar's widow with you," Tiran said after a brief pause, as though he'd been considering what Selwin had said. "Would you care to enlighten me?"

"Certainly, Your Majesty," Selwin agreed with a small bow. "The Duchess Ravina will be the first one to admit that she could never manage Pavar's holdings herself. She came to me asking my advice, and we've worked out a solution that will require Your Majesty's permission. It's a small thing, really, but I'm of the opinion that enough has happened around here without your knowledge and agreement."

"It's nice to see that you seem to have fully learned your lesson, Selwin," Tiran said in a way that made me think he was trying to sound stuffy. "Tell me about this unimportant arrangement."

"As Your Majesty commands," Selwin said with another bow. "One of my younger sons is rather good at property management, but lacks all enthusiasm for going out into the world and finding a place to exercise that talent. I've gotten him to agree to run things for the duchess Ravina, at least until one of Pavar's heirs returns. That way the estates will have no difficulty in paying their proper share in taxes."

This time Tiran leaned back a little while studying Selwin. The man sounded so weary and matter-of-fact that it was obvious we were supposed to overlook the way he'd not only assumed he would keep his estates and position, but had gotten control of Pavar's as well. I was so annoyed I couldn't help moving around a little, wondering how long Tiran intended to let him get away with it. I knew Tiran wanted this to be *his* show, but I would not be sitting by and letting Selwin get away with everything he'd done.

"Is that all you intended to tell us, Selwin?" Tiran said then, reaching over casually to pat my hand. "You've got nothing else to add?"

"Only that I would like to beg forgiveness for Pavar's other victims as well, Your Majesty," Selwin answered in that same weary and humble way. "Viscount Yellin agreed to accompany me here, but the others were too beaten down to do the same. They're so used to Pavar's unrelenting habit of revenge ... It's difficult to convince frightened people that not all men of strength are equally as ruthless."

"Well said, Selwin, well said," Tiran exclaimed, and damned if he didn't seem to be trying to swallow amusement. "Is there anything else?" When Selwin smiled sadly and shook his head, Tiran nodded. "All right, then it's now my turn. I have a few questions for you, Selwin, and I expect to get truthful answers."

"Of course, Your Majesty," Selwin agreed smoothly and comfortably. "What questions do you have?"

"Let's start with this plot of Pavar's," Tiran said with a faint smile. "The idea was entirely his, and he forced the rest of you to go along with him?"

"Certainly not," Selwin replied with a small laugh of ridicule. "Pavar was a crude, brainless fool, useful only as a weapon. All the real planning was mine, as would have been the rewards. Pavar started out demanding the throne, but was easy enough to persuade that the real power lay with being in charge of the army. He would have found out how stupid that was when I had him arrested and summarily executed. Kings find that easier to accomplish than generals do."

A muttering had broken out among the spectators and our resident nobles were staring with mouths open, but Selwin and his companions were happily unbothered. They all smiled in agreement with what he'd said, and I finally remembered that Brandis was there somewhere in the room. He'd obviously used a truth spell on Selwin, but not an ordinary one.

"That's really interesting, Selwin," Tiran commented with a wider smile. "Now tell me the real reason you're here today."

"Isn't it obvious?" Selwin returned with more than a touch of condescension. "You may be a gutter peasant, but as long as you sit on that throne and control an army, you're dangerous to those of us who really matter. By coming here today and pretending to humble myself, I accomplish a number of things. The first is forestalling any attempt on your part to arrest me, while impressing on your mind the idea that I'm too important—and too powerless—to punish."

"But of course you're not," Tiran said amiably. "You're anything but powerless."

"Naturally," Selwin agreed happily. "It will take a while to build up my resources again to the point of being able to move effectively against you, but being in control of Pavar's estates as well as my own will let me accomplish that."

"And you really expect to leave here not only unpunished, but also in control of both your estates and Pavar's?" Tiran asked in fascination. "What makes you believe you can do that?"

"The fact that you're nothing but a commoner," Selwin replied immediately. "I appeared before you as a high nobleman, so naturally you had to accept me as one. Commoners know they haven't the power to take things from the nobly born, so there will be no question of confiscating either my estates or Pavar's. And when the others see that I've saved their positions as well, they'll understand that my power is just as great as it always was and they'll keep their mouths shut. That way they'll live to be members of *my* nobility."

"That's very logical," Tiran agreed, now more solemnly. "How many of the others supported you actively, and how many were forced to agree?"

"The only one smart enough to back me completely was Yellin here," Selwin supplied, gesturing to the viscount. "The rest of them are fools and cowards, doing what they were told only because of Pavar. Once he was dead they actually tried to abandon me, but this ploy will put an end to *that*. If they try to step out of line I'll be forced to 'confess' to you that they're not in the least loyal, and you'll get rid of them for me."

"That would be very cooperative of me," Tiran said, then leaned forward a little. "And what are your plans for the members of the nobility who chose to support *me* rather than you and Pavar?"

"Why, I'll just have to confess secretly that they stayed behind at Pavar's orders," Selwin said, sending a cold glance in the direction of Sandor, Nomilt, and Obrif. "I'll tell you that they were actual partners with Pavar—unlike the rest of us, of course, who were mere dupes—but that I don't expect you to believe me. That will *make* you believe me, and will also kill any trust you might have in them. Then, when *I'm* on the throne, they'll be properly punished for siding with trash rather than with quality."

Selwin glared at the three men briefly, silently reinforcing his threat, then looked away from them with a faintly puzzled expression. None of the three had seemed in the least worried or bothered, and in fact their wives had been amused. He obviously couldn't understand that, but then he gave a small shrug of dismissal.

"I appreciate your clearing the names of Baron Sandor, Baron Obrif, and Count Nomilt," Tiran said then with real satisfaction. "I never doubted them, but after the way you and the others behaved, the people will tend to doubt all members of the original nobility. Thank you for telling them these three men are innocent."

"The people," Selwin echoed with a laugh of true scorn. "They're there to serve *us*—the true nobility."

The muttering from all around was louder and uglier now, but Selwin still didn't seem to notice. He had no worries about anything he'd said, no worries and no regrets. Tiran waited until the muttering died down, and then he clasped his hands in front of him with elbows still on the chair arms.

"I'm sure we appreciate having had the truth from you, Selwin," he all but purred. "You've made everything a good deal easier, but I wonder if you'd mind a final question?"

"Why, not at all, Your Majesty," Selwin answered, suddenly back to being weary and humble. It came to me that Brandis must have cancelled his spell, and a moment later I found out I was right.

"Do you really intend to do nothing more than work in your personal garden?" Tiran asked, the question sounding very neutral. "No more intrigues of any kind, no more involvements with any kind of politics?"

"I give you my word, Your Majesty," Selwin responded with solemn sincerity, looking directly at Tiran. "It's the word of a born nobleman, and I believe we all know what *that's* worth."

"In your case, we know exactly what it's worth," Tiran commented, and there was a sudden burst of truly amused laughter from all around. Selwin, who had been looking very faintly smug, frowned along with his companions at the laughter, but Tiran didn't leave them confused and wondering for long. "I think it's time for you five to see something the rest of us have already seen," he added, then gestured with one hand.

With Brandis still being invisible, the sudden replay of Selwin speaking truthfully seemed to come out of nowhere and from nothing but Tiran's gesture. The five people who hadn't really been aware that all secrets had been revealed stood frozen in place, deeply in shock from seeing and hearing Selwin tell all. Selwin himself was the hardest hit, of course, but he also managed to recover first once it was all over.

"You—you—*peasant!*" he screamed, all coolness and control long gone. "How *dare* you do something like that to me, how *dare* you? You had no right to invade my privacy, you—!"

"Enough!" Tiran roared, and the strength and intensity of the one word cut Selwin off in mid-rant. "You had no right to privacy, not when your intentions concerned everyone else! You're a liar without the least trace of honor, a lowly sneak-thief plotting to take what you haven't the ability or courage to earn. And you're stupid for believing your own distorted view of the world would prevail, which just may be the worst of your crimes."

Selwin was still white-faced with rage, but it seemed his pallor was beginning to have fear as its source as well. It was finally coming through to him that he'd confessed *everything*, and that Tiran's patient reception of his apology had been more of an act than the one *he'd* put on.

"I'm sure you think of yourself as unique, Selwin, but I've seen your sort in every world I've ever visited," Tiran went on, more quietly but not less intensely. "The useless and stupid of the universe, raised to believe that the accident of birth made them something special. All it really did was give you a head start you should have been able to use to turn any decent dream into reality, but you couldn't even do that much. Every man and woman in this room who survived through their own efforts is your superior, because they managed to make something out of nothing while you did the exact opposite."

Our audience applauded wildly as they shouted things in support of what Tiran had said, but I could see Selwin wasn't buying it. He'd never admit to being anything but top quality and better than the entire universe, not to himself or anyone else, and apparently Tiran noticed the same thing.

"But I can see I'm wasting my breath trying to tell you something you're too dim-witted to ever understand," he said, then sat straight on his throne and looked at Selwin with the coldest, most distant expression I'd ever seen on him. "For that reason I'll get straight to your sentencing, since your guilt has been proven by your own testimony. You've betrayed everything you were supposed to stand for, so you no longer stand for those things. All titles, property, and monetary wealth are forfeit, as much as necessary of the aforementioned monetary wealth to go to restoring the lives of those villagers you tried to enslave."

"You can't do that," Selwin muttered, his brow creased into a frown.

"Further," Tiran continued, ignoring Selwin, "you're guilty of that slavery, as well as treason to the throne and attempted rebellion. Having sworn to a series of lies proves you can't be trusted even to leave this kingdom and never return, so you won't be given the chance to hurt any more innocents. You are to be taken out and executed right now—too easy an end after all you've done, but at least we'll be rid of you."

"No," Selwin muttered, then he noticed the fighters who had come up to surround him, and he screamed, "No!

You can't do this to me! You can't! You can't! You can't . . .''

He continued to scream that as he was dragged out, and there wasn't another sound in the entire room. I couldn't keep from studying Tiraya, the woman who was supposed to be his wife and life's companion, and unsurprisingly saw just what I'd expected to. The woman's expression said she was horribly embarrassed by a scene created by a fool and loser, that fool and loser being someone she was unfortunate enough to know. She'd already distanced herself in her own mind from a man who could no longer provide what she considered the essentials of life, and would probably never bother to think about him again.

"And now, Yellin, it's your turn," Tiran said once the doors had been closed on Selwin's final hysteria. The former viscount jerked his head around to stare at Tiran, looking as though he were about to faint.

"Selwin was kind enough to tell us all that you're the only one of the rest of his group who supported him willingly and freely," Tiran said in an uninflected voice. "Since you were given the opportunity to contradict him when he said it—and you *would* have if it *hadn't* been true—you also stand condemned. But I'll wait to sentence you until you can be fully questioned under a truth spell. There's a difference between someone who joins a group because he isn't capable of acting independently, and someone who joins with the intention of letting others do the dirty work before he displaces them. We'll find out which you are, and then we'll see."

Yellin actually looked relieved when the fighters came to escort him out, which led me to believe he really was nothing more than the follower type who had to have *someone* to look up to. And his wife Bonnea actually looked worried as he was led out, which put her more than one up on Tiraya, at least in my opinion. If you share your life with someone, it should be someone you care *something* about . . .

"And now for those who aren't here," Tiran said once Yellin was also gone. "We've been told that they weren't *willing* accomplices of Selwin and Pavar, but that just means they won't be executed. Those who call themselves noble have to know right from wrong, as well as be strong enough to stand up against anyone who means to make the kingdom their private hunting ground.

"Since they didn't do even the least of that, all their holdings and possessions are forfeit, along with their titles. They'll be given just enough gold to keep them and their families alive until they can find paying jobs, but they won't be allowed to stay in this kingdom. They'll be escorted to a different world, where they'll have the best chance to start over."

People began to mutter at that, some apparently thinking the condemned were getting off too lightly, others grimly pleased that the high and mighty who had betrayed them would learn what it meant to have almost nothing. Tiran let it go on for a moment, then looked at the three women who now stood alone in their gowns and jewels.

"And last but not least we come to the female counterparts of our main villains," he said, his tone no more gentle than it had been. "Bonnea, wife of Yellin, will join her husband for the moment in waiting on my pleasure, her fate depending on what his turns out to be. As for the other two of you— But wait, I think I'm being selfish. Would you like to get in on this, Alex? You're the one these two gave the most trouble to."

Tiraya and Ravina both suddenly paled, the first really personal reactions of concern they'd shown yet. I'm sure they were certain they had nothing to fear from a man of honor no matter how angry he was—but another woman was a different story. I considered Tiran's question in silence for a moment, and then I smiled faintly.

"I think it's safe to say that these two gave full support and assistance to their husbands' efforts," I told Tiran while staring at the two women. "But now that the men have lost, I can see that these—*ladies*—are ready to forget them and move on to the next pair of fools they can manipulate. Apparently they have no loyalty to anyone but themselves, so I think *that*, along with losing all their pretty baubles, should be their punishment."

No one in the room seemed to understand what I meant, but I'd wanted it that way until I explained to Tiran. I leaned toward him and told him in low tones what I had in mind, and when I finished he chuckled.

"I believe that that can be arranged," he murmured back, then surprised me by adding, "What do *you* think, Brandis?"

"I *know* it can be arranged," Brandis's soft voice came from just behind and between us, also with a chuckle. "My congratulations on finding a punishment which truly fits the crime, Your Majesty."

Tiran waited until I'd thanked him, then announced in a normal voice, "My queen has pronounced a fitting punishment on these women, which is to be as follows: all titles and possessions will be stripped from them, and in addition they will be placed under a compulsion before being turned out into the world. The compulsion will require them to tell any men who become interested in them *exactly* what they're like beneath their smooth facades, and also to immediately exhibit those traits. If the men involved don't turn and run, they'll deserve what they get."

Laughter broke out in the room over that, but not from Tiraya and Ravina. Those two were absolutely appalled, which showed that my idea had hit the mark precisely. When you don't intend to fool people, knowing you'll be required to tell—and show—the truth about yourself won't produce more than mild discomfort or embarrassment. The two women had followed a different agenda, which now was over.

Ravina actually began to throw a temper tantrum and had to be carried out of the room. Tiraya walked out stiffly on her own, pretending nothing had happened that she couldn't cope with, but the truth is a great handicap for people like her. Bonnea trailed along behind the other two, but seemed to have distanced herself from them. She hadn't seemed particularly close to them to begin with, and now she'd apparently severed all ties.

"There's still one final matter to be taken care of," Tiran announced when the doors were closed behind the women. "I've saved the best for last in order to get the bad taste of the others out of our mouths, and to let us leave here knowing trust and loyalty aren't futile and dead. My lords and ladies, would you come forward, please?''

There was no hesitation from our resident nobility; in fact they were downright eager. Ever since Selwin had cleared them of complicity the men had stood straighter and easier.

"Gentlemen and ladies, it's time for rewards to be handed out instead of punishments,'' Tiran said to them in a much warmer voice than he'd used on the others. "You chose to stand by the legitimate ruler of this kingdom even though that put you in the minority with your fellow noblemen, and also had the strength to resist the urgings of Selwin and Pavar when others didn't. Baron Obrif, step forward please.''

Obrif took one step forward trying not to smile too widely, his wife Iltaina also moving forward, but not quite as far.

"For your loyalty and good judgment I now name you Marquis Obrif, a title which will be confirmed in proper ceremony to be held in the near future,'' Tiran said more kindly than happily. "You have our thanks as well, and now you may step back. Count Nomilt and Countess Leestin, Baron Sandor and Baroness Tovail—will all four of you please step forward?''

The four people did, leaving Obrif and Iltaina looking confused. They hadn't been called forward in the same way, and it suddenly came to them that a marquis was a step below the highest possible rank of duke.

"Gentlemen, you two will be named dukes in place of Pavar and Selwin, but not because your loyalty was any greater than Marquis Obrif's,'' Tiran explained soberly. "It was exactly the same, of course, but in your cases your wives have made the difference. Their assistance to the efforts being made by the queen and myself have been invaluable, and for that reason I've added to your reward. If this pleases you, you have your wives to thank.''

From the incredulous grins the two men wore, it pleased them as much as Obrif was *dis*pleased. But he made no effort to look at Iltaina, which was just as well. The woman was mortified, having realized that she and her husband had missed out because *she'd* been too—good, helpless, *something*—to volunteer.

Tovail and Leestin, on the other hand, glowed with delight at the enthusiastic applause of the audience. Tiran had kept quiet about what they were doing to help, but now everyone—including their husbands—knew they weren't simply wasting time. When they stepped back all six bowed or curtsied, and then they began to return to where they'd been standing originally. I was looking forward to getting out of there, but then I noticed a servant coming forward holding a folded piece of paper . . .

Tiran noticed the servant as well, and gestured the man forward. He came and handed over the paper before bowing his way back, but by then I no longer saw him. It was the paper that had all my attention, and I think Tiran knew what it was as well as I did. He opened it and held it for me to read at the same time, which ended all doubt.

"The same meadow behind the palace, in one hour's time," it read, and there was no signature.

But it didn't need a signature. Selwin and his friends were no longer a threat, and now it was time for the final showdown.

CHAPTER SEVENTEEN

Even as he changed into the exercise clothes he had
brought, most of Tiran's thoughts were on the meeting
they'd be going to in just a few minutes. But that didn't
mean he wasn't worrying about Alex. Aside from the very
obvious and very real danger they were about to walk
into, Alex had also been too quiet. He was used to seeing
her filled with burning vitality even when she sat without
speaking, and it shocked him to realize that that hadn't
been true of her for some time. She was only pretending
to be her usual self, and the painful truth was that he
couldn't think of any way to help her. She sat drinking
coffee, lost to her thoughts as he'd been lost to his, so he
went over and touched her shoulder.

"Can *you* think of anything I can do to help you?" he
asked when she looked up at him. "We only have a few
minutes left, love, so if you've got a suggestion you'd
better make it."

"I was just thinking about the way I'd decided to leave
you for your own good," she answered obliquely with a
wry smile. "If I had I never would have forgiven myself
for not being here when you needed me, but now I wonder
just how much good I'll be after all. I don't know what
they've done to me, Ti, but I can't seem to shake it off."

"Then I'll go out alone," Tiran told her, crouching
down to take her left hand in both of his. "You can write
something out formally renouncing the throne, and that
may do the trick. It's usually the king alone who defends

his throne, so the single fight ought to satisfy their need
for legitimacy.''

"Do you know what you just said, Ti?" she asked, her
smile having turned bitter. "You said you don't expect to
win, and you want to make sure that I don't die along
with you. You told me you rode back to the city with that
woman who called herself Caldai Moyan. I'd say she did
more than simply ride with you.''

Tiran couldn't *remember* anything else happening, but
obviously Alex was right because he did feel as if he were
going out to be executed. They'd both been gotten to,
then, and if it would have done any good he would have
been furious.

"I can see you're right, but that doesn't change anything," Tiran said, tightening his grip on her hand.
"Please, Alex, do as I ask and I won't *mind* dying so
much. I've always been willing to give up my life for
you, and this way your life can be saved.''

"You can't really believe that," she said gently, bringing her other hand over to cover both of his. "Aside from
the fact that I wouldn't want to live without you, I really
doubt if they'll be satisfied with anything but a clean
sweep. Statements can always be wondered about and
doubted, but a body on display is usually accepted as final.
We'll be in this together, my love, just the way we should
be—even if that isn't the way they want it.''

"What do you mean?" Tiran asked with a frown, but
even as he put the question, something told him she was
right. They *didn't* want Alex and him fighting together,
but why would that be?

"I mean that I'm not just reluctant to fight, I'm also
afraid to," she said, not quite meeting his eyes. "It isn't
that overwhelming terror I went through—it's something
much quieter, but quiet doesn't mean ineffective. I can't
imagine myself doing any good—which has to be *their*
fault—but I still intend to be there. What about how *you*
feel?''

"I feel—intensely worried," Tiran decided after considering the point for a moment. "Worried about what will
happen in general but also specifically worried about you.
I really want to talk you into staying behind, because I'm

convinced that that will save your life. Objectively I know better because I agree with what you said a minute ago, but emotionally I want nothing more than to see you promise to stay behind.''

''*Promise* to stay behind,'' she echoed with a mirthless smile. ''You want to get a promise out of me—which would be binding if I gave it—instead of trying to order me to stay behind. That isn't at all like you, Ti, but what you're like normally wouldn't get the job done. I'm glad you didn't disagree about being affected in some way, otherwise we'd be in the middle of an argument right now.''

''I almost wish we were,'' Tiran answered in a mutter. ''At least that would be more normal than what we're being put through now ... So what can we do in the next ten or fifteen minutes to change things back? Call in Brandis and ask for his help?''

''If Brandis could be of any use to us, either we wouldn't think of him or we'd be kept from reaching him,'' Alex replied with a headshake. ''Remember when we decided that it was a wizard our intruder friends are in partnership with? Since things have been getting worse instead of better, I'd say the point is just about proven.''

''And I think you're right,'' Tiran said, feeling absolutely defeated as he straightened again. ''So we can't run and we can't win. What's the sense in showing up at all—''

''Have you just remembered that we both gave our word that we *would* show up?'' Alex asked in a tone that was almost dreamy. ''As I see it, you're supposed to beg me to promise not to fight after getting me to sign something that says I'm out of it. My fear convinces me to sign the thing after promising, but I go along anyway because at the last minute you remember that I *have* to. You go into the fight thinking that you're sacrificing yourself to save my life, but once you're down they then come after *me*. I don't do any better than you did and probably worse, but that way they've fought us both but not *together*. What do you think?''

''I think I'm feeling sicker than I ever have in my life,'' Tiran answered as he put a hand over his eyes, not exaggerating in the least. "Instead of trying to figure out some way around this, all I want to do is give up. If we go out there, we'll be fighting ourselves as well as them."

"And we decided when we first got here that if we fought ourselves we'd lose," Alex supplied, telling him nothing he didn't already know. "I suppose it's a victory of *some* sort that we were able to figure all this out, but as victories go it's kind of lame. It hasn't made any difference in *my* attitudes and feelings, and you don't sound as if it's made any in yours."

"To say the least," Tiran agreed, rubbing his eyes before taking his hand away. "I'm wondering right now if maybe we aren't assuming too much and because of that foolishly throwing away a slim but definite chance. We don't know for a fact that your renouncing the throne would be a waste of time, so maybe we ought to try it. If they come after you anyway, you can always fight then."

"After you're already dead," she reminded him, looking as if she *wanted* to agree but simply couldn't. "Do you remember when those two females disguised as guardsmen tried to kill you just outside your camp near my father's palace? When I heard what had happened I was furious with myself for not being there when you needed me, and I *swore* it would never happen again. I hate to tell you how much I wish I *could* go back on that, but something that has nothing to do with those people waiting for us just won't let me. We'll be doing this together, Ti, win or lose, live or die."

"Alex," he said, finding that was the only word he was capable of speaking. She rose then and came into his arms, and they shared a kiss with more tenderness than ever before. It was a time for tenderness rather than passion, and then it was time for them to leave.

They'd spent their hour in a small, private sitting room on the ground floor, so they only had to walk around through the halls to the back of the palace. Tiran had already sent word to Damis and Gann that if he and Alex lost the fight the rest of the company was on its own, but he would recommend that they pull out completely. He would have preferred to suggest that they try to back up

Chalaine and Bariden, but he was very much afraid that those two were just as solidly up against it.

The walk out to the meadow behind the palace didn't take nearly as long as Tiran would have preferred, but he and Alex held hands as they walked and that made it better. There were a lot of people waiting outside, fighters and ordinary citizens both, but they lined up close to the palace wall and made no attempt to follow Alex and himself deeper into the meadow. They'd be able to see everything that happened from where they were, but were taking no chance of being a part of it. They didn't really know what was happening, but could tell it wasn't good.

It was late afternoon, almost evening, and clouds had blown in from somewhere to make the day darker than it should be. Not that there was much of a wind. Tiran kept his eyes on the two people in the meadow who awaited them, and their hair didn't seem to be stirring at all. They stood dressed now in the same sort of exercise clothes that he and Alex wore, and Tiran frowned because something was odd about that.

"It's good of you to be right on time," the man commented dryly once Tiran and Alex were close enough, causing the woman who called herself Caldai Moyan to smile faintly. Her attention was mostly on Tiran, but she'd sent a glance toward Alex that had been anything but friendly. "You did a marvelous job against those rebels," the man went on, "and we offer our congratulations."

"Nice of you to say so," Tiran commented back, forcing his words to be just as dry. "Especially since we saved you a lot of trouble."

"That you did," the man agreed with an honestly amused laugh. "I'm Krayn Forres, and my lady here, as you already know, is Caldai Moyan. Don't you have something for us before we begin?"

For an instant Tiran had no idea what the man was talking about, but then it dawned on him and he glanced at Alex. *She* was looking wryly satisfied, since her speculations seemed to have hit the mark. Forres was expecting them to hand over Alex's abdication before she stepped aside, and Tiran suddenly realized that nothing had been done to ruin Alex's ability with strategy and tactics. *He* was supposed to be the strategist and that was probably why he was having trouble following even the simplest lines of thought.

"I don't understand," Tiran said after the briefest pause, working at looking bewildered. "What would we have for you?"

It was Forres and Moyan's turn to exchange glances, and their amusement seemed to have evaporated. They'd been expecting Alex's abdication, all right, and for a moment they didn't seem to know how to proceed. Then Forres pulled himself together and smiled.

"We thought you would understand that we really aren't here to commit out-of-hand murder," he said. "Your queen doesn't look at all well, and to include her in on this would be cruel and unnecessary. If she abdicates in writing she can wait on the sidelines until you and I have this out, and then she can go her way unharmed. What do you say?"

Despite his previous conversation with Alex, Tiran wanted to say nothing but yes. As long as there was the slightest chance that she might survive he wanted to take it, but before he could she interrupted with something that seemed to be totally off the subject.

"You're the one who staged that kidnap attempt against me, aren't you?" she said to Forres. "The one who took those little village girls to make me come after you?"

"That's right, I am," Forres answered after a very brief hesitation. "I changed my looks for the effort, just as I changed them the one time I helped my associate here in the palace. Why do you ask?"

"Because I remember that you laughed at me for being 'the sort' to keep my word," she responded immediately. "That has to mean that you promise anything just to get what you want, then go back on your word as soon as you have it. Doing that must come in handy for you—as long as you're dealing with people who don't know you haven't a shred of honor."

Forres's face twisted with fury and Caldai's matched it, but the damage had already been done. Tiran was still desperate to keep Alex alive, but doing it Forres's way was no longer a possible means to accomplish it.

"I think that settles the subject of abdication and staying out of the fight," Tiran said, reaching over to take Alex's hand again. "My queen and I are here together, and we'll be fighting the same way. Are there any other preliminaries that have to be covered?"

Forres and Caldai looked at each other, but apparently neither of them could think of anything to add. They were still furious but also seemed to be worried about something, and Tiran could only pray that that something was to his and Alex's benefit. The two intruders stood silently for almost half a minute, and then Caldai looked at Tiran.

"You can't do anything right, can you?" she growled, apparently blaming him for something. "You keep making the wrong choice no matter how stupid that is, but this will be the last time. I can take your overgrown cow of a precious female, and Krayn can take *you*. This won't make any difference at all, so let's get to it."

Forres didn't seem to completely agree with her conclusion, but he also didn't argue. The two intruders separated, Forres going to Tiran and Alex's left, Caldai to their right, so it was time to release Alex's hand after giving it a gentle squeeze. Alex looked at him with all the love he also felt for her, and then they each went to their appointments with . . . whatever was in store.

Forres had moved a good distance away from the women, and that was perfectly all right with Tiran. He'd been picturing Alex facing Forres, who was almost Tiran's size, and that was what had been bothering him so badly. He hadn't stopped worrying about Alex, not when he didn't really know just how good Caldai was, but he did know Alex's ability. Now all she had to do was get past whatever they'd done to her and *use* that ability . . .

"We're going to do this in the old-time traditional way," Forres announced once he and Tiran had moved far enough away to suit the man. "Do you know what that means?"

"I think I heard something about it when I was a boy," Tiran answered with a frown, trying to remember more than just a fragment. "Back before Shapeshifters began to live with and among ordinary people . . . There was some rite followed whenever a new king had to be chosen . . ."

"The rite was followed by every king who ruled our people," Forres corrected, his yellow eyes glittering. "No man sat the throne without proving he was the best and therefore deserved to rule. Challengers could come from anywhere, and the royal candidate, usually a son of the previous king, had to face them all and win. You should be glad you have it easy. All you have to do is face *me*."

"So what does this facing consist of?" Tiran asked, watching the man carefully. He seemed to be getting pumped up, which meant that "contest" might start without warning.

"The first part of it involves the question of just how good at Shifting you are," Forres answered, his hands opening and closing where they hung at his sides. "The challenger gets to start off, and the defender has to match him in the best way possible. What that happens to be is for you to decide, but don't be silly enough to believe you'll be allowed to Shift to a . . . wolf, say, if I Shift to rabbit form. I think you understand what I mean."

Tiran was sure he referred to the wizard they had working with them, and that he would be stopped by magic if he did something they considered cheating. He nodded to show that he did indeed understand, and Forres began to look a good deal happier.

"So that's the way it will go," Forres said lightly, but his hands still clenched and unclenched at his sides. "I'll be starting out in animal form, and you have to match me as best you can. It probably won't go beyond that phase, but if I'm enjoying myself I might hold off on killing you until we're in natural form again. At that point weapons will be allowed, as well as the use of Shift-fighting techniques. You're supposed to be pretty good at that, so the idea shouldn't bother you."

The way he grinned then made Tiran suspicious, but he still couldn't make himself think clearly about what might be happening. That meant he was already at a bad disadvantage, and trying to push himself into thinking faster could only make things worse. Just react, he told himself with the sort of sinking feeling he was completely unused to. Simply follow his lead and do the best you can *without* thinking.

"That's it for the explanations," Forres said after wetting his lips. "Now we get down to it."

And then he began to Shift, his speed faster than anything Tiran had ever seen. The man was a virtual blur that Tiran's mind wanted to try to anticipate, but that wasn't what he'd decided to do. He forced himself to wait until he saw the outlines that showed Forres was Shifting into a beaver, and then he began his own Shift with every ounce of speed he had.

Which meant his own beaver body formed just in time to take Forres's first attack without being able to defend itself. Tiran was hit with a broad, flat tail that had all of a big man's mass behind it, and that knocked him down with his head ringing. He also rolled from the strength of the blow, feeling like a rag doll thrown around by an adult.

But Tiran's reflexes had been many years in the building, and reflexes are what take over when rational, deliberate thought fails. Forres followed up his first attack with a second, intending to take advantage of the edge he'd gained, but this time his tail smashed through empty air. Tiran had continued to roll with some of his own effort added in, and when he scrambled back to his feet it was too far from Forres to allow the man another easy opening.

Which meant that Forres had to come at him a little more cautiously. Tiran fought not to pant or shake his head in an effort to clear it, either of which would have told his opponent that he was still a bit dazed. Something inside urged him to plan his every move carefully before trying something that might not work, and Tiran really wanted to do that. What interfered with that was the confusion caused by Forres's first attack that didn't seem to want to go away. The only thing he could do was let his beaver-form take over, at least until he could think clearly again.

So what met Forres's next attack wasn't really Tiran, but Tiran-gone-feral in an oddly different way. The beaver Tiran had relinquished control to avoided Forres's next swipe, got in a solid swing of his own tail, then followed up with a different attack while Forres was still off balance. Tiran felt his sharp, wood-cutting teeth sink into a furred shoulder, and then Forres was screaming and pulling away.

Forres staggered back a few steps with his own teeth bared, but the way his shoulder bled said he wasn't going to be launching another attack, at least not in that form. Sure enough, before Tiran's beaver-mind could send *him* forward in another attack, Forres began to blur. Tiran, feeling somewhat better, took over control of his form again, and waited to see what Forres would Shift into this time.

The answer turned out to be a wolf, which Tiran copied as quickly as possible. The wound in Forres's shoulder was healed in this new form, of course, and once again Forres attacked before Tiran was completely ready. But in a way Tiran *was* ready, since he'd once again turned over control of his form to the mind that would most naturally go with it.

And that mind expected to be attacked without warning, expected to have to fight viciously and wildly in order to survive. Forres was startled by the intensity of the response his attack brought, so much so that he lost the initiative of having acted first. Tiran's wolf form pressed him hard with teeth and claws, snarling in a way designed to make an opponent's blood run cold, and Forres gave ground even as he fought back. Tiran-wolf was trying to reach his throat and sink fangs deep, and Forres had to fight wildly to keep that from happening.

In no time at all both of them were covered with wounds, but Tiran-wolf paid no attention to the pain and freely-flowing blood. He couldn't afford to pay attention to them, not if he were going to survive and win, but apparently Forres didn't see it the same. He took the first opportunity to scramble back and away and immediately began to Shift again, but this time Tiran didn't wait to see what form he would take. Something *told* him what form it would be, so when Forres settled back to natural, Tiran was right there with him.

"How the hell did you do that?" Forres snarled, right fist closed around swordhilt. "First fighting like that, and now coming back to natural as fast as I did!"

"I'd call that a trade secret," Tiran answered, not nearly

as smug as he was trying to sound. It had been the minds of his other forms that had saved him till now, but when he was natural there *were* no other minds. It was just *him* against Forres, and *him* was still as confused and unsure as he'd been earlier. As far as knowing that Forres was going to Shift back to natural went, what other form would have had a weapon of steel for Forres to use in an effort to stop him? The answer to that was too obvious to need thinking to come up with it, which was the only reason Tiran had known.

"Then keep it a secret," Forres said, the look in his yellow eyes lifeless with the intention to spill more blood. "I'll have the satisfaction of knowing the answer died with you."

By then his sword was unsheathed and being held at the ready, with Tiran's weapon following a moment later. Tiran cursed himself as he braced for the attack, knowing he wasn't moving fast enough to do anything but lose. And that was the whole trouble, of course, that he *expected* to lose. Caldai Moyan must have worked on him during the trip to the city in the same way Alex had been worked on, but just not as obviously. And that dream-incident he and Alex had been forced through after Pavar's execution—had that only been the trigger, or was there something more involved?

Forres came forward in perfect form, and his first attack was strictly by the book. Tiran parried properly and launched a cautious attack of his own, which was parried in its turn. They fenced for a minute or two, neither of them pushing particularly hard, but Tiran was able to tell easily that Forres was much better with a sword than Pavar had been. The man was also able to keep his anger in check, which was more than just too bad.

After the first couple of minutes, Forres began slowly to press Tiran. Until then Tiran had been able to keep up, but only because of his years as a fighter. His mind was so filled with doubts and fears and a desire to be free of the position that could turn him into a conscienceless monster, that paying full attention to his opponent was almost impossible. His responses were set on automatic, so to speak, and for a time that did the job.

But when Forres began to press him, Tiran began to sweat. He couldn't hope to best Forres without paying attention, but when he tried to pay attention his wild, clamoring thoughts intruded. He bobbled a parry when an attack turned out to be a feint, and the real attack came lightning fast. Tiran only just managed to keep Forres's steel out of his chest, but at the cost of a deep cut to his left arm.

And that was when Forres started to Shift-fight. It takes a lot of practice and concentration to Shift-fight properly, to know when to lengthen your swordarm or narrow your body, or change your height or center of gravity. Tiran's opponent began to show that he'd had the necessary practice, easily as much as Tiran had had, but *he* also had the necessary concentration that Tiran now lacked.

It wasn't long before Forres was grinning, almost certainly due to the way Tiran was bleeding from half a dozen wounds. He just couldn't handle Shift-fighting now, and his pitiful attempts had shown that. So far he'd been able to keep himself from stumbling, but that only applied to the physical. Mentally he'd been stumbling all over the place, incapable of developing even the simplest of attack plans. *This can't go on,* he thought to himself, *not for more than another minute or two . . .*

And that proved to be a very accurate estimate. In no more than the specified two minutes, Forres came at him with blinding speed and body all out of natural proportion. Tiran was thrown so far off balance that he wasn't able to respond at all, and the next moment his sword had been yanked out of his fist with a circle parry.

"Now *that's* what I've been waiting all this time to see!" Forres exulted while Tiran wiped frantically at the sweat in his eyes and tried to come up with *something* to do. "My enemy now stands weaponless before me, helpless to do anything other than accept what I give. And what I mean to give is lasting peace, an end to all worry and travail."

That sounded so good to Tiran that he barely felt any fear. The madness in his mind urged him to accept being ended in the same way that the day was ending, calmly and happily and without reluctance. *Do it,* the whispers urged, *do it and be at peace. There's nothing more for you to fight against, nothing more to earn.*

It felt right to agree with that, right to simply stand there while Forres readied himself with calm, deliberate motions to deliver the final grace. There *was* nothing left worth fighting for ... except, possibly, Alex. Tiran frowned as memory of his beloved came flooding back, a memory he couldn't understand having misplaced to begin with. Alex was his love and his life; how could he have forgotten that she was also fighting for survival?

Actually ignoring Forres, Tiran turned his head to see that Alex and Caldai were also swordfighting, and Alex was almost as badly off as he was. She still held her sword, but it didn't seem likely that that would be true for much longer. And as soon as *he* died, Forres would be free to help Caldai against someone she didn't *need* help to defeat.

Frantic terror suddenly gripped Tiran, but not terror over his own fate. Alex needed his help, and if he just stood there and let himself be killed, the same would happen to her moments later. The whispering in his mind tried to calm him again, but this time it didn't have a chance. His beloved needed him, so he *couldn't* let himself die.

But that decision came almost too late. Tiran turned back to Forres in time to see the man's weapon already swinging at him, and if he'd stopped to think he would have died. Instead he let his reflexes take over again, and diving aside caused the sword to slice through empty air. Forres was furious when he looked at Tiran again, but no less determined. Tiran realized his lost sword was too far away to be of any use, but there had to be *something* ...

And then the worst possible thing happened. There was a wild screaming and the sound of running footsteps, and Tiran and Forres both looked around to see Jend Oblin running across the meadow with a sword held high in both hands. The madman was obviously heading for Tiran, trying to kill him before Forres had the chance. Now it was two against him, when Tiran hadn't even been able to handle one. *Alex, my love, Alex ... !*

CHAPTER EIGHTEEN

Tiran and I parted without a whole lot of melodramatic production, and that was what was wrong with the parting. I *wanted* to be melodramatic and at least say goodbye to him, but that would have made things worse instead of better. Those of us who are supposed to be so strong and capable are also supposed to be beyond such petty needs, but I'll never understand why. Aren't people still people, no matter how capable or helpless they are?

I considered the question as I walked toward Caldai Moyan, who didn't seem quite as arrogantly nasty as she had a couple of minutes ago. She seemed faintly worried about something behind her outward show of hostility and determination, but I didn't wonder what it was. I had enough concerning *me* to worry about, enough to make me feel like a complete stranger to myself.

"So you're the one Tiran thinks so much of," Caldai commented once I got close enough, her stare full of personal animosity. "I can't imagine why he would prefer you to a *real* woman."

"He tends to be prejudiced when it comes to me," I answered, wishing I were somewhere in a small, locked room, in bed with the covers pulled over my head. But even so I couldn't have missed the fact that Moyan's hostility seemed to come in large part from the fact that Tiran preferred me to her, which explained some of the comments she'd made. A tiny part of me stirred at the thought of her trying to take him away from me, but it was so tiny I was able to quietly add, "How are we supposed to do this?"

"It doesn't matter for *us*, but we might as well do it the way the men are going to," she responded, just a little too casually even for my distracted frame of mind. "There's an old tradition among our people that they'll be following, and it isn't particularly complicated."

She started to explain the tradition then, and I let her go through the details even though I already knew them. I was curious to see if she would leave anything out or add anything in, and it was the strangest thing: she put something backwards. I would have enjoyed having some time to wonder why, but she turned out to be generous only with explanations.

"So that's it," she finished up crisply. "Now that you know, we might as well get to it. And don't forget that you won't be allowed to break any of the rules."

It was the wizard she and Forres were in league with that she meant, and thought of that magic user made me shiver and cringe inside. It wasn't possible for ordinary people to fight against magic that strong even if they wanted to, and I still couldn't make myself want to. Leaving and hiding was what I wanted, but I wouldn't be allowed that.

The first thing we were going to do was Shift to animal form, I'd been told, but not what specific animal form. That I'd have to figure out on my own, and fast enough to do a decent job of protecting myself. When the woman began to Shift I was actually rather relieved; I did a lot better as someone or something other than myself.

But the relief lasted only a very brief time. Caldai Moyan's speed at Shifting was very nearly incredible, and on top of that I lost whole seconds by not fully believing what she was Shifting into. When the form really did resolve itself into that of a bantam rooster I followed suit, but I was still way behind—and unprepared. Most people don't get involved with gender Shifts, even when it involves a kind of chicken.

That, of course, meant my opponent was ready and waiting to attack as soon as I settled into the proper form. A sharp, vicious beak pecked at me as spurred feet tried to rip my feathers apart, and I backed with a squawk and a flutter of wings. Neither of us was able to fly even as much as real roosters, but that just meant our battle would take place on the ground.

Which suddenly gave me an idea. They'd messed up everything else about me, but my planning ability seemed mostly intact—probably because they hadn't realized I *had* any. Moyan came at me with the obvious intention of pecking my eyes out, but rather than retreat again I charged into her with my own spurred feet clawing at her underbelly. With my weight greater than hers I was able to knock her over, and her squawks turned to screams when my spurs gouged through her feathers to her flesh. She'd forgotten—or had tried to ignore—the fact that I was more massive, something you can't ignore when you Shift down that small.

Moyan scrambled away with an explosion of feathers that must have hurt, and then she was Shifting again. This time I was able to tell the form she headed toward before she got there, so my mastiff-like dog was ready only seconds behind her own. That still let her get the first attack in, which she was quick to take full advantage of. As I settled into mastiff form, her teeth settled into my shoulder.

And for some reason that got me mad. It wasn't as if I expected her to fight fair and behave with high honor, but just how much of a dirty edge is enough when you're supposed to be trying to prove yourself superior? If you really are superior you don't need *any* edges, and if you *believe* you are you don't want any. Moyan and her friend were using magic, unconscious conditioning, and even the kitchen sink, and that made me good and mad.

So instead of retreating in pain and confusion, I ignored the blood running down my shoulder and leg and immediately counter-attacked. In big-dog form my greater weight didn't make as much of a difference as it had when it had been compressed to chicken size, but even a small dog can do damage when it engages in all-out attack. I sent my teeth into Moyan's dark tan hide again and again, refusing to feel the way she did the same to me.

Fighting upright quickly turned into a rolling melee of

growls and bites and the scrabbling of hind feet trying to reach soft underbelly. Grass was torn up under us as we each struggled for a decisive edge over the other, and just for an instant Moyan's throat was exposed. I went for it immediately with a snarl, intending to tear it open, but she managed to slide out of the way before I could. I silently cursed the luck and swore to myself that next time I would have her—but the next time never came.

Instead she squirmed back to her feet, retreated a short way, and began to Shift again. As soon as I saw her returning to natural I did the same, but this time I had nothing in the way of immediate attack to face. She glared at me with yellow eyes just like her male counterpart's, her face twisted into rage and fury.

"All right, so Shifting helped you out," she rasped, an odd kind of hatred in her voice. "We knew that might happen, and the luck just went against us. But from now on luck won't have anything to do with it, not when you're nothing but an overrated amateur while I'm an experienced professional."

Her expression turned to one of triumph then, but I was too deeply involved with my sudden feelings to pay much attention. My hands had gone to clutch at my hair, an effort to help me hold off the storm of fear and uselessness and helplessness and inadequacy that had flooded through my mind and body. My knees were weak and my head swam, my hands would have been shaking if they hadn't been buried in my hair, and my heart thudded like thunder while my pulse raced with the speed of a cheetah. I was terrified, and Moyan made it worse by reaching for her sword.

"But in spite of all that, this is still the time you have to face me like the fighter you pretend to be," she said, all worry apparently having vanished. "I know you'd rather run away and hide, but you'll never be *allowed* to hide from me. Draw that sword and try to make *some* kind of showing."

Her tone said she knew how small a showing that would be, and she was absolutely right. I didn't know how to deal with what I was in the midst of feeling, not when I'd never felt it before a few days ago. My mind insisted that nothing I tried would be of any use, even if I found a way to push aside the fear long enough to try something. It had been those words she'd used, "experienced professional," that had done this to me, but knowing that with a small corner of my mind didn't help. I hadn't been allowed to tell Brandis about it, hadn't been permitted to remember when I'd accidently triggered myself the night before, and now I had no one to help me get beyond it.

"I told you to draw your sword!" she barked, making me jump as well as look up to see that she'd already drawn hers. "You're a miserable excuse for a woman and fighter, and you aren't going to get away with just standing there and shaking. You need to be taught a lesson, and it's my duty to teach it to you. Now draw that sword and face me!"

It wasn't possible for me to refuse to obey, but I almost dropped the sword once I had it unsheathed. My hands shook visibly and I clutched the hilt rather than gripped it, which would probably soon turn my fingers numb. I knew that, but still couldn't do anything about it. The fear was so intense that I was all but frozen in place, well beyond any sort of constructive thinking. I knew there were people in the worlds who lived in this sort of state most of their lives, but I honestly couldn't see how they managed it.

Moyan came toward me slowly, her sword held at the ready, a tiny smile curving her lips. She seemed to be enjoying the state of terror she'd forced me into, the amount of power that gave her bringing a light to her eyes. Briefly it seemed as if there was also relief in those eyes, and I wondered in passing if the relief came from someone else being powerless rather than her. Some people were like that, striking out constantly so that no one would have the chance to strike out at them.

But then she attacked, so fast and furiously that I should have died. *I* certainly couldn't have done anything to stop her, but you don't train with weapons most of your life without the proper movements soaking into your very blood and bones. My reflexes took over and parried her attack, but she withdrew before those same reflexes could begin a counter. That broke the pattern of automatic reaction, and I immediately found myself back to where I'd been: afraid and helpless to do anything about it.

"Well, I really didn't expect you to be able to manage that," Moyan said a little breathlessly from where she'd stopped. "It should have been too fast for you to— Wait, that has to be it. It was too fast to let you think, so you simply reacted. That means *slowly* is the way to proceed, so you'll have plenty of time to think about what to do."

Her smile returned as she came toward me again, and I did have enough time to think—and almost get violently ill with the fear. She was going to hurt me, and the thought of getting hurt made the fear even worse. I tried to back away, trembling and stumbling and having forgotten all about the sword I held, and the only thing I accomplished was to spoil the aim of her leisurely lunge. Instead of reaching the middle of my chest her point and edge sliced along my left side, bringing horrible flaring pain and the quick flow of blood.

I gasped and whimpered and stumbled aside in a different direction, but it was the strangest thing. I'd been terrified of the pain and it *was* terrible, but it wasn't quite as bad as I'd been imagining. It wasn't the worst thing ever and it didn't kill me, and it wouldn't even if it happened a second time. I grabbed that thought and held to it even as my mind screamed at me to run; the pain was *not* worse than anything, and fearing it would only keep me helpless.

I fought to make sense of that even as Moyan came at me a third time, her expression showing how grimly determined she was. She'd decided she wasn't going to miss me again, I could see that in her eyes, and I didn't know what to do. Fear and pain . . . was it possible to overcome that combination somehow? People did it all the time, ordinary people without any special abilities and talents. If I could just figure out how *they* did it . . .

But Moyan wasn't going to give me the chance to figure anything out. She came after me grimly, making sure not to move too fast and trigger my reflexes. This time she was determined to make sure she got me—and then we were both distracted by the most hideous scream.

I looked quickly to my left, toward where Tiran was fighting Forres, and my heart dropped like a stone. Forres had somehow managed to disarm Tiran, and now my beloved stood empty-handed and helpless. And as if that wasn't enough, the insanity-filled scream had come from Jend Oblin, who raced at Tiran across the meadow with a sword held high over his head in both hands.

It was clear Oblin had come to murder a man who had never deliberately done him any harm, but also had had the nerve to be successful where Oblin had failed. It was easier for Oblin to blame someone other than himself for his failures, especially when that someone was no longer able to defend himself. He would kill Tiran and then sigh with pleasure, and afterward, when he failed again, he would find another innocent bystander to blame.

And that, all of it, caused something inside me to snap. The mental cripples of the worlds always look for someone innocent and helpless to take their pain out on, instead of choosing the harder road and asking for help to straighten themselves out. In the name of self defense they made victims of everyone they came in contact with, most especially those who were kind and gentle.

But there *was* a way out of that trap, the way so many really courageous people had found for themselves. I'd been told about it only in passing, since *I'd* never needed to use the trick, and so I'd forgotten. But now I did need to use it, not for myself but for someone I loved, and my need brought the memory back.

I felt as if I were suspended in a special world where time moved not at all, and in that world I was able to review what I'd been taught. Fear doesn't make a coward, in fact it's just the opposite. Without fear bravery is impossible, for only by acting in spite of your fear do you show true bravery.

Fear, like anger, is also a weapon when properly controlled. Both emotions flood your system with adrenaline, but fear sometimes releases so much that you're paralyzed rather than spurred to motion. Try to balance another strong emotion against the fear to let yourself get a handle on it: fury or outrage, if possible, ordinary anger if those others are too hard for you to handle.

Fear makes you very aware of what's going on around you, strong anger often keeps you from feeling any hurt

given you. Combine the two wisely and be alert, but don't
let worry over what will happen hold you back. The best
way to keep yourself or someone you care about safe
is to remove the source of danger before it can cause
irreversible harm.

And that, easy to say but hell-hard to do, was my only
chance to help the man I loved. I didn't *want* to do it, I
would have preferred to crawl into a deep hole and hide,
but that was no longer an option. Tiran needed me, and
I'd sworn that the next time he did I would *be* there. And
if I didn't do it this time, there'd never be another.

The world suddenly began to move at its normal rate
again, and it was time to do rather than just think about
it. I grabbed the outrage I'd felt over what was being done
to Tiran, and added it to the fear that still had me by the
throat. The outrage loosened fear's grip to the point where
I could breathe again, and then I had the boost of adrenaline from two sources that actually balanced each other.

Moyan took her attention from the screaming Jend
Oblin and gave it back to me, her intended victim. *She*
didn't care how many people attacked Tiran; her expression of annoyance said Oblin was Forres's to worry about,
which included whether or not Forres would allow the
pleasure of killing Tiran to be stolen by someone else.
Her own time of pleasure had arrived, and she would *not*
let it be taken away.

Realizing all that let me add to the outrage, bringing it
all the way up to true fury. The fear was still there, doing
its job of making me cautious and aware, but it had lost
its ability to paralyze me. I knew what had to be done,
and there wasn't much time to do it.

Moyan came in confidently, paying no attention to the
way I'd brought up my sword to a proper ready. The rage
was making me breathe harder and harder, but she thought
it was fear and so ignored the reaction as well. She came
at me faster than she had the last time, but not so fast that
I would react without thinking—and I *didn't* react without
thinking. I saw how close she would be so I waited, parried her thrust when it came, then stepped even closer and
punched at her throat left-handed. I had her, I knew I

did—but then the world stopped without my wanting it
to . . .

I felt as though I'd done nothing more than blink, but
I couldn't for the moment remember what I'd been doing
or where I was. There was a shimmering cloud of some
sort all around, and when I took a step forward it was
also the first step out of it. Two more steps let me leave
it behind completely, and then I was able to look around.

There was gray sand under my feet, a bluish-purple sky
above my head, and black clouds in that sky. There also
seemed to be tiers of seating in the distance that rose
almost up to that strange sky, but they were too far away
for me to be sure. In some strange way the place seemed
familiar, but I couldn't remember from where and it wasn't
that important.

What *was* important was the woman who stood on the
gray sand with me, about twenty feet away. Her puzzled
expression seemed to suggest she felt the way I did, but
when she spotted me she forgot about being puzzled as
quickly as I had. We were there to face one another in a
test of skill, the weapons we each held more than enough
proof of that. *Why* we were to face one another I didn't
know, but that was something else that felt unimportant.

The woman wasn't my size, but as we walked toward
each other I could see that that didn't matter to her. Her
calm expression said she had confidence in herself and her
ability, and that was just the way *I* felt. Two fighters would
face each other, and the one who was more skilled would
win. It was just that simple, and it was clear we both
knew it.

Just as clear as the fact that we both held practice weapons. If not for that I would have demanded to know why
I was there and what was going on, and wouldn't have
fought until I got some answers. But with practice weapons there was nothing to worry about and nothing to argue,
an opinion I could also see in my opponent's yellow eyes.

We both went en garde as soon as we were in range to
start the thing, and the first lightning-fast exchange told
each of us we weren't facing a novice. We were actually
very well matched, with my longer reach balancing the

fact that she was slightly quicker. We fenced, disengaged, fenced again, disengaged again, and somewhere far away there was a sound like a crowd going crazy.

I ignored the sound as I took pleasure in the exercise, finding the woman to be one of the best fighters I'd ever faced. It was almost as if we were *meant* to face each other, and that realization put an end to the pleasure I'd felt. We were also meant to show which of us was better, just as if this were a real fight. And the outcome was important, I suddenly knew that as well. I was there to win, not just fence, so I'd better get to it before *she* beat me to it.

And once again my opponent seemed to know the same thing I did. The look of enjoyment disappeared from her eyes, and rather than fencing we began to fight. Her attacks were in excellent form and came close to reaching me, and her parries were sharp and fast and accurate. But I'd been indulging that habit I have of not fighting any harder than I have to. I'd had to stretch a little to match the woman and hadn't tried to do more, but the time had obviously come to change tactics. If you really want to win you have to put everything you have into it, not just what *should* be enough.

So that was what I did. I parried her latest attack and really went on the offensive, giving her no time to do anything but defend herself. Twice she tried to disengage in order to break my rhythm and give herself a little breathing room, but I couldn't allow it. It was taking just about everything I had to maintain the advantage I'd grabbed, and I couldn't afford to give it up.

The pace was gruelling for both of us, and after what seemed like forever I finally found an opening through her guard. She must have been as close to exhaustion as I was, and her arm had begun to waver just a little before parrying. I forced myself to find just a bit more speed somewhere, and that waver she'd developed kept her from parrying the next stroke. My sword thrust straight into her chest, finally ending the fight, but she didn't just stop . . .

She froze as if I'd run her through with a real sword, despair suddenly contorting her face, and a whisper seemed to come out of nowhere.

What was fated must be done as *it was fated to be, fairly and without restrictions, else balance is destroyed. Balance must not be destroyed.*

I had no idea what that meant, but there was a blinding flash, and suddenly I was punching left-handed at Caldai Moyan's throat. Even as my blow landed and crushed her windpipe I thought I remembered *something* happening just a second ago, then shook off the ridiculous idea. Since I'd been in the middle of a fight with Moyan nothing *could* have happened, and now the fight was over.

Moyan dropped her sword and collapsed to the ground, but I was no longer watching her. I'd turned and started to race in Oblin's direction, trying to reach him before he reached Tiran. I hadn't forgotten about Forres, but I was very much afraid that I couldn't do anything to *him*. He'd know how to stop me just the way Moyan had, so going after Oblin was my only chance to help. The wound in my side burned from the sweat running into it, making me moan, but not making me slow or stop. Tiran needed me and I had to help, had to . . . had to . . . !

Alex, my love, Alex! Tiran thought frantically. *If I die then you'll die too, and I can't let that happen! I* won't *let it happen!*

And that decision forced the whispering in Tiran's head down to a murmur, too weak to make an impression on him. There were two men out to take his life, and Forres was by far the more dangerous. Insanity may lend extranormal strength and determination, but it can't and doesn't lend ability and skill.

So Forres had to be taken out first, but Tiran still didn't know how to do that. It was so damned hard to think even without the whispering in his head, and he'd only started to get the beginning of one vague idea. It had had something to do with the fact that the minds of other forms didn't have the same trouble as his natural mind . . .

That was when the rest of the idea came, a variation on an old one rather than something brand new, combined with what Alex had recently done before they made love, but it still ought to work. At the very least it was better than just standing there and dying, leaving Alex completely on her own. He might still end up dead, but not because he didn't try.

Jend Oblin was still screaming and racing toward Tiran, but Tiran ignored the madman and concentrated on Forres. The Shapeshifter was just beginning to bring his attention back to Tiran, so there was no time to lose. Tiran was bleeding from multiple wounds, but he'd thought of a way around that many years earlier. He just had to Shift into an exact copy of himself, only one that wasn't wounded. But this time he used the variation he'd so laboriously thought of, which didn't produce his natural form alone. Not only wasn't he wounded, but he'd included the fangs and claws *and mind* of his favorite fighting form.

"What in hell have you done?" Forres demanded harshly, staring at him with something very like fear. "You can't do *that,* it isn't part of the rules! You're supposed to just stand there and wait to be killed!"

The mind of the big black cat that was Tiran's best fighting form laughed at that, knowing what Forres was seeing—and fearing. A big, black-haired man, fangs gleaming from a wide grin, green eyes glinting with the feral look of a strong, confident beast of the wild. His hands ended in long, sharp claws to match that beast, claws that were downright eager to rip and tear and shred human flesh. If he had been fully a cat he would have been able to smell the fear on this man, and the weapon he held didn't bother Tiran-beast. One was cautious about many things when one began to attack, but a weapon the prey was too frightened to use wasn't one of them.

And Forres *was* frightened, rather badly. He began to back away from Tiran's advance, even going so far as to drop his point, but Tiran knew that that would change in another moment. With nothing else available he would remember the sword he held, and there was no reason to allow that complication. Immediately beginning to run and then jumping on Forres stopped his retreat along with his probable effort at defense, and brought his soft human throat comfortably in reach. It would have been far more pleasant to sink his fangs into that throat, but instead he just began to slash it open . . .

And then the strangest thing happened. Tiran found himself standing in a shimmering cloud, which disappeared as soon as he took two steps out of it. Now he stood on gray sand with a bluish-purple sky overhead filled with fluffy black clouds. But that wasn't all. About twenty feet away a man stood, and one look at him told Tiran they were opponents. Wherever they were they were there to fight, but not with man-made weapons.

Tiran's opponent examined him as they moved closer to each other, and a moment later he had Shifted into the same half-man, half-beast form that Tiran wore. But not precisely the same, which told Tiran that the big, yellow-eyed man had a different favorite fighting form to be borrowed from. His was more wolf-like, and he even had pointed ears to go with the fangs and claws.

But that made very little actual difference. The beast in Tiran's mind welcomed all comers, flexing against Tiran's loose hold on it. As soon as the fight began it knew it would be free, and when Tiran's opponent suddenly jumped at him, the beast in Tiran's mind got its wish. It was freed completely to meet the attack, to attack in turn, and to win. But first came the fight, and it wasn't easy.

The big man who was Tiran's opponent fought without fear, and very quickly the two of them were slashed and bleeding from claw-made wounds. They'd come together with a crash and after a moment were down on the ground, rolling around snarling and tearing at each other. Neither of them had any doubt that their fight was serious, and only one of them would walk away from it.

Tiran felt the gray sand tearing around in his wounds, but couldn't afford to let himself really notice. All his attention had to stay on his opponent, who had done really horrible, terrible things. Tiran couldn't remember what those things were, but he *knew* he wasn't wrong about them.

And that conviction let him spot the way his opponent occasionally overextended, let him ignore the pain of his wounds while he waited, then let him bite for the man's throat at the next overextension. Tiran's fangs closed in the throat, causing his opponent to scream, and then the scream cut off. The fight was over and the other man was dead.

Tiran pushed the dead body away and struggled to his feet, belatedly trying to understand what had happened. Why had he and that stranger been fighting, and why had it been so important to win? His beast mind hadn't asked those questions, but his man's mind did. And then a whisper seemed to come out of nowhere, reaching no one but Tiran.

What was fated must be done as it was fated to be, fairly and without restrictions, else balance is destroyed. Balance must not be destroyed.

Tiran had no idea what that meant, and then he blinked at a sharp flash of light. After the blink he slashed Forres's throat open with his claws, ignoring the feeling that something strange had just happened. The only strange thing was that he had actually won, and now it was time to turn to his last opponent.

Jend Oblin had slowed in his mad race forward, and now stood a short way out of reach, staring at Tiran in horror. Tiran could tell that Oblin watched Forres's blood dripping from Tiran's claws, and the man didn't seem able to decide how to take the sight. It had shocked him enough to jar him part way out of complete insanity, but it hadn't, unfortunately, made him forget about the weapon in his hands. He stood uncertainly and completely taken aback, but he also stood with the weapon ready.

And then Tiran saw his expression change, to disgust and outrage and new determination. His intention was so clear that words were unnecessary, but Oblin spoke them anyway.

"You unnatural, disgusting *thing!*" he rasped, beginning to work himself up again. "No wonder I couldn't win against you, you're a freak instead of a man! Now I'm really glad I came, since *somebody* has to rid the worlds of your sort. When I do it I'll be a hero, and you won't ever be in my way again."

And with that he started for Tiran once more, a delighted smile on his face. Tiran realized he should have at least Shifted the claws away so that he could use Forres's sword, but his overall mind still wasn't thinking clearly or easily. Now it was too late, with Oblin almost on top of him . . .

"The hell you will," Alex's breathless voice came, and suddenly she was between Oblin and himself. She was hurt but she still held a sword, and that forced Oblin to stop a second time.

"Haven't you gotten the message *yet?*" she demanded of Oblin while Tiran took the opportunity to Shift back to full human form. "The worlds will never consider you *any* kind of hero, not when your only claim to fame is destruction. Even a heavy rainstorm can kill someone, and how many people have you heard admiring a rainstorm? A hero is someone who builds and creates no matter *who* tries to stop him, and if you can't do that you might as well give it up."

Oblin stared at her silently, a wild desperation now in his eyes, and Tiran lost no time picking up Forres's sword and going to stand beside his wife. It would probably take the two of them to stop the madman, assuming they could do it at all. Tiran still struggled with what had been done to him, so Alex must also be incapacitated. Oblin probably didn't know it, but right now he was in a position to completely destroy his greatest enemies and win a kingdom with only two strokes of his sword.

But fate refused to let Oblin react in any way but what was, for him, true to form. He glanced wildly between Alex and Tiran, stumbling backward as he did so, and then he began to scream again. And even as he screamed he dropped his sword and unsheathed his dagger, giving up rather than making the least attempt to try, and plunged the blade into his own heart. Oblin's screams ended for the last time, and along with it that entire confrontation.

CHAPTER NINETEEN

It was two full days before Tiran and I were completely back to normal, and they weren't pleasant days. Brandis worked for hours with each of us, but not to heal our wounds. That he did in just a few minutes after he reached us, once Oblin was dead. The hard part was getting all the strangeness out of our minds, trying to make us the way we'd been. He seemed to have been fairly successful at least with me, and at least as far as it was possible to go. I wasn't really the same as I'd been, but that wasn't much of a surprise.

Outside it was raining, and I stood near the terrace doors in our reception room and stared at the steadily falling water, enjoying the coolness the rain had brought. Cadry had just left after visiting with me, because it was getting on toward lunchtime and Tiran and Brandis were going to join me there for the meal. I'd had the time to do a lot of thinking, so I'd made sure there wouldn't be anyone around during the meal except for the three of us.

"It's really damp out there," Tiran said as he came in, earlier than I'd expected him, smiling when I turned to look at him. "I'm glad our people don't have to maintain a siege against the rest of our former nobility in this. Just showing up on their doorsteps and waving a willingness to do it made the three of them surrender to Gann's forces, so that part of it is now completely over. Are you all right?"

"I'd say right as rain, but I've never been exactly sure how right that is," I answered with my own smile as I walked toward him. "I *can* tell you that I feel better than I have in a long while, and if you don't believe me I'm willing to prove it."

By that time I'd reached him, and sliding my arms around his body showed him exactly how I would prove my fitness. That made him grin as he wrapped his own arms around me, but after a quick kiss he shook his head.

"I'm not going to let you entice me into something we have no time for right now," he lectured sternly—but still didn't let me go. "You're a terrible influence and would certainly ruin a lesser man, but I'm much too superior to let that happen to *me*. We'll just have to wait until after lunch, and then we can be irresponsible and uninhibited."

"Irresponsible and uninhibited," I echoed thoughtfully as I looked up at him. "Gee, Ti, I guess I gave you the wrong impression. *That* isn't what I was talking about."

"It isn't?" he asked with a blink, then noticed my *too* innocent expression and got properly suspicious. "Okay, then it was my mistake. I guess you were discussing your willingness to join me in a card game or something, but I don't see how *that* would prove how fit you are."

"Ti, are you sure *you're* all right?" I asked, now showing a lot of concern. "I never said *anything* about card games, so if that's what you heard it might be a good idea for you to lie down for a while."

"Okay, Alex, what are you up to?" he demanded, the suspicion now a lot stronger. "I know there's *something* you're aiming at, so you might as well get straight to it. We both know you can keep this going for hours if not days, so how about giving me a break?"

"If you insist," I agreed with a sigh, certain he no longer realized we were still in each other's arms. "I do want something from you, and I happen to want it now. I've been doing a lot of thinking, and I've made some decisions that I won't be changing my mind about again."

"Decisions," he echoed, sudden fear showing in his beautiful green eyes. "Decisions that you won't be changing your mind about. Like what?"

"Like the decision about leaving, because you'd be better off without me," I obliged, ignoring the way his arms unconsciously tightened around me almost to the point of pain. "I've changed my mind about that, because I've very selfishly realized that *I* wouldn't be better off without *you.* You've become my reason for living, Ti, so walking away from you is out of the question. If that bothers you, I'm afraid you'll just have to learn to get over it."

"Bothers me!" he echoed again, limitless relief having replaced the fear in his eyes. "Yeah, I hate the idea completely, but I'm adaptable so there shouldn't be too much of a problem. But are you sure, Alex? Is this really what you want?"

"It's what I've always wanted, but like an idiot I was trying to be noble," I told him after delivering a quick kiss. "Selfishness, I've discovered, has a bad reputation for no good reason. It's a hell of a lot more comfortable and easy to live with than nobility, so I've shifted over for good. Besides, you got me curious about that pampering you want to give me, so I have to give *you* the chance to do it."

"I'll have to try to find a way to thank the EverNameless for their help in this," he said after delivering his own quick kiss. "I don't for a minute believe anything or anyone less could have changed your mind, not with *your* quota of stubbornness."

"Ti, how can you say that?" I protested, back to the innocence. "I'm the most reasonable woman ever to walk any of the worlds, but I'm *not* forgetful. I told you I wanted something from you, and you haven't yet said if you would give it to me. Is expecting a simple answer something that makes me unreasonable?"

"I said stubborn, not unreasonable," he corrected absently, his expression now so mixed that it was weird to see. "The two aren't the same, you know ... Alex, *what* are you setting me up for? I'm so happy over what you said that I feel lightheaded, but that's not quite the same as stupid. Right now I couldn't refuse you anything. With that in mind, what *I* need to know is why you're making such a point of asking. It has to be something I'll later regret, doesn't it? You want a clearly stated agreement so that later I won't be able to say you just assumed the promise, or that you didn't give me the chance to think about it. Is that it?"

"You're close," I conceded, delighted to see that he was able to use his mind's logical faculty again. "The only thing you're wrong about is my wanting you to promise about something without having the time to think about it. You can take all the time you need, but I *would* prefer an immediate answer. It's—"

"Alex, please," he interrupted. "Just tell me what it is before I die of nervousness and anticipation."

"Well, we certainly wouldn't want *that*," I agreed, deciding he was properly prepared. "We seem to have gotten through everything that was waiting to jump at our throats, and hopefully all that's left is to hear that Bariden and Chalaine have done the same. Once that happens, I want you to give me the first of our children."

He stared down at me blankly for a very long minute, making me afraid I'd handled the matter badly. I'd been sure that keeping it light would prove to be for the best, but now I was starting to worry. He had to be thinking about that illusion life we'd been forced through, where nothing including our children had turned out right, but—

"Beloved," he breathed at last, closing his eyes as he held me very, very close. "I was so afraid that that horrible projection of life we were put through would make you refuse to have children, and how could I have blamed you? Something like that is always possible, just as possible as the kind of king I could well become."

"Bullshit," I said, pushing away a little to look up at him. "It doesn't *happen* to be possible for you to become the kind of loser we were shown in the illusion, because you're not that kind of loser now. You don't worry about people plotting against you, because if they do you know you can handle it. You're also not greedy or a liar or a dozen other destructive things, so how could you possibly become like that illusion?"

"I suppose I couldn't," he said with something of a smile as he stroked my hair, but then the smile disappeared. "But that doesn't mean we still can't be disappointed in our children. People have, you know, even people with the best of intentions . . ."

"Oh, give me a break," I said with a very rude sound. "I'd rather not hear about people with the best of intentions, because they're the ones who usually make the most trouble. What you have to do is restrain yourself from planning for your kids, because what you plan might not suit them. If you and I should happen to produce a child who isn't a fighter, I won't let anyone try to turn him or her into one. I'll just give that child as much love and support as I possibly can, and then I'll be very proud of whatever that child does happen to accomplish. And there *will* be something, because any child who grows up with firm love and uncritical support turns out to be a winner."

"Yes, *ma'am*," he said with brows raised—but definite love in his eyes. "Whoever put that illusion-life together was a fool, trying to make us believe you would ever let anyone take your children away to be raised by strangers. *I'm* certainly not suicidal enough to suggest it . . . Lady of my heart, it will be my absolute delight to begin the first of our children with you just as soon as we possibly can."

He leaned down to kiss me properly then, but after a minute or two just kissing wasn't enough. It wasn't yet the right time for our lovemaking to produce the child we both wanted, but there are other reasons for people in love to share themselves with each other. Like not having any reason at all, just the desire and need.

I moved my hands down to Tiran's swordbelt without breaking away from the kiss, and by the time I had it open and had dropped it to the floor he was already cooperating. A smothered laugh escaped me when he groped for *my* swordbelt, because I wasn't wearing one. How he'd missed that fact I didn't know, but the effort wasn't a complete waste. He turned it into a double, two-handed caress that heated me even more, then abruptly lifted me in his arms and headed for our bedchamber.

"What was wrong with right where we were?" I asked in a murmur as I kissed his face. "It's been a while since the last time we were just spontaneous without giving a damn about being caught."

"Being spontaneous usually also means being interrupted," he murmured back as he put me down on our bed. "Since this is a rehearsal for the time when it will really count, I won't be very happy if I'm interrupted. And when a king is unhappy, Heads Can Roll."

I laughed softly at the capitals I could hear in his tone, and he grinned while he began to undress me. He'd be far from pleasant to anyone who did happen to interrupt us, but ordering their execution would not be a part of it. My beloved wasn't that kind of man, which was why I loved him so much.

Tiran spent less time than usual kissing me while he slid me out of my clothes, but he also kissed me while he got *himself* bare. I tried to help him get rid of his clothes, but having my body kissed was too much of a distraction. His lips and tongue paid homage to each of my breasts first, and then they moved slowly over the rest of my chest, down to and all over my abdomen, then to my belly. By the time he got *that* far I had my hands buried in his hair and my eyes tightly closed, lost to sensations that both made me want to tell him to hurry and to tell him to keep on going.

And then his hands joined his lips on my body, proving his clothes were no longer in the way. I drew him up by the hair to bring his lips in reach of my own, and then my own hands were free to move over him in the same way I was being touched. I loved to caress him, to feel his hardness and strength and know they belonged to me, just the way I belonged to him. He'd once promised we'd be partners in everything, and he hadn't lied. We were even partners in bed, sharing each other with all the love filling us so completely.

But this time the love filling *him* refused to be patient, which was exactly the way I wanted it. He moved between my thighs while we were still on our sides, and I pushed my hips forward while he thrust deep. His presence inside me was the gift I'd been excitedly expecting, the surprise I'd known was coming, the happy news I'd been waiting to get—every positive and wonderful thing all rolled into one, just as it always would be. Not to mention deliciously exciting, arousing and passion-making, crazy and abandoned. It was completion that never ended, completion I never *wanted* to end.

We made wild, abandoned love for quite some time, but finally the fires died enough to let us end it for the moment. We lay wrapped in each other's arms for a while, and then Tiran sighed.

"I hate to say it, but it's time we got back to what we were doing," he told me with regret in his voice. "But I've also just decided that we'll be taking vacation trips together, just you and me and at least twice a year. If the kingdom can't survive our being gone for a short while twice a year, we'll deserve to lose it for being too incompetent to set it up properly."

"Actually, I wish we could go to that first place we were shown in the enemy magic user's illusion," I said with my own sigh as I got up to find my clothes. "You know, that place where you live in a cave that's not a cave, and get to actually be any animal or bird or fish you care to. Too bad there isn't really a place like that."

"But there is," Tiran answered with a short laugh while he pulled on his pants, looking at me strangely. "Everything shown in that illusion *is* real somewhere, and I thought you knew that. But would you really want to go *there?*"

"Why not?" I countered, delighted to learn that it wasn't just a dream. "We *won* against him, Ti, in spite of everything he and his puppets tried, we still won. Why give up a place like that just because *he* showed it to us? It can be considered the spoils of our victory, something we've *earned.*"

Tiran didn't answer immediately, and his faint frown said he was thinking about my arguments. His silence lasted until we were back out in the reception room, and then he picked up his swordbelt and nodded while he put it back on.

"You know, you're absolutely right," he said, looking the least bit surprised. "I hadn't thought of it that way, but there *is* no reason to avoid the place. Why don't we make going there our very first vacation, which we'll take just as soon as all this insanity is a few months behind us?"

"You're on," I agreed with a grin, then moved close to him to seal the bargain with a kiss. Technically we could still be considered on our honeymoon, so there was no reason not to take advantage of the fact. We kept it up for a delightful amount of time, but then we were interrupted by some heavy throat-clearing. Neither one of us had noticed that Brandis had been admitted to the room, and the magic user's grin said that he'd been standing there for a while.

"I'm glad to see I did such a good job returning you two to the way you were," he said when we looked at him. "I also hate to intrude, but the servants are here with our lunch. Would you prefer that we all go away for a while and come back later?"

"Actually, I've been looking forward to lunch," I said before Tiran took him up on his offer, which he just might have done despite our very recent joy break. "Tiran and I can steal some more private time later, when half a dozen people aren't waiting around for us to get to them. Do you agree, Ti?"

"Of course," Tiran answered evenly and pleasantly, but the glance he gave me said he knew I was up to something. "Let's call the servants in and get this meal going the right way."

Brandis obliged us by doing that, and I took the opportunity of his back being turned to nod once to Tiran. That told him he was right about me being up to something, and he returned the nod and then produced a bland expression. He knew nothing of the details of what I had in mind, but as usual my love was ready to back me up.

The servants brought the food in and served us and Brandis, then they left to give us some privacy. The three of us chatted about nothing terribly important while we ate, but when we sat back with our coffee Brandis changed that.

"Your Majesties, now is the time, I think, to tell you something you need to know," he began after a short silence. "In just a little while I'll be leaving this kingdom for good. If you like, I'll circulate the word at Conclave that you're looking for a court magic user. I'm sure you'll get a decent response, and I'll even help interview the applicants."

"But you can't stay with us yourself," I said with a nod, completely unsurprised. "I'm sorry to hear that, Brandis. Didn't things work out with your girlfriend?"

"Ah—yes, as a matter of fact they did, and that's why I'm leaving," he said after a very brief hesitation, then remembered to smile. "Now that all the trouble is over, she's willing to come to Conclave with me to be trained. And I did tell you right from the first that I'd only be able to stay with you for a short time."

"Yes, you certainly did," I agreed, a glance showing me that Tiran was paying close attention. "We'll have to find some way to thank you for everything you've done, but right now I have a question: what level are you really at? Wizard? Whatever rank comes after wizard? *Is* there an official rank above wizard?"

"That's three questions," Brandis remarked, only the expression in his eyes showing he was shaken. "But the number doesn't matter, because I don't understand any of them. I'm certain I told you I was a sorcerer, and that hasn't changed."

"What hasn't changed?" I asked pleasantly. "That you *told* me you're a sorcerer, or that you really are one? I'm afraid I can't buy that last, even if you try to sell it to me again. I've known quite a few magic users at sorcerer level, and you just plain don't match up."

"You seem to be suggesting I'm *less* than sorcerer level," Brandis said, a bit more confidence now behind his expression. "If that's the way you look at it, you must have been disappointed with the help I gave. I'm sorry you feel that way, but I did the best I could. You—"

"Excuse me," I interrupted, "but I said *higher* than sorcerer level, not lower. I think your biggest problem was that you couldn't quite remember what you were capable of as a sorcerer and what you weren't, so sometimes you were overly cautious. When something distracted you, like anger or worry, you weren't cautious at all—and then you sometimes did things that a sorcerer shouldn't have been able to manage. I didn't do more than notice that at the time, but I've since been able to think about it."

"You know, it seems as if you're accusing me of more than just hiding things," he commented as he leaned back in his chair, his eyes now hooded. "You're not suggesting I was in league with your enemies, are you?"

Tiran stiffened at that, but all I did was smile and shake my head.

"Good try, but I really do know better than to think I can face up to an enemy magic user and hope to walk away again," I told him. "You *were* planted in the kitchens for me to find, but not by our late enemies. You never had a girlfriend here, so you won't be leaving with one. You'll be going back to report, and I'd enjoy knowing to whom."

"Your Majesty, I appeal to *you*," Brandis said to Tiran, now trying to make himself look upset. "I can't suggest there's something wrong with the queen because I know there isn't, but she *has* been under a terrible strain for quite some time. People who go through things like that sometimes begin to imagine things, but that does go away once they've gotten some rest. I strongly recommend that she gets that rest, and then I'm certain she'll be fine."

"Personally, I think she's fine right now," Tiran told him, making no effort to avoid his gaze. "If what she says is so wrong, why don't you counter her points one by one? If there's nothing behind them but confusion and exhaustion, wouldn't showing her where she's wrong help her to get over her illusions?"

Brandis hesitated at that, frustration flashing briefly in his eyes, and then he produced a smile.

"That's an excellent idea, Your Majesty," he said with what must have been an attempt at enthusiasm. "I'll be glad to help the queen in that way, just as I've done my best to help all along. Let's review the situation, Queen Alexia, and I'll point out where you've misinterpreted events."

"That's really kind of you, Brandis," I said, still sticking with a friendly smile. "Let's start right from the beginning. When I went into the kitchens as a cat, you went to great pains to 'rescue' me. You had no idea who I was, but you didn't want to see me harmed."

"That's right," he agreed, sipping at his coffee in a very casual way. "Figler was notorious in his hatred of cats, and you could have been seriously hurt because of him."

"No, that's wrong," I corrected gently. "If you knew

enough to know I was a Shapeshifter, you should also have known that there's a big difference between being able to harm an ordinary cat and harming one of my kind. I could have handled anything Figler or one of his lackeys tried to do, but you had to have a way to let me know you were the magic user I needed. Recognizing me in cat form was the way."

"But that doesn't logically follow," Brandis disagreed, also gently. "I tried to deny I was a magic user, and if you'd believed me you would have just gone on your way again. That's not what I'd call a very good plan to be noticed."

"Actually it wasn't, because you *were* afraid I'd just shrug and continue on my way," I said after taking my own sip of coffee. "That's why you told me your touching story so fast, hesitating only a breath or two before spilling it all. But I do appreciate your using Figler to get what you wanted. It brought the man to my attention, and I was able to get rid of him before he made the good kitchen help quit in disgust and walk out."

"Figler's performance was my doing as well?" he asked with one brow raised. "I really *must* be more capable than I thought, to make so many people do so many things."

"Not so many," I disagreed after helping myself to a beautiful little cake stuffed with chocolate cream. "You just made sure one of Figler's lackeys told him how smoothly everything was going, and that guaranteed his presence. Once he showed up you used a mild compulsion on me to visit the kitchens in something other than natural form. I'd *meant* to visit the kitchens, but that wasn't the best of times to have done it. I should have been looking for that enemy Shapeshifter who'd escaped, not taking time out to explore strange territory."

"But instead I brought you to me, exposed Figler for what he was, then forced you to hire me as your magic user," he said with a nod. "Aside from the fact that the explanation is more than a little contrived, why would I *do* something so outlandish? If I were in league with your enemies it would make sense, but you've already said you don't believe that."

"It's not a matter of belief," I mumbled through the last of the cake in my mouth. "It's completely a matter of logic, and is based on what you did and didn't do. What you did was help out in a very general way, mostly doing nothing more than any other fairly competent magic user would have. The one exception to that is cancelling what the ambush did to me, taking away the extreme terror I was being forced to live with. I remember how outraged you were over that, which has to be why you did it. *They* went too far so you did the same, but in general you just stood back and let us win or lose on our own. Now no one can say we bested them because we had outside help."

"I really don't understand any of this," Brandis protested, back to looking faintly shaken. "I also don't understand what brought all this up. I know you've been under a great strain—"

"Don't bother trotting out the 'great strain' story again," I interrupted dryly. "I've considered this from all angles, including the possibility that I'm just imagining things, but the clues and questions don't add up any other way. And what started me thinking along these lines is a question I asked after we defeated the first set of intruders, but which I couldn't get an answer to that made sense."

"What question is that?" Tiran asked after a moment, when it was fairly clear Brandis wouldn't. "*He* may not be curious, but I certainly am."

"Actually, Ti, you were there when I asked the question," I reminded him, but also made sure Brandis knew I was speaking to *him* as well. "We were told that we were destined to rule this kingdom, but no one went into any details about how that was supposed to have happened. The first set of intruders got here by 'accident,' they said, and the fact that they had the exact same destiny as we did was why only *we* could dislodge them."

"I remember that," Tiran said with a frown. "But now I remember something else as well. We were also told that we *weren't* necessary to dislodge them because they would soon have fallen anyway. Everyone was worried instead about the effect those others would have on us, because we were more competent than them. But if they were due to be taken down, they probably wouldn't have survived the process. That in itself would have removed the threat to us, without us having had to go anywhere near them.''

"That was one of the major logic flaws," I said with a smile, patting his hand to show how glad I was that we were back to thinking along the same lines again. "By partially untangling it I was led back to my original question, which was *how* were we supposed to have become the rulers here? Can you see us coming into this kingdom with your company, Ti, and taking it over from the legitimate king and queen? Even if they were as ineffectual as we've been told, can you see us doing that?''

"No," Tiran answered flatly at once. "Ineffectual doesn't mean tyrannical, and the people of the kingdom didn't need rescuing from their original rulers. Pavar and Selwin meant to depose the king and queen and take over, but Selwin was too clever to have started stealing everything available right out where everyone could see it. He would have been subtle about it, and his thievery wouldn't have shown for years.''

"So we would have had no reason to interfere, not with an internal takeover by resident nobles," I summed up with a nod. "Local politics would have been none of our business, and we wouldn't have tried to *make* it our business. So where does that leave my question?''

"Missing one very important ingredient," Tiran answered slowly, and then his expression cleared. "Yes, of course, I should have seen it sooner. You're absolutely right, Alex.''

"He means the missing ingredient is someone from outside the kingdom forcing a takeover of their own," I explained to a still-silent Brandis. "Someone like that would have no *right* to the throne, especially if they were the sort to start ripping people off right from the beginning. Tiran and I would have gone after them without a moment's hesitation—but there'd been no sign of them.''

"Maybe that was because of the accident you mentioned," Brandis said at last, the look in his eyes veiled. "If the original intruders struck before they could, they would have been out of luck. I don't see what your problem is with that.''

"My problem stems from the fact that they obviously stuck around anyway," I obliged, faintly annoyed that he still tried to dodge the issue. "I'll grant you they had to be really greedy and uncaring to consider stealing a throne in the first place, but that doesn't mean they were stupid. They probably chose this kingdom to begin with because the king was old, ineffectual, without heirs, and had no army. He didn't even have much in the way of a personal guard, because he refused to believe that anyone would ever consider deposing him."

"We were told he probably believed that because of how long he had to wait to take the throne in the first place," Tiran put in when Brandis remained silent. "It was an irrational belief that Pavar and Selwin were going to take advantage of, but that second pair of intruders would certainly have beaten them to it. It was the most perfect set-up for them."

"He means because they were Shapeshifters," I explained, taking over again. "They would have entered the palace and replaced the king with one of themselves, probably Caldai Moyan. She got a kick out of Shifting to a bantam rooster during our fight, thinking I would miss her point or it simply wouldn't matter, but it got me to thinking. Our kind doesn't usually gender-Shift because the strain tends to be rather intense, but that doesn't mean we can't do it."

"So she would have taken over for the king, and then she would have named Forres as 'his' heir," Tiran went on. "At that point he would already have begun building up an army and a proper guard, so when 'the king' abdicated in his favor, he'd have no trouble taking over. After the abdication the 'king and queen' would leave for whatever secret place they'd decided to retire to, and they'd never be seen again. Caldai Moyan would appear to be named Forres's queen, and they'd be in without a fuss. The situation *was* tailor-made for them."

"But the first intruders beat them to it, so they never got the chance," Brandis tried, apparently thinking he had a decent opening. "Instead they waited around and worked against you two, then tried to challenge you when they thought they could win. What's confusing about that?

Since it did happen, I don't understand why you're making a fuss."

"I suppose it's because it *shouldn't* have happened," I said, my smile telling Brandis he'd fallen into the trap just the way I'd wanted him to. "You see, what happened doesn't make logical sense any way you look at it. We agree that they picked this kingdom to begin with because it was such an easy, perfect opportunity. Now, the last week or so aside, would you consider Tiran and me the same kind of easy pickings?"

"But you can't *put* the last week or so aside," Brandis pounced, the poor thing believing the trap had closed on empty air. "They had a really strong Sighted helping them, so it made sense for them to challenge you. Logically speaking, it wouldn't have made sense for them *not* to."

"Being a magic user doesn't necessarily make you good at logic, does it?" I asked, and the gentle pity I hadn't been able to keep out of my voice told Brandis it was his foot, not empty air, that the trap had closed on. "I'm afraid, my friend, that you can't have it both ways. Either Forres and Moyan were in need of the easy pickings this kingdom was with its old king, or they could have taken over anywhere because they had a really strong ally. If they had that ally to begin with, why would they have bothered with an essentially backwater kingdom like this one?"

"Which is the same question you can ask about why they challenged us at all," Tiran put in just as gently, probably because of the stricken look on Brandis's face. "With a magic user as strong as the one working with them, they could have found a really rich, enormous kingdom to take over. But instead of doing that they stayed here, worked us over with conditioning and magic, and then faced us in challenge. And even then they weren't perfectly confident."

"So what we have is a large bunch of unanswered questions," I finished up, pretending I didn't see the way Brandis stared into space *between* Tiran and me. "If those two were after easy pickings, why did they stay around after Tiran and I took over? If they had strong magical help and didn't *need* easy pickings, why were they here to begin with? Logically speaking, there's only one answer that works.''

"The answer that says they came here *without* a magical ally, but then got together with him,'' Tiran pursued, beginning to sound somewhat less gentle. "*Someone* gave them a large amount of help against us, someone who has to be of wizard strength. If he wasn't he couldn't have gotten past our warding, and none of that horror would have happened.''

"So you have to add a couple of more items to my list of questions,'' I said. "Why would a magic user of wizard strength bother to back people like Forres and Moyan? If he wanted us out of the way for some reason, why didn't he just cause us to disappear or something? And why would he care about who ruled in this kingdom to begin with? Anybody who's reached wizard level could probably *create* a kingdom if he wanted one, but none of them do. I've heard they consider that sort of thing boring, so that just makes this whole situation even stranger. Aren't you going to say anything?''

"What would you like me to say?'' Brandis asked, his faint smile rather bitter. "You've picked apart everything I've said so far, and have even proven your contention that being Sighted doesn't necessarily make you good with logic. What else is there to talk about?''

"How about the identity of whoever it was who sent you to help us?'' I suggested, trying to give his current mood the benefit of the doubt. He didn't *have* to be putting it on as a means of defense, after all ... "At the same time you might mention why that help was so deliberately limited. You were able to get rid of whatever was done to us *after* we won the fight, but before it you pretended you couldn't even tell that there was anything wrong. Would you like to tell us why that was necessary?''

"And you might even make a guess or two about why we weren't warned about what we had ahead of us,'' Tiran added, that same hardness still in his tone. "That woman magic user, Dellir, her name was, the one who showed up after we'd all bested the intruders. She told us that the trouble was over and all we had to do was straighten out our new kingdom. Or at least that's what she suggested. Are you connected with *her* in any way?''

If I hadn't been watching Brandis closely, I probably would have missed the flicker in his eyes when Tiran asked that question. But I didn't miss it, and that gave me a new tack to take.

"So Dellir's still involved in this, is she?" I said, leaning back in my chair a little. "I knew there was a lot of her story and explanation that didn't make sense, especially all that insisting she did about how independent and uncontrollable we were. Was there *anything* she didn't lie about?"

"In the name of Chaos, how are you coming up with all this?" Brandis blurted, and I didn't doubt for a minute that he really was appalled. "You can't tell me that this is nothing but logic, not when I feel as helpless in your hands as most unSighted would feel in mine! You weren't supposed to be told anything at all and you weren't, but you still have most of the answers."

"Then how about giving us the rest?" I suggested gently after exchanging a glance with Tiran. "It's fairly obvious you have certain orders about not simply walking out on us, otherwise you would have already ended this by doing it. Why don't you start with *why* you can't simply ignore us and walk out?"

He stared at me disbelievingly for a moment, closed his eyes and shook his head hard, then was back to staring at me.

"I would *really* like to know how you do that," he said, looking at me as if I were an interesting but dangerous specimen of some kind. "You take a single bit of information, then turn it around into something else entirely. Why do *you* think I haven't just walked out?"

"I have my theories, but I'd rather hear the real reason from you," I countered without a smile. "You can consider it a test I'm giving myself, to see how close my theories come to reality."

"Or, which is more likely, to see how close to the truth *I'll* come," he responded wryly, glancing at Tiran and me both. "I *was* warned about this in a general way, but I just couldn't imagine myself being mousetrapped by a couple of unSighteds . . . Well, that's beside the point, isn't it? You want to know why I'm still here, and the answer is simple: this isn't *quite* over yet, and I can't leave until it is.''

Tiran and I exchanged more than a glance, since that was the obvious answer but one we hadn't wanted to hear. Brandis caught the exchanged look and leaned forward with a headshake.

''No, that *doesn't* mean someone or something will come at you again,'' he assured us quickly. ''You can't have missed the fact that you two and your next door neighbors are bound together in this, and their fight isn't yet over. Until it is, I'll be staying here to—keep you company.''

''Which means that something or someone *can* come at us again,'' Tiran said, putting into words exactly what I'd been thinking. ''But *I* don't understand why you claim you have to stay here to be questioned. Couldn't you have walked out, and then kept an eye on us from a distance? For that matter you could have just turned invisible again, and watched us from as close up as you pleased.''

''No, I couldn't have done either of those things,'' he answered with a sigh, true regret in his eyes. ''Considering what you've put me through I wish I *could* have, but this isn't a situation I can afford to play games with. I have to be right here, with *all* my strength available, or I might as well not be here at all.''

''The enemy magic user is *that* strong?'' I asked, a stupid question if ever there was one. The thing answered itself, so I dismissed it with a wave of my hand and asked a more important one. ''You said Bariden and Chalaine haven't yet won *their* fight. What can we do to help them?''

''Nothing,'' Brandis responded immediately, his gesture stopping Tiran in the midst of rising. ''Just as no one was able to help you two, no one can help *them*. They'll have to win or lose on their own, and they're having just as hard a time as you did. Not in the same way, of course, but just as difficult.''

''That means you probably never sent that message sphere I asked you to,'' I said as Tiran settled heavily back in his chair. "They didn't refuse our offer of help, they never got to know about it."

"They did get and answer that first message sphere, but they wouldn't have gotten any others or had one of their own passed on to you," Brandis said with compassion. "If the small children of this kingdom suddenly decided to stage a revolt, how hard would it be for you to stop it? Would you even have to use members of your company, or would any bunch of people off the street do? The kind of magic being used over there is completely beyond the ability of unSighteds to appreciate, let alone withstand. Would you really want to throw away the lives of your people for nothing?"

That was another question that answered itself—assuming we were being told the truth. At the moment there was no way of knowing if we were, but it might be possible to find out.

"All right, so they have to win on their own just the way we did," I conceded for argument's sake. "That doesn't explain why *we* had to, or who's behind all this. I think this would be the perfect time for you to give us some details on that."

"But you've already explained it all yourself," Brandis protested, now trying to look innocent. "What else is there to add?"

Rather than go through it all again I just stared at him, and Tiran did the same. All we'd been told was how good we were at deducing things, how upset Brandis was at being put on the spot, and that we wouldn't be allowed to offer help to Chalaine and Bariden. All in all the revelations had come to nothing we didn't already know, and it was time to go beyond that.

"I could always put you under a light compulsion to forget about all this and just go about your business," Brandis mused after a moment, faint annoyance in the glance he divided between Tiran and me. "That would be much more pleasant from *my* point of view, and would certainly teach you how much of a waste of time it is to try to force a Sighted into doing something. Is that the way you'd prefer it?"

"I thought that even turning yourself invisible would

take more strength than would be wise for you to expend,''
I commented without shifting my stare. ''Keeping the two
of us under a compulsion like that would have to be
harder, since our minds would be fighting you every step
of the way. But even assuming it wouldn't be harder,
I can't see a reason for you talking about it instead of
doing it.''

''Which means you either *do* do it, or start answering
our questions,'' Tiran added even more flatly than I'd spoken. ''I really am grateful for the small amount of help
you gave, but I keep remembering what my wife and
queen was put through for some reason I don't yet understand. Right now I'm waiting to understand, but I won't
be waiting much longer.''

''And I'm the closest representative of those you consider responsible for what happened,'' Brandis concluded,
looking at Tiran oddly. ''You certainly have some idea
how powerful a Sighted I am, but that hasn't affected your
intentions—or stopped you from giving me fair warning.
Now I really don't know what to do.''

He leaned back and went into a brown study, obviously
considering his options. Tiran and I looked at each other,
but there was nothing we could do but wait. If Brandis
decided not to tell us anything after all ... Well, that
decision could wait until it actually became necessary to
make it. Brandis thought for a good couple of minutes,
and then he came out of it to lean forward and reach for
the coffee pot.

''I'll probably catch Hellfire for this, but I don't see
that I have any choice,'' he said heavily as he refilled his
cup. ''I'm not even expending strength on keeping my cup
refilled the easy way, so you have to know I was bluffing
about that compulsion. See? I can handle logic when I
have to, only not quite in the same way you two do.''

He smiled at us without humor as he sat back, took a
sip from the cup he'd refilled, then looked directly at each
of us.

''I *cannot* tell you everything, so don't expect that I
will,'' he stated, showing us a different, more self-assured
Brandis than the one we'd gotten used to. ''I won't tell
you you wouldn't understand, because that would be a lie.

I'll simply say there are things you can't know about, and leave it at that.''

"What about your real name?" I put in, just to rattle all that newly exhibited self confidence a little. "You called yourself Brandis because that's very close to the name Bariden without being overly obvious. You knew we trusted Bariden completely, so you used the name to gain the same kind of trust for yourself the easy way."

"Will you please stop that?" he said with exasperation, more than a little annoyed. "I know why you're doing it, but you're wasting the effort. I've already given up on the idea of trying to lie to you, because I do know I probably can't get away with it. Instead I just won't discuss certain things, which ought to be at least a small amount of protection. And you're right, my name *isn't* Brandis, but you might as well just go on calling me that."

Tiran, wearing a very amused smile, reached over to take my hand and kiss it. I appreciated *his* appreciation, but also followed his example and refrained from commenting.

"Thank you," Brandis said very dryly, obviously referring to my choice in keeping silent. "You're restraining yourself admirably, so I'll get on with it. To begin with, you're right about Forres and Moyan. They *were* the ones you were supposed to have rescued the kingdom from, after they stole the throne from the original king and queen. They would have been fairly well dug in by the time you arrived, so you would have had something of a struggle before you shook them loose."

I could feel Tiran's glance at me, but this time I didn't return it. Brandis had just told me a lot more than he probably knew, and the implications were more than simply disturbing.

"But the original intruders got here and moved in on the king and queen before Forres and Moyan could," Brandis continued. "They were furious, of course, and tried to find a way around being edged out, but your predecessors were far too much for them to handle. There were also their Sighted allies in the next kingdom to consider, so Forres and Moyan retreated to think things through and plan their next move.

"They spent quite some time at it, but finally had to admit they *had* no next move. The two of them alone couldn't hope to get anywhere against your predecessors even without their Sighted allies, so they decided to move on and look for easier pickings. That was when they were contacted by the wizard, who told them not to be hasty. He had a plan of his own and they were a part of it, and if they followed his instructions they would have the kingdom legitimately, without anyone being able to cast doubt on their right to rule."

"But why would a wizard do something like that?" Tiran interrupted to ask, his tone bewildered. "Magic users don't *need* to use ordinary people to further their plans, especially not when they're that strong. Who is he, and what does he want from us?"

"Who he is is one of the things I can't tell you," Brandis answered heavily. "I also can't tell you why he did things in what really is a roundabout way, so you might as well not ask. Do you want me to go on with what I *can* tell you?"

Tiran hesitated for a moment before nodding, the only answer he could have made. He probably wasn't seeing what I had because he wasn't looking in the proper direction, which was something of a relief. If he had demanded an answer to *that* part of it, Brandis certainly would have refused to say anything more at all.

"All right, then I'll continue," Brandis agreed. "Forres and Moyan were ordered to wait a while, and they found out why they'd been given the order when you two defeated your predecessors and took the throne for yourselves. Things were in a great deal of confusion for a while because you began to change everything around, but that was a help to them rather than a hindrance. They were supplied henchmen to hire, in the form of ex-guardsmen who couldn't afford to let themselves be arrested."

"So when they kidnapped those village girls, Forres *was* being helped by ex-guardsmen," I said, mostly to keep Brandis from realizing I was thinking about other things. "Did they really expect to take me, or were they just trying to make sure I'd be in the city to fall into the ambush they later arranged?"

"The latter," Brandis answered with a frown. "It wouldn't have done them any good to kidnap you, not even if they privately considered the possibility of actually asking for ransom and then leaving when they got it. That would have ruined their *ally's* plans, and they really knew better than to try that. They sacrificed most of the men they'd hired, but they considered that to be done in a good cause."

"And was it them in the marketplace that day?" I asked next. "The old man and woman who set me up for that ambush?"

"No, those were hired henchmen, but it was the wizard behind them and he also drew those fighters into the trap with you," Brandis said, reaching across the table to touch my hand. "He knows certain things about you, you understand, and he wanted to make the time as horrible as possible for you. Leading you to believe that those fighters died for no other reason than because they were guarding you accomplished that aim."

"What about Caldai Moyan being in that last village?" Tiran asked after a moment, probably to cover the fact that I wasn't saying anything else. He was right to believe that the idea still bothered me, but I'd gotten another idea that currently bothered me more.

"I know Caldai was planted in that last village so I'd find and rescue her," Tiran said, "but weren't they taking something of a chance? If we'd been even a few minutes later, she would have been in the midst of entertaining the leader of those fighters who were training the villagers."

"She was never in any danger," Brandis disagreed with a faint smile. "She was a better fighter than the man who intended to take advantage of her, but the wizard still didn't risk her safety. He had the man under his control, so they would have been in the same positions no matter when you and your people showed up. She had to be able to condition you on your ride back to the city, after all, so it would have been stupid to take chances."

"And they never really meant to face us the day I executed Pavar, did they?" Tiran went on. "When we finally did face them, I noticed that they were dressed for the occasion in exercise clothes, something they weren't that first time. They were just there then to lure us into a position where that illusion could affect us. The longer we lived with the memory of that illusion, the more reluctant we were to stay here and fight for the throne.''

"They also wanted to give you the chance to see to Selwin and the others," Brandis agreed. "They wouldn't have been able to do it themselves if they'd won, not as quickly as it would need to be done, so they gave you the time to do it for them. And, as you say, it also gave that illusion time to work on you.''

"What about Caldai's offer to be a stand-in for Alex?" Tiran put next. "Did she seriously want me to agree, or was that just a bit of misdirection that meant nothing?"

"Oh, it meant something, all right, and a rather important something," Brandis assured him. "If you'd publicly accepted her in Alex's place, you would have been specifically denying Alex her place as your queen. She would have been legally put aside in another woman's favor, and that other woman would have gained the legitimacy of her position. It wouldn't have saved Alex's life once they put *you* down, but it would have saved *them* a good deal of trouble.''

"It would have saved them from dying," I interrupted, suddenly having trouble with keeping quiet. "It wouldn't have been legal for me to help Tiran then, and it was our fighting *together* that defeated them. Isn't that the way it went, Brandis? We won because we fought *together?*"

"Yes, it would be accurate to say that," he agreed cautiously, studying me somewhat narrowly. "Why do I have the impression that you mean more than you said?"

"Probably because I do," I admitted freely enough. "Despite what you said about them only trying to wound me, they made a serious effort to kill me in that ambush. They used that conditioning as a backup just in case they couldn't do the killing, which it turned out they couldn't. Then Moyan tried to get Tiran to put *her* in my place, and that didn't work either. They were desperately trying to keep Tiran and me from fighting together as a team, but I don't know why ... Is there anything else you can add to what you've told us? Like why you were sent here to help us?''

"I was sent here to help because you weren't likely to find someone with my strength and experience on your own," he replied, still cautiously. "That should have been obvious."

"I just wanted to have you confirm it," I said, leaning forward to reach the coffee pot. "And that's everything you can talk about, everything you're *permitted* to talk about?"

He nodded agreement, but his eyes showed that his caution had changed to suspicion. He was wise for feeling that way, but I finished fixing the new cup of coffee before sitting back with it and looking at him bleakly.

"The next time you see your friend Dellir, make sure she knows that if she ever loses her ability to do magic, she'd better stay well away from *me*," I stated. "That goes for you and the rest of your group as well, and don't make the mistake of thinking I'm joking. You people are beyond vile, and I don't give a damn about what you can do to me for saying it."

"Alex, take it easy," Tiran urged while Brandis closed his eyes and went gray. "We may have gotten caught up in magic user business, but Brandis did help us and is now here to guard us. You can't say they aren't trying to be fair about this."

"Oh, but I can," I disagreed, reaching out to take Tiran's hand without looking at him. "There's nothing fair about this whole damn mess, and Brandis knows it even better than I do. Do *you* want to tell him, Brandis, or shall I?"

"You *can't* know what you're pretending to," the magic user muttered, then opened his eyes and raised his voice. "You're pushing with nothing behind the move, Alex, bluffing to make me discuss what I can't. I hadn't realized you knew how badly I felt about all this, but obviously you do and are now trying to take advantage of it. But it won't work, because there's nothing else I can tell you."

"Nothing else you're *willing* to tell," I corrected, making no effort to avoid his gaze. " 'Can' has nothing to do with it. And if I'm bluffing, then you won't mind tackling my new list of questions. The first one is so obvious I'm

almost ashamed to mention it, but what the hell, we're all
grownups here. You do remember confirming that Forres
and Moyan were the ones we were *supposed* to have faced
here, don't you? Good, I was afraid you'd forgotten. Now
why don't you tell us how you know that to be true."

"W-what?" he stuttered, his face losing all color again
as the shock registered in his eyes. It looked like he really
had thought I was bluffing, and I almost wished he were
right.

"I said," I repeated over Tiran's slowly indrawn breath,
"tell us how you know we were *supposed* to have faced
Forres and Moyan. If it didn't happen, which it didn't,
how could you possibly know it was supposed to have?
A chain of logic brought us to the conclusion, but you
confirmed it for us. So how do you know what should
have happened but didn't?"

"It—was a conclusion my people pieced together from
available data," Brandis finally answered, his voice relatively even but his face still pale. "They used the same
chain of logic, and therefore reached the same conclusion.
How else did you think I would know?"

"That's the question I asked *you*," I responded, letting
my tone and stare tell him I didn't believe a word he'd
said. "Your people used available data, but where was it
that they could avail themselves of it? Logic says that the
only ones who knew for sure were Forres, Moyan, and
the wizard they worked for. Which one of those three did
your people get their information *from?*"

Brandis didn't answer this time, but that wasn't surprising. The point had been passed over so matter-of-factly
that we weren't supposed to have noticed it, but that
wasn't the only one of its kind.

"If you're finding my first question too hard, how about
a different one?" I suggested. "Like the one about why
the wizard—that very strong, very dangerous wizard—
wasn't allowed to touch us directly. That's right, isn't it,
Brandis? He wasn't *allowed* to touch us."

"Of course he wasn't!" Tiran contributed, now all
caught up. "That's obvious from everything that happened. Not once did he do anything to either of us directly,
only to and through the people around us. Even that illu-

sion was set up in the middle of a meadow, certainly before we got there. It was Forres and Moyan who lured us into it, making us think we were going out to face them. I wanted to know why a wizard would do things like that, and now I know. He wasn't *allowed* to touch us."

"Which means Brandis and his friends are playing some sort of game with that wizard," I said, taking over again while Brandis stared at Tiran. "He must have bent the rules that time when Brandis was so outraged over what had been done to me, so Brandis was able to bend them a little in turn. But he didn't bend them so far that he negated *everything* that had been done, only the part that was against the rules. It's really a good thing you were there to help, Brandis, otherwise I might have suffered."

"You don't understand," Brandis whispered, somehow having turned older than he'd been. "It isn't what you're thinking, it really isn't."

"No?" I said, feeling very little pity for him. "Weren't you the one who mentioned that the wizard knew certain things about me? Did that bit of information also come from available data? If it did, then let me tell you about a bit *I* pieced together. You claimed you were sent to work with us because of how strong you are, but that has to be another lie. Since you didn't *use* any of your strength we might as well have had the help of an actual sorcerer, but that's just the point. You took the job of helping us because you didn't *want* us to have someone else, not when that someone else would certainly have done more for us than you did. You weren't sent to help us, but to keep us from getting *effective* help."

"It looks like the answer to that question wasn't quite as obvious as you thought, Brandis," Tiran said to a magic user who had closed his eyes again and hadn't yet opened them. "Your people wanted the game to go in a particular way, so they sent you here to make sure it did. But there's something I'm still not certain about, Alex. If they're all in this together, why is *this* one still here and talking about protecting us?"

"Maybe because the game isn't over," I suggested, letting myself slump in the chair. "We may or may not be out of it, but I do believe that Chalaine and Bariden aren't.

And there's always the chance that that wizard will get so wild over losing that he'll simply throw the rules away and come after us in person. He can't be happy about having had to stick to them until now, not when they made him lose."

"How can you possibly sit there talking about rules and games?" Brandis suddenly demanded, apparently tired of trying silently for some pity. "Everything that happened was dead serious, and you two almost ended up just as dead. Is that what you call a game?"

"It's not *my* definition, but it has to be yours," I told him, ignoring the outrage in the same way I'd ignored his silence. "It was all that business about legitimacy that first started me thinking, and then Moyan turned the rules of the challenge around. I thought at the time that she did it simply for the edge it gave her, but now I'm not so sure."

"What are you talking about?" Tiran asked while faint panic flashed in Brandis's eyes. "I'd never heard the details about those rules of challenge until Forres told me about them, so you'll have to be more specific. What was turned around?"

"It was that bit about who was supposed to start and who was supposed to follow," I supplied, privately wondering about Brandis's hidden panic. "I learned about the rules during history lessons while I was growing up, and it was the prime candidate—meaning the lawful heir or the seated king—who got to go first. Challengers had to follow their lead, which meant the edge was against them. Moyan's turning it around suggested *she* was the seated queen, and I was nothing but the challenger."

"Forres did the same, and now I wonder why," Tiran said, sounding thoughtful. "Even though he lied and said the wizard would zap me if I tried to do anything but match him, he was still taking a big chance. If I *had* tried something and didn't get zapped, he could have lost even sooner than he did."

"Wouldn't *you* like to comment, Brandis?" I offered, still watching the man. "You look upset again, and I'm wondering why."

"Why is easy," he answered with a sigh after taking a good swallow of his coffee. "You've picked up incredibly more than I expected you would, but you've put it together wrong. I should be glad of that, but I'm not. It disturbs me to have you thinking of me as you do.''

"What other way do you *expect* me to think of you?" I countered, trying to figure out where he was going now. "You and your friends devised a game whereby that other wizard would back a pair of thieves and you and your friends would back us, and then you'd see who won. Of course, the other guy was allowed to give his people almost unlimited help while we had to get along with next to none, but that was just part of the game, right? It was all in fun, so there's no real reason for me to have hard feelings, right?"

"No, you aren't right," he insisted, looking angry at something other than me. "I now understand why I wasn't supposed to tell you *anything,* but it's too late to take it all back. This whole misunderstanding is my fault, and not being able to clear it up yet is killing me. But better that than letting it all out now. There are facets of this that you know nothing about, and I'm not the one best suited to discuss them. When the proper time comes, you'll be told everything possible."

"Everything possible," I echoed, still making no secret of my disbelief. "That translates to, 'as little as we can get away with.' And when do you expect Dellir to get around to doing it? She's much better at lying than you are, by the way, so I'm not surprised that she's 'more suited' to hand out explanations. Do you expect her here before winter, or will she wait until some time next spring?"

"She'll wait until Bariden and Chalaine have either lost or won," he answered, for once without all the extra signs of emotion. "If I were you I'd spend my time hoping hard that they win. If they don't, you probably won't be concerned with explanations or the lack of them. As a matter of fact, none of us involved in this will be."

He said that so simply that I felt a chill, and looking at Tiran showed that he felt the same. We'd get our explanations if Bariden and Chalaine won, but if they didn't, then—what? What would happen if they lost? I didn't for a minute believe they would lose, but there was a wizard out there who couldn't be trusted not to break the rules of that incomprehensible game they were playing.

So what would happen if Bariden and Chalaine lost? And even beyond that, what would happen if they won?

The man calling himself Brandis watched the two children he was there to protect, privately marveling at how well they controlled themselves even with everything they knew. And he'd been unprepared for how close they'd come to getting all the answers there were to be had. If they'd had access to one or two more bits of information, they would have understood exactly what they were in the middle of.

And that alone, simply understanding everything that was happening, could very well mean disaster for everyone. Brandis sipped his coffee in an effort to steady his nerves, an action he wasn't used to needing to take. That whole situation was a nightmare, but he couldn't say he hadn't been warned. It was Dellir herself who had warned him, and he'd actually been amused.

"You don't really expect me to believe I have to guard myself against unSighted children *I'll* be guarding," he'd said to Dellir with an indulgent chuckle. "They can't *know* anything at all, so if they want to guess wildly about things completely beyond them, why not simply let them? I promise I won't laugh where they can see it, not when it would hurt their feelings."

"And I promise you won't laugh at all," Dellir had returned with a sigh. "For you and me and the rest of us who are known as Elder Ones, they *are* children, but not like any you've ever known. If they weren't more than special, do you think we'd be in the middle of this horror now? Hopefully they won't figure it *all* out, but they'll certainly get most of it. Just make sure you're *very* careful of what you say, otherwise you know what might happen."

And he did know, which was why the sweat had broken out on his forehead. The balance of the universe was already unstable, and one misstep could conceivably cause a chain reaction of destruction that would move from world to world in a widening arc, maybe even into infinity.

It wasn't possible to know every form that misstep could take, so their only choice was to minimize their actions and everyone else's. And, as actions spring from knowledge, that, too, had to be limited.

Like the fact that the children hadn't been allowed to remember the other confrontation they'd each had with their opponent. Dellir and others of the Elder Ones had overseen that, taking the four children to a place where their battles might be fairly fought and fairly won or lost. It had been hoped that Tiran and Alexia would win there as well, reinforcing their major victories against enormous odds and also doing a significant amount toward stabilizing the imbalance. The action *had* helped to a certain extent, but not as much as they'd all hoped. Alexia and Tiran weren't Sighted, and therefore had a lesser effect on the balance.

Which meant that the whole thing now rested on the shoulders of Chalaine and Bariden. Brandis pitied them so deeply that his heart ached, but helping them was just as impossible as it had been with Alexia and Tiran. It would be a very long time before he was able to forgive himself for just standing there and watching their suffering, and that despite the fact that he'd had no other choice. In the name of everything decent and good, he was an *Elder One!* Why hadn't he been able to *find* a way to help them that wouldn't have destroyed them and him and everyone else . . . !

Brandis took a slow, deep breath, the only outward sign of his inner turmoil. He couldn't *afford* to be distracted by that now, not when the end of the insanity was so near. It would come in the next day or two, and if Bariden and Chalaine did win, that would be the signal for needing the greatest alertness yet. It wasn't possible to know how *he* would take total defeat, not when his thoughts and actions were so deeply involved with so many of the variables. Whatever happened it wasn't likely to be pleasant, but they did have a chance to survive.

Survive . . . *if* things were done in just the right way . . . *if* Chalaine and Bariden had the sort of potential they all hoped . . . *if* . . . *if* . . . *if* . . .

AVONOVA PRESENTS
MASTERS OF FANTASY AND ADVENTURE

SNOW WHITE, BLOOD RED   71875-8/ $5.99 US/ $7.99 CAN
edited by Ellen Datlow and Terri Windling

A SUDDEN WILD MAGIC   71851-0/ $4.99 US/ $5.99 CAN
by Diana Wynne Jones

THE WEALDWIFE'S TALE   71880-4/ $4.99 US/ $5.99 CAN
by Paul Hazel

FLYING TO VALHALLA   71881-2/ $4.99 US/ $5.99 CAN
by Charles Pellegrino

THE GATES OF NOON   71781-2/ $4.99 US/ $5.99 CAN
by Michael Scott Rohan